THE BIGFOOT BLUNDER

A CHARLIE RHODES COZY MYSTERY BOOK ONE

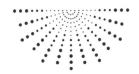

AMANDA M. LEE

WINCHESTERSHAW PUBLICATIONS

PROLOGUE

13 YEARS AGO

"*M*ath is stupid."

Kate Rhodes arched an eyebrow, her powder blue eyes full of mirth as she glanced up from the dishwasher she was emptying and fixed her only daughter with a dubious look.

Charlotte "Charlie" Rhodes, her long dark hair standing up at odd angles because she'd been dragging her hands through it for hours, stood on the other side of the kitchen island. She had a fascinating way of looking at life – as only a ten-year-old could – and Kate always got a kick out of talking to the youngster. Charlie had a lot of gripes when it came to her existence, but they were almost always entertaining.

"Math is important," Kate argued, adopting a pragmatic tone. "You won't get very far in life if you don't know how to multiply ... or figure out sales tax when it comes time to go shopping."

"I don't care about multiplication," Charlie shot back. "I have a calculator. That's all I need."

Kate was famous for her patience, which almost never frayed. A little thing like pre-teen angst wasn't going to send her over the edge. "Did you finish your homework?"

1

Charlie rolled her eyes and Kate had to bite the inside of her cheek to keep from smirking. "Why do you think I hate math?"

"That wasn't an answer."

"Yes, Mom. I finished my math. Geez." Charlie, a lovely child on most occasions, wielded a deft hand when it came to delivering snark.

Kate's husband, Caleb, picked that moment to stroll into the kitchen, an empty pie plate in his hand. He stepped around his wife so he could rinse it, sliding the plate into the dishwasher while glancing between his wife and daughter.

"Geez, Louise," Caleb teased, smirking as Charlie made an exasperated face. "What are you complaining about now, my little terror?"

"I'm not little," Charlie argued. "I'm growing up. I even can wear Mom's shoes now. I know, because I tried them on and only fell once because of the heels."

"She can," Kate agreed, bobbing her head. "She has to put on only three pairs of socks to get them to fit, but they look amazing otherwise."

"Oh, well, that sounds lovely." Caleb rested his elbows on the counter and leaned closer. "Did you do your homework?"

Charlie let loose a long-suffering sigh only preteens can pull off without risking public mocking. Anyone trying to sigh like that in the real world would get fired ... or punched in the face. "I finished my homework. Don't I always finish my homework?"

"No." Caleb didn't hesitate before answering. "In fact, when your mother and I went to parent-teacher conferences your teacher told us that you've been pretty lax in your homework over the past few months. That's why we're always asking about your homework."

"Yes, well, Mrs. Butter Butt should mind her own business," Charlie grumbled, crossing her arms over her chest and averting her gaze.

"Mrs. Butterfield is a perfectly nice woman. You're the one in the wrong here," Kate clarified, her tone stern. "She's right in this instance, Charlie. "She says you're distracted, and she's worried about you. Do you want to tell us what's distracting you?"

In truth, Mrs. Butterfield explained to the Rhodes that Charlie was her brightest student. She also was prone to staring out windows and completely losing her train of thought in the middle of a lecture. Mrs. Butterfield suggested having Charlie tested for potential learning disabilities, but Kate didn't believe for a second that Charlie's problem was medical or mental. Charlie simply refused to apply herself.

"I'm not distracted," Charlie snapped. "I don't know why she says that."

"She says it because you're too smart to be getting Cs and Ds," Caleb argued. "I agree that your problem is internal and something you can easily fix. I'd be lying if I said I wasn't worried, though. Is it a boy?"

Charlie made an exaggerated face. "It's not a boy."

"That's good." Caleb's grin was mischievous. "I don't believe I'm ready to share you yet. When you do find a boy, keep in mind that girls always fall in love with their fathers. That means I have to approve of your boyfriend."

"Oh, geez!" Charlie stared at the ceiling as she rubbed her nose. "It's not my fault that math is stupid. I don't know how you can expect me to focus on math when it's just so … stupid."

"It sounds like you're having a problem with your vocabulary lessons, too," Kate teased, pushing a strand of Charlie's flyaway hair from her face. "If there's something wrong, you can tell us. We'll fix it together."

"We will," Caleb agreed. "You have to tell us before we can help, though."

Charlie pressed her lips together and exhaled heavily through her nose, reminding Kate of a bull as the girl shifted from one foot to the other. "There's nothing wrong."

"I don't believe you," Kate said, maintaining a level demeanor. "But you're clearly not ready to talk about it. We'll be here when you're ready to talk. It's okay. If you don't want to confide in us we'll simply wait until you are ready."

"It's not that," Charlie said, shaking her head as guilt swamped her. Her parents never yelled or threatened. They were always reasonable.

Things would be easier if they weren't always so reasonable. "There's nothing wrong with me."

"Then I look forward to you doing better in school," Caleb pressed. "If there's nothing wrong, you have no excuse."

"And if there is something wrong, all you have to do is tell us," Kate added.

"There's nothing wrong." Charlie gritted out the words before turning on her heel and stalking toward the hallway. Her shoulder brushed against the doorjamb as she did and she reached out to steady herself, myriad images she couldn't untangle slamming into her head and causing her to jolt sideways.

Concerned at the way his daughter moved, Caleb rushed toward her, catching the thin girl around the waist before she could flop backward and hit her head on the kitchen island. "What is it, Charlie?"

Charlie didn't immediately answer, her eyes rolling back in her head. Kate panicked when she saw the girl staring into nothing, her fingers shaking, and looked for the cordless phone. "Oh, my ... she's having a seizure! I'll call 911."

"I'm not sure she's having a seizure," Caleb gritted out, his expression serious. He gripped Charlie's shoulders, but except for her shaking fingers she didn't so much as twitch.

"Is she breathing?" Kate asked, fumbling for the phone.

"She is." Caleb bobbed his head. "In fact, I think she's ... ."

As if on cue, Charlie bolted into a sitting position, her eyes back to normal but her pallor unearthly white. "Call for help," she blurted out, her breath coming in ragged gasps. "The Fitzgerald house is on fire."

Caleb remained where he was, staring at Charlie with a dubious expression on his face. "The Fitzgerald house? You mean next door? How can you possibly know that?"

"I just do." Charlie's eyes filled with tears as she gripped her hands into tight fists. "I'm not lying. Mrs. Fitzgerald is trapped in the house. She can't get out. She's ... screaming!"

Caleb shot a worried glance at Kate, rubbing Charlie's shoulders before releasing them and rising to his full height. "I'll go look."

"You'll be too late," Charlie screeched, her voice breaking. "She's going to be gone ... and soon!"

"Charlie, calm down." Caleb forced a smile before disappearing into the hallway. "I'm sure the Fitzgerald house is fine. You just ... imagined the fire or something. I think you fainted."

Kate kept the phone in her hand as she stared at the back of Charlie's head. Despite Caleb's misgivings, she believed Charlie. Kate had no knowledge of the house next door being on fire, or the elderly woman trapped inside, but she instinctively believed Charlie.

Caleb was back in the kitchen in seconds. "Charlie's right," he said grimly. "The house is fully engulfed. Call for a fire truck. Tell them to hurry."

"Where are you going?" Kate asked, her heart rolling when she saw Caleb scurrying toward the door.

"I have to see if I can help her." Caleb briefly glanced between his wife and daughter. "It will be all right."

Charlie remained on the kitchen floor, staring blankly at the wall. She looked smaller than her ten years, vulnerable even. She also looked abandoned and alone.

"It's not going to be all right," she intoned, pressing her eyes shut. "It's already too late. Mrs. Fitzgerald is gone."

"You can't know that," Caleb hedged.

"I know it!" Charlie's temper flared and at the light fixture over the sink exploded. "I know it. It's already too late. I'm always too late."

1

ONE

PRESENT DAY

*I*t took every ounce of energy I had not to use my rather impressive and yet woefully uncontrollable magic to fling my coffee mug at my new boss's head.

Okay, that could be the nerves talking. *Myron Biggs is not a bad man.* That's what I kept telling myself when I caught him staring at my chest ... and my butt as he ushered me into his office ... and then my cleavage when he leaned over to ostensibly make me feel warm and welcome in my new work environment.

He's not a bad man. Really. That line was stuck on repeat in my mind while my heart begged to differ. My foot wanted to agree with my heart and kick him. This was probably not the best way to start a new job.

"I think you're going to fit right in with the team," Myron offered, his smile more "cat that ate the canary, the canary's family and the canary's neighbor's family" than "I'm going to win boss of the year accolades in the near future." His eyes lit up as they locked with mine. "I think you're going to offer a youthful vibe to our team that is sorely needed and missed."

The words themselves weren't terrible. The fact that he was staring at my breasts when he said them, on the other hand, was enough to make my stomach roll. I had my doubts that he could pick me up out of a police lineup if a murder conviction was on the line, but believed completely he would be able to identify my breasts in a sea of strippers at a porn convention.

I bit the inside of my cheek and quickly counted to five to calm myself, fixing a pleasing smile on my face as I maintained my world-famous calm. "Yes, well, I'm looking forward to being part of the team. Hopefully my teammates won't stare at my breasts as much as you. Fingers crossed!"

Whoops. Did I say I had world-famous patience? That was my mother, may she rest in peace. I'm the exact opposite. It's more like I have a notorious reputation for foot-in-mouth disease. That's the same thing, right?

My name is Charlotte Madison Deborah Winifred Rhodes (my mother was one of four sisters, and simply refused to favor one over the others), but everyone calls me Charlie. I'm a recent graduate of the Gendry Metaphysics Institute.

Yes, that's a real thing.

I have a degree in parapsychology, focusing on psychokinesis and paranormal phenomenon.

Why did I pick that field? Because I have psychic dreams and relatively regular flashes that show me the near future or various times from the past. Oh, and I can occasionally move things with my mind – only when I'm upset or angry, though – so there's that to contend with, too. I'm like the Hulk if he were mixed with Carrie and there was a lot of pig's blood at places other than the prom.

No, I'm not delusional. Wait … that does kind of make me sound unbalanced, doesn't it?

On top of all that, this is my first official job that doesn't involve asking, "Do you want fries with that?" at the end of every conversation.

I'm only mildly nervous. Okay, I'm completely nervous. My palms are sweaty, my eyes refuse to focus and I'm fairly certain I'm suffering brief bouts of deafness because I hear only half of what Myron Biggs is saying to me. Wait … he's talking again.

"I was not looking at your breasts," Myron sputtered, his cheeks flushed with embarrassment. "If you think that ... ."

"I must've been mistaken," I said hurriedly, forcing my temper to remain in check. The last thing I needed was to cause Myron Biggs' head to explode. That's never happened, mind you, but it's one of my biggest fears. Other people worry about car accidents or ghosts (for the record, I would love to meet a ghost, and expect to do that one day in the near future thanks to this job), but I worry about magical abilities that I can't always control and hide from everyone for fear of being burned at the stake or locked away and studied like a lab rat. Yeah, I'm a massive coward. Sue me. "I'm just really nervous and tend to blurt out random things when I'm in a new situation. I promise it won't happen again."

Biggs narrowed his eyes, understandably dubious. "How can you guarantee that?"

"Because we'll never be in this situation again."

He stared me down for a long time, finally shaking his head and leaning back in his chair. "You have outstanding academic records, and my nephew insisted you were the one for the job. I allow him to be in charge of all the hiring for the Legacy Foundation. He wanted you ... so here you are."

"Chris Biggs is your nephew?" I probably should've put that together before now. That's the nerves again. "I didn't realize."

"Yes, well, the Legacy Foundation was started by my father thirty years ago and it was always very important to him. Since his death, my brother and I have focused our interests on other parts of the business," Biggs supplied. "The foundation is almost entirely funded by private grants, and believe it or not, it's funded well. My father included a stipulation in his will that the Legacy Foundation continue after his death, so my nephew took over operations about five years ago. He's very ... passionate ... about the endeavor."

Biggs said "passionate" like someone else might say "loony." I didn't bother to point that out. "Well, I happen to be passionate about it, too. I look forward to being a contributing member of the team."

Biggs' smile was tolerant, but just barely. "Yes, well, I'll call my nephew so he can collect you and start your tour. I'm sure he will be able to answer any questions you have."

CHRIS BIGGS WAS nothing like his uncle. While Myron boasted snowy white hair, perverted green eyes and a mouth that made me want to vomit because he constantly used his tongue to lick the corners, Chris was the exact opposite. He had a friendly and open smile, chiseled cheekbones, broad shoulders and warm green eyes that reminded me of a walk in the meadow.

What? He's young and hot. He almost looks like a male fashion model, with that perfect blondish brown hair and those broad shoulders and that tight little ... um ... where was I again? Criminy, I'm allowed a little work crush. Sue me.

"I'm so glad you arrived when you did," Chris enthused, gesturing wildly with his hands as he led me down a basement hallway. I guess I shouldn't have been surprised that the Legacy Foundation was housed in the basement – where else would they hide the paranormal investigators, right? – but it was still disappointing when Chris led me into the elevator and pressed the button for the bottom floor.

"I'm glad to be here," I enthused, taking a moment to study the ridiculously attractive lines of his face. I surreptitiously glanced at his left hand for a wedding ring, my heart settling a bit when I saw it was bare. That didn't necessarily mean that he was open for offers – or that I would make them – but the realization filled me with warmth.

"I thought we would start off with a brief tour of the facility and then introduce you to the other members of the team."

"That sounds great."

The tour was like most tours ... boring. I'd seen the state-of-the-art equipment before and I couldn't exactly work myself into a frenzy when I saw the new all-terrain vehicles they were outfitting for jobs in remote locations. The EDI meters, infrared lights, EMF detectors and EVP recorders were nothing new. I'd been outfitted with all of them multiple times while in college and working an apprenticeship for a semester in London. I was most interested in the people, and I wasn't disappointed when Chris led me into a large conference room where a group of bored-looking drones munched doughnuts and discussed the day's events.

"This is the team." Chris grinned broadly as his gaze bounced between faces. "Team, this is Charlotte Rhodes. She's our new associate."

"Charlie," I corrected automatically, my cheeks burning when a couple of curious stares floated in my direction. "I go by Charlie."

"Charlie." Chris' grin widened. "So, we'll start over here. This is Hannah Silver. She is an M.D. with a Ph.D. in cryptozoology and hominology. Her focus is on animals in the wild, and she can conduct an autopsy and DNA scan in a pinch. She's utterly brilliant."

I didn't miss the goofy smile Chris shot in Hannah's direction. It looked as if I wasn't the only team member with a crush. I couldn't blame Chris. Hannah boasted silvery blond hair tied back in a bun, long legs and a slim frame. She managed to look smart and somehow busty at the same time. She must use a lot of underwire. No woman that thin should naturally have boobs that big. Despite her body, she looked as if she belonged in a white lab coat making important decisions to save the human race. It was probably the glasses, I told myself. They were simple black frames, and she looked effortlessly chic in them.

I extended my hand in greeting. "It's nice to meet you."

"It's nice to meet you, too." Hannah's smile was legitimate, but she seemed distracted. "Chris, did you get my request for a new microscope? I need it before we head out on another job. The lens on my last one broke."

"I got it, and it's being sent down from the seventh floor even as we speak." Chris beamed, his expression wistful as he stared at Hannah. She seemed oblivious to his affection as she bobbed her head, happy to be getting a new toy, but unaware Chris was apparently hopelessly in love with her. "It should be here any second."

"Thank you."

Chris watched her shuffle away from the table for a moment before shaking his head and returning to the introductions. "This is

Laura Chapman. Her father is Ben Chapman. He's one of the vice presidents in the company and he heads the accounting division. As for Laura, she's into metaphysical and holistic life coaching."

Hmm. *That's a thing?* I didn't know that was a real thing. The look the auburn-haired beauty shot me left no doubt about whether or not I should voice that opinion. I didn't bother shaking Laura's hand because I could tell it was the last thing she wanted. Instead I merely shoved my hands in the pockets of my cargo pants and smiled. "It's nice to meet you."

Laura curtly nodded her head. "And you. I understand you focused on telekinesis while studying. Any particular reason why?"

The question was abrupt and took me by surprise. "I've always had an interest in that field," I answered evenly. "Aren't you interested in telekinesis?"

"I don't believe it really exists," Laura replied, not missing a beat. "I look forward to lively debates, though. The whole point of this group is to discover what is real and what is legend, right?"

She didn't believe it existed? I could show her a thing or two. Of course, because I keep my abilities to myself – and plan to do so for the foreseeable future – there was no way I could do that. "Yes, well ... "

Laura was already across the room talking to Hannah by the time I regrouped.

"Don't worry about her." Chris forced out a dry chuckle. "Laura takes some time to warm up to people. She's a little ... cold."

That was a nice way of putting it. "That's okay. Hannah seems like a dream. I don't think one personality makes up an entire group. If that were the case, well, things would get boring pretty quickly, wouldn't they?"

"Definitely." Chris patted my shoulder as he directed me toward the far corner of the room, where a black man in his fifties sat nursing a mug of coffee while a white woman, also in her fifties, studied her reflection in a pocket mirror. "This is Millie Watson and Bernard Hill. Bernard is our mechanic and general Mr. Fix-It. If anything breaks, take it to him."

I liked Bernard on the spot, and it had nothing to do with the way he winked and shot me a thumbs-up. Okay, almost nothing. "Hi."

"Don't you worry, you'll figure everything out and feel as if you've been part of the team forever pretty quickly," Bernard offered between sips of coffee. "It might seem overwhelming now, but we're pretty easy to get along with."

"Speak for yourself," Millie interjected, sighing as she ran a hand through her bottle blond hair. The woman was eccentric looking. There was no other way to put it. She ratted her hair as if the 1980s trend never went out of style, wore the brightest red lipstick I'd ever seen – which happened to clash with her pink satin coat – and the black liquid eyeliner clouding both her upper and lower lids looked as if it had been drawn on while Millie was drunk. Given the way she smelled, I couldn't be sure that wasn't the case. "I happen to think we're extremely difficult to get along with."

"That's just you," Bernard said, chuckling as he patted her hand. He seemed fond of the boisterous woman. "Don't mind Millie. She's hungover, and she enjoys taking it out on other people."

Well, that answered that question. "Are you hungover often?" I asked, genuinely curious.

"As often as humanly possible," Millie replied, unbothered as she lifted her arm and sniffed her pit. "Seriously … it's coming out of my pores."

"Drink something lighter next time," Bernard suggested.

"That's probably a good idea." Millie looked tired when she focused on me again. "Welcome to the team. I can already tell I'm going to like you more than I do Laura."

Chris' smile, which had remained firmly in place for the entire tour, slipped. "Millie, you know you're not supposed to cause trouble with her. She'll report you to Human Resources – as she always does – and then Uncle Myron will come down and yell."

"You send Myron to me," Millie suggested. "I'll handle him. We both know he won't fire me."

"He won't?" Wrapping my head around the group dynamic was an ongoing effort, but I was keen to know the ins and outs of the relationships. "Why is that?"

"Because he's my ex-husband," Millie replied, not missing a beat. "If he fires me he'll have to pay alimony, and there's no way he'll do that."

My mouth dropped open as I considered the statement. "I ... um ... ."

"Don't worry about it," Chris said, patting my arm as he chuckled. "You'll get used to it. Uncle Myron and Mille have a ... unique ... relationship."

"We do," Millie agreed. "He hates me, but still loves me. I hate him, but tolerate him because I'm fond of the boy." She jerked her thumb in Chris' direction. "We have a very uncomfortable relationship, but I enjoy it because torturing Myron is one of my few joys in life. Well, that and Jell-O shots."

"Oh, well, that sounds fun." At first glance I wasn't sure what to make of Millie. Within a few moments of talking to her I knew she was bound to be one of my favorite people ever. She was refreshing ... and not only because she obviously didn't give a flying fig what anyone thought about the way she carried herself or dressed. "I'm very glad to meet both of you."

"Oh, you need to work on your lying, honey," Millie tsked, shaking her head. "You'll have to get much better at it if you expect to survive this group."

I'd been lying my entire life, keeping my abilities secret. I didn't think I'd suddenly start having a problem now. "I'll consider it."

"And here is the final member of our team," Chris said, shifting his gaze to the open door where another man – this one taller and darker than Chris – stood in the doorframe. "Charlie Rhodes, this is Jack Hanson. He's former military and handles all of our security."

"In other words, if he yells 'duck' do it and don't ask why," Millie suggested, winking at Jack. "Isn't that right, hot stuff?"

Jack, his shoulder-length black hair tied into a ponytail at the nape of his neck, ignored the question and focused on Chris. "We just got an assignment from upstairs," he said, his face blank. "We have a job ... and it's hot."

Chris was suddenly all business. "Where ... and what?"

"Someone claims that Bigfoot is killing people in Michigan," Jack replied. "Apparently the cops thought this was right up our alley and want us to lend our scientific opinion."

"Bigfoot?" Chris' face split with a wide grin. "You're kidding?"

"I'm not kidding." Jack's dark eyes briefly landed on my face before shifting back to Chris. "Everyone needs to pack up. We're out of here in thirty minutes."

"All right!" Chris pumped his hand in the air. "This is the big one, folks. This is what we've been waiting for. Grab your gear and meet by the elevator in thirty minutes. You got that?"

Various team members murmured their assent as I focused on Jack. "You know how to make an entrance, huh?"

Jack's lips curved. "I don't do subtle."

"Probably not. You said Michigan. Where in Michigan are we going?"

"A little town called Hemlock Cove," Jack replied. "It's supposed to be wacky and weird. I figured that fits this group perfectly."

"It sounds as if that's definitely the case." I could barely contain my excitement. "Here we go, huh?"

Jack didn't seem nearly as enthusiastic as I felt. "Yeah. Here we go."

TWO

"Tell me about Hemlock Cove."

Chris sat in the passenger seat of the rented Chevy Tahoe and cast an expectant look in Jack's direction as the younger man navigated the rutted two-lane blacktop that led toward the small Michigan hamlet.

"It's wacky," Jack replied, his tone dry.

Chris cocked a dubious eyebrow. "Wacky? Can you be more specific?"

I sat in the back seat next to Millie and glanced at her to see if she was following the conversation. The wackiness level of Hemlock Cove was apparently the furthest thing from her mind, though, because she was fast asleep. She slept during the entire plane ride to Michigan – the Legacy Foundation boasts its own private plane – and barely woke long enough to climb into the Tahoe at the airport before Jack sped away. Bernard, Laura and Hannah rode in a second vehicle with the bulk of our equipment. I wasn't upset about the driving configuration because it meant I didn't have to spend more time with Laura.

"The town used to be called Walkerville," Jack volunteered. "Several years ago they decided to turn their misfortune into a tourist trap. It seems that when the manufacturing base dried up the town council decided to rebrand. They've turned the town into a magical refuge for geeks who like witches, wizards, ghosts and other odd stuff like that."

I leaned forward, intrigued. "They rebranded the town as magical? But ... how?"

Jack shrugged, not bothering to meet my gaze in the rearview mirror. "Something about everyone in town being witches and wizards and stuff. They have a boatload of festivals from what I can gather. Information on the town isn't exactly flowing because it has one newspaper – The Whistler – and it's a weekly. I looked through about eight previous editions. Each one was essentially an advertorial for a festival."

"Sounds kind of fun," I admitted. "Is anyone there really a witch?"

Jack's swivel was slow and I couldn't help but worry about him ignoring the road so he could pin me with a hard look. "You believe in witches?"

I nodded without hesitation. "How can you do this job if you don't believe in witches?"

"It's not too difficult."

Chris chuckled as he shifted in his seat. "Don't let Jack get to you, Charlie. He's a non-believer."

"Then why does he work with us?"

"Because he's good at what he does, and we need a solid security guy in place on many of our jobs," Chris replied, matter-of-fact. "Jack knows what he's doing and he's loyal. If he doesn't happen to believe the same things we do ... well ... it's not the end of the world."

It sounded like the end of the world to me. Of course, I wasn't in charge of hiring. "What about the residents of Hemlock Cove, though?" I pressed. "Do any of them claim to really be witches?"

"Not that I can tell." Jack appeared to be amused by the question, his fingers light as they tapped the steering wheel. "It seems to be one big in-joke. The entire town plays a part in it. The town pretends it's magically imbued by some great power. The tourists eat it up. The shops are theme stores and there are kitschy bakeries and tons of inns in the area. It must be working for them."

Something about the story didn't make sense. "So someone was killed by Bigfoot in a town run by witches? You don't find that strange?"

"Fair point," Jack conceded. "Michigan has a lot of Bigfoot legends. I saw a few of them when I ran a cursory search before packing for the trip. I plan to continue later tonight if I get the chance."

"I read up a bit on the plane," Chris offered. "Most people in the area agree something lives in the woods, but they don't call it Bigfoot. I'm not a fan of that name either. I prefer hominid or hominid-like creature. I can even tolerate Sasquatch. As for Michiganders, though, they call it the Dog Man."

I rubbed my cheek as I absorbed the statement. "It's essentially Bigfoot, though, right?"

"We don't know what it is," Chris answered. "I don't like jumping to conclusions until I get more information. This is your first case, so you're bound to be excited. I can forgive anything when it's accompanied by enthusiasm. I get that you will be bouncing all over the place. Just don't let your excitement get the better of you."

"I'll try to refrain," I said dryly, lifting my chin as the town ahead took shape. There wasn't much to it – two main roads and a handful of businesses – but what I could see was downright adorable. "Oh, wow! It's cute."

"That's not how I'd describe it," Jack said, his eyes shifting to Hemlock Cove's main drag as he navigated through the sparse town. "There's no gas station."

"Yeah, um, I believe there's one on the south side of town," Chris offered. "I looked at a regional map on the plane, too. The inn we're staying at is a good ten miles from the gas station, so keep that in mind so we don't run out of gas."

"Yes, that would suck," Jack muttered.

"Especially if the Dog Man is out there to get us," I teased, smiling as we stopped at a light near a cute magic shop named Hypnotic. The sign in the window said "Drink Up, Witches" and featured a painted silhouette of a witch sitting in a martini glass. "I love this place."

"You haven't even seen this place," Jack countered, annoyance evident in his voice. He clearly wasn't a fan of unrestrained enthusiasm. I refused to let that bother me despite his determination to be a killjoy.

"I've seen enough," I said, smiling at the picturesque town square. "Look. There's a festival going on. I wonder what it's for."

"It's spring, so it's probably a spring fling or something," Chris noted. "Look. They have a kissing booth. I haven't seen one of those since I was a kid."

"They also have an old lady running around in a combat helmet," Jack observed, pointing at an elderly woman in camouflage fatigues as she scurried through the parking lot that led to the newspaper office. "Holy cripes! That woman has a shotgun in her hand."

"And a whistle," I added, grinning. I had no idea what the woman was doing – or why she was going into the newspaper office – but I was a big fan of eccentric personalities. "What do you think she needs the whistle for?"

"Probably to tell Bigfoot she's coming after him," Jack replied. "That's probably why she's carrying the gun, right?" He looked worried when he asked the question, tilting his head when he saw a blond woman appear at the newspaper door. She made big gestures as she talked to the older woman with the gun, but she didn't appear to be in any immediate danger.

"She's cute," Chris noted.

"The woman with the gun? Just darling," Jack muttered.

"Not her." Chris chuckled, genuinely amused. "I was talking about the blonde. Perhaps I'll have to stop in at the newspaper office for some research."

"Won't that cut into the time you spend mooning over Hannah?" Jack asked, not missing a beat.

For some reason I couldn't identify, my stomach rolled. Having Chris' crush on Hannah verified was mildly disappointing. It's not as if I took the job to find a boyfriend, I reminded myself. I wanted to do something important, something that would lead me to answers about my own abilities. Still, a little eye candy never hurt anyone. If that eye candy belonged to someone else, though, that was a different story.

"I don't 'moon' over Hannah." Chris' cheeks burned bright as he stared out the passenger window. "Geez. Why would you say that?"

"I've got eyes," Jack replied, turning his attention to the GPS unit on the dashboard. "According to this, we need to stay on this road until we see a lighthouse. That's where we park. Then we hike a bit behind the lighthouse to find the body. The police chief will be waiting for us."

The body. I'd almost forgotten we were in Hemlock Cove to investigate a murder – or potential Dog Man attack. It could honestly go either way, and that's what made this first case so magical. "Is it wrong that I'm excited?" I asked finally, feeling rather guilty.

"Not at all," Millie answered, taking me by surprise with her wakefulness. I thought she was completely out. "Someone remind me to get a combat helmet when we have a chance to shop later. I totally liked that woman's style."

Chris snorted. "You never cease to amaze me, Millie. That's why you're my favorite aunt."

"Right back at you, kid." Millie smoothed her hair as she straightened. "Now, let's find Bigfoot. I'm dying to ask who does his hair."

I HOPPED out of the Tahoe and groaned as I stretched my legs. The nearest airport was a little more than an hour away. By the time we disembarked, loaded the vehicles with supplies and then drove to Hemlock Cove, my legs and back felt stiff and sore.

The lighthouse – known in all the reading material as the Dandridge – was easy to find. A group of people stood talking in front of the picturesque building as we gathered our group. I took a moment to study the new faces, noticing the odd configuration of three men and one woman. The chief of police was easy enough to pick out because of his uniform, but the two men standing beside him were harder to gauge.

One man had dark hair and eyes. He stood with his arm protectively around a short woman with long dark hair. She looked upset as she spoke to the police chief. The dark-haired man was obviously trying to console her. So was the police chief, for that matter. He rested his hand on her shoulder a few times as she spoke, but I was fairly certain she was crying.

"I bet she found the body," I murmured. I was mostly talking to myself, but because Jack exited the Tahoe on the same side as me he heard the words.

"She does look upset." Jack narrowed his eyes. "My understanding is that a couple of people live in the lighthouse. I suggested we camp there when I talked to the chief, but he shot that down quickly."

"You wanted to camp in the lighthouse?" I was mildly impressed with Jack's suggestion ... and willingness to isolate himself in the face of danger. "That would've kept us closer to the scene. It's too bad that's not possible."

"Hannah and Laura prefer hotel rooms," Jack supplied. "They're not big on camping – especially Laura – so we would've had rooms to shower and rest in regardless. We'll play it by ear and figure it out."

"What about the other guy?" I asked, my eyes zeroing in on the man who stood out in the small crowd. He was tall, broad shoulders tapering to a narrow waist. He looked as if he and not the chief was in charge, yet he had long hair, almost as long as Jack's, and wore street clothes. "He doesn't look like a cop."

"He's not," Jack said, following my gaze. "He's FBI."

"You know him?"

Jack shook his head. "He has the certain look. And the police chief told me they had a Fed dedicated to the area on the way."

"How can he be a Fed with long hair like that?"

Jack shrugged. "Some people just like long hair." He offered me a half-hearted wink as my cheeks burned. "Some women like it, too." He turned his attention from me and met Chris' gaze across the hood of the Tahoe. "Let's introduce ourselves."

The foursome studied us with unveiled interest as we approached. I plastered a wide smile on my face and locked gazes with the woman first to take the edge off my nervousness. She seemed friendly, perhaps a little scattered. I opened my mouth to greet her, but the men took control of the situation before I could.

"I'm Chris Biggs. We're with the Legacy Foundation. This is Jack Hanson. I believe you talked to him on the phone?"

"Yeah, I did. I'm Terry Davenport. I'm the chief of police here in Hemlock Cove." The chief shook hands with Chris and Jack, offering Millie and me a stiff nod before turning to his comrades. "This is Landon Michaels. He's with the FBI. This is Sam Cornell and Clove Winchester. They live in the Dandridge."

Everyone exchanged handshakes and head bobs by way of greeting, and I found my attention bouncing between the FBI agent and the small woman standing between him and Sam Cornell.

"Did you find the body?" I asked the question before I considered the intelligence associated with uttering it.

Clove – she honestly looked like a Clove, which was weird – nodded. "I did. I was taking a walk to see if part of the path needed to be re-graveled – we've been working on making this a haunted attraction for a bit – and that's when I found it."

"She called me," Sam added. "I came out to see and … well … that's when I called Chief Terry."

"Do you know if the victim is a man or a woman?" Jack asked, all business.

"It's a woman," Landon answered. "We had to move her to the morgue. I know you wanted to see the entire scene as it was, but we couldn't risk scavengers or inclement weather. There's a potential storm blowing through tonight. We took photos, though."

"I'm still confused as to what you do," the chief admitted, rubbing his chin. "Landon suggested I call you when we found a strange set of animal tracks – he said you might be able to help us – but I haven't been able to do much research on you because you don't have a website."

"That's by design," Chris offered. "We like to keep our operation out of the headlines. It's not about getting accolades or media attention. We simply like finding the truth."

"And that's what you're doing here?" the chief pressed. "You're looking for the truth?"

"That's the one thing we care about most of all," Chris replied. "As for the body, I understand. I can send Hannah to the medical examiner's office. She's used to cutting through government red tape."

"Perhaps you could share her with my office once she's done," Landon, the FBI agent, joked, his eyes heavy-lidded as he maintained control of the converging factions. "I hate red tape."

"She's perfectly happy with our group," Chris replied primly, his tone taking me by surprise. Laura and Hannah remained in the Dandridge parking lot, yet Chris acted as if the FBI agent was hitting on her in front of him.

"I was just ... never mind." Landon shook his head and exchanged a quick look with the chief. "I can take you to the scene and show you around. If you have people who want to go to the medical examiner's office Chief Terry can handle transportation and directions."

"Sounds great," Jack said, smiling. "Also, when we leave, I was hoping one of you could point me in the right direction. I can't seem to find the inn we're staying at on the map. I don't want to risk getting lost."

"What inn?" Landon asked.

"Umm ... The Overlook."

I didn't miss the quick look Landon and the chief exchanged as Clove widened her eyes.

"Is something wrong?" I asked, legitimately curious.

"Nothing is wrong," Landon replied after a moment's hesitation. "It's actually convenient that you'll be at The Overlook."

"Why is that?" Chris asked, his eyes narrow.

"I live on the grounds with my girlfriend," Landon replied. "Her family owns the inn."

"They're my family, too," Clove pointed out.

"I could never forget that." Landon flashed her a saccharine smile. "Well, let's get this train moving. You'll want to survey the scene and then get settled in your room. If you're late for dinner, you'll go hungry."

Chris balked. "They won't feed us if we're late for dinner? That doesn't sound like a very good inn."

"It's the best inn around these parts," the chief supplied. "It's the best food you'll ever eat, in fact. The women who run it simply don't like people being late."

"I'm sure we'll be able to work around the rules." Chris forced a smile. "Um, how about I send Laura and Hannah to the medical examiner's office with you, Chief Davenport? The rest of us will check out the scene of the attack."

"That sounds fine." The chief moved to walk toward the parking lot, but slowed when Sam offered a quick word of advice.

"Good luck at The Overlook. You're going to need it."

"You're so not funny," Clove complained, flicking his ear. "I'm going to tell Aunt Tillie you said that."

I had no idea who Aunt Tillie was, but Sam looked positively apoplectic at the threat.

"I take it back."

Hmm. Hemlock Cove was going to prove even more interesting than I originally thought. I could already feel it.

THREE

"So people actually live out here?"

I cast a glance over my shoulder as I followed Chris, Jack and the FBI agent into the thick forest. Clove and her boyfriend went inside the lighthouse, their heads bent together as they whispered to each other and left us to our exploration. I couldn't dislodge the shaken look on Clove's face from my mind, the expression almost traumatic.

"Sam and Clove do," Landon replied. "Sam bought the Dandridge about a year ago or so. Clove moved in with him a few months ago."

"It must be cool to live in a lighthouse."

Landon shrugged. "Clove seems to like it."

"Do you know her well?"

If Landon was put off by my questions he didn't show it. "My girlfriend and Clove are cousins, although they're more like sisters. They lived together – actually, with another cousin, too – until recently. Now I live in the guesthouse with Bay, and Thistle lives in town with her boyfriend Marcus."

"Bay, Clove and Thistle?" Jack didn't bother hiding his amusement. "Someone had a sense of humor."

"Their mothers are ... unique." Landon didn't sound disparaging when he said the word. He looked almost wistful. "You'll find that out when you check into the inn."

"And will you be there?" I had no idea why I found him so fascinating – perhaps it was the smile that curved his lips when he talked about his girlfriend and he thought no one was looking – but I couldn't stop myself from staring.

"I'll be at the guesthouse," Landon replied. "It's on the property. We eat dinner there quite often, and I'm sure tonight will be no different."

"Like a family thing?" Chris asked. "That must be nice."

"It's nice to be around a family." Landon appeared to be choosing his words carefully. "Even when they're eccentric, they're still family."

There it was – the odd expression that he kept trying to hide. I couldn't figure out his deal. His girlfriend or her family members clearly didn't embarrass him, yet there was something about them he found amusing. I was almost positive he was looking forward to us meeting the women, although why was anyone's guess.

"Are they witches?" I blurted out the question before I thought better of it.

Landon looked taken aback by my bluntness. "I'm sorry?"

"I think everyone in town is supposed to be a witch," Jack supplied. "You'll have to forgive Charlie. She's new to the game – this is her first case. She was fascinated when I told her about Hemlock Cove being a town for witches."

"Oh, that." Landon visibly relaxed. "They're all witches. Everyone in Hemlock Cove will claim some form of paranormal identity."

"Because that's part of their tourist shtick?" Chris asked.

"Yeah. I was a little thrown by it at first, but … I'm used to it now. The town wouldn't be what it is if they didn't have the witch theme going on."

"Fun." Jack slid a thoughtful gaze in my direction before returning his attention to Landon. "So you live here? There's no FBI office in this town. It's not big enough."

"My office is in Traverse City. I used to have an apartment there," Landon replied. "I get special dispensation because I'm mostly on the road – and often in Hemlock Cove – so I'm allowed to break the rules and live here thanks to some added effort by my boss."

"And you did that for your girlfriend?" I was impressed that he not only put in the request but also didn't seem embarrassed to admit it.

Landon's smile was enigmatic. "I did that for myself. The scene is over here."

Landon stood several feet from the area, which was cordoned off with yellow tape, and crossed his arms over his chest as Chris and Jack moved closer to the scene. There was a dark stain on the ground, and it took me a moment to realize it was blood.

"How was she killed?" Jack asked, straightening.

"Her throat was … missing," Landon replied, grimacing. "That's the best way I can describe it."

"Meaning you think an animal ripped out her throat?" Chris asked, utilizing the expensive camera around his neck to snap photographs. "What kind of indigenous animals do you have here?"

"We have some bears, coyotes and the like," Landon answered. "We've never seen an aggressive bear in this area to my knowledge. Coyotes aren't big enough to do what was done to this victim – and we don't have an identity yet. We're waiting on the medical examiner for that. Then there's … that." Landon pointed toward an odd print on the ground closest to Jack's foot. "We don't know what that is."

"Look at that." Chris was excited as he used his hip to clear me out of the way so he could have a clear shot of the print. "This is clearly not a coyote print."

"Or a bear," Jack added, pursing his lips as he locked gazes with Landon. "You've been careful not to say too much, but your office contacted us."

"I didn't contact you," Landon clarified. "That was my boss. He seems to have some relationship with a guy named Myron Biggs."

"That's my uncle," Chris supplied. "I think they went to the same high school."

"I have no idea about any of that." Landon's stance was firm. Even though Chris was technically in charge, it was clear he had more respect for Jack. I couldn't figure out why – Chris was an amiable guy, after all – unless it was because they both had long hair and tough guy demeanors. "My boss suggested calling you in to utilize your expertise. Chief Terry and I will still handle the investigation. You can track down non-essential leads and focus on the animal aspect as much as you want."

"But you're not happy we're here," Jack prodded.

"I don't care either way," Landon clarified. "This place is my home. Something killed that woman. I don't know if it was an animal or a human, but I plan to find out. I love a lot of people in this town, and I don't want them being left at the mercy of a madman ... or a mad beast, for that matter." He seemed calm as he said the words, but I didn't miss the fervency in his eyes.

"What do you think it was?" I asked.

Landon shrugged, holding his hand palms up. "I don't know what it was. I know that I don't want it to happen again. So I'm here to offer you whatever help you need. I will be following up my own avenues of investigation, though, so I will not be at your service for the majority of your stay."

"Sounds more than fair," Jack said, cracking his large knuckles. "We need to get casts of the prints, Chris. Then we need to look around."

Chris snapped three more photos in rapid succession. "I'm on it. This could be it, Jack. We might finally be able to get proof of a hominid-like creature in the United States. Think about it."

Jack forced a smile that didn't make it all the way to his eyes. "Great. Get your clay stuff for the cast. I'm going to take a look around the perimeter to make sure the cops didn't miss anything."

Landon arched an eyebrow when Jack straightened. "What is it you think we missed?"

"I just want to make sure we have all of the bases covered," Jack replied. "I didn't mean it as an insult."

Landon's shoulders were stiff. "Then I guess I shouldn't take it as one."

"Great."

THE NEXT FORTY-FIVE minutes were extremely uncomfortable. I helped Chris with the foot casting while Jack prowled the immediate area, sticking his head through the sparse foliage in a bevy of different locations. It was spring, so the weeds and undergrowth hadn't filled in yet and the ground was soft and muddy in places. That made searching with our eyes easier, but navigating the footpaths slippery and wet.

Landon remained rooted to his spot. He appeared mildly curious while watching Chris mix the fast-drying clay we used to make print casts, but otherwise remained lost in thought. After such an extended period of silence I couldn't take the uncomfortable atmosphere descending over the area one second longer.

"How did you end up here?" I asked, causing Landon to jolt when the quiet was jarringly interrupted.

"I don't understand what you mean," Landon said after a beat. "I was assigned to the Traverse City office. I grew up in mid-Michigan and wanted to stay in the state from the start. I did. I was assigned here."

"Oh, not that. I mean, how did you end up in Hemlock Cove?"

"Bay." Landon's answer was simple and the way his lips curved at the corners at mention of his girlfriend made him that much more attractive, if that was even possible.

"So you've been dating her a long time?"

"About a year and a half."

"Did you meet her on a case?"

"What is this, Lifestyles of the Fed and Dateless?" Jack shot me an annoyed look, which I ignored. "Leave him alone. He doesn't want to answer your questions. You're being invasive."

"I'm not trying to be invasive," I protested, lobbing a dark glare in Jack's direction. "I was simply trying to get a feel for how he ended up here. He doesn't look like the sort of guy who belongs in a town like Hemlock Cove."

Landon's lips twitched. "And what kind of guy do I look like?"

"The kind who prefers the big city," I answered honestly.

"I much prefer Hemlock Cove," Landon explained. "As for Bay ... well ... I met her while undercover on an assignment a while back."

"Was it love at first sight?"

Landon snickered as Jack groaned. "Yes."

I readjusted my gaze so it was appraising instead of curious. "You're very open, but you're being kind of ... weird ... about certain things," I noted. "I can't decide if you're telling the truth."

Jack's mouth dropped open as Chris continued with his cast. He clearly didn't hear me. I expected Landon to tell me to mind my own business, but he was too amused.

"You're going to fit right in at The Overlook," Landon supplied. "The Winchesters love vocal women. I suggest you sit next to Aunt Tillie during dinner. She'll find you fascinating."

I refused to be dissuaded. "Who is Aunt Tillie?"

"Bay's great-aunt."

"Is she funny?"

"She has her moments." Landon adopted a far-off expression, running his tongue over his lips as he considered how to continue. "I'm not being weird. I also don't mean to be disparaging, so please don't think that's what this is. I simply can't figure out what you are supposed to offer us."

"Perhaps some expertise that you don't have access to," I suggested. "Not everything is black and white. There are some things harder to explain than others in this world."

"I'm well aware of that." Landon scratched his nose as he studied me. There was something weighted about his gaze, as if he was trying to see inside of my heart and mind. "Not everything about Hemlock Cove is as it seems," he offered, adjusting his tone. "The people here are genuinely good, though, and I want them protected."

"That's what we want, too," Jack offered, returning from one of his forays into the woods. "I can't find tracks from this spot. No tracks that match what Chris is casting, no tracks for humans either. There are a few sets heading that way, but I have a feeling that's from you guys and the medical examiner's team."

"That's exactly what I found," Landon confirmed, rolling his neck.

"The evidence seems to suggest that she was killed here and yet ... that scenario is hard for me to swallow given the lack of footprints."

"Could someone have erased them?" I asked, glancing around. "The ground is still hard in some places and damp in others because the spring thaw isn't complete. Maybe whoever – or whatever – it was simply didn't make an impression."

"That's definitely a possibility," Landon agreed. "I don't know what to think. The state police evidence team collected a few items, but we're hampered by the fact that all of the local high schoolers like to hit the woods for a party every weekend."

"Ah." Jack made a clucking sound in the back of his throat and nodded. He seemed to understand what Landon was saying better than I did.

"What does that mean?" I asked, confused.

"It means that any beer cans collected ... or discarded matchbooks ... or even condoms indicating sexual activity could be a lost cause because the kids will have roiled up the area," Jack supplied. "It could be a long time before the evidence starts rolling in."

"Yes, and we either have a killer human or animal on the loose while that's happening," Landon added. "I love this town. I love most of the people here. I will do what I have to when it comes to their protection."

"Are you worried about your girlfriend?" I asked.

"I'm always worried about Bay." Landon's smile was back. "But she can take care of herself. She has a tendency to stick her nose in things that shouldn't concern her. I have no doubt this case will be no different."

"Why not order her to stay away?" Jack's question seemed more of an order than a suggestion. "You are with the FBI, after all. She has to obey you."

Landon snorted. "You've never been in a serious relationship, have you?"

"I have." Jack looked caught. "I mean ... I understand women."

"You obviously don't if you think you can boss them around," Landon countered. "Bay is ... a free spirit. She does what she wants when she wants, and I have to live with that. I'll tell her to stay out of it, she'll get mad and do what she wants, we'll fight and then we'll make up. That's how we roll. She won't be able to stay away from this one. It's not in her nature."

"Because it was probably Bigfoot?" I asked.

Landon chuckled. "No. Because she's the editor of the only newspaper in town and she'll be crazy for this story."

"We saw the newspaper office," Jack noted. "She doesn't own a combat helmet, does she?"

"How about a shotgun?" I added.

Instead of laughing off the suggestions as ludicrous, Landon narrowed his eyes. "Why do you ask that?"

"Please tell me you're not dating the woman in the combat helmet," Jack sputtered. "She could be your grandmother."

Something clicked into place for me. "He's dating the blonde who opened the door at the newspaper office," I corrected. "The one Chris commented on."

"What did Chris say about her?" Landon asked, leaning forward.

I risked a glance at Chris and found him completely wrapped up in his own world, oblivious to the conversation as he poured the casting clay into the print. "Just that she was pretty," I replied hurriedly.

Landon raised his eyebrows. "Yes, she's lovely." He stared at Chris a moment, an obvious appraisal, and shook his head.

"What about Bigfoot?" I pressed. "Do you think he's a threat?"

"You're very persistent," Landon noted. "As for Bigfoot … let's just say I'm less worried about Bigfoot attacking Bay than a human with an attitude trying to end her life."

"That's probably smart," Jack agreed. "I'd be worried about the woman with the shotgun, though. She seemed determined."

Landon was determined to be blasé, but I saw his expression crack. "You said she had a combat helmet on?"

"And a whistle," I added.

Landon sharply inhaled and then exhaled slowly, the sound long and drawn out. "I'm sure Bay is fine."

"Who is the woman?" I couldn't help but be curious … and a little worried. Landon Michaels was an FBI agent, and he was supposed to be calm under pressure. He appeared anything but calm.

Landon ignored the question. "I'm just going to make a quick call." He reached into his pocket and retrieved his phone. "I'd better get a mountain of bacon tomorrow morning. I can already tell this is going to be a long week."

4

FOUR

"This is The Overlook?"

I couldn't help but be a little disappointed. The way Landon, Clove and Sam built it up I expected something out of a horror movie. Instead, the inn was absolutely beautiful, the cookie cutter shutters accenting a huge facade that was more pretty than perilous. "It looks like it was a Victorian at one time, maybe something more when you see the back jutting out the way it does."

Jack arched an eyebrow as he handed me my medium-sized suitcase from the back of the Tahoe. "You look sad. Not what you were expecting?"

"I thought it would look like witches live here," I admitted. "This looks like someone's grandma lives here."

"I believe someone's grandma does live here." Jack's eyes betrayed a flicker of mirth. "Didn't you see the look on the FBI agent's face when you mentioned the combat helmet, gun and whistle?"

"Yeah, that was pretty odd."

"See, the way I read his face, it wasn't odd at all," Jack countered. "He was worried about his girlfriend getting in trouble … but not the kind of trouble that would get her killed."

Confusion wafted over me as I tucked a strand of my long dark hair behind my ear. "What other kind of trouble is there?"

"The kind that gets you arrested and gives your FBI boyfriend a migraine."

I was flabbergasted. "Seriously? You think she's a criminal?"

Jack snorted, amused by my dramatic flair. "I think they have a unique relationship, and if you're developing a crush on him you might want to look elsewhere. That man is clearly taken."

"What man is taken?" Laura asked, sticking her nose between us. "Did someone meet a man in this hellhole town? If so, I want a description and a map of where to find him, because I haven't seen any men since we landed. All I've seen is a parking lot."

Jack rolled his eyes as he grabbed the shoulder of my hoodie and tugged me away from Laura. He seemed to dislike the woman even more than I did, which was entirely possible because he knew her better. "We were talking about the FBI agent we met this afternoon."

"And he's definitely taken," I added. "He lives on the grounds of this inn, in fact. He said he lived in a guesthouse, right? What's the guesthouse look like?"

"It's like a little cottage," Hannah supplied, distracted by her phone screen. "The cell service isn't very good here."

"That's what's great about living in the country," Chris added, inhaling heavily. "I love the country! This is where Sasquatch lives ... and hopefully breeds. I can feel it, folks. This is the one!"

Jack muttered something unintelligible, rubbing his forehead. I didn't miss the weary look on his face. I wanted to ask why he insisted on working in this particular field if he was a non-believer, but instead I merely forced a smile and extended the pull handle on my suitcase.

"I don't have a crush on him," I volunteered, keeping my voice low. "I just find him interesting."

"Why? Because he's dating a witch?" Jack looked amused at the prospect.

"No, because he clearly loves his girlfriend enough to give up any chance of FBI advancement. And he's hiding something with the chief of police."

Jack stilled, narrowing his eyes. "How do you know that?"

"Let's face it, he would have to love that woman an awful lot to want to stay in this small town his entire life."

"Not that." Jack curled his lip. "The part about him lying."

"Oh, well, I guess 'lying' is a strong word," I clarified. "They're clearly hiding something, though. I think this town has a secret. They exchanged a few looks when they thought no one was watching. And Landon was kind of evasive on certain topics."

"I thought I was the only one who noticed that," Jack said, closing the door and fobbing the lock. "Perhaps you're more observant than I realized."

I rolled my eyes. "Perhaps you're kind of a butthead."

Instead of reacting with anger, Jack smirked. "Yeah. That's a distinct possibility."

I followed the line of people into the inn, pulling up short when I saw the harried woman standing behind the counter. She looked to be in her fifties, dressed well and easy on the eyes, but the woman standing beside her was another story.

"It's the combat helmet lady," Jack said, amused.

"I said no, Aunt Tillie." The woman at the counter fixed the older woman with a dark look. "When I say no, I mean no."

"Oh, chill out, Winnie." Tillie – this must be the great-aunt Landon mentioned in passing while at the scene – rolled her eyes so hard I swear she almost fell over. "I was hardly trying to date rape you."

Hannah choked at the words, her eyes widening. She was a pretty girl – and sweet – but I was starting to think she was something of a Mary Sue. "I ... um ... ."

Tillie lifted her finger to her lips and let loose with a loud and obnoxious "Shh."

"Aunt Tillie!" Winnie barked, causing me to bite the inside of my cheek to keep from laughing. "I said no. That's my final answer. Now, if you'll excuse me, I have guests to check in. If you need someone to entertain you, I believe Bay and Thistle are in the library."

"I don't want to spend time with them." Tillie unveiled an exasperated expression only a family member could love. There was something so expressive about the elderly woman – her face carved by wrinkles and her curly short hair struck through with gray – that I couldn't help but briefly wish I was a part of her family. "They're obnoxious and mouthy brats."

I raised my eyebrows as I risked a glance at Jack. He looked as amused with the conversation as I did.

"I don't really care if you want to spend time with them or not," Winnie shot back. "I only care that I don't have time to spend with you right now. So ... go."

Tillie crossed her arms over her chest. "Um ... no."

"That did it!" Winnie raised her arm – whether it was to strike her elderly aunt or vigorously point a finger at her I couldn't be certain – but the front door opening and Landon stepping in interrupted her.

"You guys made it." Landon's reaction was blasé as he took in the members of the team he'd yet to meet. "I'm glad you didn't have any trouble finding the place."

"Hello, sailor," Laura murmured under her breath.

"He's got a girlfriend," I reminded her.

"He's not married, not that it would matter to me," Laura countered. "I'll need to spend some time with him, that's for sure."

Landon either didn't notice or care that he was the center of attention. Instead he remained focused on Winnie. "Where is Bay?"

"In the library with Thistle."

"Oh, geez." Now it was Landon's turn to make a face. "Is Thistle in a good or bad mood?"

It was interesting to watch the family dynamic. Landon had been nothing but professional at the scene where the body was found – other than his brief break to check on his girlfriend and her shotgun-wielding great-aunt, of course – but he was clearly comfortable here. Winnie seemed equally at ease with him.

"Thistle is being Thistle," Winnie shrugged. "Before you go, though, I need you to do me a favor."

"What?"

"I need you to take this." Winnie shoved Aunt Tillie toward Landon. "Keep it out of trouble until dinner."

"Um ... pass." Landon's expression mirrored Tillie's from a few moments earlier as he pushed the senior citizen back in Winnie's direction. "I'm in no mood for itchy underpants tonight."

"See, he knows what's good for him," Tillie nodded.

Landon scorched her with a dark look. "Don't push me. If you do, I'll lock you in a room with Thistle and see who comes out standing."

Tillie was unruffled. "It will be me."

"You're not as young as you used to be."

"And yet I'm still young enough to beat Thistle with one hand tied behind my back."

Landon stared her down for a moment, his expression unreadable. "Fine," he said after a beat. "Do what you want, but leave Bay and me out of it. I'll be in the library with your daughter if you need me before dinner, Winnie."

Winnie glared at his back. "Does that mean you're not taking Aunt Tillie with you?"

"I love you, Winnie, but nowhere near that much."

I snickered as I watched him go, amused. I shifted my position a bit, eager to see the famous Bay. I finally caught a glimpse of her through the double glass doors as Landon grabbed both sides of her face to plant a kiss on her before sitting. She said something to him that made him laugh, and another woman – this one with bright teal hair – shuffled closer to the couch and extended a finger in Landon's direction. Whatever she said didn't impress Landon, who merely rolled his eyes.

"She even looks like the devil, doesn't she?"

I jolted at the sound of the voice so close to my side, shifting my eyes down to find Tillie staring into the library. She didn't appear bothered by the fact that she was invading my personal space. "I ... don't know her," I hedged. "She seems friendly enough. I like her hair."

"She's the devil," Tillie whispered. "Look out, because she'll steal from your secret stash when you're not looking ... and then she'll rat you out for having the secret stash when she wants to get you in trouble."

With those words Tillie turned on her heel and flounced toward the door that I presumed led to the inner sanctum of the inn. "I'm taking a nap before dinner," she announced over her shoulder. "Don't let anyone drink my wine."

Winnie offered a distracted wave. "Whatever." She forced a smile when she finally turned her full attention to us. "Let's get you checked in, shall we? I'm sure you're in for a lovely stay in Hemlock Cove."

I was flooded with doubts, but remained hopeful that was true.

IT DIDN'T TAKE long to get settled. I left everything in my suitcase and propped it on the chest at the end of the bed. I ran a brush through my hair, studied the pretty but simple room, and then headed back to the main floor.

That's where I expected all of the action to be, so that's where I wanted to be.

I wasn't disappointed.

"Knock it off." Landon sounded grumpy. I followed the sound of his voice to the dining room. I was the first of my group downstairs. It was early for dinner, so the table was mostly empty except for Landon, the blonde I assumed to be Bay, the teal-haired siren Tillie referred to as the "devil" and a handsome blond man with long hair and a patient smile.

"I'm not doing anything," the girl with the wild hair barked. "You're being a kvetch."

"What's a kvetch?" The question was out of my mouth before I realized it looked as if I'd been eavesdropping. It was too late to take it back, though, so I boldly stepped into the dining room as if I had nothing to hide.

"Hey, Charlie," Landon smiled. "Did you get settled in your room?"

I nodded. "It's a beautiful inn."

"Thank you." The blonde flashed a pretty smile. "I'm Bay, by the way. Landon and Clove told me all about meeting your group. It must be exciting … looking for Bigfoot and everything, I mean."

I searched Bay's face for hints she was making fun of me, but she seemed sincere. "Oh, well, it's my first job, so I'm not sure how exciting it will be. I'm looking forward to it, though."

"Did you always want to be a monster hunter?"

"I always wanted to discover something new," I clarified. "I do have an interest in paranormal things."

"There's no shortage of those things here."

Bay's smile was benign, but I didn't miss the look Landon pinned her with before focusing on me. "Yes, Hemlock Cove is full of randy witches. That's why it's my favorite place on Earth."

Bay playfully pinched his flank. "I don't think you needed to throw in the 'randy' part."

"And yet I'm not sorry I did it." Landon poured two glasses of wine, pushed one in front of Bay and then held up the bottle. "Wine?"

"Oh, sure. That sounds nice." I moved closer to the table, fixing a hesitant look at Bay before grabbing the chair next to her. "So … what's a kvetch?"

Bay snorted. "That's what Aunt Tillie calls our cousin Clove," she replied. "She saves the meaner names for Thistle." She pointed toward the teal-haired girl for emphasis.

"I'm sorry." Landon remembered his manners. "This is Thistle and her boyfriend Marcus. He's okay, but she's evil."

I raised my eyebrows, amused. "I heard that."

"Who did you hear it from?" Thistle asked suspiciously.

I saw no reason to lie – and I'm terrible at it when caught – so I wisely decided to ignore that potential landmine. "Your aunt."

"Which one?"

"The one in the combat helmet."

"That mean old biddy," Thistle groused. "She's our great aunt, and I'm totally going to make her pay. I think it's time to put Operation Make Aunt Tillie Cry into active rotation, Bay. She's been a righteous pain for weeks. She needs to be brought down a peg or two."

"You're going to make your great-aunt cry?" I nodded in thanks as

Landon handed me the glass of wine and watched as he rested his hand on Bay's back, drawing idle circles as he listened to the conversation. They seemed in tune with one another, happy in the face of the chaos. A homey feeling wafted through the room despite the squabbling.

"Oh, she's got it coming," Thistle grumbled. "Trust me. That woman knows how to get under someone's skin – and not in a fun way like one of those spiders that burrows under your skin and lays eggs."

"Oh, um … ." I wasn't sure what to say, which had to be a first. "She seemed nice. Although … um … why does she wear the combat helmet?"

"In case Russia decides to drop the big one," Bay answered, causing Landon and Marcus to snort in unison.

"Really?"

"Well, maybe not Russia," Bay conceded. "She's been waiting for someone to drop the big one since the sixties, though."

"Yeah, she's convinced that when the zombie apocalypse hits it will happen because of an oozing chemical weapon rather than a virus gone awry," Thistle added. "Sadly, we're going to be stuck with her no matter what happens because she knows how to survive."

"She's on your zombie apocalypse team?" The notion made me grin.

"Yeah, it's Bay, Aunt Tillie, Landon, Marcus and me," Thistle replied. "We figure that's the team that has the best chance of surviving."

"I told you that you need to bring one of your mothers, too," Landon interjected. "You guys aren't going to cook. I don't want to eat anything you call cooking."

"There's going to be a bacon shortage in the zombie apocalypse anyway," Bay pointed out. "You'll be sad about food no matter what."

"I see no reason to live if there won't be bacon," Landon teased.

"What about me?" Bay pressed.

"That's a tough choice, sweetie. I'll give it some thought."

Bay elbowed his stomach before turning to me. "So, Charlie, tell us about being a monster hunter."

I giggled, amused at her serious tone. "What do you want to know?"

"Everything," Thistle interjected. "We especially want to know if Bigfoot is real and whether or not we can borrow him. Clove is terrified of Bigfoot, and she's been bugging the crap out of me. She's due for a little payback, too."

"Well, how much time do you have?" I asked, leaning back in my chair.

"Dinner will be ready in thirty minutes," Bay replied. "Is that enough time?"

"Plenty."

"Then let's do it."

Surprisingly enough, I felt comfortable opening up to them. Not about the big secrets, of course, but I instinctively knew they could be trusted with the little ones. "Okay, but I've never seen Bigfoot. I'm convinced I saw an elf once, though."

"Join the club," Thistle said. "We grew up with a menstruation monster and sock-eating gnome in this house. There's nothing you can say that would surprise us."

I bet I knew a few things, but I opted to keep them to myself as I launched into my tale. After all, I liked them, but I didn't know them. There was no way I could trust them with the big stuff.

FIVE

"*I* feel as if my head has been run over by a truck and then backed over again."

I met Millie in the hallway before breakfast the next morning, cocking an eyebrow as I took in her disheveled hair and smeared makeup. I was fairly certain she hadn't taken a shower – although that was none of my business, I reminded myself – and she looked as bad as she sounded.

"You did a lot of drinking last night," I acknowledged, working overtime to hide my smirk. Millie was one of the few people in the group who talked to me as if I wasn't the newbie. "Do you want some aspirin? I'm sure we can ask for some downstairs."

"I want to crawl into an aspirin bottle," Millie replied, shuffling toward the stairwell. "Until that becomes a possibility, though, I want a huge vat of coffee."

"I'm sure they have that, too."

Most of the Winchester family was already around the table, including Clove and her boyfriend. They missed dinner the previous evening, and that seemed to be the topic of conversation.

"You're such a baby, Clove," Thistle spat, openly glaring at her cousin. "It wasn't really Bigfoot. You're letting your imagination run wild. Stop thinking things like that."

"I only think things like that because you told me Bigfoot was out to get me, and now it looks as if he is," Clove shot back, her eyes flashing. "You and Bay like terrorizing me. Now it's coming true. I hope you're happy."

I widened my eyes momentarily, worried this battle would really turn hostile. I learned fairly quickly last night that the Winchester way was to mess with one another whenever the opportunity presented. It was like that in my family until my parents died when I was eighteen. Then the laughter died ... and didn't come back for a very long time. Even when it did return, it was never the same.

"Good morning," I chirped, drawing a few sets of eyes. "How did everyone sleep?"

Thistle stared at me with open distaste for a long time before turning back to her cousin. "Bigfoot didn't kill Penny Schilling. I'll bet that new vintage cauldron I found that it's a human trying to cover his or her tracks by making it look like an animal attack."

"I have to agree with Thistle on this one," Bay said, rubbing her forehead. She looked as hungover as Millie, but it appeared she'd showered and brushed her hair. "The odds of it being Bigfoot are pretty slim."

I considered arguing the point – that's why I was here, after all – but it seemed like a lot of effort before I had my coffee. "Who is Penny Schilling?" I asked, latching on to the one part of the conversation I couldn't make sense of.

"She's the victim," Millie replied, taking me by surprise with her gruffness. "Keep up."

"I like her," Thistle said, her lips twitching as she stared at Millie. "She could give Aunt Tillie a run for her money."

"She tried to give Tillie a run for her money with the wine over dinner last night," I argued. "That's why she's so grumpy. Do you have any aspirin, by the way? I think a couple of people are going to need it."

"Right here." Landon grabbed a bottle from the table and twisted the cap. "I was just about to pour some into Bay. She's hungover, too."

Bay made an exaggerated face that caused me to stifle a giggle. "You're the one who was crying about wanting to kill yourself because your head hurt so much this morning."

"That was only until you revived me in the shower." Landon's grin was cheeky as he tapped three tablets into Bay's cupped hand. "My headache is gone. You magically cured it."

"I think that was the bacon you stole when we walked through the kitchen," Bay grumbled. She tossed the aspirin into her mouth and swallowed half a glass of tomato juice to wash them down. "Aren't you going to have aspirin?"

Landon shook his head and handed me the bottle. "I'm manly. I don't need aspirin."

"Oh, puh-leez." Thistle snorted so loudly it jarred Millie as she tried to get comfortable with her mug of coffee. "You palmed aspirin when you thought no one was looking and you're going to take it and pretend you're somehow stronger than everyone else."

Landon balked. "I did not."

"Open your hand."

"I certainly will not."

Bay's expression shifted from weary to suspicious as she turned to her boyfriend. "Let me see your hand."

"I let you see my hand earlier. I don't think you need a repeat showing." Landon tried to cover his discomfort with flirting, but Bay was having none of it.

"Show me."

"Fine." Landon made a disgruntled face and displayed the aspirin tablets. "Are you happy, Thistle? You ruined my manly facade."

"I still think you're manly," I offered, patting his shoulder as I moved to sit between him and Millie. "That should make you feel better."

I didn't realize that the comment could be misconstrued as flirting until I saw the amused look flit across Bay's face. If she was bothered by my fascination with her boyfriend, she didn't show it. I cleared my throat to dislodge the uneasiness settling in the pit of my stomach. "So … um … who is Penny Schilling again?"

"She's the victim," Landon replied, seemingly relieved to be rescued from the "manly" conversation. "She lives in Bellaire – it's about twenty miles away – and she works at the resort there."

"What kind of resort?"

I jerked my head to the door at the sound of Jack's voice, surprised to find Bernard, Jack and Chris walking into the dining room. Much like Landon, they appeared to be putting on a brave front to hide their hangovers. They were moving slower than normal, though.

"It's a ski resort in the winter and a golf resort in the fall," Landon replied, rubbing his hand over Bay's knee under the table. He seemed to want to be in constant contact with her, which was cute, but also unnerving. They were very tight, which meant whatever secret he was hiding probably had something to do with her. Even after a good night's sleep, I was convinced he knew more than he was saying. But I was unsure how to voice my suspicions to Chris without looking like an alarmist.

"Is it in operation now?" Jack asked, happily pouring himself a mug of coffee. It was the first expression akin to giddiness I'd seen him muster since our first meeting. He took a sip, groaned, and sighed. "That's good stuff."

"Do you want aspirin?" Millie asked, holding up the bottle.

Jack shook his head. "I'm not hungover."

"Oh, we have another manly one," Thistle groaned, her eyes flicking to Jack. "He even kind of looks like our manly one."

"I'm not your manly one," Landon shot back. "I'm Bay's manly one … er, Bay's man. That sounds awful no matter how I phrase it."

Bay patted his arm, amused. "I liked it."

"Ugh, I'm going to puke if you don't knock it off," Thistle warned. "As for the resort, it's open. It has a big dining room and they're getting ready for the season. This is Michigan, so people start wearing shorts as soon as it hits sixty degrees."

"Sad but true," Landon said, chuckling. "Chief Terry and I are heading to the resort to question the workers today. Penny worked in the main dining room most of the time. I understand she picked up swing shifts for other departments when help was needed. She was always eager for overtime."

"What else do you know about her?" Jack asked, sparing a glance for Laura and Hannah as they joined the breakfast party. Laura scanned the table, looking for a spot close to Landon. When she saw where he was situated she scowled and sat next to Sam. Sam completely ignored her and kept his hand on Clove's neck as he attempted to rub out the tension. She really did look worked up.

"She was twenty-four and lived with roommates," Landon replied. "That's all I know so far. I'll get more from Chief Terry when I hit the police station after breakfast. That reminds me, … ." He shifted in his chair and fixed Bay with an unreadable expression. "What are you doing today?"

"Do you want me to go with you to solve the crime?" Bay was clearly amused. "I feel so loved."

"Oh, I love you." Landon said the words, but there was an edge to them. "However, that has nothing to do with my question. I want to know what you're doing today. If you plan to run through the woods with Thistle and Clove I want to know."

"I'm not going into the woods," Clove announced. "I'm thinking of moving back into the guesthouse until this is settled."

"No, you're not." Landon wagged a finger. "That guesthouse is private property now … Bay and I need our privacy. The fact that we had six people essentially living there for months is in the past."

"Oh, you're so bossy," Tillie complained as she breezed into the dining room. Her combat helmet was gone, replaced by an odd gardening hat with scissors sticking out of the band. She also wore pink camouflage pants with flip-flops. The ensemble was … interesting. "I think all cops get off on being bossy."

"No one asked you," Landon shot back, his eyes drifting to her outfit. He didn't seem shocked – which made me think her clothing choice was a regular occurrence and not an indication of some sort of stroke-related behavior – but he did seem suspicious. "Do you plan to garden today?"

"What's it to you?" Tillie challenged, grabbing the coffee pot and pouring herself an oversized mug. "Are you going to stick your nose in an old woman's gardening habits? That's 'The Man,' for you. He's always sticking his nose into business that doesn't concern him. I think my spring saplings are probably quaking in their grow pods in the greenhouse."

"It is a little early in the season for gardening," Bay offered.

"Mind your own business, junior busybody," Tillie snapped. "Worry about your boyfriend. He's trying to get you to promise that you won't investigate the dead girl. Pay attention."

Bay knit her eyebrows and swung her head in Landon's direction. "Is that what you were trying to do?"

Landon nodded without hesitation. "Someone – or something – ripped Penny Schilling's throat out. I don't want you running into the sort of individual who would do that."

"What if it's an animal?" Chris challenged.

Landon ran his tongue over his teeth as he leaned back in his chair. "Then I don't want her running into that animal either. No offense, man, but this conversation has nothing to do with you. I don't want the people I care about eaten by an animal or stalked by a man. You'd be surprised how often it happens."

"They're often eaten by animals?" Laura asked, her smile flirty.

"They're often stalked and put in danger," Landon fired back, ignoring her wink and smile. "Bay, if you want to go out to the scene … I'll take you. I'd prefer if you waited until I was free to go with you."

"We're going out there today," Chris offered. "We can take her."

"No, you can't," Landon growled, flicking his eyes to Tillie. "You did this. Are you happy?"

"I'm not unhappy," Tillie replied. "As for the gardening, I'm merely doing some work with my rototiller, no planting. There's no reason to get your panties in a bunch."

"Why is gardening such a big deal?" I asked, confused.

"You don't want to know," Landon growled.

"I want to know," Laura argued.

Landon pretended he didn't hear her. "If you guys go exploring today, I want to know about it. Just … text me or something."

Bay's face was a mask of emotions as she stared at her boyfriend. She opened her mouth to answer, but Chris, oblivious at the end of the table as he studied his phone, cut her off before she had a chance.

"We could use someone who knows the terrain in that area," he said. "She's more than welcome to come with us. We'll keep her safe. In fact, I can have Jack stick close to her, if that makes you feel better."

Landon stared at Jack, their handsome faces leveling and suspicious eyes locking as he shook his head. "That doesn't make me feel better at all."

Thistle snorted. "That's because he looks like you – only a younger model – and you're worried Bay will fall for him."

"I am not." Landon scowled. "Do you have to be such a pain so early in the morning?"

"She was born a pain," Tillie answered. "Don't worry about Bay. She can take care of herself. If she gets in trouble, I'll handle it."

"Oh, that makes me feel so much better."

I wrapped my hands around my coffee mug, enjoying the warmth on my fingers, the spoon spinning on its own. I was doing that. Er, well, I did that on occasion with my magic. I doubted anyone noticed, but I grabbed the spoon with my fingers just in case. When I lifted my head, I found Tillie staring at me. She didn't bother trying to hide her actions. She openly studied my face without blinking. She reminded me of a creepy owl, and I shifted on my chair, suddenly uncomfortable.

"Do I have something on my face?" I instinctively wiped a finger down my cheek.

"Ignore her," Landon suggested. "She gets her jollies unnerving people. But she usually prefers doing that to men." He snapped his fingers in front of Tillie's face, causing her to glare at him. "You're making Charlie feel self-conscious."

"Sorry." Tillie sounded anything but sorry. "I didn't mean to be rude. That's clearly your job, copper."

"You know I hate it when you call me that," Landon muttered.

"Even more than 'The Man?'" Laura asked. "You do look all man, by the way."

Landon pressed the heel of his hand to his forehead as Bay shot Laura a menacing look and Thistle cracked her knuckles. The Winchester family was ridiculously odd – there was no getting around that – but something else was going on this morning, something I couldn't quite wrap my mind around. They were all scattered and keen on poking one another with insults while covering up for something bigger.

"Either way, we'll need a guide," Chris said. "If you won't lend us your girlfriend, do you have any suggestions for someone who knows the town well?"

"Look for Margaret Little." Landon's smile was enigmatic as Bay elbowed his ribs.

"Don't look for Margaret Little," Bay countered. "I can take you out there."

"No, I don't want you out there," Landon's voice became serious. "Bay, there's either a killer or creature in those woods. Can't you – I don't know – spend your day in the newspaper office?"

"Not last time I checked."

Landon sighed. "You give me a headache."

"I think you should use Clove as your guide," Thistle suggested. "She lives out there, and she's a big fan of Bigfoot."

"Shut up," Clove snapped, jerking her foot against her cousin's shin under the table, causing Thistle to cry out. "You suck."

"And you're a big baby," Thistle shot back.

"You are a big baby, kvetch, but Thistle definitely sucks." Tillie studied my group, her gaze lingering on me. "I can show you around the area."

The offer clearly baffled the people who knew Tillie best, because Bay's mouth dropped open and Landon looked as if he was searching for hidden cameras in the wall sconces.

Chris, focused on his camera, missed all of this. He was clearly great with the science, but terrible with people. "That's great," he said. "We'll leave right after breakfast."

Aunt Tillie's smile was serene as she arched an eyebrow and practically dared Landon to cause a scene. "I'm looking forward to it."

6

SIX

Tillie Winchester was an enigma of sorts. She changed out of her gardening hat and back into her combat helmet for the drive to the Dandridge. She rode with Sam and Clove – which I think made everyone more comfortable – so we gossiped freely as we followed the vehicle. Only Jack, Chris and I opted to return to where the body was found. Everyone else followed up on other tasks.

"Does anyone else think the Winchesters are odd?" I asked.

Jack snorted from the driver's seat. "Isn't that like asking if the sky is blue?"

"I think they're quirky but fine," Chris replied. "If everyone acted the same it would be a very boring world, wouldn't it?"

He had a point, still ... . "They're hiding something." I don't know what possessed me to say the words. I liked the Winchesters. No, really. That didn't mean they weren't keeping some big secrets, and I couldn't help but worry that the secrets would impact the job we were in Hemlock Cove to do.

Instead of laughing, Jack shot me a keen look in the rearview mirror. "What do you think they're hiding?"

"If I knew that they wouldn't be hiding anything."

"You must have something to pique your suspicion," Jack argued. "What is it?"

"They all look at one another when they think no one is watching them."

Jack snorted. "That's the way families interact. They have in-jokes. That's normal. Isn't your family like that?"

My family was dead … at least those I knew about. "No." I averted my gaze and stared out the window. "Maybe you're right. Maybe I'm overreacting."

"But you don't believe that." Jack pursed his lips. "They seem fairly normal to me. Sure, that great-aunt is all sorts of eccentric, but I think it's an act. The rest of the family seems used to it. Heck, the FBI agent didn't even blink when he saw the scissors sticking out of that gardening hat."

"No, but that's part of what I'm saying," I argued. "He wasn't weirded out by the hat – which should weird out anyone – but he seemed agitated by the thought of her gardening. Why would anyone care if a little old lady gardens?"

"Maybe they're worried about her health," Chris offered from the passenger seat. "She is elderly, and it's not quite warm enough for her to be gardening so early in the morning. Maybe she's stubborn and refuses to take care of herself in the manner they would like."

"I guess that's a possibility." I chewed my bottom lip, unconvinced.

"They don't believe we're looking for Bigfoot," Jack pointed out.

"Technically we're not," Chris said, his fingers busy as they flew over his phone screen. "We're looking for a hominid-like creature. I'm not a big fan of the Bigfoot name, as I've repeatedly told you. I think people use it in a joking manner, which I don't like. I don't mind Sasquatch, though. I have no idea why."

I stared at him a moment, dumbfounded. "Is that really important right now?"

"I think using the correct names is always important."

I shifted my eyes to the mirror and caught Jack's reflection smirking. "Okay, but … we're talking about the Winchesters and the fact that they don't believe we're looking for a creature."

52

"I'm not sure we're looking for a creature either," Jack admitted. "Someone could've used the history of this place, that Dog Man legend, and made a murder look like an animal attack. I'd like to see the autopsy report."

He parked in front of the Dandridge and hopped out of the Tahoe, catching me off guard when he opened the door for me before I even reached for the handle. It was a gentlemanly gesture, but I didn't know what to make of it.

"Do you think they'll tell us what's in the autopsy report?" I asked, smoothing my top as I hit the ground. "They don't have to, do they?"

"They don't have to do anything they don't want to do," Jack replied. "They seem open to sharing information – even though you're convinced they're hiding something – but we can't rely on them to make our case. That's our job."

"And it's going to be a fun job." Chris' eyes lit up as he marched toward the path that led past the Dandridge. "Is everyone ready to see the impossible?"

I opened my mouth to answer, sliding a baffled gaze toward Jack. For his part, the security guru seemed amused by our boss's enthusiasm. "He does know the odds of us actually seeing Bigfoot while out there today are slim, right?"

Jack shrugged. "I think he wants to see Bigfoot so bad he'll will it to happen if he has to."

"That's a little … worrisome."

Jack's eyes were contemplative as he grabbed a bag of supplies from the back of the Tahoe. "Aren't you desperate to see the impossible?"

I'd seen impossible things quite regularly since I was a small child. I found it more terrifying than freeing, quite frankly. "I didn't join this group to see the impossible. I joined to … get answers."

Jack tilted his head to the side, his long dark hair slipping past his shoulders. "What answers are you seeking?"

"Different kinds."

"Uh-huh. Well … I hope you find them. You seem to desperately need them."

"That would be a nice change of pace."

"THIS IS WHERE her body was found?" Tillie looked less than impressed when she saw the area the police had taped off the previous day.

Jack nodded, a small smile playing at the corner of his lips. "It is. Does something strike you as funny about that?"

"Not funny," Tillie replied, groaning as she dropped to her knees and stared at the blood. "Did she die here or was it made to look as if she died here?"

"I'm not a police officer," Jack replied. "You'll have to ask the chief … or the FBI agent you have living on your property. You don't seem to like him, though."

"Landon?" Tillie wrinkled her nose. "I like him fine."

"You're mean to him."

"He's mean to me right back."

"Yes, but that's why I figured you don't like each other," Jack pressed. "Most people who like each other are nicer to one another."

"That's not how any family I've been a part of operates," Tillie countered. "Make no mistake, Landon is part of my family. He and Bay are in it for the long haul."

"Are you okay with that?" I asked, ignoring the fact that it was none of my business how Tillie felt about her great-nieces' loves.

"I'm fine with Landon, but Marcus is my favorite," Tillie replied. "I'm growing to like Sam. I hated him at first, but he's not so bad now. He's exactly what Clove needs, so that makes me like him."

"You like Marcus best even though you hate Thistle?" Jack challenged. I could tell that he was trying to get a read on Tillie, and coming up short. She was a hard woman to pin down.

"I don't hate Thistle," Tillie clarified. "I simply rarely like her."

"Isn't that the same thing?"

"No." Tillie offered the one-word answer as if it was the end of the discussion and let loose another groan as she struggled to her feet. "She wasn't killed here. I'm almost positive of that."

"How do you know?" Chris asked, shifting his eyes from the camera he held to the elderly Winchester woman. "You don't have a background in law enforcement, do you?"

"No, but I could totally be an FBI agent for a living if I wanted to work long hours for crap pay and boss people around for no good reason," Tillie replied. "I've been around enough investigations since Landon came into our lives to recognize that this is a body dump, not a killing ground."

"But why would a hominid-like creature kill a person in one area and move the body someplace else?"

Tillie stared at Chris as if he'd suddenly sprouted another head. "What's a hominid-like creature? I'm not a bigot, by the way. If Bigfoot is gay and wants to dance the night away, I don't care, so be careful how you answer."

"Hominid," I automatically corrected. "It means ape-like."

"Oh." Tillie scratched her chin. "Our creatures out here look like walking dogs, not apes."

Instantly intrigued, Chris took a hurried step toward Tillie. "Have you seen it?"

"Sure."

"What does it look like?"

"A mangy dog."

Jack narrowed his eyes. "You've seen this ... Dog Man ... yourself?"

"You'd be surprised at the things I've seen over the course of my life," Tillie replied. "The Dog Man is only one of them. I've seen the Loch Ness Monster, too. Nessie was over in the Hollow Creek for a visit a good twenty years ago."

"The Loch Ness monster?" I swallowed the urge to laugh because I didn't think it would go over well. "How did it get here?"

"It swam."

"But ... it would've had to cross land at some point."

"And the ocean," Jack muttered.

"So what?" Tillie was clearly losing interest in the conversation. Either that or she didn't like anyone calling her truthfulness into question. "I've seen the chupacabra, too."

"Here?" For the first time, doubt crossed Chris' face. "You saw the chupacabra in Michigan?"

"Michigan is a perfectly nice state," Tillie replied. "Even chupacabras like to visit. But all of that has nothing to do with the fact that Penny Schilling wasn't killed here. She was killed someplace else. And I don't think the Dog Man did it."

"Who do you think did it?" Jack asked, genuinely curious.

"Most murders are committed by people who know the victim," Tillie explained. "The motive is generally love ... or money ... or plain old meanness. Stranger murders are rare. The answers aren't here. The answers are with the people who knew Penny."

"Did you know her?" Something about the way Tillie carried herself made me believe that she did.

"I knew her mother," Tillie replied. "She went to school with my girls. They didn't like one another – which wasn't uncommon, because my girls are pains in the butt – but I knew the girl to be relatively quiet and easygoing. Penny was younger than Bay, Clove and Thistle, but I saw her around town occasionally even after her mother moved to Bellaire."

"What was she like?"

"Penny?" Tillie shrugged. "She was a quiet girl. I didn't know her well. I'm not used to quiet girls, because I raised six really loud ones."

"How did you end up raising your nieces? What happened to their mother?"

"She died when they were teenagers. We all lived in the same house before that. I helped raise them from birth."

"And your great-nieces?" Jack asked. He appeared to be just as engaged in the conversation as I did. "How did you end up raising them?"

"Because my nieces picked deadbeats to procreate with, and they needed help raising the little monsters that sprang from their loins," Tillie replied, causing me to internally cringe at the visual she painted. "I know you think I don't like the girls – and there are times I want to make each and every one of them eat a pile of dirt – but I would die to protect them."

56

Her vehemence took Jack taken aback, but it made me like her even more.

"Even Thistle?" Jack asked finally, doubtful.

"She's the most like me," Tillie explained. "It's normal that she should irritate me most. She's a good woman with an occasionally evil mind." Tillie flicked her eyes to the Dandridge, which poked majestically through the trees in the distance. "Clove shouldn't stay out here. Not until we catch who did this, at least."

"We?" Jack arched a confrontational eyebrow. "When did you join the team? You don't even believe it was Bigfoot."

"It wasn't Bigfoot. I can guarantee that."

"We can agree there," Chris offered. "It was a Sasquatch."

Tillie rolled her eyes. "It was a man who was smart enough to at least try to disguise a murder as an animal attack. That rarely works, but ... well ... he did a good enough job to get you guys out here, didn't he?"

"I know you don't believe, but how do you explain these?" Chris gestured toward the footprints. "A human clearly didn't make those."

"No, probably not," Aunt Tillie conceded. "At least not the way you think. Footprints can be faked. I should know. I've been faking footprints for more than a year to throw 'The Man' off the track when I'm harvesting my crops."

And back to the gardening. "And just what do you grow?" I asked.

Jack's smirk told me he'd already figured out the answer ... or at least an approximation of the truth. "She grows a variety of plants, don't you, Ms. Winchester?"

Tillie's smile was genuine when she graced Jack with a grin. "I have varied interests," she confirmed. "I think I like you."

Jack balked. "Like how?"

"Not in a perverted way." Tillie made a clucking sound in the back of her throat. "I would like you for one of my younger girls if they weren't already taken. How do you feel about older women? None of my nieces are linked to men right now – although Terry will eventually be a full-fledged member if I had my way."

"Chief Davenport?" I smiled at the picture. "Is he close with your family?"

"Closer than most." Tillie bobbed her head. "If you like older women, I think you'd make a good match for Marnie."

"I'm going to say thanks ... but no thanks," Jack said, his cheeks turning crimson. "It's a very nice offer, though."

"You remind me of Landon." Tillie said the words so low that I wondered if she meant to utter them aloud. "He was snarky and standoffish when we first met him, too. You look like him ... and you have the same feel. I can tell you're a good man."

"What about me?" Chris asked, his tone needy.

"You're a good man who tends to get lost in the clouds," Tillie replied. "You remind me of Twila, which means you can't be with her because you'll spend all of your time lost in the clouds and forget what it's like to plant your feet on solid earth. Two floaters can't be together, because someone needs to serve as an anchor."

"I ... didn't really consider dating Twila," Chris said. I could practically see him picturing the redheaded woman with the scattered personality as he wrinkled his nose. "I was only asking what you saw when you looked at me."

Tillie's smile was mischievous. "Trouble."

SEVEN

We met the rest of the group at the Hemlock Cove diner shortly after noon. I spent most of the morning helping Chris search for additional footprints and grilling Tillie Winchester on her family and what it was like living in Hemlock Cove. She answered every question, yet told me very little. She was happy to discuss her great-nieces and the various ways she enjoyed making them pay for personal transgressions, but she revealed very little actionable material.

Once we hit town she waved us off, saying she would find her own way home before skulking off in the direction of something called The Unicorn Emporium. I had no idea what the store sold, but I doubted Tillie could stir up trouble in a kitschy store. She looked determined as she glared at an elderly woman selling her wares behind the counter, though, and didn't so much as spare a glance for us before disappearing.

"Should we be worried?" I asked Jack as we walked toward the diner. "We said she would be safe with us. Now she's wandering all over town on her own."

Jack wasn't nearly as concerned. "She's an adult. She's allowed to do whatever she wants."

"I know that. It's just … what if she gets lost?"

"She's lived here her whole life."

"How will she get home?"

"I have a feeling she knows plenty of people who can give her a ride."

"What if something happens to her?"

Jack's expression softened when he registered my worry. "She'll be fine. She knows how to handle herself. You saw her in the woods. She kept a keen eye open even when you were grilling her about her background."

"I was not grilling her. I wasn't!" I hated the dubious curve of his eyebrow and huffed out a ragged sigh as he held open the diner door to usher me inside. "I simply find her fascinating."

"I'm sure she gets that a lot." A small smile played at the corner of Jack's lips. "She seems to enjoy being the center of attention."

The diner was half full, which was a relief because we wanted to talk openly. We secured a large table at the center of the dining area. We'd just managed to sit down and peel off our coats when the door opened to allow Landon and the police chief entry.

"Maybe we can get them to sit with us," I whispered, drawing Jack's eyes to the door. "They might share information if we offer them a friendly lunch."

Instead of clapping me on the back and telling me it was a great idea, as I expected, Jack's eyes filled with mirth. "Oh, what a diabolical plan."

I pressed my lips together, annoyed. "I only meant … ."

"I know what you meant," Jack said, cutting me off. "Charlie, you're new at this so I'll forgive the really odd enthusiasm, but they're either going to share information or keep certain things to themselves. Soup and a sandwich won't change that."

"But … ."

"I think you have a little crush on Agent Michaels, which is cute, but he's clearly happy with his blonde. If they want to sit with us they're more than welcome. We don't need to go out of our way to invite them."

Well, that was a little condescending. "I don't have a crush on him."

"I've seen the way you look at him."

"It's no different than the way you look at his girlfriend," I hissed, expressing myself a little more emphatically than necessary. When I risked a glance at Landon and Chief Davenport I found the FBI agent staring at me. I quickly squared my shoulders and mustered a smile. "Won't you join us?"

Jack made a small groaning noise, but matched me smile for smile. "Plenty of room," he offered.

Landon glanced around, clearly conflicted, and then nodded. "Sure. That sounds good."

"There's an open seat over here," Laura offered, winking as she patted an empty chair.

Landon shoved Chief Davenport in that direction and took the open seat next to Jack, purposely ignoring the one on the other side of me. "What have you guys been doing so far today?"

"Hanging out with Tillie Winchester," Jack replied, grinning at the memory. "She's ... funny."

"That's not a word I would use to describe her, but she has her moments," Landon said dryly. "Did she do anything odd?"

"Define odd."

Landon ran his tongue over his teeth and tilted his head to the side, as if conducting some form of internal debate. "You'd know if she did anything odd. Where is she, by the way?" He glanced around the table. "You didn't leave her out there, did you?"

"Of course not," I sputtered. "She took off when we hit town. She said she would find her own way home."

I expected Landon to be upset by the news, but he barely blinked. "Okay."

"I told you," Jack snickered.

"You're not worried about her?" I was mildly incensed on Tillie's behalf. "She's elderly. What if she forgets where she is and wanders into the woods?"

Landon snorted, seemingly amused by the question. "She's only elderly when she wants to put one over on strangers and new acquaintances. She's fine. Her mind is sharp, and she'll have no problem getting a ride back to the inn."

"How can you be sure?"

"Because she's Aunt Tillie," Landon replied matter-of-factly. "Even the zombie apocalypse couldn't claim her. She'll be fine. Bay and Thistle are in town to give her a ride if she needs it. I saw Kenneth's car at the senior center. That's probably where she headed."

"Who's Kenneth?" Jack asked.

"Her boyfriend ... sometimes."

"She has a boyfriend?" Jack looked as if he would fall over when he let loose with a hearty guffaw. "That guy must be a glutton for punishment."

"You have no idea." Landon smiled at the waitress as she approached. "I'll have my usual."

"Got it." The waitress turned to Chief Davenport. "You, too?"

"That's good." The chief looked to be in a serious discussion with Bernard, the two of them getting along well, but Landon appeared uncomfortable in what should've been an easygoing setting.

I waited until all of the orders were placed to fix my full attention on him. "What did you guys find out today?"

"We spent the morning at the medical examiner's office," Landon replied, toying with his crinkled straw wrapper. "There are some abnormalities that he's having trouble explaining."

Chris visibly perked up. "Abnormalities?"

Landon nodded. "It looks as if the injuries to Penny's throat were inflicted after her death, as we suspected."

"That would indicate a human did the deed," Jack noted.

Landon nodded in agreement. "There was, however, animal DNA in the wound that the doctor can't quite pinpoint. It's all mixed up – like perhaps it was multiple animals – so they're running additional tests."

Jack's eyebrows shot up his forehead as Chris excitedly slapped the table.

"Are you serious?" Chris almost knocked over his chair he was so worked up. "Can we have a sample of the DNA?"

Landon remained dubious and calm. "You'll have to talk to the medical examiner about that."

"I'll head over there after lunch," Hannah offered. She looked almost as excited as Chris did. I realized I liked her. Er, well, I liked what I knew of her. She seemed sweet, kind and smart. She was also oblivious to her looks, which made the fact that she was so beautiful easier to swallow.

"How will you approaching the investigation?" Laura asked Landon, her eyes predatory as they roamed the strong planes of his face.

"We're heading to the resort this afternoon," Landon replied. "We're not focusing on any suspect or scenario at present. The medical examiner couldn't identify the DNA, so we have to wait for another test to get some actionable results. That means we're tackling the investigation as we would any other."

That was an odd way of putting it. I opened my mouth to ask a follow-up question, but was momentarily distracted by movement in front of the diner's big window. Tillie Winchester scurried past, moving faster than I would've thought possible given her age, while casting a worried glance over her shoulder. The movement wasn't lost on Landon.

"What is she doing?" Jack asked, concerned. "Should we help her?"

Landon remained seated when he saw another senior citizen – I was fairly certain it was the woman from the unicorn store – racing in the same direction. "She's fine."

"Who is that?" Millie asked, her eyes widening. "I don't like the looks of her."

Landon and the chief snorted in unison.

"That's Margaret Little," Chief Davenport supplied. "She and Tillie are … lifetime enemies."

"Mortal enemies," Landon corrected. "They're fine. Mrs. Little won't catch Aunt Tillie. She never does."

"But aren't you worried one of them will have a heart attack?" Bernard asked. "I know I'm no spring chicken, but that's a lot of effort for ladies of advanced age to be expending."

"Oh, please use that 'ladies of advanced age' line on Aunt Tillie when you see her at the inn later," Landon pleaded, amused. "They're fine. At least no one has a chainsaw this time."

Chris' eyes widened to comical proportions. "A chainsaw?"

"Nothing is worse than the time Tillie decided she was going to make fireworks and turn Margaret's store into the Fourth of July," the chief explained. "But Landon is right, Tillie is fine."

As if on cue, Tillie appeared in front of the window again. She wasn't alone. She had a clearly complaining Thistle trailing behind her. I couldn't hear what the teal-haired woman said, but she obviously wasn't happy.

"See." Landon bobbed his head. "Reinforcements have arrived."

"I thought they hated each other," Laura challenged, staring at the two women as they disappeared back in the direction of The Unicorn Emporium.

"Tillie says she doesn't hate Thistle, only dislikes her most of the time," I offered.

"She loves Thistle," Landon corrected. "Thistle makes it hard to like her a lot of time. Aunt Tillie and Thistle like to ... um ... play games, if you will. They both have evil minds."

"But good hearts?" I asked hopefully.

Landon shrugged. "Sometimes."

As if she heard him through several feet of brick and glass, Thistle popped up in front of the window a second time and glared into the diner. Landon shifted uncomfortably when her eyes found his.

"Criminy! What are they even doing out there?"

"They're fine," Chief Davenport admonished. "If you spent as much time in town as I do you'd be used to this. It happens about three times a week."

That's when Bay, her blond hair shining in the sun, joined the small group. She screwed up her face in concentration as Thistle said something to her. Bay's mouth dropped open and she glanced over her shoulder, clearly barking something at someone standing just out of sight.

"Who is she talking to?" Bernard asked.

"I don't know," Hannah answered, but it's like a television show on mute."

"Like a soap opera, to be more exact," Landon grumbled, pushing himself to his feet. "I'll handle this."

"Yes, you should truly terrify them when you punish Bay with kisses," the chief drawled. "Don't do that, by the way. You know I don't like it."

"Yeah, yeah." Landon waved off his admonition. "She's still eight with pigtails to you."

"And overalls ... and a stuffed dog ... and ice cream on her face."

Landon smirked. "She had ice cream on her face last night."

"And a stuffed dog," the chief said, wagging a finger. "I saw how much you ate and drank. You were stuffed."

"Why are we even having this argument?" Landon complained, moving toward the door. "They're clearly up to something. I'll put a stop to it."

Chief Davenport rolled his eyes and shifted on his chair so he could watch. Whether he forgot we were present or simply didn't care, he talked to himself as he watched the scene play out. "Oh, he'll put a stop to it. Those women will ride roughshod over him. They always do."

I watched the chief's eyes light up when Bay and Thistle appeared in front of the window again. They clearly didn't see Landon closing on them, because they remained focused on Tillie, each grabbing an arm and dragging her along the sidewalk as they tried to cajole her into making the trek easier.

Bay, her mouth open, made an odd face when she smacked into Landon. She jerked her head around, smiling when she saw the new player. She said something to Landon, who responded with a headshake.

"It's like the best television show ever," Laura said. "That guy is so hot."

Chief Davenport darted a dark look in her direction. "He's also taken."

Laura didn't appear annoyed by the words, or the tone he employed. "For now."

"Forever," he corrected. "I don't know why I'm even worrying about you. You're no threat to Bay."

Laura snorted. "Honey, I'm a threat to everyone."

"And that's why you're a threat to no one," the chief corrected, shaking his head. I couldn't help but enjoy the way he dressed down Laura. I barely knew the woman and could barely tolerate her. Apparently I wasn't alone in my assessment of her personality. "You think so much of yourself you can't see the truth."

Laura rolled her eyes. "Whatever. Let me watch the hot FBI guy in peace."

I tore my gaze from Laura's determined stare and cracked a smile when Landon finally gave in to whatever Bay asked him to do. He grabbed Tillie around the waist, hoisted her over his shoulder and turned to walk down the sidewalk. Thistle and Bay scampered after him, their mouths moving rapidly.

"Where is he taking her?" Jack asked.

"Hypnotic. That's the store Clove and Thistle own," the chief replied. "They're probably trying to get her off the street."

"Oh, the cute magic store?" I asked, my interest piqued. "I saw it when we hit town. I want to stop there before we leave."

"It's a nice place," Chief Davenport said, shifting in the chair and smiling as the waitress delivered his lunch. "You might want to add a bowl of chili and a grilled cheese on cracked wheat, if you have time. Landon is rounding up Bay for lunch."

"You don't know that," Laura challenged. "He didn't say he was bringing her back."

Landon picked that moment to reappear in the doorway, Bay's hand wrapped in his. He looked serious as he spoke to her. Tillie and Thistle were nowhere in sight.

"I think he's right, though," I pointed out, smiling as Laura's scowl became more pronounced.

"Of course I'm right," the chief grumbled. "I could set my watch by Landon's moods where Bay is concerned. You have no chance, honey."

He emphasized the last word in a derogatory manner before lowering his voice. "You try to hurt her, and we'll have words."

I bit my lip to keep from laughing at the murderous look on Laura's face, and shifted my eyes to the door as Landon and Bay entered. It appeared they weren't quite done arguing.

"I'm only saying that it's not my fault," Bay whined.

"I didn't say it was your fault," Landon countered. "But you're coming with us to the resort this afternoon to make sure nothing else happens that can be misconstrued as your fault."

"You can't make me go with you," Bay argued.

Landon rolled his neck. "Bay … ."

"I will gladly offer my services to the FBI if you ask nicely, though," Bay teased, grinning at Chief Davenport as she passed.

"You'll be the death of me," Landon muttered, reclaiming his chair. "Order some lunch. You haven't eaten since breakfast."

"I ordered a grilled cheese and chili for her," the chief supplied.

"Oh, such a good provider." Bay beamed. "You have to ask me nicely, Landon. You're not the boss of me."

"Fine," Landon growled. "Will you please come to the resort with me?"

Bay grinned and pressed a kiss to his cheek. "Yes."

Landon looked as if he wanted to remain stoic and angry, but his grimace flipped upside down as he handed Bay the pickle from his plate. "You're a lot of work."

"I know."

The small interaction made my heart flip when I saw how comfortable they were with each other. I didn't realize I wanted that … wanted the peace of someone understanding everything about me … until I saw the real thing in action. I didn't get a chance to ponder the realization for long before Jack leaned in.

"I think we should schedule our own visit to that resort," he whispered. "Are you game?"

I nodded, sobering. "I think that's a good idea. We have to start somewhere."

EIGHT

*B*ecause he was much more interested in the possibility of seeing Bigfoot – or Sasquatch, whatever – Chris took Hannah, Bernard and Laura back to the site. That left Jack, Millie and me to head to the resort. Jack plugged the resort's coordinates into the GPS and headed in that direction.

The resort was beautiful. I couldn't tear my gaze from the quaint shopping village on one side and the majestic hills on the other. A full landscaping team was working on the smaller hills we drove past, but it was too soon to tell what they would look like when finished.

"What's the deal with the big hill?" Millie asked, leaning forward in the passenger seat.

"Landon said this was a ski resort in the winter," I replied. "That looks like a tow rope to the right and a chair lift down that way on the left. I'll bet those hills are ski slopes in the winter."

"What are they now?"

"Empty," Jack answered, pulling into a parking spot.

Everyone hopped out of the Tahoe and studied the resort. It wasn't busy because it was between seasons, but it was obvious where the main door was thanks to a big sign over the glass entryway. What I didn't understand were the two buildings across the parking lot. They were both large and well-kept, but they stood alone compared to the rest of the resort.

"What do you think those are?"

"That's where the golf course is," Jack replied. "That building there is the cart shed. The other is the pro shop and what looks to be a small restaurant."

"How do you know that?" I asked.

"Because I golf." Jack's answer was succinct. He turned from the empty buildings and focused on the bigger one. "This is the main hotel. I think the dining room is that way."

"So we should go that way?" Millie asked.

"That's the direction I believe Landon, Terry and Bay headed," Jack replied. "I think we should try going in a different door."

"You don't want them to know we're here?" I couldn't contain my surprise. "Why not? We're not doing anything wrong."

"It's not that I don't want them to know we're here," Jack clarified. "I simply prefer they didn't know we were stepping on their toes."

"How is that different?"

Jack shrugged. "It makes me feel better. Come on. Let's go in through the loading dock."

Loading dock? I was confused until I followed Jack around a corner, through a set of wide delivery doors that opened and closed for large trucks, and realized he wasn't referring to anything that could be mistaken for a port. He was referring to the place where the resort's delivery trucks pulled in for unloading.

"How did you know this was here?" I asked, flipping my eyes to the large wooden doors that cut off the area to guests when the dock wasn't in use. Thankfully for us it appeared that a food delivery was on tap for the afternoon so they weren't locked.

"I worked at a resort weekends when I was in high school," Jack replied. "I was a bellhop."

I pressed my lips together to keep from laughing at the unintended visual. "Did you wear a uniform?"

Jack nodded, unembarrassed. "It was good money. If you think you're going to tease me, you can't. I have fond memories of that place. That's where I learned the necessity of a good work ethic."

"I wasn't going to tease you."

Jack cocked a dubious brow.

"Much," I clarified. "I wasn't going to tease you much. I just can't picture you in a uniform. You seem like you've always been a jeans and T-shirt kind of a guy."

"I have, but I have no problem with a uniform if it involves making money." Jack held open the door that led inside the building, opting to eschew the area where several men toiled unpacking the truck.

Once inside it took a moment for my eyes to adjust to the dim room. "What's with the office over there?" I asked, pointing toward a small corner room that featured multiple glass windows looking out on the dock."

"My guess is that's the purchasing agent's office," Jack replied, running a restless hand through his hair as he got his bearings. "He has to sign for every delivery and check to make sure everything arrived, so he has to be close."

I stared into the office, focusing on the man behind the glass. He didn't glance in our direction, seemingly busy with whatever paperwork he studied. "Why isn't he trying to chase us out of here?"

"Because he probably doesn't care," Jack answered, pressing his hand to the small of my back and prodding me forward. "He's not who we're looking for. We need younger workers who are too stupid to realize that talking about co-workers out of school is a bad idea."

"So ... under thirty?"

"Under twenty-five if possible. I ... ."

"I found something I want to check out," Millie announced, staring down a hallway that led to what looked to be storage rooms. I could see two shirtless men unloading boxes, and Millie appeared focused on them. "I'll catch up with you in a little bit."

Jack looked annoyed by the announcement. "Millie, they're not who we're looking for."

"They're exactly who I'm looking for," Millie shot back. "Don't leave without me."

"Like I would do that," Jack muttered, shaking his head as he walked toward a set of doors that led to a different hallway. "Women give me a headache."

I pursed my lips as I followed him. "Just women? That's kind of sexist."

"Maybe I'm a sexist individual. Have you ever considered that?"

I nodded without hesitation. "Since the moment I met you. You're not overtly sexist, though. It's more that your machismo won't allow you to do anything that would endanger women. You feel you need to protect everyone, but especially women."

Jack's mouth dropped open as he walked through the door with me. "I don't know what to say to that."

"You don't have to say anything. I like observing people, and you're easy to read. It wasn't meant as an insult."

"Uh-huh." Jack rubbed the back of his neck as he locked gazes with me. "I like observing people, too. You know how you're convinced the Winchesters are hiding something from us?"

I nodded. I remained convinced of that. It became more obvious with each conversation.

"Well, you're hiding something, too," Jack announced, causing my heart to stutter. "I don't know what it is. I don't know if it's something big, but it's big to you. That could be because of your age or enthusiasm ... but you're definitely hiding something. Now, I don't care about it as long as it doesn't put my team in danger. But I know you're hiding something, and I want you to know that you're not fooling me."

My instinct was to balk, so that's what I did. "What do you think I'm hiding?"

"I don't know," Jack admitted, his dark eyes searching my face. "You're not a normal girl, though. I know that."

"I'll take that as a compliment." I swooped past him, adding a little swing to my step as my mind worked overtime. He couldn't possibly know the big secret. He wasn't prone to believing paranormal tales. He worked for a group of people who sought out paranormal answers, yet he didn't believe in any of it. Whatever he thought I was hiding was of the mundane human variety. That was good for me ... probably. I would have to be more careful. "Where do you want to start?"

Jack's face was impassive as he waited for me to turn and stare at him. Something unsaid passed between us – although what it was I couldn't say – and then he inclined his chin in the direction of two women standing beside the women's bathroom. They were dressed in maid uniforms. "Maids love to gossip."

"I think that was code for 'women love to gossip,'" I corrected. "You're probably not wrong about this duo, though. They look like chatters."

"Let me do the talking," Jack instructed, swaggering in their direction.

"Why? Because you're a man?"

"No, because they've been watching me since they caught sight of us," Jack replied, keeping his voice low. "Much like Laura, they fancy themselves man-eaters. They're not hard to read."

Jack plastered a bright smile on his face as he approached the women. I was mildly curious about what tack he would take with them. I was utterly surprised when he opted for the truth.

"My name is Jack Hanson," he announced. "I'm conducting an investigation into a woman who died in the woods near Hemlock Cove. Her name was Penny Schilling and she worked here. Did either of you know her?"

The two women exchanged a quick look and then the bolder of the two – a bottle-blonde who wore way too much makeup – stepped forward. "We both know her. Or, well, knew her. We heard the rumor about her dying when we got here this morning. Is it true?"

Jack nodded. "It's true. She was found in the woods."

"Is it true an animal ate her?"

Jack shifted a bit, as he debated how to answer. "My understanding is that the police are still trying to ascertain that," he hedged.

"Aren't you the police?"

Jack shook his head. "I'm with a private investigation group. We're looking for answers, and I'm hoping you can help us."

I had to hand it to him. He knew how to question people. He flashed a flirty smile to charm the women and didn't outright lie. He didn't mention we were with the Legacy Foundation – which might've caused them to think we were quacks – but he didn't open himself up to future issues by telling outright falsehoods either. His method was almost flawless.

"Who is she?" the second woman asked, nodding in my direction.

"She's my assistant," Jack replied without hesitation. "Her name is Charlie Rhodes. She's learning on the job. What can I call you?"

The first woman heaved a sigh and glanced at her friend, both of them nodding in unison. "I'm Christy Sayre and this is Kelly Nichols. What do you want to know?"

THE WOMEN WERE a fountain of information – just as Jack suspected and I initially doubted. While I expected them to know a little gossip, and a lot of unsubstantiated rumors, they appeared to know everything about everyone who worked at the resort.

"It's pretty simple," Christy supplied, popping the top of a can of Coke as she sat in a small resting area in front of a fire. "Penny was a nice woman who did a good job in the main dining room, but she was a total slut."

My mouth dropped open at the woman's bluntness. "How do you know that?"

"It was common knowledge," Kelly replied. She was much chattier now that everyone had been introduced, although her keen eyes never left Jack's face. She wasn't even mildly interested in me. "She slept with everyone."

"Define everyone," Jack prodded.

"Well, for starters, she slept with the head of purchasing," Christy volunteered. "His name is Shane Norman. He's the guy who works in the glass office on the dock."

The guy I saw through the window, I realized. "The one with the bald spot?"

Kelly nodded. "He's not much to look at, but he's one of the better paid administration people around these parts. He's fairly popular because he keeps to himself and doesn't bug anyone."

"How old is he, though?" I asked. I knew the question sounded judgmental, but I couldn't help myself. Penny Schilling was twenty-four and in the prime of her life. The guy I saw through the window had to be in his fifties.

"I think he's forty or something," Christy answered.

"Forty?" That couldn't be right.

"He doesn't get a lot of exercise and he eats terrible food," Kelly explained. "He looks older than he is. I thought he was close to dying, too. Maybe he's like forty-five or something. Who can really tell when people get that old?"

"Oh, well, I didn't think he was close to dying," I clarified. "I just thought he was older than forty."

"How do you know that Penny and Shane were involved?" Jack asked, directing the conversation back to something he was comfortable talking about.

"People saw them having sex through that big window," Kelly said. "It has blinds, but apparently Penny was all pressed up against it. She left sweat stains on the blinds. The gossip spread like wildfire."

"Okay." Jack dragged out the word as he considered the scene. "That's only one man, though. What you told me makes her adventurous. What makes her a slut?"

"Shane wasn't her only boyfriend," Christy answered without hesitation. "She was also sleeping with the head bartender. His name is Bob Grimes and he's married. But it's not as big of a scandal as you think. His wife works here, too. Bob sleeps with everyone who looks in his direction. He's a male slut, so they kind of meshed well together."

"Delightful," Jack intoned, exchanging a quick glance with me. "Was it just the two of them?"

"You mean doing it?" The expression on Christy's face reflected bafflement. "I don't think they ever all did it together."

"Not that." Jack tugged on his patience as he forced his smile to remain serene. "Did Penny have relations with anyone else?"

"Oh, that." Christy nodded. "Just one more that I heard of, but I'm not sure if that's really the end of the list. She seemed determined to snag her a man, so I think she was spreading herself thin trying to find one. She didn't even care that all of the guys she was sleeping with were friends in high school."

"Why was she so determined to catch a man?" I asked, knitting my eyebrows when she mentioned all of the men being old friends. That seemed a bit ... incestuous, at least in a small town way.

"Because she needed one to take care of her." Christy acted as if I had asked a stupid question.

"But ...."

Jack sent me an imperceptible headshake before returning his attention to our new friends. "Who else was Penny dating?"

"Jim Green," Kelly supplied. "He's the head of security."

"Here?"

Kelly nodded.

"So you're telling me that Penny dated three men from this resort and they all had limited power," Jack mused, rubbing the back of his neck.

"They all used to be friends, too," I reminded him. I couldn't let go of that part of the story. It seemed to make things somehow more sick and twisted.

"That's him over there," Kelly noted, pointing to a man in an expensive suit standing by a set of bay windows on the other side of the sitting area.

"He's probably trying to figure out who we are," Jack mused, looking the man up and down. Jim Green had slicked-back hair and something of an oily demeanor. You could tell from forty feet away that he thought he was more important than the rest of the workers he conversed with as they passed by.

"Why was she so obsessed with dating men at this resort?" I asked, remembering we were in the middle of an interrogation.

"Look around," Christy prompted. "The only people in this area who have money are the guests at the resort or the people who make decent money at the resort. If you want a comfortable life, you don't have many options."

Jack nodded. "In your opinion – and I swear I'll keep this to myself, so don't worry about that – would any of Penny's boyfriends had the drive to kill her if he found out she was cheating on him?"

Christy shrugged, seemingly unbothered by the question. "They all seem pretty lame, but you never know. Like we said, they're all friends. If we knew about Penny sleeping with all of them, odds are they knew, too. You just never know what people think and feel about each other if they're determined to hide their feelings."

"No, you never know," Jack agreed, forcing his smile back in place. "Thank you so much for your time, ladies. You've been a big help. You'll never know how much."

I WAITED until we were back on the loading dock – Jim Green keeping an eye on us and making me uncomfortable until we disappeared down the employee hallway – to voice the obvious question.

"What do you think this means?"

"I think it means that three men had motive to kill Penny and it's a lot more believable that it was one of them rather than Bigfoot."

"Sasquatch," I automatically corrected.

Jack wrinkled his nose. "Whatever. We need to keep asking around, maybe even talk to these men. One of them has to be the guilty party."

"That makes sense in theory," I admitted. "It's just ... whoever killed her had to think fast on his feet to get her out in the woods and fake a monster attack. Do you really think anyone working at a resort for a living would have the fortitude to do that?"

"That depends on if the murder was planned beforehand or heat of the moment," Jack answered, not missing a beat. "If it was planned, everything might've been in place long before Penny died."

"I hadn't even considered that," I admitted. "If it was planned, that means one of Penny's boyfriends could've found out about the others and plotted against her."

"I think that's the best scenario for us to work with. Come on. Let's see what else we can find out … and where is Millie? If she's naked with one of those guys I'm going to lose it."

That sounded like it had the potential to be fun – at least for me.

9

NINE

We managed to get out of the resort without Landon, Terry and Bay seeing us. I did see Bay, though. She stood at a set of large windows, frowning out at the heavily wooded area that surrounded the resort's far west side. She seemed lost in thought, almost as if she was looking at something only she could see. Landon moved up behind her, slipping his arm around her waist and whispering something to her. She smiled, nodded, and then they disappeared toward the lobby.

The sight of them was enough to spur Jack to movement. He insisted it was time to go. I balked, thinking he meant to leave Millie, but she was prowling the loading dock when we found her. She waited until we were in the Tahoe to speak.

"Apparently Penny Schilling slept with anything that moved – and maybe even a few things that didn't."

Jack arched an eyebrow as he navigated the road that led away from the resort. "We found that out, too. She apparently had three boyfriends."

"She had three older men she was trying to make boyfriends out of," Millie clarified. "She wasn't picky when she wanted a night of fun

… and apparently the younger demographic at this place likes to have a lot of fun."

Jack was flummoxed. "What is that supposed to mean? Are you saying they have orgies and stuff?"

Millie snorted, amused. "You've got a dirty mind, boy. I like it."

"I didn't say I was a fan of orgies."

"I am." Millie made the announcement with a sparkle in her eyes and a smirk curling her lips. She clearly liked messing with Jack, and surprisingly enough, he wasn't opposed to her antics. "They don't have orgies, though. What they do have is outdoor parties where the younger crowd groups together to drink before separating for a little one-on-one action, if you know what I mean." She waggled her eyebrows suggestively.

"I think everyone knows what you mean," I said dryly, but intrigued. "Do you know where they have these parties?"

"They jump around," Millie explained. "In the winter, they use some of the vacant big rooms in the conference section of the resort. When it gets warmer – in the spring and late fall – they use the cart barn. I had to ask what that was. Apparently it's where they keep the golf carts during inclement weather."

"Yeah, I pointed that building out when we first arrived," Jack noted.

"I was barely listening because I found the conversation was boring," Millie said. "In the later spring and summer, as soon as it's warm enough, they move the party outside. Apparently there's a lot of property up that way … ." She waved vaguely as we passed a private road with an automated gate. "They go up there quite a bit."

"How do they get past the security system?" Jack asked, eyeing the locked gate.

"They know the ambulance codes."

"Ah, well, that makes sense." Jack was thoughtful. "Where are they partying up there?"

"My understanding is that their favorite spot is the eighteenth green of the golf course," Millie replied. "It's accessed through a short trail. Nobody ever busts them out there because the cops can only go past the gate if there's an emergency. Also, the head of security apparently knows and doesn't care as long as they don't tear anything up. He's even joined them a time or two."

"What about homeowners in that area?" Jack pressed. "Wouldn't they call the cops if they heard something?"

"I guess that's the only part of the golf course that doesn't have condos looking out over it," Millie replied. "The kids explained it to me. The course starts by the cart barn thing and then winds all the way around, ending behind that gate."

"Well, you never have to worry about young people not being able to find a place to party," Jack mused. "What did they say about Penny?"

"Just that she wasn't the discriminating sort and slept her way through half the bellboy staff, the entire maintenance staff and some of the kitchen staff. She was looking forward to greeting the seasonal summer staff in a few weeks."

Jack exchanged a quick look with me in the rearview mirror. "I feel kind of ashamed we only stumbled over the three older men while we were questioning people."

"According to the guys unloading that truck – who were very hot and sweaty, by the way – Penny was focused on those men above all else," Millie said. "I wrote their names down."

"Shane Norman, Bob Grimes and Jim Green?"

"Those would be the ones." Millie shot Jack a gaze full of grudging respect. "You have a good memory."

"Yes, well, I wrote down their names, too, so it's not exactly as if I'm magic," Jack teased.

I remained mostly silent in the back seat, something bothering me. "If Penny was really sleeping with all of those men, odds are that a human killed her because of jealousy." I meant to think the sentence instead of utter it, but my mouth often gets ahead of me.

"I think a human did kill her," Jack said, his eyes cloudy. "Does that bother you?"

"Well, I would be lying if I said it wouldn't be more interesting if Bigfoot killed her," I admitted. "It's just … we're here for the paranormal angle. Will we leave because it's clear a human probably killed her?"

"No." Jack shook his dark head. "Right now we believe a human killed her, but have no idea who did the deed. Unfortunately the suspect list is bound to be massive. We cannot rule out anything until we find her murderer."

"What does that mean?"

"It means that Chris will continue doing what he does until the cops tell him otherwise," Millie replied, a fond smile curving her lips. "He's a good boy – I've loved him his entire life – but he gets tunnel vision. He's so desperate for it to be an undiscovered beast that he'll refuse to see the truth until he has no other choice."

"Will we tell him what we've found?" I was still unsure how the group worked.

Jack nodded. "I'll tell him. He'll immediately tell me that just because she had multiple boyfriends doesn't mean Bigfoot isn't the culprit. I'll argue that the odds aren't good for his scenario. Then we'll agree to keep working until the truth comes out."

"I guess that makes sense." I scratched my cheek as I leaned my temple against the window. "I want to do some research on this area. I'm curious about the Dog Man stories."

"And I want to pull up a map of the resort and run a search on the men from the resort," Jack said. "I'm thinking we can probably do both at the library."

I knew he was right, but still … . "I want to check the newspaper archives, too. They might have old stories about Dog Man sightings in the area."

Jack's eyes were filled with curiosity when I met them in the mirror. "What?"

"Nothing." Jack seemed conflicted. He shook his head more decisively. "If you want to go to the newspaper office, I don't see why you can't."

"Thanks so much for your permission, Dad," I said dryly.

"No problem." Jack forced a wan smile. "Next stop Hemlock Cove. Let's see what we can come up with, shall we?"

I GRABBED a coffee from the bakery and sat at a table that over-looked the newspaper office as I waited for Bay to return. A lovely woman named Mrs. Gunderson saw where my attention was focused and offered me a small grin when she circled around to top off my mug.

"Are you looking for Bay?"

The question caught me off guard. "I'm hoping to look through her archives, but I believe she's off with the police chief and an FBI agent."

"Landon and Chief Terry?"

I was used to living in bigger cities, so the fact that everyone knew everyone in Hemlock Cove was something I was still trying to wrap my head around. "Yes. You know them?"

"I've known Terry since he was a boy," Mrs. Gunderson explained. "Landon is a more recent transplant, but he fits in well. He and Bay are cute together."

"Do you know Bay well?" I figured it was risky to ask questions about the Winchesters in a town this size, but I couldn't seem to stop myself.

"I've known Bay since she was a baby," Mrs. Gunderson acknowl-edged. "She's been running around town with her cousins ever since. They were quite the mischief makers as children – Tillie encouraged that so it wasn't really their fault – but they've grown to be wonderful women."

"Do you find them … odd?"

Mrs. Gunderson appeared amused by the question. She glanced around the bakery to make sure everyone was content and then sat in the open chair across from me. "What's wrong? I was under the impression your group was staying at The Overlook. Are you fighting with the girls? If so, just avoid Thistle. She's crabby, but has a heart of gold under all of that snark."

I wasn't sure the "heart of gold" comment was accurate, but I could hardly argue the point. "Do you know what my group does?" Gossip was a way of life in small towns, so I couldn't stop myself from wondering what kind of whispers were being spread about the foundation.

"You people try to prove whether or not something strange is afoot."

Mrs. Gunderson's response sounded so well-rehearsed I couldn't help but bark out a laugh. "Kind of. We're here because my boss believes Bigfoot killed a woman named Penny Schilling. Did you know her?"

"I didn't know Penny, but I know her mother."

"That's what Mrs. Winchester said."

"You're talking about Tillie?"

I nodded. "Do you know Tillie?"

"We went to school together," Mrs. Gunderson replied, choosing her words carefully. "There was a time we were very close. We've grown apart over the years, but I have a lot of respect for her."

"Because she's odd?"

"Because she's loyal," Mrs. Gunderson corrected. "I understand that from your perspective the Winchesters probably appear ... persnickety. That's simply the way they interact. They love each other terribly, and if something were to happen to one of them they would all fall apart."

I didn't need to know the Winchesters better to figure that out for myself. "They're hiding something."

I don't know why I said it. Actually, I whispered it, to be more precise. I kept my gaze locked on Mrs. Gunderson's kind eyes as I said it, gauging her reaction. Instead of balking and saying I was crazy or responding with gossip of her own, she chuckled and patted my hand.

"Everyone has something they want to hide, my dear." Mrs. Gunderson's eyes were contemplative as they locked with mine. "I think even you have secrets you're loath to share with anyone else."

That was definitely true, and still ... . "You know what they're hiding, don't you?"

"I know that the Winchesters are extremely loyal individuals and every single one of them is a hard worker," Mrs. Gunderson replied.

"If they have secrets – and everyone does – they've earned the right to keep them."

"That wasn't a denial."

Mrs. Gunderson heaved a heavy sigh that told me her patience was wearing thin. "Charlotte … that's your name, right? I believe that's what I heard."

"Charlie. Everyone calls me Charlie."

"Charlie, I can see why someone in your unique position would look at the Winchesters and think there's something to uncover there, but I promise you that you're wasting your time," Mrs. Gunderson said. "I've known Tillie a long time. She's always been eccentric. For example, did you know that about six months ago she took to ordering leggings online? Some of them were almost pornographic."

I didn't know that, but the picture in my head was enough to make me smile. "How were they pornographic?"

"Let's just say there should be an age limit on leggings and leave it at that," Mrs. Gunderson suggested, smiling. "When those girls were young, their fathers left. Their mothers wanted a good life for them, so they went to school and learned business so they could turn the old homestead into a bed and breakfast at first and then eventually an inn."

"That's great. What happened to the fathers?"

"They left town for a bit. Then they showed back up about a year or so ago," Mrs. Gunderson answered. "They own a competing inn."

I widened my eyes, dumbfounded. "Really? Do Thistle, Clove and Bay see their fathers?" For some reason I was fascinated by the gossip.

"They do, but I wouldn't say the girls are close with their fathers," Mrs. Gunderson said. "But they are all close with the man who stepped in and acted as their father for a number of years."

"Terry Davenport." I knew it was the chief without wasting time on an internal debate. I shifted my eyes to the police station when I heard a car door slam and saw Bay, Chief Davenport and Landon exiting a police cruiser. Bay said something that had both men guffawing loudly. The look on the chief's face when he smiled at her was definitely fatherly. "I should've figured that out myself. He was ordering Landon not to do anything dirty with her earlier."

"Yes, Landon and Terry have a unique relationship," Mrs. Gunderson confirmed. "Despite all of that, Terry looks at Landon as a son."

"If Bay is his daughter, doesn't that mean there's a little incest going on?" I was going for levity, but Mrs. Gunderson didn't look amused.

"Only if you have a perverted mind," she answered, her eyes dark. "I didn't tell you this because I enjoy gossip. I do, mind you, but this isn't really gossip. I'm simply telling you that what you see as a secret may well be a complicated relationship. The Winchesters are all about complicated relationships."

She had a point. I felt guilty for prying. "I'm sorry for asking about them. It's just ... I can't help being curious. They're all so colorful."

Mrs. Gunderson chuckled. "They're definitely colorful."

"Earlier today Thistle and Bay practically wrestled Tillie down on the sidewalk because she was going after some woman named Mrs. Little. It was like watching a television show."

Mrs. Gunderson's smile was bright enough to light the entire bakery. "Yes, well, they should've let Tillie do whatever she wanted to that harlot."

I tried to swallow my smile ... and failed. It seemed Mrs. Gunderson had a few secrets of her own, and hating Margaret Little was one of them. "I'm sorry for being gossipy. I just can't seem to wrap my head around this town."

"It takes some getting used to." Mrs. Gunderson got to her feet. "Don't assume the Winchesters are hiding something big. They thrive on fighting about small things, too."

"I've noticed that." Impulsively I reached out and gripped Mrs. Gunderson's free hand. "Thank you."

Mrs. Gunderson opened her mouth to respond and then snapped it shut when I gasped. My senses kicked into overdrive as a series of visions filled my head. Then I heard the screaming – oh, it was terrible! – and I fought to remain conscious as the scenes sped through my brain like a movie playing on fast-forward.

I saw Bay fall in a hole and Landon scream for her. I saw Mrs. Gunderson crying as she talked to Tillie. I saw Landon's terrified face as he tried to protect Bay with his body from … something I couldn't quite identify. I saw a terrible white mist congealing into the form of a man and advancing on Bay.

All the while I heard screaming … and then it was replaced with something else.

I'm coming for you, Floyd!

I jerked my hand back, my heart hammering as my fingers shook. Mrs. Gunderson's face flooded with concern as she leaned closer. She clearly hadn't seen the images in my head, but she'd lived through at least some of them.

"Are you okay?"

I struggled to find my tongue, and when I did, my voice cracked as I responded. "I'm fine. Thank you. I should probably get over to the newspaper so I can go through those archives."

"Yes … well … are you sure you're okay?" Mrs. Gunderson didn't look convinced.

"I'm fine," I forced out, my stomach twisting. "I just drank too much caffeine today. I'm feeling a little jittery."

I often felt jittery after being overwhelmed by a vision. This vision, though, was more powerful than any other. I wasn't expecting it either. I didn't seek it out. It came to me at a time when my mind and heart were open.

What the heck is going on in Hemlock Cove?

TEN

Bay didn't seem surprised to see me when I walked through the front door of the newspaper office, which appeared to be empty save for her.

"I was hoping to go through the archives if it's not a bother," I said sheepishly. "We want to see if you ever ran anything about animal attacks in the past, maybe see if we can find common locations, things like that."

"That makes sense." Bay's smile was light and airy as she gestured for me to follow her down a short hallway. "You'll find that we don't have archives like newspapers in big cities do, which is both a blessing and a curse depending on which way you look at things." She pointed to a row of file cabinets against the far wall. "Help yourself. I just ask that you file everything back the way it was when you're done."

The tall file cabinets looked daunting but I was determined to make an effort. "Thank you so much."

"No problem." Bay turned to leave before I could question her further – which is what I really wanted – but I hurriedly grabbed her hand, hoping to have another psychic flash like the one I experienced in the bakery. It worked, but not in the way I expected.

I blinked rapidly, a series of frantic pictures shifting through my brain. I saw a small blond girl bullied by a dark-haired girl and then the same blonde laughing with two other girls who were clearly Thistle and Clove. The final image was of a blond girl, this time lonely as she stood in the center of a cemetery. She seemed upset, even a little lost, and then Terry Davenport wandered up to her and they began chatting. There was nothing else. No danger ... or fear ... or terrible screams.

I released Bay's hand, forcing a smile and hoping she didn't realize I'd been trying to invade her mind. My psychic flashes were hard to control. I'd been hoping to see more about the white mist monster I saw the brief flash of when I touched Mrs. Gunderson's hand. It wasn't there, though.

"I want to thank you for your hospitality," I offered, hoping I sounded sincere. "Your family has been wonderful to us."

I couldn't be sure, but I was almost positive I saw something flash in the depths of Bay's eyes. It was recognition, but it was gone before I could spend too much time focusing on it.

"Don't worry about it," Bay said, her tone cheery. "I understand that you have a job to do. It's not an easy one given what you're investigating. I hope you find what you're looking for."

"You, too."

I SPENT hours going through the archives and came up with only a handful of articles even remotely interesting. When it was time to leave, Bay offered me a ride with her and Landon – which I initially declined and said I would call a cab to get back to the inn because I was desperate not to inconvenience her. She laughed and pointed out Hemlock Cove didn't have cabs, so my only choice was to track down Jack for a ride or go with her. I opted to go with her.

"Landon is picking us up in the parking lot," Bay offered, locking the door and causing me to cock an eyebrow. "Is something wrong? Did you forget something?"

"No, it's just ... isn't someone else in there?"

Bay shook her head. "It was just us all afternoon. No one else was in the building."

"I swear I thought I heard you talking to someone."

"No."

"You called her Viola."

This time I was positive that the expression flitting across Bay's face was something to worry about. She looked both pensive and curious. "I was on the phone briefly with Clove," she said, and I got the distinct impression she was making it up as she went along. "That's probably what you heard."

"Probably." I didn't believe that for a second, but I could hardly call her a liar.

Bay hurried down the steps and headed straight for Landon's Ford Explorer. He hopped out of the vehicle when he saw me, curious, but he went straight to Bay and offered her a hug. "Charlie went through our archives all afternoon," Bay offered. "She was looking for stories on animal attacks."

"That sounds like a boring way to spend an afternoon," Landon noted.

"We're giving her a ride back to the inn," Bay added.

"That's fine." Landon opened the back door of the Explorer for me and gestured. "Climb in."

I immediately reached for the seatbelt when settled, taking a moment to watch Bay and Landon through the window. They didn't speak, but they said a lot with their expressions. Landon's jaw was tight when he leaned forward to press a kiss to Bay's mouth, something unspoken passing between them. They were both friendly and calm when they climbed into the Explorer.

"Did you find anything in the archives?" Landon asked, firing up the vehicle and directing it toward the main road.

"I found a few stories of wild bear attacks and some others where people claimed to see the Dog Man," I replied. They seemed relaxed, Landon using his right hand to hold Bay's left, rubbing idle circles on top of her knuckles. I could sense a bit of unease between them, although it wasn't overwhelming. "There was nothing in there to explain the most recent attack, though."

Landon appeared surprised by the statement. "Did you think there would be?"

I shrugged. "Legends survive through decades – centuries even – for a reason," I answered. "Don't you ever wonder how some legends start? For example, I was going through the archives and at first I didn't see anything about the Dog Man or similar creatures, but there was plenty about witches."

"Witches, huh?" Landon kept his eyes facing forward. "What did it say about witches?"

"Just that there was supposedly a coven around these parts and that people believe some lines still survive today. Of course, that article was written by someone named Edith in the sixties, so you have to take that with a grain of salt. That was a long time ago."

"That's the legend Hemlock Cove was founded on," Bay said softly.

"I … oh. That hadn't even occurred to me." I leaned forward. "So you know the story about the witches, huh?"

Bay nodded. "There have been stories about witches in these parts since long before I was born. When the Walkerville council members decided to focus the town's future on tourism they thought they'd take advantage of the history and build from there," Bay explained, smiling. "It wasn't as hard as you might expect to take those legends and run with them."

"And the town has definitely run with them," Landon added with a chuckle. "When I first started spending time here all I heard about was witches."

"It obviously worked for you guys, though," I pointed out. "Hemlock Cove seems to be thriving."

"The town does pretty well," Bay confirmed. "Most of the inns sell out throughout the spring, fall and summer. There are some small gaps in the winter. My mother and aunts do robust business throughout the year. They're never hurting for guests."

"And your father?" The question was out of my mouth before I thought better about asking it. That's a common practice for me.

Bay stiffened and Landon slid a worried look in her direction.

"The Dragonfly does fine, too," Bay replied, her tone clipped. That was as far as she planned to take it, which was a relief. But Landon was the exact opposite.

"How do you know about Bay's father?" Landon asked. "Have you been asking around about her?"

"Oh, I was at the bakery this afternoon and I spent some time talking to Mrs. Gunderson," I admitted, squirming. "She mentioned that Bay was close to the police chief and said he was kind of like her father, even though she had a father who left town when she was younger and recently came back to open his own inn."

Did I mention that I babble when I'm nervous?

"It seems you and Mrs. Gunderson had quite the talk." Bay mustered a nervous laugh. "All of the inns in the area do well."

"Yes, well … um … I'm sorry if you think I was invading your privacy," I offered lamely.

"It's fine." Bay waved off the apology with minimal effort.

"It's not fine," Landon corrected. "Why are you chasing stories about Bay when you're looking for Bigfoot?"

"I … wasn't chasing around stories about Bay," I protested.

"You were obviously doing something," Landon countered. "I doubt the story about her father just came up. Mrs. Gunderson isn't gossipy about anyone not in her age bracket."

"I'm sorry." My voice ratcheted up a notch. "I didn't mean to upset you."

"You didn't upset me," Bay assured me quickly. "It's fine."

"It's not fine, Bay," Landon growled, his eyes in the rearview mirror now narrowed. "She has no reason to poke her nose into your business."

"She was merely asking questions," Bay shot back. "It's fine. Don't worry, Charlie. I ask questions for a living. It's not a big deal."

Bay said the words, but I couldn't help but wonder if she really meant them. Thankfully I didn't have long to dwell on the conundrum before Landon pulled up in front of The Overlook. I was eager to escape the couple's thoughtful and weighted looks.

"Thanks for the ride." I bolted from the Explorer and hurried to the inn as fast as I could, sucking in huge mouthfuls of oxygen to calm myself once on the other side of the lobby's front door. I'd clearly stepped in it. I couldn't blame them for being angry. I'd be upset if someone poked into my background, too. I couldn't shake the niggling worry that they were upset about something else, though. It wasn't just that I found out about Bay's father. It was that I asked questions at all. I was almost sure that was the case.

I didn't have long to fixate on my thoughts, because the sound of raised voices in the dining room caught my attention. I scampered in that direction, thankful to have a reason to put distance between the door Landon and Bay would walk through at any moment and me. When I hit the dining room, I found a fascinating sight.

Tillie stood on her chair at the end of the table, a glass of wine in her hand. She looked almost regal as she stared down at the other members of my group.

"What's going on?" I asked, breathless.

Jack spared a glance for me. "I've been trying to text you. Do you ever answer your phone?"

"I ... um ... had it on. At least I think I did." I dug in my pocket and when I retrieved my phone I found it was turned off. "Oh, sorry. I thought I had it on."

"I've been worried," Jack snapped. "I thought you needed a ride back to town, but when you didn't answer my texts ... ." He broke off, perhaps realizing how ludicrous the statement sounded given the size of Hemlock Cove. I was hardly going to wander off and get lost in the crowd or be attacked by gangbangers by wandering to the wrong side of town.

"Landon and Bay gave me a ride back."

"Great. I guess." Jack squared his shoulders.

He was acting odd even for Jack. "What's going on here?" I gestured toward Tillie. "She seems ... upset."

"She's off her rocker," Laura snapped, her eyes flashing as she stared down the rambunctious Winchester matriarch. "She's crazy. There can be no other explanation."

I wasn't ruling out Tillie mental state, but something told me Laura had instigated this incident. "What did you do?"

"Me?" Laura was incredulous. "How could you possibly think that I had anything to do with it? She's crazy!"

"I shall call down the thunder and smite you," Tillie intoned, her voice deepening to almost comical proportions.

"Do I even want to know what you're doing?" Landon asked, strolling into the dining room with Bay close at his side.

"I'm cursing the wanton woman so she will have nothing but unhappiness for the rest of her life," Tillie replied, never moving her gaze from Laura's face.

"Great. While you're at it, make Bay smell like bacon for me," Landon suggested, reaching for one of the bottles of wine at the center of the table. "Don't forget to make her taste like bacon, too."

Jack snickered at Landon's calm demeanor, amused at what clearly had to be a family joke. "You put in curse requests? Does she do this often?"

"At least three times a week," Landon replied. "The bacon curse is my favorite." He handed the bottle of wine to Bay and smiled. "Can you please open that for me, sweetie? I think I'm going to need to get drunk to get through the night."

Bay wordlessly nodded, flicking a worried look at Aunt Tillie before heading to the buffet for a corkscrew.

"And, you," Landon said, swiveling back to Tillie. "Who are you threatening?"

"The wanton woman," Tillie replied, her voice positively dripping with fake dramatic flair.

"You'll have to be more specific," Landon prodded. "Which woman is wanton today? I don't see Thistle, so she can't be in the line of fire. I guess that means you're talking about one of those three, huh?" He gestured toward Hannah, Laura and me.

Tillie nodded. "That one," she hissed, pointing at Laura. "She's on my list."

"She keeps saying that," Laura whined. "I have no idea what list she's talking about or why it's so bad to be on it."

"Oh, you definitely don't want to be on it," Landon wagged his head while taking an empty wine glass from the table.

"Definitely," Bay echoed.

"If you're already on it, though, that might be good news for the rest of us," Landon added. "If Aunt Tillie is focused on you she can't torture the rest of the world. Maybe you should consider staying on her list."

"I'm an excellent multi-tasker," Tillie sniffed. "I can curse more than one person at a time."

"Just remember bacon," Landon whispered, grinning before he shifted his blue eyes to Laura. "What did you do to her?"

"I didn't do anything to her!"

"Tillie was telling us a story about the time she wrestled Bigfoot and won. Laura said it was a crock of crap, and things pretty much fell apart from there," Bernard offered from the opposite end of the table. He seemed to be enjoying the show. "Then Tillie started talking about her list, and Laura said she was making stuff up as she went along. That brought out more talk of the list. I'm honestly dying to see how this ends."

"You and me both." Jack grinned. "Do you have any suggestions about how we should handle this, Agent Michaels?"

Landon nodded as Bay returned with the bottle of wine and the two settled into chairs at the table. "I do. Abandon Laura to her fate and try to stay off the list for the rest of your stay here."

Everyone but Laura chuckled.

"What is that supposed to mean?" Laura asked, her eyes flashing. It was as if she couldn't believe Landon wasn't running over to rescue her.

"It means you're in trouble," Tillie replied. "You'll be sorry you ever met me before this is all said and done."

"Oh, don't worry." Laura adopted a snotty tone. "I'm already there."

"Good!" Tillie bobbed her head knowingly. "You're now at the top of the list. You should start running now."

ELEVEN

"*A*re you ready?"

The only thing I was ready for after the longest – and freaking loudest – dinner I'd ever sat through was a good night's sleep. That's why Millie's appearance at my door, seconds before I was ready to slip into my pajamas and call it a day, threw me for a loop.

"Ready for what? Are you here to romance me?" The snarky response slipped out before I had a chance to think better about uttering it to a woman in Millie's age bracket.

"You're funny," Millie said, clearly enjoying my answer. "That's not what I was talking about, though." She cast a furtive look up and down the hallway.

I followed her gaze, curious. "What are you talking about?"

"We're going on a little adventure." Millie's smile was mischievous so I couldn't help but feel my interest pique.

"We are? Did you see the Winchesters doing something? Are they hiding bodies on the property or something?"

Millie made a face right out of a sitcom. "Why would they be hiding bodies?"

"Because I'm pretty sure they're hiding something big."

"I'm pretty sure you're right, but I don't think it has anything to do with bodies," Millie said, shoving me out of the way so she could stroll into the bedroom and grab my hoodie. "Put this on. You'll need it."

"But ... where are we going?"

"We're going back to the resort," Millie replied, making a "well, duh" face as I slipped into the hoodie.

"We are?" I rolled the idea through my head. It didn't make sense. "Why? Do you think one of Penny's boyfriends is going to kill again?"

"You're full of drama, girl," Millie said, clicking her tongue against her teeth as she shook her head. "You're gung-ho – I'll give you that – and I think you'll be fun once we pull that stick out of your you-know-what."

I knit my eyebrows. "I don't have a stick in my you-know-what."

"You need a stick in your you-know-what," Millie countered. "Unfortunately you seem to have one up your behind instead, because you're trying to be employee of the month or something. Here's a hint: The foundation doesn't give out awards for being happy and helpful on the job."

I balked. "I am not trying to be happy and helpful. Wait ... that came out wrong."

Millie snorted. "You're a bundle of nerves. I get it. You're twenty-five and this is your first real job. It happens to all of us. You'll outgrow it."

"I'm twenty-four."

Millie's mouth dropped open. "You're twenty-four? Why are you working if you're twenty-four? You' should be out partying and having sex with any guy who looks at you sideways. That's what I did when I was twenty-four ... and twenty-five ... and forty-eight, for that matter."

Millie boasts one of those faces that make you wonder if she was ever twenty-four. "I have bills to pay."

"Bummer. You should be fornicating until you can't fornicate a second longer. You know your body is never going to get better than this, right?" She gestured toward my lean frame. "You're a little light on top, but your butt and thighs are nice. You should exploit them."

My cheeks colored under her serious gaze. "I cannot believe we're having this discussion."

"Well, believe it," Millie said, holding up a set of keys. "I stole Chris' keys when he wasn't looking, so we should have no problem getting back to the resort."

"And why are we going back to the resort?" I grabbed my room key from the dresser before shutting my bedroom door. "Do you think we'll catch the killer?"

"Well, I don't think we're going to find Bigfoot, if that's what you're asking," Millie shot back. "As for finding the killer, I'm fairly certain he won't be where we're going."

"But ... where are we going?"

Millie shot me a sympathetic look. "We're going to take care of your stick problem."

I tilted my head to the side, confused. "Which stick problem? You said I had two."

"If we're lucky we'll handle both of them," Millie said, grabbing my arm. "Come on. I guarantee you won't want to miss this."

"**THIS IS** A TERRIBLE IDEA."

That's how I felt the minute I realized Millie probably shouldn't be driving – especially because she technically stole Chris' rental vehicle. She weaved all over the road, got distracted by signs and was convinced every flash she saw on the side of the road was a deer about to race out in the road in front of her. Once she punched in the ambulance code to get behind the gate she had shown us earlier and made me hike through the woods in the dark, my feeling intensified.

"Oh, suck it up," Millie intoned. I couldn't see her eyes in the darkness, but I was sure she was rolling them. "You're twenty-four. You should be excited about an illicit rendezvous in the woods."

"I'm with you! How illicit can it be?"

"Would you be okay if you were with a man?" Millie slowed her pace and swiveled to face me. The muted moonlight allowed me to make out some – but not all – of her features. "How about if you were with Chris?"

Thankfully the darkness hid the flush of my cheeks. "Chris? Why would I want to be out here with him?"

"Because you think he's cute."

"He's my boss."

"That doesn't mean he's not cute."

She had a point. Still … . "I do not have a crush on Chris."

Millie remained silent for a beat and then relaxed her shoulders. "That's probably good. The boy is head-over-heels for Hannah, even though she doesn't realize it. I think they'll find each other eventually, but it's like watching stone statues trying to mate."

I bit my cheek to keep from laughing at the visual. I didn't want to encourage Millie, but she was definitely funny. "I noticed that myself."

"What about the FBI agent?" Millie challenged. "I've seen you looking at him."

"I have not!" My voice carried over the night air, causing me to cringe. "Besides, in case you haven't noticed, he's got a girlfriend."

"One he loves," Millie said sagely. "Anyone who looks at that boy can see he's gone … and he's never coming back."

"I don't know why you're telling me this." I shifted from one foot to the other, uncomfortable. "I don't have a crush on Landon."

"You do, but it's okay," Millie countered. "He's an attractive man, and it's not as if you actually think you'll get him. Laura's infatuation with him is much more annoying. She actually thinks she might have a shot, even though that blonde could knock her on her fat butt without breaking a sweat."

"Bay? She doesn't strike me as the type to get down and dirty."

"No?" Millie cocked a confrontational eyebrow. "Look at her again. That woman clearly knows what she's doing when it comes to a fight. She learned from her great-aunt."

"Tillie?" I rolled the idea through my mind. "I bet that she fought a lot in her younger days. She seems the type."

"Age is a state of mind, and that woman's state of the mind is all over the place. She still fights. Heck, I think she fights daily."

"Well, it doesn't matter." I'm obstinate when I want to be. "I don't have a crush on Landon. I'm merely interested in the Winchesters. They're clearly hiding something."

"I agree," Millie said, causing my heart to hop. "I just don't think they're hiding what you think they're hiding."

"Oh, whatever!" I turned back to the worn trail that cut through the woods. "Where are we going?"

"To the eighteenth green," Millie replied. "They're having a party tonight. Those boys I met earlier invited me."

"They invited you to a party?" I couldn't hide my surprise. "That's … impressive."

"I have a way with men. Why do you think I still work for the foundation despite divorcing Myron decades ago?"

That was a pretty good question. "Are you uncomfortable working for him?"

Millie shook her head. "He was always funny to mess with." She fell into step with me, picking a slower pace to navigate the dark slope. "What about Jack? How do you feel about him?"

"Oh, good grief!" I felt as if I were in high school all over again. "He seems nice enough, but he has even bigger problems with sticks than I do."

Millie snorted, amused. "You've got that right, honey. That's kind of why I think you might make a good match."

"I'm not here to find a match," I argued. "I'm here to find … something else."

"Bigfoot?"

"Isn't that why you're here?" I challenged.

"I'm here because I'm genuinely fond of Chris, I like to travel and I have nothing better to do with my time," Millie corrected. "As for finding Bigfoot? Meh. I don't get nearly as excited as the rest of you do when we find a weird footprint in the dirt. That doesn't mean I don't want Chris to eventually find what he wants."

"I'm sorry. I just … you're kind of a busybody."

Millie chuckled loudly. "That's rich coming from you, who spent the entire day trying to find information on the Winchesters instead of working the case you're being paid to pursue. Since when do the Winchesters have anything to do with this case?"

"I ... um ... you don't know that they don't have anything to do with this investigation." As far as justifications go, it was lame. It was all I could come up with.

Millie made a tsking sound and shook her head. "You need to learn to be a better liar. Now, come on. The party is this way. I can smell beer from here. Sure, it's probably cheap beer, but in an hour I won't care in the slightest."

MILLIE WAS RIGHT. An hour later she was drunk enough to hand me the keys to Chris' rental so she wouldn't lose them and euphoric enough to dance with several of the younger resort workers as they performed an ornate line dance I didn't recognize.

Despite myself – and the chill in the air – I found the scene entertaining.

"Do you want a drink?"

I vaguely recognized the guy who moved up to my right side – although I wasn't sure from where – and shook my head when I saw the proffered plastic red cup. "I think one of us needs to stay sober for the drive back."

The guy laughed, the expression lighting up his handsome face. "Yeah. Millie's a trip. She asked if she could touch my muscles earlier. I have no idea why, but I let her."

Recognition dawned as I gave the man another look. "Oh, you were one of the guys unloading the truck. I didn't recognize you with your shirt on."

"Trevor Harris." He extended his hand and I gladly shook it. "You're Charlie, right?"

I nodded. "I see Millie has been talking about me."

"Yes, she said you had a problem with a broken stick and she wanted me to fix it," Trevor said. "I figured she was talking about something dirty, so I pretended I didn't understand what she was saying. Is she your grandmother?"

I smiled at the question. "She's my co-worker. Actually, I just met her a few days ago. I'm new on the job."

"And what do you do for a living?"

I couldn't decide if Trevor was honestly interested or merely passing time. There had to be at least fifty people partying on the eighteenth green, but he paid all of them zero attention and focused on me.

"I work for the Legacy Foundation."

"I don't know what that is."

"We investigate unknown phenomenon."

"Like UFOs?" Trevor leaned forward, intrigued. "Are you here looking for aliens?"

"We're here because Penny Schilling died in the woods and she may or may not have been attacked by an animal of unknown origin."

It took Trevor a moment to grasp what I was saying. "Oh, like the Dog Man?"

I nodded. "That was the rumor, although given Penny's extracurricular activities that's looking less and less likely."

"Yeah, she was a busy little bee." Trevor sipped the beer, grimacing. I was fairly certain that whatever was in the keg couldn't be considered quality brew, which made me doubly glad I was the designated driver for the evening. "She had quite the reputation around the resort."

I cast him a sidelong look, curious. "Did you ever ... ?"

"Me? No. I didn't make enough money to turn her head."

"I heard that didn't matter sometimes," I supplied. "There's a rumor that she wanted a relationship with the high earners but wasn't opposed to spending time with just about anyone if she had an opening in her schedule."

"I think that's definitely true," Trevor confirmed. "I tried to keep my distance from her because I heard a lot of things – including that she had a disease."

I stilled. "What kind of disease?"

"You know; the kind people claim they get from a toilet seat but you really know they got because they'll bone anything that moves."

That was a lovely way to put it. "I heard one of the guys was married," I said. "Did she know that?"

"Bob Grimes." Trevor screwed his face into an unfortunate grimace as he shook his head. "Bob doesn't have a very good reputation himself. His wife works in the hospitality department. She works behind the front desk and helps guests at the concierge desk most days."

"Did they meet at the resort?"

Trevor shrugged. "I know they've been married a long time and that Bob likes to spend more time with his boat and hunting buddies than his wife. She pretends there's nothing wrong with their relationship while he nails anything that moves and drinks more than he should."

For a young guy, Trevor had a way with words. Of course, if I had to guess, he was probably my age. I considered myself good with words, too. "So Bob and his wife are married, but it's all for show, and he got involved with Penny."

"He probably didn't get involved with Penny," Trevor clarified. "It's more like he got drunk and fell on Penny a few times and she told him they were going to get involved. Bob is a nice guy who never thinks before he acts. Penny was a manipulative woman who knew exactly how to get what she wanted."

"Which was?"

Trevor shrugged. "If I knew the answer to that I would've told Penny a long time ago. She seemed to be searching for something. She never found it. Now I guess she never will."

"No, you're probably right." I turned my attention back to a drunk Millie. "Did you really invite her to this party?"

Trevor brightened. "Are you kidding? Look at her. She's hilarious."

"She's definitely the life of the party."

"That's exactly how I want to be when I'm that age," Trevor said. "I want to know who I am and not care what anyone else thinks."

Oddly enough, I felt the same way. I wasn't quite there yet. "How long do you think I should give her before I force her back to the inn?"

"Oh, she's probably got twenty minutes before she starts puking."

"What?" My smile slipped. "Do you really think she'll puke?"

"She's well on her way. In fact … yup. There she goes. She didn't last nearly as long as I thought she word. Darn. I thought she would be good for another dance or two. There goes the night's entertainment."

TWELVE

I wanted to get Millie back to the rental vehicle on my own – mostly because I wasn't keen on letting a guy I hardly knew walk through the woods with me when I was distracted and vulnerable – but ultimately I didn't have a choice. Millie looked small and light in stature, but she was far too heavy for me to navigate on my own.

Trevor seemed amused when he slung one of Millie's arms over his neck, taking the bulk of her dead weight on his broad shoulders. He kept up a light conversation – nothing serious or worrisome – as we headed toward the spot where we had parked.

I'd pretty much managed to lull myself into a feeling of relaxation and security even though I had no idea how I was going to get Millie back inside the inn without anyone noticing. My brain was already skipping forward to various scenarios when a pair of hands shot out of the trees to my right and grabbed my shoulders.

I lashed out without thinking, slapping as hard as I could and making contact with skin. I heard a grunt as I lifted my knee, instinctively going after the one place I knew would equalize the strength factor when fighting against a guy. Jack quickly shifted his hips, keeping me from hitting my target, and shoving me back, a wild look in his eyes.

"Are you trying to kill me?"

I stilled, surprised. He was the last person I expected to find hiding in the woods. "Are you trying to kill me?" I fired back, my temper flaring. "You don't grab someone while they're hiking to their car in the middle of the night! It's not gentlemanly."

"Is something wrong?" Trevor asked, grappling with Millie's weight as another figure moved out of the trees and closed on him. I recognized Bernard right away.

"Don't even think about touching him," I warned. "He's helping, not hurting."

"What happened to her?" Bernard asked, giving Millie a long look. "She isn't dead, is she?"

I snorted, amused. "She's dead drunk. She drank a little too much, and I couldn't carry her back on my own."

"Par for the course." Bernard mustered a smile as he helped Trevor with his burden. "Here. We'll put her in this vehicle."

Trevor shot me a look, as if to ask if I was okay with the shift in riding arrangements. All I could do was nod and offer a wan smile before locking gazes with Jack. He looked furious.

"Don't you even think about yelling at me," I warned, surprising myself with the tone of my voice. "You're not the boss of me."

"No, I'm head of security," Jack gritted out. "That means I'm in charge of your safety. I can't be in charge of your safety if you're crawling around the woods in the middle of the night."

Something occurred to me. "How did you even know we were gone?"

Jack balked, taken aback by the question. "It's my job to know."

"That's not what I asked."

"Help me get Millie in the truck," Bernard ordered Trevor. "Stay away from that argument, son. It's never wise to get between two bulls when they're about to knock horns."

Trevor didn't look convinced. "I … he won't hurt her, will he?"

"He won't hurt her physically," Bernard confirmed. "I have a feeling both of them will have bruised egos before this is done."

"Just take Millie back to The Overlook," Jack barked, retrieving a set of keys from his pocket and tossing them in Bernard's direction. "I'll drive the other vehicle back."

Bernard had no problem picking the keys out of the air even as he supported Millie's weight with his other arm. "No problem. Don't call her any names you can't take back. I've noticed you're not good with the apologies. Women like a man who can apologize."

"Thanks for the tip," Jack said dryly, shaking his head before flicking his eyes to me. "What were you thinking sneaking out of the inn in the middle of the night?"

"It wasn't even ten o'clock," I argued, my temper returning with a vengeance. "That's hardly the middle of the night. The local news doesn't start until eleven, for crying out loud."

I could practically hear Jack's temper sizzling as he glared at me. "Do you think you're funny?"

"Funnier than you. That's not really saying much, though, is it?"

Jack scowled. "You could've gotten yourself into a ton of trouble. You realize that, right?"

"How? Do you really think I was in danger of something terrible happening while with a bunch of kids drinking on a golf course? I wasn't even drinking. Someone had to be the designated driver. I watched Millie drink and I asked a few questions."

"So ... um ... I should probably be going." Trevor hovered a few feet away, gripping his hands together as he cast a longing look in the direction of the golf course. I could hear his friends whooping it up. "It was nice meeting you, Charlie. I enjoyed talking to you and everything." He flashed a warm smile and held my gaze for a bit longer than necessary. "If you need anything else, you know where to find me."

Trevor's good manners did nothing to improve Jack's mood. "Thanks so much for your help," he muttered, scorching Trevor with a dark look. "I don't know what we would've done without you." Jack strode toward me with purpose, grabbing my shoulder and directing me toward the vehicle Millie and I brought to the party. "Get in. We'll finish this discussion on the way back to the inn."

That didn't sound like any fun at all. "I have the keys. I'm driving."

"No, you're not."

"I haven't been drinking," I argued.

"I don't care." Jack slipped his hand in my pocket, causing me to squirm as my stomach warmed. I instinctively jerked away, glaring.

"Don't get fresh."

"When I get fresh, you'll know it." Jack jerked open the passenger-side door. "Get in."

"Don't tell me what to do." I was tired and ready for bed, but obeying Jack wasn't on my to-do list, so I made a big show of searching the ground next to the vehicle instead of getting inside.

"What are you doing?" Jack gritted out, his patience clearly fraying.

"I'm looking for a stick."

"Why?"

"Millie said I have issues with sticks and I think she might be right," I answered primly. "I need a stick so I have something to hit you with during the drive."

Jack was quiet. Finally I had no choice but to look in his direction. I was almost convinced he'd left, abandoning me to find my own way back to The Overlook. Instead he leaned against the front of the vehicle, arms crossed across his chest, staring at me.

"What?"

"Get in, Charlie," Jack ordered, keeping his voice low and even. I was almost positive the corners of his mouth twitched, but his expression turned serious too quickly for me to be absolutely sure. "I think we need to have a long discussion about the chain of command."

I huffed out a frustrated sigh, abandoned my stick search and headed for the open door. "I think we do, too, because you're not the boss of me."

"You're wrong."

"We'll see."

"We definitely will."

I KEPT MY lower lip jutted out, my arms crossed over my chest and my eyes focused on the windshield as Jack drove toward Hemlock Cove. I could almost feel the anger seeping from him, but I chose not to comment on it. I was determined to make him come to me, which, given his hostility, only made things worse.

"Why did you sneak out of the inn in the middle of the night?" Jack finally broke the silence with a near growl.

"It wasn't the middle of the night."

"You know what I mean."

"No, Jack, I'm not sure what you mean." I kept my voice light because I knew it would irritate him. "I'm a lowly female who needs protection. You might need to use shorter words to explain things to me."

"That's not what I said," Jack barked, rolling his eyes as he dragged a hand through his hair. "You're purposely trying to drive me crazy. You think I don't know what you're doing, but I do."

"I'm not trying to do anything to you," I countered. "We went to the resort because Millie found out that the younger workers were having a party. We thought they might have some information for us."

"So this was Millie's idea?"

"I ... no." I had no intention of putting this on Millie. I agreed to go with her, after all. It wasn't her fault, and I wasn't big on blaming others for my actions. "It was my idea."

"Really?" Jack arched a challenging eyebrow. "It was your idea to go to a party you didn't know existed?"

"How do you know that I wasn't the one invited to the party?" Now I was challenging him simply because I could. His short fuse proved that I could manipulate his attention in certain directions if the situation warranted.

"Because you were with me all afternoon while we were at the resort, and Millie was the one who took off on her own," Jack replied matter of factly. "I also happen to know that you were exhausted and ready to go to bed when you left the library earlier tonight. I saw you. You couldn't stop yawning."

"Watch me a lot, do you?" It was meant to be a derisive comment, but Jack nodded, catching me off guard.

"I have been watching you because it's your first investigation, and it's my job to keep you safe," Jack offered. "You had a long day. I was sure you were going upstairs and retiring right away. I knew Millie was going to cause trouble, but I thought she would be hanging around with Tillie. I had no idea she planned to steal one of the rental vehicles – vehicles she has no business driving, mind you – until I saw her lift Chris' keys before announcing she was going to bed."

"You saw her steal the keys?" I wasn't sure what to make of that. "Why didn't you say something before she left the property?"

"I wanted to see what she would do," Jack answered honestly. "I lost sight of her for a few minutes, so I waited in the parking lot. Imagine my surprise when she left with you."

"I ... this is my fault." I felt suddenly desperate. "If someone is going to get in trouble, it should be me."

"No one is going to get in trouble, because Chris isn't going to find out about it," Jack countered. "As for the rest, Millie can't be fired. She knows too many family secrets. Even though she's divorced from Myron, the entire family is still fond of her. She could burn down the entire lab and be safe."

That made me feel marginally better. "I ... that's a relief."

"You're another story," Jack plowed forward. "I'm sure they explained that you're on probation for ninety days, right?"

I wordlessly nodded, my heart sinking.

"You can't steal rental vehicles when you're on probation," Jack barked. "That's not how things are done around here."

"I ... well ... ." I broke off, swallowing hard. "We were only asking some questions. I thought you might be interested in the answers. I didn't think we were doing anything wrong."

"I don't believe that for a second." Jack's expression softened as he ran his tongue over his lips. "Charlie, I know Millie bullied you into going and you went because you have a natural curiosity. You were loyal enough not to let Millie tackle this part of the investigation on her own. It's a nice sentiment, but you need to understand that Millie always leaps and never looks."

"I didn't think there would be any harm in it." That was true, right? I honestly couldn't recall any longer.

"I don't think you believe that. And I'm not here to suck all of the fun out of this," Jack countered. "I know you don't believe it, but it's true. Just … you should've gotten me. I would've gone with you."

I couldn't help but be suspicious, and I made my feelings known as Jack pulled into a parking spot in front of The Overlook. "You're only angry you were left out of the fun. Admit it."

Jack snorted. "Whatever." He hopped out of the vehicle and moved toward the sidewalk that led to the inn's main door. Bernard was already out of the Tahoe and supporting Millie's weight as he led her toward The Overlook.

I considered pressing Jack on the issue of his anger, convinced his nose was really out of joint because we didn't include him. I didn't get the chance. He extended an arm in front of me to still my movement and tilted his head to the side. "Do you hear that?" His voice was barely a whisper.

I didn't hear anything but my own inner voice telling me that Jack was purposely trying to be a pain in the butt. "Don't change the subject," I chided. "I … ."

Jack clamped his hand over my mouth and pressed his eyes shut for a moment, ultimately changing course when his senses tripped over something I couldn't see or hear.

"What are you doing?" I hissed, shoving his hand from my mouth.

"Something is going on back there," Jack whispered, pointing toward a spot on the other side of the greenhouse I'd noted when we first arrived. "There are people outside."

"What are they doing?"

Jack shrugged. "I have no idea. You're convinced the Winchesters are up to something, right?"

My previous indifference evaporated. "Yes."

"Let's see what that noise is."

I kept close enough to Jack that I could touch him if things went bad, but remained quiet as I followed him. It took him a few minutes to pick his way through the area, finally stopping and staring when we reached a small clearing halfway up the bluff behind the inn.

A bonfire roared in the center of the circle. My mouth dropped open when I saw the dancing women. There were four of them … and they were naked. "Is that … ?"

"Winnie, Marnie, Twila and Tillie." Jack hissed. "I guess Millie isn't the only one who thought it was a good night to drink. They look as if they've been through at least four bottles of wine, if the empties scattered on the ground are to be believed."

"What are they doing?"

"They appear to be dancing." Jack was grim. "I'll never be able to unsee this. I didn't even know boobs could spin that way."

I couldn't help but be amused, opening my mouth to tease him when a hint of movement caught my attention on the far side of the clearing. Landon, a disgusted look on his face, stumbled closer to the women, Bay at his side.

"Oh, good grief," Landon complained. "You couldn't wait until the monster hunters were gone to do this?"

Winnie energetically waved and continued to dance. "It's the vernal equinox," she argued. "We can't delay it. It doesn't matter who is staying at the inn."

"Yes," Twila laughed. "We … must … dance!" She jiggled her butt for emphasis.

I exchanged a quick look with Jack to see if I could grasp what he was thinking. His face remained impassive.

"They already think we're weird," Bay offered. "If they see this … ."

"Who cares what they think?" Tillie called out. "I certainly don't."

"You don't care what anyone thinks," Landon said, moving closer to the blanket spread on the grass. "Did you drink all of the wine? If I'm going to watch this, I'll need wine."

"There's more in the basket." Twila flapped her arm as she pranced and pointed. "You should hurry up and drink so you can catch up. You live on the property now, too, Landon. You need to dance."

Landon shot a worried look in Bay's direction. "Is that true?"

"I should mess with you, but it's not true." Bay giggled. "They have a bet to see when you finally get drunk enough to dance with them under the full moon."

"Oh." Landon's face was impassive. "That's never going to happen."

"Oh, it's going to happen," Tillie said. "I'm definitely going to live to see that."

"Whatever." Landon shook his head as he pulled a cork. "Who wants to drink with me?"

Bay raised her hand.

"I know you do." Landon kissed the tip of her nose, making my heart hurt because the smile he flashed at her was so earnest. "So ... bottoms up?"

Bay slid a glance in the direction of her mother and aunts. "That's probably the wrong term around this group."

Landon chuckled. "Cheers?"

Bay smiled. "Drink up, witches," she corrected, giggling.

"Drink up it is." Landon took a huge mouthful of wine and risked a glance at the gyrating older women. "We might need a few more bottles of this if I'm going to survive the horror."

"You and me both."

THIRTEEN

e watched a long time. Probably longer than we should have. It was too fascinating to turn away from. Jack secreted us behind a group of trees and we hunkered down, fascinated despite the chill in the air as the women did their own thing and ignored the outside world.

Mostly it was just dancing. Bay and Landon didn't join in, instead resting on the blanket spread across the far side of the clearing and whispering to one another. After almost an hour Landon staggered to his feet, tossed Bay over his shoulder and announced they were going to bed. It was clear what he had in mind. The others merely waved and continued their twirling.

Eventually my legs cramped and Jack prodded me away. We made the walk back to The Overlook mostly in silence, only risking talking once we were inside.

"What do you make of that?" he asked finally, breathless.

"They like to drink and dance."

Jack made an exaggerated face. "But … Landon was out there with them. He didn't seem to care at all."

"Why should he? This obviously isn't the first time they've done it."

"No, but that's his future mother-in-law," Jack argued. "Why would he want to see her naked?"

He had a point. Still … . "He never looked at Winnie," I said after a moment's contemplation. "He stayed focused on Bay the entire time. I mean … well … he knew they were dancing, but he remained focused on Bay while they were out there."

"He's always focused on Bay," Jack noted. "He barely looks at anyone else."

"He loves her."

"It's not just that," Jack countered. "It's as if he's waiting for something bad to happen to her. He's determined to protect her at all costs."

I noticed that, too. "Well, she is a reporter who happens to own the newspaper where she works," I offered. "Maybe she gets into trouble from time to time."

"She's a reporter for a weekly in a town that's all about festivals," Jack argued. "I wouldn't think that would put her in harm's way very often. Landon tries to keep her as close as possible whenever he can."

"I think it's kind of sweet that he loves her that much."

"I think it's weird."

I made a face. "Because you can't imagine loving someone that much?"

Jack shook his head. "Because he seems to be waiting for something terrible to descend on this family. It's almost as if he knows that danger is coming, and when it arrives, it will be coming for Bay. Why do you think he believes that?"

"I think some people want to protect the people they love at all costs." My mind briefly traveled to my parents and the way they cautioned me about keeping my abilities hidden. "Maybe Landon knows something we don't. Have you ever considered that?"

Jack held his hands palms up. "That's exactly what I'm worried about. What do you think he knows?"

I had no idea, but I was determined to find out. "I need some sleep. I guess I'll see you in the morning."

"You'll definitely see me in the morning." Jack shuffled down the hallway, heading for his room. He paused with his hand on the door-knob. "You don't have to worry about getting in trouble. Even if Chris finds out, you'll be fine. Millie will tell him the truth and, like I said, she's allowed to do whatever she wants."

"Yeah? Thanks." I flashed a small smile. "I probably shouldn't have gone with her. It seemed like a good idea at the time, though."

"The dumbest ideas always do." This time Jack's grin was legitimate. "Get some sleep. I have a feeling it's going to be an interesting morning."

He wasn't the only one.

I WOKE EARLY AND SHOWERED, taking the extra time to blow dry my long hair and apply the bare minimum of makeup. I hadn't imbibed the night before, so I didn't have a hangover, but I was under the impression that the same couldn't be said for the rest of the house.

Tillie, Landon, Bay, Thistle and Marcus sat at the dining room table when I hit the main floor. I took a moment to eavesdrop before entering.

"I can't believe I missed that," Thistle complained. "I forgot it was the equinox. We need to write this stuff down on a calendar, Marcus. You know how I love the naked dancing."

"You don't love the naked dancing," Marcus argued. It was the first time I could remember him raising his voice. He seemed quiet and contemplative most of the time, which was why I liked him. "You do nothing but complain when it's happening."

"That lasts only until I've had some wine," Thistle shot back. "I like it fine after that."

"Well, I don't like it fine," Marcus argued. "You know how I feel about the magic of spinning boobs."

I had to bite my lip to keep from laughing.

"We didn't spend any time watching them anyway," Bay offered. "Once Landon had some wine in him he started making up poems about bacon and that got him in the mood."

"The mood for what?" Tillie asked, nursing her mug of coffee with a haggard expression. "By the way, my boobs don't spin. They're as firm as they were when I was a teenager. I could be a model. They're that firm. No, seriously, I could totally do it professionally. Victoria's Secret called and I had to turn them down."

Thistle snorted. "Please. Your boobs have like eight minds of their own when you get to drinking and dancing. Still, was that a smart idea when we have the Legacy Foundation group in the inn?"

"I don't care who we have in the inn," Tillie replied. "Besides, they're looking for Bigfoot. Unless I'm mistaken, we weren't dancing with Bigfoot."

"You were still loud enough to draw attention," Landon warned. "That's how Bay and I knew you were out there. We forgot it was the equinox, too."

"And you wanted to go home and take a bath," Bay teased. She seemed mildly hungover, but in good spirits. "Think how much we would've missed if we did that."

"I'm sure my head wouldn't be pounding nearly as much as it is now if we'd been good instead of bad," Landon countered, rubbing his forehead. "Still, I'm glad you made me write down that ode to bacon before going to bed. I'm going to recite it to you every night."

Bay snorted. "Yes, that will certainly put me in the mood."

"It will put me in the mood," Landon said. "I'm the one who generally puts you in the moods so ... we'll be fine."

I took advantage of the lull in the conversation and pasted a bright smile on my face as I walked into the dining room. "Good morning. How is everyone this fine and beautiful spring day?" Hmm. That probably came out a little forced, huh?

"Still alive," Tillie replied, draining the rest of her coffee. "I'd say that's about all we have going for us."

I fixed a puzzled look into place while pouring my own mug of coffee. "Oh, is something wrong?"

Tillie narrowed her eyes as she regarded me, rolling her neck and openly staring. "She saw us." She made the announcement after only a few moments of contemplation. I was completely taken aback.

"I did not see you."

"Ha!" Tillie extended a finger. "If you didn't see us, how do you know there was something to see?"

"You just told me."

"Oh." Tillie drew her eyebrows together. "I'm still pretty sure she saw us."

"I'm pretty sure you're right," Landon said dryly, pouring Bay a glass of tomato juice as he pinned me with a quizzical look. "Were you out and about last night?"

"I ... ." Crap. I was caught. They knew it and I knew it. Thankfully Jack picked that moment to swoop into the dining room and save me.

"What's going on?" he asked, his expression unreadable as his gaze bounced from face to face.

"She was spying on us last night," Tillie replied, unruffled. "She thinks we don't know ... but we know."

"Spying?" Jack was a much better actor than I was and when he lifted a confused-looking eyebrow I almost believed him. "What was she spying on?"

Tillie ran her tongue over her teeth as she regarded Jack. I figured she was probably debating whether or not she wanted to tattle. I was wrong.

"You were out there, too."

Jack balked. "I was not out there watching you."

I groaned as I slapped my hand to my forehead. "And you think I'm a bad liar," I muttered, shaking my head.

"Told you." Tillie was clearly full of herself as she shifted her eyes to Landon. "You didn't do anything illegal, did you? They could take your badge if you're not careful."

"I didn't do anything illegal," Landon barked, his annoyance obvious. "At least I don't think I did. We didn't do that one thing I suggested with the bacon, right?" He looked confused when he glanced at Bay.

Instead of being embarrassed, she giggled. "No. We don't have any bacon in the guesthouse. We couldn't have done that even if we wanted to."

"I think the better question is: Would you have done that?" Landon perked up.

Bay immediately began shaking her head. "No. It's dirty."

"Since when did you become a puritan?"

"Not dirty-minded," Bay corrected. "It's physically dirty. We'd never get the grease out of the sheets."

"What if we do it in the tub?"

"Do you want to eat soggy bacon?"

Landon shrugged. "Life is full of hard choices, sweetie. We'll give it some thought later." He patted her hand and turned to Jack. "They were on their own property. What you saw was none of your business."

Jack widened his eyes. "I didn't want to mention seeing anything." He jerked his thumb in my direction. "That's on her. She has a big mouth."

"She didn't announce that she saw us," Bay pointed out. "She merely pretended she didn't, and Aunt Tillie figured out she was lying."

"And how did she do that?" Jack asked.

Bay shrugged. "She has a nose for lies. I can't explain it."

"Yeah, she definitely manages to figure out when people are lying," Thistle confirmed. "Once, when I was a teenager, I told her the truth about my car breaking down because that was the reason I missed curfew. She got me to admit to lying even though I was telling the truth."

"That's not why I did that," Tillie said, snorting. "I knew you weren't lying that night. I also knew you snuck out two nights before and made out with the Randall boy. You didn't get caught for that, so I was merely paying you back."

Thistle's mouth dropped open. "How did you know I snuck out that night?"

"I know all and see all."

Surprisingly enough, the Winchesters didn't appear bothered that someone had spied on them the previous evening – which was dumbfounding to me because I wouldn't get naked in the gym shower, let alone a field full of family members. So I took a risk and settled in one of the open chairs, picking a spot close to Jack. He filled his mug with coffee, clearly enthralled by the odd conversation.

"You're making that up," Thistle said. "You simply played the odds that I'd done something wrong over the past week and guilted me until you got the outcome you wanted."

"You'd like to think that, wouldn't you?" Tillie was clearly hungover, but she was determined not to use that as an excuse to lose an argument. "I always knew what you were up to. It's my special skill."

"Oh, and I thought it was making me think my head was imploding on a daily basis," Landon deadpanned.

"Don't make me put you on my list," Tillie warned.

"I'll try to refrain from the overwhelming urge to get on your list," Landon said, sipping his coffee before shifting his eyes to Bay. "What are you doing today?"

"What are you doing today?" she countered.

"You told me that answering a question with a question is a sure-fire way to know that someone is up to no good," Landon pointed out. "What are you doing today?"

"I am ... working." Bay suddenly found something interesting to stare at on the tablecloth. I had no idea what, but she was determined to avoid eye contact with the pushy FBI agent.

"What are you working on?" Landon didn't raise his voice, but it was clear he was suspicious.

"I'm working on an article about the dead woman in the woods," Bay replied. "What else is there to work on?"

"Okay. I'd like to know where you plan to pursue your leads," Landon pressed. "I don't want you wandering around the woods by yourself, Bay. It's not safe."

"I'm not going to be by myself." Bay cast a pleading look in Thistle's direction. "I'm not going to be in the woods either. I'm going back to the resort. And I'm taking Thistle with me."

"I can't go with you," Thistle said, dashing Bay's hopes. "I have to do inventory. We have a huge shipment coming in at the store. I don't have a choice."

"Well, I guess that settles that," Landon said. "I might be able to carve out some time this afternoon to take you to the resort. If you can wait until then … ."

Bay cut him off with a shake of her head. "I can't wait until then."

"Why not? I have to go with Chief Terry to talk to Penny's family. I can't go to the resort with you now."

"I don't need you to go with me," Bay argued. "I'm an adult. I have my own car. I can go out to the resort myself."

"Sweetie, I would really rather you didn't." Landon lowered his voice. I couldn't decide if it was because he was embarrassed to be caught begging or he was trying to placate the feisty blonde.

"I'm going." Bay was firm. "I'll be fine. It's a nice day, and I won't be wandering around the woods. There's nothing to worry about."

"Besides, I'll go with her," Tillie offered. "You'll have nothing to worry about as long as I'm there to supervise."

Landon's grimace turned into a scowl. "That doesn't make me feel any better. In fact, that makes me feel worse. The idea of the two of you running around that resort is enough to give me indigestion. Can't you please wait, Bay?"

Bay looked caught. She clearly didn't want to hurt Landon's feelings, but she was determined to return to the resort. I couldn't fathom why, but was dying to find out. That's why I decided to interject myself into the argument, which, in hindsight, was probably a mistake.

"I need to go back, too," I offered, wrapping my hands around the mug. "I can go with her."

Landon turned his incredulous eyes to me. "Excuse me?"

"Yeah, excuse me?" Jack was equally annoyed. "We didn't discuss that."

"I wasn't aware I had to discuss my plans with you," I sniffed, locking gazes with Bay. I knew she would decide her own fate – she had that air about her – and I wanted to make sure I wasn't forgotten in the melee. "If you're game to go out to the resort, I'd be more than happy to go with you."

Bay made up her mind on the spot. "The more the merrier. Sounds like a fun morning."

"Oh, geez." Landon pinched the bridge of his nose. "This has mistake written all over it."

"Don't worry." Tillie patted his arm. "I'll be there to keep things under control."

"And I'm going to need to start my day with a drink," Landon muttered. "I think my liver is going to be shot before the week is out at this rate."

I couldn't help but worry he was right.

FOURTEEN

"I can't believe you didn't let me drive," Tillie griped as she climbed out of the passenger seat of Bay's car. Bay parked in front of the main lobby, which I hadn't entered when I'd been at the resort yesterday, so I was excited to see it. Of course, I was also nervous because the possibility of running into people I'd previously met was high. I hadn't thought about that when I volunteered to accompany Bay.

"Your truck still has the plow on it and there's nothing to plow," Bay argued, adopting a long-suffering sigh only family members familiar with specific quirks can muster. "Besides, you shouldn't have a license. You're a terrible driver."

"Okay, you're definitely on my list," Tillie grumbled, staring at the resort's main building. "Huh. Is this place bigger?"

"When was the last time you were here?" I asked.

"Probably the seventies."

"Oh, well, I assume they made some changes," I offered, smiling. "It's a beautiful resort. Do you golf? I'll bet the course is gorgeous."

"Why would I want to golf?" Tillie asked, scuffing her shoes against the concrete as we walked up the sidewalk. "What fun is there in hitting a ball with a stick? If I want to hit something with a stick, I want it to move first. Otherwise it's too easy."

I was taken aback. "What do you hit with sticks?"

Tillie shrugged. "I'm not a big fan of moles. They mess up my garden."

"So you hit them with a stick?" My eyes widened. "Do you kill them?"

"Not with a stick. That's what the gun is for."

Bay shifted her shoulders and glared at her great-aunt. "Where is your gun, by the way? I told Landon you were walking with it in town and he went to find it and came up empty. I'm sure you were anticipating that, though. Is it in the greenhouse? The door was locked yesterday."

Tillie's face flickered between annoyance and faux innocence. "Why would you be trying to get in my greenhouse? You don't garden."

"I could garden," Bay shot back. "You're trying to distract me. Where is your gun?"

"I don't have a gun. I think you're mistaken." Tillie shifted her eyes toward the kitschy gift shop area. "That's where I'll be if you need me."

Bay's mouth dropped open. "I thought you were here to help me."

"I am here to help you. I'm going to help myself, too. They have a candy shop. I'll ask questions about Penny Schilling there. Bakers and candy makers are always thick with the good gossip."

I had no idea if that was true, but Bay seemed resigned.

"Fine," Bay growled. "Don't get in trouble, though. Don't call anyone names ... and don't put anyone on your list. By the way, you don't have any mortal enemies who work here, do you?"

Tillie shrugged, unbothered by Bay's tone. "It's a small world, Bay, and my enemies list is ever growing. I can't answer that question until I see who works here. You know that."

"Okay, but if you get arrested, call Mom for bail money. I'm going to pretend I don't know you."

"So it will be like you're in middle school again." Tillie's smile was sunny. "I'll see you in a little bit. By the way, if you get arrested, don't come crying to me. Call 'The Man' and make him bail you out."

"I don't get arrested," Bay countered.

Tillie snorted. "I seem to remember a time or two where you were arrested with me."

"That happened once."

"It happened a few times when you were little," Tillie countered. "I merely told you we were visiting Terry so you wouldn't cry. You girls were such whiners when you were younger."

"Whatever." Bay, a dark expression on her face, watched her great-aunt cross the parking lot. When she realized I was staring at her she squared her shoulders and forced a smile. "So ... um ... shall we?" She gestured toward the main entry.

I nodded as I fell into step with her, the weight of trying to think up passable conversation causing my shoulders to slump. "So, your aunt seems fun."

Bay snorted. "She has her moments. She actually was fun to grow up in the same house with. She always took us on adventures ... and I don't know anyone who doesn't love a good adventure."

The shift in Bay's attitude once Tillie was out of hearing distance was remarkable. "You love her."

"Of course I love her. She's my great-aunt."

"But ... you like her, too."

"I understand her," Bay corrected. "She likes attention, whether it's negative or positive, and she truly enjoys keeping people on their toes. She's a royal pain in the butt when she wants to be. She's also loyal to a fault, and she'd die before letting harm come to anyone she loves."

"Does that include Thistle?"

Bay smiled and this time the expression made it all the way to her eyes. "It definitely includes Thistle. They're the most alike."

"Does Thistle believe that?"

"If you hear her talk, the answer would be no," Bay replied. "I think deep down she recognizes that she has a lot of Aunt Tillie in her. We all have a certain amount, just in different ways."

"Yeah, well ... about last night ... um ... ." I had no idea how to broach the subject and found myself struggling for the right words. "I didn't mean to infringe on your privacy. We were coming back late and Jack thought he heard something. We were checking out the noise and saw you. I promise we didn't stay for very long."

That was a total lie, but it sounded better than the truth.

"You were out there for almost an hour." Bay said the words without recrimination and her eyes sparked with mirth when they locked with mine. "I knew you were out there the entire time."

"How?"

"I ... felt you. I guess that's the easiest way to say it."

"You felt us?" That was interesting. "Are you psychic?"

If Bay was surprised by the question, she didn't show it. "No, I'm not psychic. Are you psychic?"

Unlike Bay, who appeared to have the grace to remain unruffled during the oddest of circumstances, I could feel my cheeks burning under her pointed gaze. "Of course not. I ... why would you ask that?"

"Because you're hiding something." Bay's answer was simple, succinct and said without malice. The observation was also terrifying. "I've known you were hiding something since you arrived."

"That's kind of funny," I admitted, hoping my voice wouldn't crack as I fought to remain calm. "I've thought the same thing about you since we met."

"What do you think we're hiding?"

"I thought we were going to discover it last night, but all we saw was naked dancing and heavy petting," I replied, refusing to back down.

"Who was doing the petting?" Bay was mortified. "I wasn't paying attention to everyone else."

"Then you should know who was doing the petting."

Bay's face was blank. "I ... ."

"It was you and Landon," I offered helpfully. "You guys were in your own little world. I couldn't hear what you were saying to each other, but there was definitely some petting."

For the first time since the conversation began over breakfast an hour before, Bay finally showed signs of embarrassment. Her cheeks flooded with color as she scratched the side of her nose. "Oh, well, I guess we were feeling a bit … cuddly … last night?"

I barked out a laugh, genuinely amused. "Cuddly? Is that what you guys call it?"

"I knew we had an audience, but I kind of forgot," Bay offered lamely. "Aunt Tillie makes her own wine and it's stronger than anything you can find in a store. Once you have a few sips of that … whoa, baby … you kind of forget your surroundings."

I couldn't help but laugh at the embarrassment on her face. "It's okay. You guys weren't being gratuitous or anything. In fact, it was kind of sweet."

"What was sweet about it? Landon was making up dirty limericks about bacon."

"Yeah, he seems obsessed with bacon, huh?"

"He is, but now that he has an audience he plays to it because it's easier than discussing the pros and cons of a Bigfoot murder," Bay explained, holding open the large glass door so I could enter in front of her. "It's just his thing. He does eat a lot of it, though."

"You guys seem happy together."

"We are." Bay's expression was thoughtful as she met my gaze. "What about you and Jack? Are you happy together?"

The question caught me off guard. It was so absurd that I couldn't wrap my head around it. "Jack and me?" I sputtered, legitimately amused. "We're not together."

"You're not?" Bay didn't look convinced. "Almost every time I've seen you since you arrived, you've been with Jack."

That couldn't be right. "I just joined the team," I explained. "I graduated from college this semester. Technically I haven't graduated yet. The ceremony isn't for another two weeks."

"That's not what I asked." Bay's smile was impish. "I asked about Jack."

"And I'm explaining that I barely know him."

"That doesn't mean there's nothing there." Bay climbed the stairs that led to the front desk. "I guess you're not ready to deal with that, this being your first big job and all. When you're ready, though, don't look past Jack."

"He doesn't like me," I argued. "He thinks I'm immature. Last night he yelled at me as if I were a child."

"What were you doing?"

"I ... well ... Millie convinced me to come to a party out here," I admitted. "It was on the eighteenth green of the golf course."

"So you have been out here before." Bay wasn't accusatory, but the way she bobbed her head made me realize she suspected it already. "Were you here yesterday afternoon?"

"I ... yes." I saw no reason to lie. "Jack wanted to question some of the workers. I saw you staring out a window when we were here. I didn't approach you because Jack seemed to want to keep it a secret."

"Landon figured you guys would come out here," Bay noted. "It's okay. You didn't break any laws."

"We used the ambulance code to get behind the property gate." I lowered my gaze to my feet. "I'm pretty sure that's against the law."

"It's not a big law. Don't worry about it."

I pursed my lips. "That seems like an odd thing for the girlfriend of an FBI agent to say."

"Yes, well, I'm a Winchester first," Bay offered. "We were taught that the only rule you had to worry about was the one about not hurting others. Little rules were meant to be broken."

"Do you still believe that?"

"Yes."

"What about Bigfoot? Do you believe in that?"

Bay shrugged. "I believe there are a lot of magical things in this world that people don't understand," she said. "I'm of the mind that you should never rule anything out."

"I kind of believe that too."

"I know. I can tell." Bay turned her attention to the bustling lobby. "Now, let's see if we can find the wife of the bartender, shall we? I hear Penny was shtupping him and the wife most certainly had to know. Let's go this way."

IT DIDN'T TAKE long to realize that Bay Winchester was fun to be around. She showed no nervousness when it came to questioning people – even thinking fast on her feet when confronted by the suspicious head of security about our presence at the resort. By the time we tracked down Phyllis Grimes she was determined.

"Let me do the talking," Bay instructed, moving in the woman's direction with clear purpose.

"That sounds like something your great-aunt would say," I pointed out.

"That's who I learned from." Instead of approaching Phyllis with a bright smile, Bay took a different approach. She kept her face impassive as she rested her hands on the other side of the concierge desk. "Are you Phyllis Grimes?"

The round-faced woman behind the desk was pleasing to the eyes. She was clearly used to disgruntled guests, because she fixed Bay with a bright smile even though Bay took a no-nonsense tone with her. "Can I help you? Is there a problem with your room?"

"I don't have a room," Bay replied. "My name is Bay Winchester. I'm a reporter with The Whistler. Er, actually, I'm the owner now. I'm still getting used to it. That's a long story, though. That's the newspaper in Hemlock Cove."

Phyllis' smile slipped. "I'm familiar with it ... and now that you mention it, I recognize you."

"Great," Bay said, not missing a beat. "We're here looking for information on Penny Schilling. She was murdered and her body was dumped behind the Dandridge lighthouse."

"I ... heard about that." Phyllis, already pale, turned even whiter. "I'm not with Human Resources, so I don't know much about her service here."

"We have questions," Bay explained.

"I'm not authorized to answer questions about Penny's work history." Phyllis made a big show of organizing the envelopes on her side of the desk. "You should speak with someone in Human Resources."

"I talked to them yesterday," Bay said. "We also talked to some workers who told us about some of Penny's more ... colorful ...

avenues of interest. One of those avenues happens to be your husband."

Bay's bold tactics flabbergasted me. I would've tried to butter up the woman a bit, but Bay went straight for the jugular. Phyllis' cold stare told me Bay hit the exact nerve she was after.

"Are you saying that my husband was involved with Penny Schilling?"

Bay nodded without hesitation. "Yes."

"We're happily married!"

"That's not what all of the workers say," Bay countered. "They say your husband sleeps with everyone, you know it, and that Penny was only his latest conquest."

"I … you … I … you can't say things like that to me," Phyllis spat, her temper flaring. "My husband is a good and loyal man. He's a great father."

"He also can't keep it in his pants," Bay said calmly. "Where were you three nights ago, Mrs. Grimes?"

Phyllis narrowed her eyes to dangerous slits, lowering her voice as she leaned forward. "You are not a police officer. I don't have to answer your questions."

"That's fine." Bay was airy, seemingly unbothered, even though Jim Green, the head of security, was back and watching us from a few feet away. "The police and FBI will be here to talk to you in a few hours about some new evidence they have. I thought you might want to get your statement on record with the public before that happens."

Phyllis jerked her eyes to the door, fearful. "They wouldn't dare question me here."

"They don't care where they question you, just that they get answers," Bay countered. "Well, if you don't want to talk to me, I'll take what everyone else said and move on from there."

"Don't you dare!" Phyllis grabbed Bay's arm, digging her fingernails in as she locked gazes with the reporter. "That slut got what she deserved. Everyone knows it. That doesn't mean I did anything to her. You stay away from my husband and me. Don't even think of asking him questions. We're innocent."

"Phyllis, don't let her get to you," Green ordered, stepping closer to the hysterical woman and keeping his eyes on her rather than us. "You're playing right into her hands."

Bay remained unnaturally calm as she stared into the woman's eyes. "Where were you three nights ago?" she repeated finally, catching me off guard with the question. I thought for sure she would apologize for upsetting the woman. I was convinced she'd back off. Instead she drilled deeper. "Were you with Penny?"

"Don't answer that," Green snapped, moving behind the desk and grabbing Phyllis' arm. "Don't even think about answering that."

Phyllis stared into Green's eyes and then stiffly nodded. "Right. Right."

"It's going to be okay, Phyllis," Green soothed. "I'll get rid of them."

"You stay away from us," Phyllis seethed, spittle forming at the corners of her mouth as she fought to regroup. "You'll be sorry if you don't."

"Like Penny was sorry?"

"Like ... mind your own business!" Phyllis pulled away from Green and turned on her heel, disappearing into the office on the other side of the desk.

I risked a glance at Bay and didn't miss the small smile playing at the corners of her mouth or the defiant stare she bored in Green's direction. "Why did you do that?" I asked, genuinely curious. "She would've been more prone to answer if you were nicer to her."

"I've heard some disturbing things about her," Bay explained. "One of the young women who is at the diner now worked here for a few months. She said Phyllis attacked her for putting in a drink order with Bob Grimes ... even though he's the bartender and you're supposed to put your drinks in with him. The woman said Phyllis accused her of sleeping with her husband and threatened her. She said she was crazy."

"So you wanted to make her crazier?" That made absolutely no sense to me.

Bay shrugged. "I want to see what she'll do. She won't answer questions and I don't have the authority to ask the ones I really want to ask. That will be up to Landon and Chief Terry."

"So now what do we do?" I asked, confused.

Bay pointed toward the couch that faced the concierge desk. "We watch and see how she melts down."

"You're kind of mean," I said, the words escaping even though I was mildly impressed.

Bay wasn't bothered. "I learned that from Aunt Tillie, too."

FIFTEEN

*T*rue to her word, Tillie met us at Bay's car later that afternoon.

"The chocolate in that place sucks a wizard's nut," Tillie announced, tossing a bag of candy in Bay's direction. "Only give that to someone you hate. It will give you the runs."

I pressed my lips together to keep from laughing as Bay calmly nodded.

"I'll drop it in front of Mrs. Little's store or something," Bay offered, distracted.

"That's a great idea." Tillie brightened considerably until she took a moment to absorb Bay's countenance. "What's wrong, pouty?"

"How well do you know Phyllis Grimes?" Bay asked, rolling her neck until it cracked. I thought she would keep what happened inside to herself – perhaps embarrassed because she chased off Phyllis – but she appeared to be focused on something else.

"Phyllis Grimes?" Tillie wrinkled her nose. "That name doesn't mean a heck of a lot to me. Why?"

"She's Bob Grimes' wife."

"Who is Bob Grimes?" Tillie asked, confused.

"He's the bartender," Bay replied. "He was having an affair with Penny Schilling."

"And she's the woman eaten by Bigfoot?" Tillie didn't look impressed. "Well, was she sleeping around with everyone or just someone else's someone?"

"Everyone," I answered automatically. "She was sleeping with the head of purchasing, the head of security and the chief bartender. The guys we partied with last night also told me that she would sleep with anyone if she was bored."

Tillie's expression turned appraising. "You partied with the manual laborers and got some good information. I couldn't be more proud if you were one of my own."

The compliment caught me off guard. "I … well … thank you."

"She's not done yet," Bay said dryly.

"You should've asked about the wife," Tillie added. "She's obviously the key. How did you approach her, Bay?"

"Like you would've done."

"You accused her and she ran and hid?" Tillie tapped her chin. "Hmm. Why did you think I would know this woman?"

"Because she's Anna Stewart's daughter," Bay replied, her eyes traveling back to the resort's main door. "She was ahead of us in school by quite a bit. I don't know much about her. I'm not sure she recognized me before I introduced myself."

"She doesn't live in Hemlock Cove, right?" I was still trying to follow all of the small town familial trails.

Bay shook her head. "She lives here. I see her in town from time to time – her mother still lives in Hemlock Cove – but I don't think she spends much time hanging around at town festivals."

"Oh, Phyllis Stewart?" Tillie bobbed her head. "I know who you're talking about. Fat girl? Wears her hair so short that she kind of looks like a pig?"

Bay heaved a sigh. "You can't say things like that. She's not fat. She's very … pretty."

Tillie made a face that would've made me laugh under different circumstances. Much like Bay, though, I wasn't keen on making fun of people's looks. "Oh, please. You're such a whiner. I didn't raise you to be politically correct, Bay."

"You raised me to torture my enemies with yellow snow and curses," Bay countered. "This woman isn't my enemy, though. From everything I heard about her yesterday, she's not exactly pleasant. But that doesn't mean she's a terrible person. If your husband cheated on you with everything that moved, you'd probably be unpleasant too."

"No one would ever cheat on me," Tillie countered. "I'm a dynamo in the sack. Men have written sonnets about it. I could totally do it professionally if I was so inclined."

Tillie Winchester was in her eighties. I didn't have an exact age, but I was sure of that. To hear her say those words was enough to cause me to double over with laughter.

"What is she carrying on about?" Tillie asked, annoyed.

"She thinks it's funny that you called yourself a 'dynamo in the sack,'" Bay explained. "She's trying to picture you doing just that."

"Oh, gross." Tillie smacked my arm. "I didn't realize you were a pervert. Knock that off or I'll put you on my list."

I had the strength to silence myself and straighten, although just barely. I took a few moments to collect myself and then shifted my gaze to the huge windows at the front of the lobby. I could clearly make out Phyllis Grimes standing in one. She watched us with outright hatred.

"What do you think we should do?" I asked, once my laughter was contained. "Do you think she's guilty?"

"We can't know that until we know exactly what happened," Bay answered, resting her hand on top of her car. "We need to talk to Landon."

"What is he going to do?" I was honestly curious.

"Other than kiss her and leave her breathless? He eats a lot of bacon and yells like a bossy cow," Tillie replied.

Bay shot her great-aunt a dark look. "Don't say things like that about him."

"I was merely testing to see if you were listening," Tillie countered. "You know I love Landon dearly."

Bay narrowed her eyes. "I'm going to tell him you said that."

"Go ahead. I'll deny it."

"He'll believe me because I don't have a history of lying," Bay countered.

"He'll believe me because I'm mean to him and that will never change." Tillie threw open the car door and stared inside for a moment. "I want to drive."

"Over my dead body," Bay countered, opening the driver's side door. "You can drive your own truck when we get back to town."

"You're such a kvetch when you want to be," Tillie grumbled.

"I still don't know what a kvetch is," I admitted.

"It's Bay right now," Tillie offered. "A whiner and complainer."

"Doesn't that make you the queen of kvetches?" I asked, the words escaping a second before I realized how dumb it was to say something like that.

Bay's eyes widened to comical proportions as she risked a glance at Tillie. I realized I was holding my breath and let out a long gasp as Tillie glared at me.

"I ... um ... ."

"Don't say anything to ruin it," Tillie said after a beat, turning to face forward. "I'm starting to like you."

"That's high praise indeed," I teased.

"I said starting," Tillie stressed. "That doesn't mean I won't put you on my list."

"Duly noted."

Tillie grabbed the offensive candy and rested it on her knee. "Drop me off in town. I have an errand to run."

Bay eyed her, suspicious. "Mrs. Little?"

"I have other enemies."

"Fine. If you get arrested, though, don't call me."

"Do I ever?"

"At least three times since I moved back to town."

"So you're due."

BAY PARKED in front of the newspaper office, barely spared a glance for Tillie as she scampered across the parking lot, and then pointed herself in the direction of the diner. I followed her for lack of something better to do but I had no idea what we were doing.

"What now?"

"I need lunch," Bay replied. "Landon is at the diner."

"How do you know that?"

"Because his Explorer is at the police station and it's noon," Bay replied. "He and Chief Terry like to eat lunch and talk about the case at noon whenever possible. They're creatures of habit."

"Do you think they're alike?"

Bay nodded. "In a lot of ways they are. Why do you ask?"

"Because they say that girls marry their fathers, and Mrs. Gunderson said the chief was essentially your father."

Bay's shoulders were stiff as she swiveled and my heart sank at the expression on her face.

"I'm sorry," I offered lamely. "I didn't mean it."

"I think you did mean it, and that's the problem." Bay wet her lips. "I think you're nice ... and smart ... and funny. I need you to know that."

My stomach twisted but I managed to nod. "Thank you."

"I also think you're young and impulsive," Bay added. "You need to think before you speak. I know it's hard. I'm a Winchester so ... trust me. I know it's freaking hard. You still need to do it. You won't make it far in this line of work if you don't take other people's feelings into consideration."

"Did you take Phyllis Grimes' feelings into consideration when you went after her today?"

Bay's expression was unreadable as she tilted her head to the side. "I'm looking for a killer. What are you doing?"

"I ... um ... ."

"That's what I thought." Bay ran her hands through her hair as we approached the diner. "Take it from someone who does and says stupid things every single day, there's going to come a time when you want to take something back. You won't be able to, and it will eat at you."

"That happens on a regular basis with me," I admitted. "You, too?"

Bay nodded. "Because I'm related to Aunt Tillie and Thistle, people rarely notice when I say stupid things. That doesn't mean I don't say them. It also doesn't mean I don't regret them."

"I'm sorry. I ... that wasn't a smart thing to say."

Bay snorted, the inelegant display causing my discomfort to ratchet up a notch. "I notice that you said it wasn't a smart thing to say, but you're not exactly taking it back."

"Should I take it back?" The question came out as something of a challenge even though I wasn't looking for a fight. I have tone issues sometimes that I can't explain. People think I'm trying to goad them when in reality I only want to learn.

"You're not wrong," Bay said. "Chief Terry is my father in all the ways that count. That doesn't change the fact that I do have a father. It also doesn't change the fact that my relationship with Chief Terry and my father is none of your business."

"I ... I really am sorry."

"I know you are." Bay's lips curved and she turned back to the diner. "That doesn't mean you don't need to think before you speak. You don't want to grow up to be Aunt Tillie. I can pretty much guarantee that."

Bay didn't wait to see if I had a response, instead disappearing inside of the diner. Perhaps she realized that I couldn't stop talking until someone else ended the conversation and was doing me a favor. It's one of my weaknesses.

She was right about Landon being inside, of course. He brightened when she breezed in, accepting her proffered kiss and making room for her between himself and the chief. I didn't immediately notice that they weren't alone. Jack and Bernard sat with them, and they seemed to be involved in a serious conversation. I didn't have many options, so I joined them.

"You should order something to eat," Jack said, moving so I could sit between him and Bernard. "I was starting to get worried, you were gone so long. What did you find out at the resort?"

"Well, Bay approached the wife of the bartender right away and basically accused her of knowing about her husband's affair. We didn't get much further than that," I answered.

"You did what?" Landon rarely raised his voice to Bay, but he looked furious now.

"This would be another instance where you should think before you speak," Bay said, pressing the heel of her hand to her forehead and avoiding Landon's accusatory eyes. "I have a headache."

"You do not have a headache," Landon countered. "What did you say to the Grimes woman? I told you that we were going to question her. Why did you take it upon yourself to do it first?"

"I spent the entire day with Aunt Tillie and another woman who has no filter," Bay countered. "I have a huge headache. I think my head might even fall off it hurts so much."

"Don't yell at her," Chief Davenport ordered. "We need to give her some aspirin."

"Oh, you're playing to your audience," Landon muttered. "You know Terry won't yell at you and you're counting on that. Just because he's a softie doesn't mean I won't yell at you. Now that woman knows we're coming, Bay. She'll have time to think of a story."

"Did you honestly think she wouldn't have time to think of one?" Bay challenged. "I wanted to see her face when I mentioned Penny. Sue me."

"What did she say?"

"She melted down, threatened me and then hid in the back office for two hours," Bay replied, unruffled. "She clearly knows something."

"Does she really know something or is this like when you were convinced Clove was keeping something from you and you got thrown from a horse because you were distracted?" Landon challenged.

Bay scalded him with a dark look. "Clove was hiding something. And you know darned well that's not why I fell off the horse."

"Why did you fall off the horse?" I asked.

"Never mind," Bay and Landon answered in unison, their eyes zeroed in on each other.

"I think that they want you to mind your own business," Jack cautioned, his voice low. "I'm guessing that you don't want to get into the middle of whatever they're about to fight about."

"They're not going to fight," the chief said, handing Bay one of his onion rings and grinning when he saw Landon's scowl. "This is just how they interact occasionally. When two dominant personalities share space in the same relationship things like this happen."

"Don't eat that onion ring," Landon ordered. "I won't be able to kiss you when it's time to make up if you do."

"You could eat half of it and then we'd both smell," Bay suggested.

Landon took his half of the onion ring and wordlessly popped it into his mouth. He muttered something, which sounded suspiciously like "you're still in trouble," but I couldn't be sure because he turned back to his burger and fries, the argument seemingly forgotten.

"What did you guys find today?" Bay asked, grabbing another onion ring from the chief's plate.

"We found out that Penny had bruises on her body but definitely bled out from the wound in her throat," Landon replied.

"So an animal did kill her?" I couldn't help but be surprised.

"We were just talking about that," Jack countered. "The medical examiner can't say with any certainty that a weapon wasn't used. If it was a weapon, she's not sure what it was. She hasn't ruled out teeth, though."

"There were also multiple strains of animal DNA in the wound," Landon added. "The medical examiner can't identify it. She came up with, like, three animals instead of one. It's … odd … and a little gross when you add in the teeth ripping the flesh."

Huh. And there went my appetite. "So … it was Bigfoot?" I had trouble wrapping my head around the sentence, but that seemed the obvious choice now despite Penny's personal life.

"We honestly have no idea," Landon admitted. "We either have to find a weapon that could make that wound pattern or start searching the woods for a predator big enough to kill a grown woman."

"And we've ruled out a bear, right?" I pressed.

"Bears are big and clumsy," Terry supplied. "Whatever killed Penny was cunning and it boasted the ability to use thought."

"And move a body," Bay added.

"There is that, too," Terry conceded. "There wasn't enough blood at the scene to account for the volume missing from Penny's body. That means she wasn't killed where we found her."

"Maybe someone cut her throat in one location and didn't realize that she wasn't dead until they transported her someplace else," Bay suggested. "Maybe half of her blood volume was lost in the original spot, but she really did bleed out and die in the woods."

"We're not ruling anything out, but we can't rule anything in either," Chief Davenport said. "All I can say with any certainty is that no one should take anything for granted ... and that includes you and your cousins. No running around the woods without proper supervision."

"I'm not nine," Bay argued. "I can take care of myself."

"Were you in the woods with your mother and aunts last night?" the chief challenged. "I got a complaint that there was some naked dancing."

Bay shot an accusatory look in my direction, causing me to instinctively raise my hands in protest. "It wasn't me."

"It was Margaret Little," Landon said, handing Bay a french fry. "You know she complains every time she thinks you guys are dancing. She calls in four times a month, even though you guys are only out there one night a month. He's messing with you."

"Do I even want to know how you know that?" Chief Davenport challenged.

Landon shrugged. "I can promise there's always wine involved."

"And bacon poems," Bay teased.

Their earlier skirmish forgotten, Landon wrinkled his nose as he kissed the corner of Bay's mouth. "I'll recite that for you again tonight."

"Don't do that." The chief reached around Bay and flicked Landon's ear. "I'm not joking about wandering around in the woods,

Bay. If there is an animal out there … well … I don't want you coming up against it."

"I'm not worried about an animal,' Bay said. "I'm worried about a human that acts like an animal."

"Either way, everyone needs to be careful," the chief warned. "We have no idea if this was a one-time thing or just the beginning."

And that right there was a terrifying thought.

SIXTEEN

*L*andon and Chief Davenport agreed to allow Jack to accompany them on their second search of Penny's house. I was understandably surprised by their easygoing attitudes, but given the shift in the investigation they were open to new ideas and felt Jack fit better into their world than ours given his doubts about man-eating monsters right from the start.

Landon insisted Bay tag along – which I found equally weird – and that left me to decide what I wanted do. Ultimately it wasn't difficult. I was keen to see Penny's home base. I'm a busybody by nature. Even though it looked likely that our expertise might be needed to track an animal rather than a human after all, I couldn't shake the suspicion that an important clue remained overlooked.

I rode with Jack as we followed Landon along the streets leading out of town. We were alone, so I took the opportunity to study Jack's features. He didn't look happy.

"Do you wish I hadn't come?"

"Huh? What?" Jack jerked his head to me, seemingly ripped out of some reverie. "No. It's fine. Just don't touch anything when we get there."

"Are you angry with me?"

"I'm not happy with you for taking off with Bay this morning without asking whether it was a good idea. But you came back in one piece, so I guess I don't have anything to complain about."

"But ... why were you angry in the first place?"

"Good grief." Jack kept his right hand on the steering wheel and rubbed his forehead with the left. "You never stop asking questions, do you? It's as if you can't just sit there and be quiet for five minutes."

"Is that what you want?"

"Is that really another question?"

I opened my mouth, something snarky on the tip of my tongue, and then snapped it shut. I didn't need him or his stupid attitude. I crossed my arms over my chest and stared out the window, the foliage blurring as I let my mind wander. The only problem I had is that my mind refused to drift very far. It kept circling back to Jack and his stupid comment, like a shark scenting blood in the water.

"I don't ask a lot of questions," I exploded, after what felt like at least fifteen minutes of insufferable silence.

"Two minutes and forty-five seconds," Jack noted, glancing at his watch. "Is that a new record?"

If I could have kicked him in his naughty bits without risking a car accident I would have done it. "Whatever!"

Jack heaved a weary sigh, dragging a hand through his hair as he kept his eyes on Landon's tail lights. "Can I ask you something?"

"That's rich coming from the guy who doesn't like questions."

Jack ignored the sarcasm. "Where do you think Chris is today?"

Despite my determination to pretend Jack fell into a black hole and I couldn't see or hear him, the question caught me off guard, and I jerked my head in his direction. "What do you mean?"

"Where is Chris today?" Jack repeated.

"I ... don't know." Hmm. Where was he headed with this line of questioning? It couldn't be good.

"Why don't you know?"

"Is this some sort of game?" I tugged on my limited patience to keep from exploding. "I don't know what you're getting at, so why don't you just tell me."

"Well, you're an employee of the foundation, which means you should be doing what your boss says, right?"

My heart twisted as I bit down on the inside of my cheek. "Did Chris say something to you?"

"No, because I told him I had you running errands," Jack replied.

"You did?"

"I did. Charlie, I get that you're enthusiastic and this is the first time that you've been in the thick of things, but you need to remember that you're an employee. You can't just do whatever you want to do whenever the mood strikes. We have a chain of command, and you, my dear, are at the bottom of it right now."

"But ... I went with Bay," I protested, immediately realizing how lame the argument sounded. That didn't stop me from piling on. "I was trying to help her."

"And Bay is her own boss – er, at least from what I can tell – and she was doing the work she needed to do," Jack argued. "Landon and the chief spent the morning investigating and talking to the medical examiner because that's part of their job description. Hannah did the same because that's part of her job description.

"Millie spent the morning nursing a hangover because she can pretty much do whatever she wants," he continued. "That left Laura and Chris to go back to the scene. They set up cameras so they could record the area and they made plans for potential overnight visits to that spot – which I really don't want to think about right now. They did the work, though. They were there. Did you know that?"

"I ... no." I swallowed hard, shame washing over me.

"I didn't think so," Jack said. "Chris came looking for you this morning to help him go through the footage. He thought you would be excited."

"I would've been happy to do that," I said.

"Yes, but you weren't around," Jack pointed out. "This was after you stole one of the rental vehicles and took off with Millie last night. This was after you watched the Winchesters dance naked under the moon."

"You did that, too," I protested.

Jack's grin lit up his handsome face at the same time it made me want to punch him. "I like your enthusiasm and I think you're competent ... when you want to be. You still have a boss, Charlie."

"I know. I just ... when Bay said she was going back I thought I could offer her some help. I wasn't trying to shirk work. Honestly, that's not who I am."

Jack's expression softened, although only marginally. "I get that. I think you are a hard worker. I think your biggest problem is that you get distracted and abandon important tasks because you see something shiny and new to focus on. That said, you're lying about why you went with Bay this morning."

"I am not." The words were out of my mouth before I took the time to ascertain whether or not they were true.

"You went with Bay because you're fascinated with the Winchesters," Jack said, ignoring the tinny quality of my voice. "You think there's something off about them – and I don't disagree – but they're not why we're here. I think they have a few secrets too, but I don't think one of them is that they're hiding Bigfoot in Tillie's greenhouse."

I swallowed the ball of self-doubt pooling in my throat. "I don't think they had anything to do with Penny Schilling's death. I just ... thought I would offer my help. It was a mistake. It won't happen again."

"Good. See that it doesn't." Jack tapped his fingers on the steering wheel as he followed Landon's Explorer into a condominium development. From what I remembered of my drive to the resort, it was located about halfway between Hemlock Cove and the main resort building.

"Just out of curiosity, what did you tell Chris I was doing?" I asked, my voice low as I unfastened my seatbelt.

"I told him you were conducting research at the newspaper," Jack replied. "He thought that was a good idea."

"I did that yesterday."

"He doesn't know that."

"Okay, well, thank you ... I guess." I reached for the door handle, but Jack stilled me with a hand on my arm.

"Charlie, I'm not trying to be the bad guy here. You need to pay attention – maybe get your head out of the clouds – and focus on the job you were hired to do."

"I'll do better." I meant it. It was my third day on the job and I was already slacking. That's not how I was raised. The guilt settled in my stomach like a hard, immovable ball.

"Okay." Jack forced a smile, his dark eyes searching my face. "This is a fun gig if you relax and enjoy it. But there is work to do."

"Yeah, I've got it."

"Okay."

I gripped the door handle, raising my head as I did. Bay stood in front of the Tahoe staring, her expression unreadable as she glanced between Jack and me. Somehow I knew what she was thinking, but she was so far off she needed another ZIP code to be in the right area.

This was so not how I saw this day going.

PENNY'S CONDO was really a condominium in name only. It was clear that the facility had once been apartments – and low-quality ones at that – and I couldn't help feeling unbelievably sorry for the woman when I saw how messy the one-bedroom was.

"Who lives like this?" I asked, horrified as I stepped around a plate of half-eaten food – it looked to be rotting spaghetti, but I couldn't be sure given the mold – sitting in the middle of the tiny living room. "Did someone break in and do this?"

"No, this is how she left it," Landon replied, riffling through a stack of mail. "Women are messier than men in some instances. When I first started dating Bay she left her underwear around the guest-house. She wasn't the only one. Thistle and Clove did it, too. They didn't think anything of it. So when I sat on the couch I'd find my head leaning against a bra and panties. It was … distracting, to say the least."

"Was it dirty?" Jack's expression was grim. "Like … were they stripping in the middle of the living room and just leaving their panties behind?"

Landon narrowed his eyes as he glanced over his shoulder. "That's my girlfriend you're picturing."

"I didn't say it wasn't," Jack argued. "I was simply asking a question."

"I know exactly what you were asking, because I asked it, too," Landon countered. "I pictured them having pillow fights and giggling. That's not what was happening."

"What was happening?"

"Don't answer that question," Chief Davenport growled. "I don't want to know what they were doing. Those are my sweethearts. All three of them."

"Even Thistle?" I asked, dubious.

"Even Thistle," the chief replied, not missing a beat. "She looked like an angel when she was little. So did Clove and Bay. Bay had all of that light hair, and I swear there were times I looked at her and saw a halo." He took on a wistful expression. "I won't allow whatever story you're about to tell to tarnish that halo."

"No, it's not," Landon argued. "There's nothing nefarious or dirty about the story. Well, actually that's not entirely true. All three of those girls were filthy. They refused to clean up after themselves. They'd strip on the way to the shower and just leave panties and bras behind. I was so disappointed when I learned the truth."

Bay poked her head out of the bedroom. "You know I can hear you, right?"

"That's why I'm talking so loud," Landon replied.

Bay rolled her eyes. "Did you notice that the window in here doesn't latch properly?"

Landon stilled, amusement from his storytelling skills fading as he moved in Bay's direction. "No. Are you sure?"

"Would I have said it if I wasn't sure?"

Curious, I followed the rest of the group into the bedroom. Penny was apparently even more slovenly when it came to this small space, because I had to take a step back when I saw the mountain of laundry heaped on the bed. "Did she leave that, too?"

"No, we came in here and did laundry when we were bored," Chief

Davenport deadpanned, watching as Landon looked over the window. "That wasn't like that when we were here yesterday."

"No, it wasn't," Landon agreed, his hand automatically moving to Bay's back. "Someone was in here after we left."

"Who?" My mind momentarily flashed to a picture of Bigfoot climbing through the window. "You don't think it was an animal, do you?"

"Not bloody likely." Landon rubbed his chin and shot Jack a hard look. "You guys were out watching us last night. Before that, where were you?"

"Do you think I'm a suspect?" Jack's eyebrows flew up his forehead. "Why would we break into this place?"

"I'm not suggesting you killed her," Landon clarified. "I'm simply suggesting that you might've broken in here to investigate. If you did, we need to know now."

"They weren't here," Bay interjected, taking me by surprise with her fortitude. "Charlie and Millie attended a party at the resort. Bernard and Jack followed them. They weren't in this apartment."

Landon let out a relieved breath. "Okay. Wait ... how do you know that?"

"Yeah, how do you know that?" Jack challenged.

Bay pointed at me. She almost looked haughty in turning the tables to become the resident blabber. "Charlie told me."

"You have a huge mouth," Jack grumbled, shaking his head. "You don't have to answer every question people pose. You know that, right?"

I shrugged, unbothered. "I saw no reason to lie. We weren't doing anything wrong."

"Except for trespassing and drinking with underage minors," Bay offered.

I narrowed my eyes. "Really? Is this because I told Landon what you said to Phyllis Grimes?"

Bay grinned. "Maybe. They won't do anything to you anyway. The resort is in a different town. They don't have jurisdiction."

"Oh, well, that's a relief." I brightened as I locked gazes with Jack. "See. No harm, no foul."

"I'm an FBI agent," Landon reminded me. "I have jurisdiction wherever I want."

I deflated a bit. "Oh, well ... hmm."

"Yeah, big mouth." Jack muttered. "Get out of their line of sight so they forget you're a lawbreaker."

"You were with me," I complained, following him out of the bedroom.

"I'm smart enough not to admit things like that," Jack said, moving toward the kitchen. "See if you can find anything in the living room, okay? And keep out of trouble."

I shot him a dark look. "The only thing I'm going to find in the living room is the bubonic plague. Did you see the mold on the spaghetti?"

Jack's grin was utterly charming when he flashed it in my direction. "So definitely don't eat it."

"Yes, I'll try to refrain from eating the weeks-old spaghetti."

Jack snickered as he opened a cupboard. "Investigative work isn't as much fun as you thought, huh?"

"Now who can't stop asking stupid questions?" I challenged, my cheeks burning as I slid around the offending plate. "Seriously, though, who lives like this?"

"Someone who didn't care about cleanliness," Jack replied, his expression sobering. "Penny Schilling had a plan to get out of here. I think she was focused singularly on that. She didn't care who she stepped on to get what she wanted."

"So are we back to a human killing her?"

Jack held his hands palms up. "Your guess is as good as mine. I doubt very much a Dog Man opened that window and searched her apartment. I really don't know what to think."

He wasn't the only one.

17

SEVENTEEN

When no one was looking I touched a few of Penny's items, being careful to avoid anything that looked overtly filthy. Unfortunately – or, perhaps, fortunately – I didn't get any flashes from the items I touched. Part of me was terrified I would see the woman's death – it had happened before when I touched a wrecked vehicle after one of my classmates died in a terrible collision when I was a senior in high school. The other part of me wanted to see her death so we could put aside any debates about the killer being paranormal or human.

It simply didn't happen.

When we were finished we headed back to the inn to regroup and get ready for dinner. Bernard had stayed in town, expressing zero interest in searching Penny's apartment, so Jack sent Chris to pick him up when he was done at the scene. It was just the two of us on the long drive back to The Overlook.

"What are you thinking?" Jack asked about halfway through our trip.

"I'm thinking that Penny Schilling must've been an extremely sad individual."

Whatever answer he expected, that wasn't it. Jack shifted on his seat. I could feel his eyes on me even though I didn't turn to meet them. "Why do you say that?" Jack's voice was soft.

"She was clearly looking for something she never found," I answered, keeping my gaze trained out the window. "I think it would have to be sad to be looking for something externally when the answers are probably internal and you don't have the ability to seek them out."

"Profound." Jack made a clicking sound with his tongue as he debated how to continue. "Not everyone knows what they want out of life at a young age. I think you understand what you want despite your youth. You seem to be driven to find answers."

"You don't think Penny wanted answers?" It was almost a rhetorical question, and yet I still expected an answer.

"I think Penny wanted comfort," Jack clarified. "You saw her apartment. That wasn't a home. It was a place to live. There are some people in this world who spend all of their time searching for what they think will be a happily ever after. In Penny's case, I think that's why she kept going for older men she believed could provide financial security.

"Somewhere in her past, Penny went through life wanting things, maybe even food and warmth," he continued. "She didn't know what she wanted, but she was certain she didn't want to be cold and hungry. I think that's normal for people who grow up poor."

He spoke the words as if he had special insight into the issue, and I filed the notion away to reflect on later.

"Penny was probably one of those people who have a hole inside of her that she was desperately trying to fill," Jack continued. "A lot of people have holes like that. They use alcohol, food, sex, manipulation, tears ... whatever ... to fill that hole."

"And you think Penny used sex," I mused, stretching my arms. "She thought if she could snag one of those top resort guys that she could fill the hole and then start living the life she thought she deserved."

Jack nodded. "She didn't realize that you find the answers within when you want to plug a hole like that. A person can't do that for you."

I dragged my eyes from the window and focused on him. "You don't believe one person can complete another?"

"I believe in love, if that's what you're asking."

"It's not."

Jack pursed his lips, seemingly straddling a line as he considered his next words. "I don't believe that one person can fix another," he said finally. "I do believe people can love and complement one another. Is that what you're asking?"

It wasn't, but it was close enough.

I WAS EXHAUSTED by the time we hit The Overlook, my late-night antics the previous evening finally catching up with me. I took a brief nap, my dreams so muddy and dark that I was relieved when I woke. I hopped in the shower, cleaned up, and then headed down-stairs. Most of my team and the Winchesters were already in the dining room.

"Sleep well?" Jack asked, lifting his eyebrows as he studied me. "You look better ... kind of."

"Oh, well, thank you so much for the compliment," I deadpanned, annoyance bubbling up. "I don't know what I would do if I didn't have you around to fluff my ego."

The words were biting, but Jack easily shrugged them off. "I only meant you have some color back in your cheeks. You still look tired."

"Sorry." I mumbled the word into my hand as I rested my chin on my elbow.

Instead of being offended, Jack smirked. "You're more than welcome."

Dinner was a festive affair, but mealtimes apparently always are at The Overlook. Tillie sat at the head of the table regaling everyone with hilarious stories of her misspent youth. She peppered exciting babysitting tales throughout some of the more serious stories – including the time she made her great-nieces act as lookouts while she stole flowers from the cemetery.

"That's when Clove earned her nickname," Tillie supplied. "That was the first time she was a complete and total kvetch."

"I was five," Clove protested from the far end of the table, Sam beside her. They didn't regularly come for meals, but did pop up several times a week. Marcus and Thistle were fairly frequent guests around the table – including tonight – but Bay and Landon appeared to be the only ones who showed up for breakfast and dinner daily.

"You were still a kvetch," Tillie argued. "Bay and Thistle treated the entire thing like an adventure. You spent the whole night whining that Terry was going to arrest us."

"He would've if he caught us," Clove argued.

I slid a sidelong look at Chief Davenport, who joined us this evening and sat to my left, and arched a dubious eyebrow. "Would you have arrested them?"

"Probably not," he conceded. "I might've arrested Tillie."

Bay snorted, amused. "No, you wouldn't have done that either," she argued. "You would've been too worried about us crying. You hated it when we cried."

"I didn't care about making you cry," the chief countered immediately, although there wasn't much conviction behind his words. "You girls all act as if I melted into a puddle of goo whenever I saw you. That's not how I remember things."

"How do you remember things?" Landon asked. "All of the stories I've heard end with you spoiling them. I even heard one in which you carried all three of them through four-foot snow drifts because Aunt Tillie had them spying on Margaret Little and you refused to leave them in the woods."

Tillie's eyes widened to comical proportions. "You have a big mouth, Bay! Why did you tell him that story?"

"How do you know I'm the one who told him that?" Bay hedged, averting her gaze. "It could've been Thistle, Clove or Chief Terry."

"Why would I tell him that story?" the chief challenged. "You were making them spy on Mrs. Little. That was after attacking her with yellow snow for three days straight, if I remember correctly."

"I'm pretty sure your memory is faulty," Tillie sniffed. "That doesn't sound anything like me."

"No, of course not," Chief Davenport deadpanned, causing the table to erupt in riotous laughter.

"Did your great-aunt take you on adventures often when you were kids?" Hannah asked. She was a sincere individual who mostly minded her own business – which made me largely ambivalent toward her – and honestly seemed to be enjoying the conversation.

Bay nodded, smiling. "Our mothers were busy trying to learn everything they could about the bed and breakfast business when we were younger. They wanted us to amuse ourselves a lot while they studied."

"They had jobs, too," Thistle added. "This house didn't look like this when we were younger. It has grown a lot over the years."

"It was a simple homestead when the property first came into our possession," Winnie explained. "Then every generation started adding. Eventually it was a Victorian. The finest house in town.

"We always knew we wanted to start our own inn, so eventually we turned the Victorian into a bed and breakfast. Then, several years ago, we did the big expansion to turn the place into a full-fledged inn."

"Will your daughters eventually take over the operation?" Laura asked. I didn't fail to notice that she'd managed to steal the spot on Landon's right side this evening, something he refused to acknowledge as he kept his attention on Bay.

"I don't know how that will work," Winnie admitted, her eyes flicking to Bay. "I've never considered the girls to be all that interested in running the inn. The property will certainly pass to them. What they do with the house ... well ... I guess that's up to them."

"That's a long way off," Landon noted. "Who knows what will happen in that time."

"Exactly," Tillie added, bobbing her head. "I'm barely middle-aged. We have decades in front of us before we have to make any tough decisions."

Laura let loose a derisive snort, but she recovered quickly when she realized that everyone around the table was glaring at her. "I ...

um ... that's a good point. So what about you, Landon? Do you see yourself living here forever? Are you going to be an FBI agent who happens to run an inn on the side? That sounds like an odd book or a cozy mystery, doesn't it?"

Landon rested his arm on the back of Bay's chair as he studied Laura's face, his fingers light as they traced small circles on the back of Bay's shoulders. "I see myself living with Bay forever. If that's here, I'm fine with that."

"So she's your one and only?" Laura asked the question in a casual manner, but it was clearly pointed.

Landon answered without hesitation. "Yup. Why would I possibly want someone else? Why would someone even ask a question like that?"

Laura balked. "I didn't mean ... ."

"He knows what you meant," Tillie interjected, cutting off the stuttering vixen. "Everyone has seen the way you look at him. You're panting up the wrong police-shaped tree."

Landon's lips quirked as he reached for his glass of wine, but the expression on Laura's face was dark and dangerous.

"I don't know what you think you've seen, old lady, but ... ."

"Laura, that will be quite enough of that," Chris barked, taking everyone by surprise. I hadn't heard Chris raise his voice since I started working for him. In fact, when I really stretched my brain, I couldn't remember sharing more than a few hundred words with him. He was so caught up in the work – the actual work of examining the scene where Penny was found – that my enthusiasm for the investigation led us in different directions. I couldn't help but feel a bit guilty about that.

"I wasn't doing anything," Laura protested, her eyes flashing.

"Yes, you were," Millie shot back, shaking her head. "You always do something. Every single time we have a job you pick a person to flirt with. You don't care if that person is interested or not. You focus on them until we leave town, as if it's a game."

"I do not!" Laura's temper flared. "Stop saying things like that. You'll give these people the wrong idea."

"We've met people like Laura before," Thistle said. "We recognized her for what she is the second we met her. There's no need to get worked up about it. We've dealt with worse."

"Hey! I am sitting right here." Laura's temper was something to behold. I couldn't help but wonder if the Winchesters purposely egged her on to see if she would crack. The supposition appeared ridiculous on the surface, but it seemed to fit the facts. They were conducting a social experiment, and they were having a good time doing it.

"Eat your dinner and be quiet," Chris ordered, his voice low and firm. "Speaking of work, I was wondering if someone would take a shift out at the scene with the equipment tonight. Laura and I spent the entire day going through footage – found a few interesting tidbits I'd like to clean up and examine more closely on the laptop – but I've decided that I want someone out there at all times so we can have eyes on the areas not covered by cameras. The hominid might recognize a camera and avoid it, after all."

The news was met with a chorus of groans.

"I know everyone hates camping," Chris continued. "I happen to love it, but I'm the oddity. After what we found today, though, I don't see how we can let this opportunity slip through our fingers."

"What did you find today?" Tillie asked, leaning forward. "Was it the Loch Ness Monster after all?"

"The Loch Ness Monster can't get to the Hemlock Cove woods," Thistle argued. "How would it manage to get here without being seen? That doesn't make any sense."

"You're on my list," Tillie warned, extending a finger. "It makes perfect sense, by the way, if you believe in an underground water system that runs two hundred feet below the surface. That's how creatures like the Loch Ness Monster survive over the eons."

Thistle didn't look convinced. "Why has no one ever seen this water system?"

"Because it's magically hidden."

"By whom?"

"Elves, you idiot!" Tillie barked.

"Okay, that will be enough of that," Landon ordered, topping off

156

his wine glass. "I'm a little confused about why anyone has to be at the scene. Why can't you just leave the cameras running and check them in the morning?"

"Because the cameras are pointed at one particular area," Chris explained. "The odds of a hominid-like creature passing over that exact area are slim, and if it recognizes the cameras it'll take great pains to avoid the camera. Hominids are notorious for disliking cameras."

"Is he saying Bigfoot is gay?" Tillie whispered, leaning closer to Bay for clarification.

Bay shook her head. "He's only referring to an ape-like creature."

"Like Landon when there's no bacon?"

Bay tried to hide her smirk … and failed. "Kind of." She patted Landon's knee under the table. "You already made the gay Bigfoot joke before, though. I remember it. You need to stop recycling material."

Tillie scowled. "Whatever."

Bay ignored her and focused on Chris. "So you want to put people out there camping all night so they can operate camera equipment in the hopes of seeing Bigfoot?"

Chris nodded, the question apparently perfectly reasonable in his mind. "I was thinking Millie and Bernard could take the first shift."

Millie groaned, annoyed. "Oh, geez."

Jack's words from earlier in the day flooded over me and I immediately started shaking my head. "I'll do it. I was caught up with other stuff this afternoon when I should've been helping you."

"Yes, well, you don't know that much about the equipment yet," Chris hedged.

"I can learn on the job." I was determined to make up for the mistakes I'd already made. "I want to do it. And you don't have to send anyone else with me. They deserve some sleep. I can handle this on my own."

"That sounds good to me," Laura said. "Can someone pass the rolls?"

"Well, it doesn't sound good to me," Jack argued. "You can't go out there alone."

"I agree," Chris said. "She'll need someone to go with her. Millie?"

"Ugh." Millie made a face and let loose with a series of unintelligible grunts instead of offering up an answer.

Jack interjected himself before she had a chance to clear things up. "I'll go with her," he said. "I know how to use the equipment."

"Are you sure?" Chris was visibly surprised. "You usually don't volunteer for this sort of assignment."

"I'm security. I want to make sure our new member is safe." Jack shot me a tight smile and I was sure I would hear an earful about volunteering as soon as we were alone. "I'm looking forward to it. I'll bet it's an eventful evening."

I was starting to worry about that myself.

EIGHTEEN

"I can't believe we're staying in tents."

I was almost giddy when Jack finished erecting the two small tents, my gaze bouncing between them. I tried to help him when it came time to erect the temporary nylon shelters, but he said I was more of a hindrance – which was mildly hurtful, but I was too excited to care.

"Yes, it's the highlight of my evening," Jack said, tossing a sleeping bag in my direction and shaking his head. "I see you got the campfire burning. Looks a little lopsided, but … good job."

I was fairly certain that was the closest thing to a compliment I would get out of him, so I let it slide. "I know how to make a campfire. I was a counselor at summer camp as a teenager."

"Really?" Jack cocked an eyebrow. "I don't see you at a summer camp."

"Well, I probably wouldn't go back after what happened, but I had a good time up until the end."

"What happened?" Jack asked, tossing his sleeping bag in the tent closest to him without bothering to look inside. Both the tents and sleeping bags were new – Chris purchased them one town over this afternoon – so Jack didn't appear to be worried about bugs being inside. That was at the top of my list of things to worry about. I'm not big on bugs.

"It was a cold night. My friends started disappearing one by one until I was the only one left." I adopted an eerie voice as I flicked my new flashlight on under my chin. "I followed a trail of blood from the kitchen and found a body. It seems there was a legend around those parts. A killer thought drowned in the lake as a child kept coming back."

Jack heaved a sigh as he settled on the ground next to the fire. "That's the plotline of *Friday the 13th*."

"Seen that one, have you?"

"Anyone who likes horror movies has seen it," Jack replied, his tone weary.

"Do you like horror movies?" I left my sleeping bag behind to put away later and sat on the ground next to him. I positioned myself so I was close, but not so close I might inadvertently touch him. We were alone in the woods, and I didn't want to give him any ideas, after all. Now that Bay had mentioned she thought we might make a good match I was suddenly uncomfortable around Jack. I couldn't explain the shift in my attitude.

"I like some horror movies," Jack replied. "I like older stuff, like *The Shining, Halloween* and *The Exorcist*."

"I like those too."

"I also like eighties slasher films like *A Nightmare on Elm Street* and *Friday the 13th*. I'm not a big fan of the newer stuff."

"That's because they're not scary," I offered. "Remakes are stupid, too."

"Remakes are definitely stupid," Jack agreed, shifting his feet closer to the fire. "Can I ask you something?"

"Are you suddenly turning into the question man or something?" I teased, amused.

Jack's lips quirked, but he shook his head. "Did you sign up for this job because you felt guilty about what I said to you earlier?"

"I ... no." That wasn't even remotely true. I felt completely guilty about what he'd told me earlier. "I do want to pull my own weight," I said. "How bad can it be? We're camping, for crying out loud. That can't be considered work."

"You've never been camping before, have you?"

I shook my head. "My parents were city people. They preferred subways and taxis. I like to think I was born for the country, though. I know that sounds weird, but … there it is."

"You just said your parents were city people," Jack pointed out. "How could you be born for the country if you come from city folk?"

I shrugged, unsure about how to answer. "I was adopted, so … ."

"Oh." Jack lowered his voice, understanding washing over his features. "How old were you when you were adopted?"

"Four."

"Do you know … why?" Jack seemed curious, yet uncomfortable. I didn't blame him. It's not easy to know how far to push someone when it comes to talking about personal issues, especially when you barely know that person.

"Do I know why my birth parents suddenly abandoned me when I was four? I have no idea." I tried to adopt a breezy tone, but was pretty sure I failed miserably.

"They abandoned you?" Jack tilted his head to the side. "How do you know they abandoned you?"

"I don't remember anything before that age," I admitted, rubbing my cheek. The fire made a convenient focal point, so I kept my eyes there. It was easier than meeting Jack's gaze and letting him see into my soul. "I was discovered in the parking lot of a fire department in Minnesota. There was no note … or other clothes … nothing other than a stuffed dog."

I heard Jack swallow, but refused to look at him. "That had to be rough. Do you think you blocked out your memories from before then?"

I shrugged. "Maybe. I've been through the police reports filed at the time. I had a bruise on my arm, but it wasn't bad. The cops said it didn't look as if I'd been abused. I was given a thorough examination and … um … there was no sexual abuse or anything."

"That's a relief." Jack shifted, and I couldn't tell if it was because he was uncomfortable due to the ground or the story. "Didn't the cops ask you to describe your parents? I mean, I know it's been a long time and you can't be expected to remember something like that now, but back then it would've been fresh in your mind."

"They said I didn't know anything except my name: Charlotte."

"Charlotte Rhodes?"

I shook my head. "Just Charlotte. I have no idea what my last name was. Not even the hint of a memory."

Jack took me by surprise when he rested his hand on top of mine. It wasn't a romantic gesture or a flirtation. It was merely meant as a form of solace. "What happened to you then?"

"I was put in the system for a bit," I replied, reciting the story from a clinical place instead of emotional. I didn't know how else to deal with it. "It seemed like forever, but I think I was honestly lucky. I bonded with the first foster family I had – Kate and Caleb Rhodes – and they adopted me a year later."

"So a happy ending." Jack looked almost relieved that I didn't have a horrible tale to tack on the end. "Do you ever wonder about your birth parents?"

Did I ever wonder about my birth parents? I got psychic flashes when I touched people and objects, and occasionally moved things with my mind. "All of the time," I answered honestly. "My adoptive parents were wonderful people, and I loved them a great deal. They were both blond and fair – unlike me. I often wonder if I look like my birth mother or father, perhaps a mix of the two. I doubt I'll ever know."

"Your adoptive parents were good people?" Jack cast me a sidelong look. "When did you lose them?"

"I was eighteen. They were in a car accident on the way to my high school graduation."

"Oh, man." Jack heaved out a shaky breath. "That couldn't have been easy on you."

"Is death ever easy on anyone?"

"I guess not. Still … how did you deal with it?"

I shrugged, noncommittal. I wasn't sure I'd ever really dealt with it.

I still suffered from fugue dreams in which I was sure they remained alive, even talking to me at times, and when I woke I expected to find myself in my old bed. I was convinced that if I walked downstairs I'd find them in the kitchen, laughing and chatting as usual. That, of course, never happened.

"Do you ever feel split between two worlds, Jack?" I asked, changing the subject.

"All of the time." Jack offered an odd smile. "My father died when I was thirteen. He was a career Marine. I wanted to make him proud so I joined the Marines right out of high school. It took me a long time to realize that I was living that life for him, not me."

"So you finished your tour and joined the Legacy Foundation?" I pressed. "Is this where you want to be?"

"I have no idea," Jack answered. "Right now I want to make a good living and think about what I want. I'm twenty-seven years old. I spent seven years in the Corps and I've been hopping between jobs ever since. I think the need to feel as if you ... belong ... somewhere ... is a natural one."

"So you don't know where you belong either," I mused, rubbing the palms of my hands over my knees. "Do you think you'll ever figure it out?"

"I don't know, Charlie." Jack kept his voice even as he joined me in staring at the fire. "I think that everyone finds answers on their own terms. I'm still looking for mine. You're still looking for yours. I think people like Chris and Laura are still looking for theirs.

"On the flip side, I think people like Bernard, Millie and Hannah have it all figured out," he continued. "There are people like Tillie Winchester, who know everything and still want to question everyone. There are people like Landon, who seeks answers but is willing to refrain from asking questions he knows might upset him. It would be a pretty boring world if everyone was alike, wouldn't it?"

"Now that was kind of profound," I teased, poking his side to alleviate the tension. "You're right about Landon, though. I see it in his eyes. He has a lot of questions, but he's wise enough to know that sometimes he doesn't want the answers. I'm not that wise. I want all of the answers – even if they'll make me unhappy when I finally get them."

Jack rubbed his thumb over his bottom lip as he considered the statement. "I worry that your quest for answers will get you in trouble. I'd be lying if I said otherwise."

"You're not the only one," I said, patting his knee as I leaned forward. "I worry about that too. But I can't change who I am. I decided a long time ago that I wasn't going to try. I'm going to turn in. Wake me if Bigfoot comes around to eat us."

Jack snorted as he watched me grab my sleeping bag and head for my tent. "I might let him take you to the woods and do terrible things to you if you're not careful."

I stilled near the tent opening. "Did you know there's an entire section of erotica dedicated to things like that? It's called monster porn."

Jack's eyes lit up, the firelight flickering in the dark depths and making them appear almost black. "I did not know that. May I ask how you know that?"

"I happen to be a fountain of useless information," I replied. "Goodnight, Jack. Wake me if you need me."

"We'll be fine," Jack called back. "I'll put out the fire and turn in myself in a bit. I want to relax and enjoy the night."

"Don't let Bigfoot get you."

"Don't let bad memories get you, Charlie."

I THOUGHT I would be too emotionally keyed up to sleep, but I slipped under the moment I climbed inside the sleeping bag. My dreams were a tangled web of the past and present, my adoptive parents asking about my day as I walked into my old house and Jack sitting on the couch drinking soda and smiling as I tried to answer them to the best of my ability.

It wasn't a nightmare – not by a long shot. I had nightmares quite often and I know the difference. Still, I tore myself from the dream and bolted to a sitting position, my heart pounding as I tried to get my bearings.

It was dark, unnaturally so. The fire outside the tent was long since burned out and the only light came from the bright moon overhead. I'd left the small window flap down so I could see the stars, and when I shifted now I caught the hint of movement on the other side of the tent.

My breath caught in my throat as I tried to control my breathing, focusing on the movement. It was hard to make out, but whatever walked behind my tent was tall – at least six feet, probably more – and boasted broad shoulders. I couldn't make out any other features, human or otherwise, and my terror was so overwhelming that I didn't know what else to do.

"Jack." I barely managed to croak out his name. I couldn't help but hope the shadow belonged to him, that he was relieving himself in the woods and my fear was overwrought and ridiculous. I would yell at him for purposely scaring me during breakfast tomorrow morning. But the figure didn't move like Jack. I was certain of that. Something else was in the campsite. Suddenly I wanted Jack for a different reason. His tent was only a few feet away, but I couldn't make my voice work to call him.

The dark figure walking close to the trees continued to poke its head here and there as it searched for something only it could see. Occasionally I heard a snuffling – as if someone or something was sniffing the area for food or a mate – and my heart hammered as I attempted to remain calm.

I cleared my throat and tried again. "Jack." My voice was a little louder this time, but still a terrified whisper.

I gripped my hands into tight fists, my fingernails digging in, and opened my mouth a third time. This time only a strangled sob emerged.

I jerked my head to the window, but the creature – it seemed too tall and misshapen to be anything other than an animal now that my imagination was in overdrive – remained focused on its search. I needed it to stay near the woods so I could make it to Jack's tent without garnering attention. There was only one way to do that.

I sucked in a calming breath, pressed my eyes shut and searched for the magic that only seemed to come when I least wanted it. I felt a whisper of power press against the corners of my mind. I prodded it, cajoled it a bit, and then I pushed it out in the direction of the trees.

The magic ripped free, grabbing a high branch on one of the pines and severing it from the trunk. The branch made a decent amount of noise as it fell, causing the creature to stare in that direction before dropping to a stealthy crouch to check it out. I had a chance. I couldn't waste it.

I pushed myself to my knees, fumbling with the zipper on the side of the tent farthest from the shadow. I managed to navigate it high enough to slip through and then crawled to Jack's tent, all the while thinking the creature would attack from behind and rip me apart. I didn't risk a glance. I couldn't. All I could do was push forward in the hope I would make it.

I considered knocking – which seemed ridiculous considering the circumstances – but I wasn't sure about proper tent etiquette. Finally I found the zipper embedded at the bottom of Jack's tent and opened it.

I crawled inside, feeling instantly better when I was close enough to hear Jack breathe.

He slept on his back, his chest rising and falling in even increments. He seemed peaceful as he dreamed. Now that I was in his I felt foolish and reticent about waking him. No force on Earth, however, was strong enough to get me to crawl back out without alerting him to what I saw.

"Um ... Jack?"

Jack bolted to a sitting position, instantly alert. His eyes were full of concern when they fell on me. "What's wrong?"

"I ... um ... saw something."

"Where?"

I pointed toward the tent flap. "Behind my tent. I ... Jack ... um ... it looked like Bigfoot."

Jack stared at me a moment, dumbfounded. Finally he rubbed his fingers against his eyes and rolled out of his sleeping bag. "Stay here."

That sounded like a terrible idea. "What if it gets you?"

"It won't." Jack didn't hesitate as he crawled through the opening. I sat on the floor of his tent, my heart pounding as I rested my head against the knees I drew to my chest. After what seemed like forever – far too long for Jack to have survived the creature's wrath, that's for sure – the tent flaps moved again. I instinctively slapped out with my hands.

"It's me," Jack said, grumpy. He poked his head through the flap and scorched me with a dark look. "Were you going to slap Bigfoot to death?"

"I ... um ... ."

Jack's expression softened and he took me by surprise when he tossed a sleeping bag to me. I recognized it as the one from my tent. "It's okay. I didn't see anything out there. But I didn't want to traipse all over everything and ruin any prints we might find in the morning."

"Oh, well, that's a good idea." I said the words, but I wasn't sure I meant them. "What do you want me to do with this?"

"Get in it and sleep," Jack replied, reclaiming his sleeping bag. "If you're not going to sleep in your own tent, the only way I'll get any rest is if you sleep in here."

"But ... what about the monster?"

"Monster?" Jack challenged. "There was nothing out there. I looked. I think you let your imagination – maybe even some dreams – get the better of you."

"I didn't dream about monsters," I argued. "I dreamed ... about something else."

Jack's eyes filled with pity – which was somehow worse – and he gripped my shoulder. "It's okay. I kind of saw it coming after we talked around the fire. The second the sun rises I'll look for prints. Until then, this tent is big enough for both of us."

I wasn't convinced. "What if we're attacked?"

"I'll be the closest to the door." Jack pointed toward an empty space on the other side of the tent. "Put your sleeping bag there and sleep. It's okay, Charlie. I won't let anything bad happen to you."

"But ...."

"Sleep." It was an order.

"Fine," I grumbled, spreading out my sleeping bag. "If Bigfoot attacks, don't say I didn't warn you."

"I would never say anything of the sort. Now sleep. You've managed to work yourself up for no reason. I promise everything will be okay in the morning."

I wanted to believe him, but I knew what I saw. It was no dream.

NINETEEN

I woke feeling unusually warm and comfortable, almost as if basking in the sun's full warmth.

It generally takes me several minutes to gather my faculties upon regaining consciousness. This morning was no different. I stretched before scratching my cheek, frowning when my fingers brushed against something solid.

I forced my eyes open, my brain finally realizing that I wasn't in a bed. The first thing I saw when my vision cleared was Jack's stubbled chin. It was pressed against my forehead. I was halfway out of my sleeping bag; he was halfway out of his. During the night we must have met in the middle and wrapped ourselves around one another.

My mouth dropped open as I realized my predicament, my face pressed in the hollow between Jack's shoulder and chest, his arm wrapped around my back. He slept hard, his breathing regular as small snores escaped his mouth. He clearly had no idea that we were entangled. The only thing I could be truly happy about was the fact that nobody's hands looked to have wandered anywhere inappropriate.

I was gentle when I tried to shift away from Jack. Even in sleep he recognized the loss of warmth, though. He tugged me closer, making a small murmuring noise as my temple landed next to his mouth. That's when I felt it. His body moved and tension replaced relaxation as his senses went into overdrive and he woke.

I pressed my lips together and widened my eyes, watching his profile as realization washed over him.

"What the … ?"

"So … um … was it good for you?" I had no idea why I asked the question. I was going for levity in an effort to pretend I wasn't bothered by the sleeping arrangements. I thought if we could play it off as a joke things would be okay.

Jack clearly felt differently.

"We didn't … did we?" His voice rose to an unnatural level and I couldn't help but be a tad offended.

"I'm pretty sure I would remember if we did," I said dryly. He hadn't pushed me away from him yet and I remained trapped in his grip. "Unless … are you a minute man? Maybe we did it and I didn't even notice."

Jack scowled as he grabbed my shoulders and shoved me back, keeping a firm grip on the fabric of my sweatshirt and looking over my face as myriad emotions flitted through his eyes. His cheeks were flushed. Sweat began pooling on his brow despite the cool morning air. He looked completely flabbergasted.

I took it as an insult despite my best intentions. "I take it that it wasn't good for you."

"Stop saying that," Jack snapped, jerking his hands back the second he realized he was still touching me. He dragged a hand through his long hair – which was unfortunately even hotter when tousled with sleep – and stared at me. "I'm so sorry."

Of all the reactions I expected, that wasn't even on the list. "I … you're sorry?"

Jack nodded. "I didn't mean to touch you. If you want to file a formal complaint with Chris, I understand."

He was trying to be sweet and make me feel comfortable. I recognized that, and yet … my fury could not be contained.

"You're sorry?"

"I said it," Jack said, rolling to a sitting position and glancing around the tent with furtive eyes. "I'm not sure how it happened. I'm so very sorry."

"Jack, we slept pressed against each other," I challenged, my voice dripping with disdain. "It's not as if you raped me."

Jack paled even more, which seemed impossible given his color. "That doesn't mean this is okay."

"What is this?" I let my gaze bounce around the tent, frustrated. "We slept in separate sleeping bags in the same tent and somehow ended up cuddled together. It's hardly the end of the world."

Jack didn't look convinced. In fact, he looked near tears. It was shocking because I'd never seen him so much as break military character since our first meeting. "I'll put in my resignation right away."

"Oh, well, that did it." I jerked my foot out of my sleeping bag and slammed it against his knee, causing him to cringe and pull back. "You didn't molest me! In fact, how do you know I'm not the one who did this? I was afraid." My mind traveled back to the figure in the woods, the branch I caused to drop. "This probably is on me. I was afraid and shouldn't have climbed into your tent. If anyone should resign, it should be me."

"That's not right," Jack argued, alarmed. "You were unsettled. It's my job as chief of security to take care of you. This is my fault."

"No, it's my fault."

Instead of abject horror, anger washed over Jack's handsome features. Oddly enough the anger made me feel better than the pity.

"Didn't I just say it was my fault?" Jack exploded.

"Why does it have to be anybody's fault?" I shot back. "You didn't touch me inappropriately. I'm pretty sure I didn't touch you anywhere scandalous. We slept next to each other. It's not the end of the world."

"It feels like the end of the world." Jack was grim. "It feels as if I took advantage of you."

"How?"

"I ... don't know."

I narrowed my eyes. "You're seriously starting to bug me."

"Have you ever considered you're starting to bug me?"

"I certainly hope so. At least that will stop you from feeling sorry for yourself."

I COULDN'T GET out of the tent fast enough. I rolled my sleeping bag and tossed it outside, following it with a full head of steam and a truckload of aggravation. I was so lost in my own head I didn't notice Jack until he was outside. Instead of meeting my measured gaze, he headed to the spot where I had seen the figure the night before, causing my agitation to flare in a different way.

"Do you see anything?"

Jack didn't immediately answer, instead dropping to one knee near the foliage line. He seemed intent, and when I worked up the courage to join him he spared me a reluctant glance. "There are prints, but they're hard to see. This is a heel here ... and the ball of a foot here. I don't see any treads."

"Does that mean it was an animal?"

Jack shrugged. "I don't know. Treads would indicate a human wearing a shoe or boot, but they're not clear enough to definitively call them animal prints."

I knelt next to him, keeping distance between us and stared at the fresh prints. "I told you I saw something." I tried to keep from sounding accusatory. "You didn't believe me, but ... there it is."

"I didn't say I didn't believe you," Jack groused. "I said I couldn't see anything and you clearly weren't attacked."

"Oh, whatever." I crossed my arms over my chest. "The camera is pointed in this direction. Do you think it caught anything?"

"No idea. I figure we should let Chris go through the footage. He loves that stuff."

"I ... well ... okay." I couldn't decide if Jack wanted to hand the task over to Chris because that was the smart thing to do or he wanted to cut short any time we might spend together. I also wasn't sure which possibility I preferred. "I guess we should start packing, huh?"

Jack nodded, his eyes narrowing as he focused on something a few feet away. I watched, curious, until he shuffled over to a fallen branch.

I pursed my lips, doing my best to remain calm as he tentatively lifted the branch and stared at the splintered end.

"I think I'm going to start packing," I offered, nervous.

Jack didn't immediately respond, instead staring at the broken end of the branch with such intensity I couldn't help being a bit worried.

"Jack, I'm going to pack the tents. Is that okay?"

"What?" Jack jerked his gaze from the branch and focused on me. "No. Leave the tents up. We'll monitor this site every night. You can grab the sleeping bags."

"Oh, um, we're going to monitor the site? Does that mean you and I will be doing that?"

Jack's expression was unreadable. "I meant the whole group."

"Oh, well, good." I searched for something to say that he wouldn't find offensive. "That's probably good, right?"

"I guess we'll know when we see the video," Jack replied after a beat. "Something clearly ripped this branch off the tree. It was high, too."

"How do you know that?" I hoped I didn't come off as panicked.

Jack pointed to a damaged section of the tree, a good eight feet off the ground. "I don't know any humans who could rip that branch off like that."

Crap! I should've thought about that before I used the branch as a distraction. "Maybe it just fell … you know … because it was old or something." That sounded plausible, right?

Jack shot me a dubious look. "Do you really think that a tree that isn't dead sheds branches like a dog does hair?"

"I've never really given it a lot of thought," I admitted. "What makes you think that branch was pulled down, though? It could've fallen."

"Look at the end." Jack held it to my face so I had no choice but to stare. "The ends are ripped, Charlie. This branch was pulled off the tree, and by something extremely powerful."

I swallowed hard. "So you think an animal did that?"

"I don't think a human could do this," Jack replied. "I'm not sure what kind of animal we're dealing with, but no human is tall enough. And I doubt they'd be strong enough."

He was right about a normal human not being able to do it. I was pretty far from normal, though. "Jack ... um ... ."

Jack ignored the uncertainty in my voice and stood. "Let's grab the packs and clean up the campsite. Chris will want to hear what happened right away. This is right up his alley."

I didn't have much choice in the matter, so I readily agreed. "Okay. I ... let's do it."

JACK WAITED until we pulled onto the long driveway that led to The Overlook to speak, which was beyond frustrating. I wanted to find a way to dissuade him from telling Chris about the fallen branch, but came up empty. He waited until the worst possible moment – of course! – to break from his taciturn demeanor and turn chatty.

"We need to have a quick talk."

Jack's tone was dour enough to cause my palms to sweat. I rubbed them against my jeans and flicked a glance in his direction. "Um ... okay."

"I'm still willing to put in my resignation over what happened," Jack offered. "You were put in a bad position. That's not right."

"I don't blame you for that. You're really starting to irritate me with this martyr act," I argued. "We didn't even really touch one another. We just kind of ... snuggled. It's hardly the end of the world."

Jack didn't appear thrilled at the choice of the word "snuggled," but I couldn't think of another way to phrase it. "I wasn't putting the moves on you."

"Thanks. I figured that out by myself. I did it long before we accidentally decided to keep warm by sleeping next to each other."

Jack rubbed his thumb over his lower lip as he pulled into a parking spot. "I'm not interested in you that way, Charlie. I think you're a nice girl and you make me laugh sometimes, but ... I'm not looking for a relationship. It's important that you understand that."

I knit my eyebrows, annoyed. "I didn't think you were," I said.

"Why did you just say that?"

"What?"

"Why did you warn me that you weren't looking for a relationship?" I pressed, annoyed. "Do you think I'm looking for a relationship?"

"That's not what I said." Jack shifted on his seat, clearly uncomfortable. "I simply need you to know that there's no future for us in that manner. I'm not interested in you."

It took me a moment to realize what he was saying. "And you think I'm interested in you?"

"I think that you ... are very nice and capable," Jack replied, choosing his words carefully. "But I'm not part of this group because I plan to date anyone. That includes you. If you're thinking something is building here between us ... I need you to know that's not the case."

I narrowed my eyes, momentarily wishing I could fire lasers out of them to burn him alive. "So you think I have a crush on you? Is that what you're saying?"

"It would be normal for you to think that considering the fact that I'm a little older than you and I seem wise because I've been with the group longer."

"You seem wise?" Oh, well, that was just too much! "You think you seem wise to me?"

Jack balked. "I think this is coming out wrong. I'm sorry. I'm not trying to offend you."

I stared at him for a few beats and then opened the door, hopping out. I maintained my composure – although I have no idea how – and by the time Jack followed me to the walk that led to the inn's front door I was feeling pretty proud of myself. He was still alive and I wasn't about to burst into tears. That's growth, right?

Then Jack opened his mouth again.

"You're an attractive woman," he supplied. "You're just not my type of attractive."

"Oh, well, that does it!" I planted my hands on my hips as I scorched him with a dark look. "I can't believe you just said that!"

"What?" Jack was the picture of innocence as he shifted his eyes left and right. "I was stating a fact. I wasn't trying to hurt your feelings."

"You were stating a fact? You were stating a fact?" I grew shriller by the second. I'd lost the ability to control my temper, a purple tulip exploding in the plant bed behind him. Jack was so focused on me he didn't notice. I was relieved that I didn't accidentally cause a tree branch to fly into his head.

"I ... um ... ." Jack took an inadvertent step back, his cheeks flushing with color when Bay and Landon appeared on the walkway in front of him. They looked between us curiously as they headed toward Landon's Explorer.

"Everything okay?" Bay asked, worried, her eyes briefly touching on the former tulip before locking with mine.

"Everything is fine," Jack answered automatically.

"Everything is pretty far from fine," I growled, my annoyance taking over. "Jack here was just explaining that he's not interested in me, so if I'm developing a crush on him I should probably stop."

"Oh." Bay bit her lip, amusement flitting across her features.

"That's not what I said," Jack argued. "I merely said that ... if you had feelings ... or looked at me with some sort of hero complex ... or thought I was attractive ... I don't think I'm explaining this right." Jack looked to Landon for help.

"I'd stop digging if I were you, marine," Landon agreed, his lips curving as he slung an arm around Bay's shoulder. "You're tap dancing through a minefield in clown shoes. I'm enjoying the effort, though. It kind of reminds me of when I first met Bay."

Bay's smile was serene as she tilted up her chin. "You were desperately in love with me even though I wanted nothing to do with you." Landon snorted. "It was the other way around, woman."

"It was not."

"It was so," Landon shot back. "You were totally warm for my form."

"I was never warm for anything of yours," Bay argued. "You chased me until I relented and agreed to go out with you. You totally had a crush on me first."

"That is such crap." Landon's eyes lit with amusement. "You cried when I left."

Bay stilled and I could see the revelry flee both of them as Landon's words hit home. "I was talking about when we first met at the corn maze. I was not talking about when you left."

Landon clearly realized his mistake too late. Bay escaped from his grip and headed toward the Explorer. "Oh, sweetie, do we have to fight about this again?" He shot a dirty look in Jack's direction. "This is your fault."

"How is this my fault?" Jack was dumbfounded. "I was trying to be a good guy."

Landon snorted. "Please. No woman wants to hear she has a crush on you before she admits it to herself."

"I do not have a crush on him," I barked. "I don't even like him!"

Landon pursed his lips. "Yeah, you keep telling yourself that."

"That's all I was trying to keep from happening," Jack offered. "I was trying to be a good friend and co-worker."

"You keep telling yourself that too," Landon said, his eyes following Bay as she pouted in the Explorer's passenger seat. "If you said it, that means you're worried about it."

"That is a pile of crap!" Jack's voice took on an uneven edge. "I was trying to be a good guy about this."

Landon glanced between us and then shook his head. "You need to figure this out on your own. Keep Bay out of it next time. I don't like her upset."

"I'm pretty sure you upset her," I countered, crossing my arms over my chest.

"Charlie's right," Jack added. "You upset her."

Landon's frustration was evident as he stepped off the curb. "You're both on my list," he muttered.

"Let's get breakfast," I suggested. "I'm starving. We can forget the rest of this ever happened."

Jack looked relieved. "Affirmative."

It was definitely a plan – and one I had every intention of following. A crush on Jack? Freaking ridiculous!

20
TWENTY

I headed straight for the dining room and grabbed an open seat, hoping to focus on breakfast rather than Jack's oversized ego. Jack ignored the empty chair next to me and took the one next to Tillie – the one I was fairly certain Bay vacated before leaving the inn with Landon. I couldn't stop myself from smirking at the way Tillie looked Jack up and down.

"Breakfast looks great," Jack said, forcing a nervous smile for Winnie's benefit. "Camping always makes me hungry."

"I think that's your big head," I countered, not bothering to lower my voice. "It's so big you probably need extra fuel to fill it."

Jack ignored me and grabbed a slice of bacon. I was almost positive I heard him grumble the word "whatever" under his breath, but the chatter was too loud to be sure.

"Did you find anything?" Chris asked, wiping his mouth with his napkin. He looked well rested and keen, two things that irritated me beyond measure given the rough nature of my morning.

"Well, it wasn't an uneventful night," I countered, smirking at the way Jack's cheeks colored at my intended double entendre. "In fact, last night was the night to end all nights."

Thistle, a glass of orange juice resting in front of her, ran her tongue over her teeth as she stared. I could almost see the gears in her mind working.

"Well, don't keep us in suspense," Laura prodded. "What happened?"

"Nothing," Jack growled.

"I think I saw Bigfoot," I offered, enjoying how Jack shifted on his chair.

"Do you have ants in your pants, boy?" Tillie asked Jack, seemingly amused by his discomfort. "Camping is rough on delicate sorts such as you. If you have ants in your pants, you might want to take a bath or something."

"I don't have ants in my pants." Jack worked overtime to keep his voice pleasant and even, but I could read the set of his shoulders and knew he was close to falling off an angry cliff. He would erupt soon if pushed too far. I couldn't decide if I wanted to see that or avoid it. "My back merely hurts from sleeping on the ground."

Tillie narrowed her eyes, dubious. "That's not why you're shifting."

"Yeah? Then why am I shifting?"

"I haven't figured that out yet." Tillie glanced between him and me, and I couldn't stop myself from shifting my gaze quickly. "Hmm."

As if sensing I was about to melt down myself, Thistle raced to my rescue. "You said you saw Bigfoot. I'm dying to hear ... and only partly because I'm going to use it to terrorize Clove until she cries."

"You will do no such thing," Twila chided, scorching her daughter with a hard look. "Clove is a good girl. She has the right to feel safe in her own home. If you terrorize her as you intend, she won't feel safe."

"I see your point," Thistle said pleasantly, taking everyone by surprise.

"You do?" Twila cast her daughter a sidelong look. "Oh, well, that's good."

"I see it and reject it," Thistle clarified, her expression evil as she rubbed her hands together. "If I can't mess with Clove I have absolutely no reason to live."

"Thanks, honey," Marcus deadpanned, rubbing Thistle's shoulder. "That makes me feel great."

"I didn't mean that," Thistle said hurriedly, leaning closer to her long-suffering boyfriend. "You're still my favorite person in the world."

Instead of reacting with hostility or snark, Marcus merely grinned. "I know I am. I also know that you won't be happy until you make Clove cry."

"She doesn't have to cry," Thistle countered. "She can scream and I'll be satisfied."

Marcus tugged a hand through his hair. "Do whatever you want," he offered, seemingly resigned. "I know I won't rest for days because of the complaining if I try to stop you. Just keep in mind that I won't bail you out of jail. And if Clove makes you eat dirt, I will not help you clean up. I'll also laugh."

Thistle's expression darkened. "That's a mean thing to say."

Marcus held his hands palms up and shrugged. "What can I say? I learned from the best."

"I'm the best," Tillie corrected. "You learned from Thistle, so you learned from the second best."

"I'm not second best at anything, old lady," Thistle shot back. "I guarantee I can make Clove cry faster than you can."

"It's not how fast you make her cry," Tillie corrected. "It's how long you make her cry that counts."

"I can beat you on that one, too." Thistle puffed out her chest. "I'm the best when it comes to making Clove cry."

"Oh, is it a bet?" Tillie looked intrigued. "You're on, mouth. We need to come up with a point system, though."

Thistle popped a strawberry into her mouth. "Why don't we use the same one we had last year?"

"We could, but I don't see any reason to make Clove believe that a kraken lives in the bay by the Dandridge." Tillie sounded pragmatic despite the surreal conversation. "That was the top point earner last time. We need to weed out the non-essentials this go-around."

Thistle blew out a sigh. "Fine. Come up with your list and I'll go over it. It has to be fast, though. I promised Bay I'd help her with something this afternoon."

"You are terrible people. I'm not bailing either of you out of jail if you get arrested," Marcus warned. "In fact, I'm tempted to run out to the Dandridge to warn Clove. She hasn't done a thing to you."

"You always fall for that innocent act of hers. It gets annoying," Thistle grumbled.

I tuned out most of the argument and risked a glance around the table, focusing on each of my team members in turn. Millie and Bernard appeared intent on their breakfast plates and nothing else. Hannah and Chris had their heads bent together and appeared excited, although I wasn't sure what had them riled. Laura looked bored. And Jack? Well, Jack was doing his level best to refrain from looking at me, so he had nowhere to focus but the argument. It was almost comical to watch him pretend to feign interest in Thistle and Tillie Winchester as they plotted the best methods to torture Clove.

"Not that this isn't a fascinating conversation, but you still haven't told me what you found at the site," Chris prodded, his pointed gaze landing on Jack. "If something happened, we need to know."

"I'm not sure what happened, but you're definitely going to want to go through the footage," Jack suggested. "We kept the cameras running, but didn't look through the footage. As for what might be on it … well … I think Charlie is the one you need to talk to."

Chris turned to me, excited. "You saw a hominid-like creature?"

He was so earnest I couldn't exaggerate, so I merely shrugged. "I'm not sure what I saw. It was dark and I heard something outside of my tent. I'm not sure how to explain it. The tent had a little window and I looked at the stars before I fell asleep. It was nice."

"Oh, good grief," Laura complained. "We don't need to hear the romanticized version of your story. Can't you get to the good stuff?"

I ignored her. "I fell asleep for a few hours, and when I woke it was as if I sensed something outside of the tent."

"What was it?" a rapt Twila asked. "Was it a snake?"

Tillie snorted. "It was a trouser snake … and it belonged in this one's trousers." She jerked her thumb in Jack's direction, causing him to turn bright red. "Ha! I knew it!"

"That is not what happened," Jack offered hurriedly.

"I don't care about that," Chris said, impatiently waving off Jack's embarrassment. "Tell me about the creature."

"We don't know that it was a creature," I stressed.

"We don't," Jack agreed. "Charlie heard something that woke her. When she looked out her tent she saw ... something."

"What did you see?" Chris was breathless.

"It was a shadow," I replied, doing my best to play down the terror that seemed to overwhelm me the night before. "Whatever it was, it was too far away to make out any features. It didn't talk. It was dark. It was at least six feet tall. And I heard it snuffling, as if it was scenting the area. That's all I know."

"What did you do?" Tillie asked, leaning forward. "Did you go out to investigate?"

"I ... no." In truth, that hadn't even occurred to me. I'd been too afraid to risk going in that direction. All I could think about was getting to safety. That meant Jack's tent. "I kind of watched it a little bit, and then I got Jack."

Jack mustered a dubious expression. "She woke me, and by the time I made it to the spot she indicated it was gone."

"So you didn't see anything?" Chris was disappointed. "I thought you were going to give me good news."

"That's not the end of the story," Jack said. "This morning I went back out there and found footprints. I don't want you to get too excited, but there were no tread marks in the prints."

Chris sucked in a breath. "Oh, my!"

"What does that mean?" Thistle asked.

"Shoes," Marcus answered before anyone else could. "When someone is wearing shoes, they almost always have tread marks that leave a pattern in the dirt. Jack is saying that whoever – or I guess whatever is more accurate – was out there last night didn't leave behind a tread pattern."

"Oh." Thistle screwed up her face in concentration. "Did it have paw prints?"

Jack shook his head. "Indentations. I can't say with any certainty that it was an animal."

"I don't care about animals," Chris pressed. "I care if it was a hominid-like creature."

"You need to expand your vocabulary," Tillie suggested. "Call it Bigfoot and stop being so full of yourself. You're simply annoying people and nothing more."

"Excuse me?" Chris' eyebrows flew up his forehead.

"Bigfoot," Tillie repeated, exaggerating the two syllables. "You can say it if you apply yourself."

Chris pressed the tip of his tongue against the back of his teeth while I hid behind my coffee mug. I found the Winchester matriarch hilarious. I had a feeling I was the only one.

"Maybe it was a bear," Marcus suggested, drawing my attention to him. "We don't many bears in the area, but they're drawn to the water. If there was a bear around, it would want to be close to the lake or creek so it could fish."

"Why would a bear murder Bellaire's favorite wanton woman?" Thistle challenged.

"I'm not saying a bear killed Penny Schilling," Marcus clarified. "I believe a human did that."

"How can you say that?" Chris turned his full attention to Marcus. "There were unidentified animal prints out there. Now Charlie saw something in the woods."

"There are plenty of ways a human could cover his or her tracks after dumping a body in the woods," Jack cautioned. "Don't get ahead of yourself, Chris. You should look over the video. Don't get your hopes up, though. I have no idea if you'll find anything on that footage."

"I'm not getting my hopes up," Chris shot back. "I'm merely looking at the facts."

"You seem to be forgetting the fact that Penny slept with anyone who moved," Thistle argued. "There are a lot of humans out there who would have the motivation to kill her."

"I'll bet she saw a trouser snake or two in her time," Tillie said.

"Don't be crude," Jack warned, extending a finger.

Instead of declaring him to be on her list or going after him, Tillie merely laughed. "You remind me of Landon."

Jack stared at her. "Is that good or bad? You don't seem to like Landon."

"I like him well enough. And Bay loves him," Tillie replied. "That's good enough for me." Her eyes drifted to me and lingered, making me uncomfortable. "Of course, Landon didn't realize what he was getting into when he started sniffing around Bay. He was attracted to her, but didn't want to admit it. He was already a goner by then, but he didn't know it."

"I ... okay." Jack face flushed at the conversational turn. "I'm not sure why you're telling me that."

"Oh, you know why I'm telling you that." Tillie grabbed a strip of bacon from the platter in front of Jack and waved it enticingly. "I'm kind of curious about how much like Landon you really are."

"He's not like Landon," I interjected, cleaning off my plate. "Jack is his own person. He has his own brain, heart and ego. Oh, and his ego needs its own ZIP code."

Jack scowled. "Do you want to take this outside?"

Thistle snorted as Marcus frowned.

"Did you just challenge her to a fistfight, man?" Marcus asked, his eyes clouding.

"I ... no." Jack was scandalized. "That's not what I meant. I was going to ask her if she wanted to go outside to talk. Just ... talk. It has nothing to do with a fistfight. I ... how could you even think that?"

Marcus shrugged. "I live with Thistle, and she's big on wrestling. It's not that far of a leap."

"You hit her?" Jack challenged.

Marcus was flustered. "Of course I don't hit her," he snapped back. "I don't even really wrestle with her unless we're naked. Um, wait. That totally came out wrong."

"We know what you meant, honey." Thistle patted his hand, amused. Clearly this didn't happen often, because she was having a good time messing with Marcus over his discomfort. "You like to smack me around when I'm naked. It's totally normal."

Marcus hopped to his feet, flummoxed. "That is not what I said."

"What did you say?" I asked, genuinely curious.

"I … ."

Jack snickered as Marcus took a step from the table.

"I'm done here," Marcus announced. "Thistle, you're on your own for the day. Don't get arrested. And if Clove beats you up once you make her cry I'm not going to have any sympathy for you. As for the rest of you … well … have fun looking for Bigfoot."

Marcus spun on his heel and fled through the swinging door that led to the kitchen. Thistle was unbelievably amused at his departure, although her gaze was thoughtful when it landed on me. I could practically see her mind working.

"What?" I challenged.

Thistle shook her head, the teal hair glinting under the chandelier. "Nothing. It doesn't matter."

"You clearly have something to say," I prodded.

"I don't have anything to say." Thistle stood and locked gazes with Tillie. "Are you ready to come up with our point system? I have work and then … well … then I have Bay."

That was the second time she'd mentioned Bay. I couldn't help but be suspicious. "What are you doing with Bay?"

"Cousin stuff," Thistle replied evasively. "You guys have fun with your video. If you find proof of Bigfoot, we'll be thrilled to see it."

"If we find proof of a hominid-like creature, the world will be thrilled to see it," Chris corrected. "We'll be famous."

"Yeah, you need to show your trouser snake to the blond girl over there," Tillie said, pointing. "I think that's the only thing that's going to save your nerves and make you famous in your own mind now."

Chris stared blankly. "What's a trouser snake?"

"Oh, geez!" Aunt Tillie pinched the bridge of her nose. "I miss the normal guests. They're so much easier to mess with."

Thistle grinned. "Well, if you don't feel up for a challenge, old lady, you can just give me the money now."

"Keep it up, mouth. You'll be crying when I'm done with you."

As frustrated as I was about the previous evening's events – and the confusing way I woke – there was something comforting about the Winchesters' brand of zany hijinks. I lost myself in their silly argument for the rest of breakfast, pushing my own problems out of my mind.

That didn't stop the big question from popping up, though. Where were we supposed to go from here?

TWENTY-ONE

"*M*en are stupid."

With nothing better to do with my morning I decided to go back to the site for a better look around in the bright light of day. Chris was eager to pore over the video. He kept Hannah and Laura close so they could use various filters to clean up the imagery. I found the video distracting because the only thing I could see with any certainty was that a branch fell at some point. Of course, Chris was determined the creature dropped the branch. I could hardly tell him the truth without outing myself. In an effort to escape my discomfort, I suggested returning to the site.

Ostensibly I volunteered for the task to see if I could make casts of the prints – which Chris readily agreed to – and then asked for keys to one of the vehicles. Chris suggested I take Jack with me, which was a terrible idea, so I opted to shanghai Millie instead. She seemed up for the adventure until I fell into a fit of melancholy once we parked next to the Dandridge. I couldn't get Jack's earlier words out of my head. I became steadily obsessed with the size of his ego as we walked to the site.

Millie arched a penciled eyebrow as she shifted a glance toward me. She was fine picking her way through the woods and trudging over broken trails, never uttering a word of complaint. I could tell she was curious about my mood, but she didn't ask a single question ... until I opened my big, fat mouth.

"I was thinking of making that the title of my autobiography one day," Millie mused, slowing her pace to step over a fallen tree. "I think 'Men Are Stupid ... and So Are the Women Who Love Them' is a fantastic title."

I tilted my head to the side, curious. "Are you planning to write an autobiography? I bet you've got some good stories to tell."

"I do," Millie confirmed. "I would never really write an autobiography, though. That was a joke."

"Oh." In hindsight I should've realized that. "I can see why you wouldn't want that. You're a private person, after all."

Millie snorted, taking me by surprise. "I'm not private in the least," she offered. "In fact, I've got some very off-color stories involving public restrooms that I'm dying to share once I know you better."

"I'm never offended by true stories," I protested.

Millie didn't look convinced. "You're under the age of twenty-five, honey. You're part of that whole politically correct youth movement that's so annoying today. Don't get me wrong, I like it when kids state their opinions and stand up for injustice. I read about the whole 'burning your bras' thing and wished I'd been old enough to do it at the time. What I don't like is people getting offended just to be offended."

I studied her a moment, conflicted. "You would burn your bra?"

Millie's smile was so wide it almost split her face. "How did I know you would focus on that? For the record, yes, I would burn my bra. That's not just because I hate wearing a bra – I do – it's also because I love a good protest."

I took a moment to look Millie up and down as I waited for her to edge around a large rut in the middle of the pathway. "I can see you at a protest," I said after a beat. "I'll bet you participated in a lot of protests. Like ... did you protest the war?"

Millie balked. "How old do you think I am?"

"Oh, I ... ." I knew answering that question would be a mistake. My mother always told me that when a woman asks you to identify her age it's almost certainly a trap. "You don't look a day over twenty-nine."

Millie snorted, amused. "You're quick on your feet. I'll give you that."

"That's what my mother always told me."

I felt Millie's eyes rest on my back as I continued pushing forward. "Your adopted mother, you mean?"

I swallowed hard. "How do you know about that? I only told Jack … and now I'm definitely regretting it if he told you. I didn't realize he had such a big mouth."

"He doesn't," Millie clarified. "He didn't mention anything about that. But I am curious about what happened to the two of you last night, so don't go thinking we're done talking about that. You shouldn't blame him, though. The boy is loyal. He wouldn't betray your trust."

I had the grace to look abashed. "Oh." I ran my tongue over my lips as I tried to rein in my temper. "If Jack didn't tell you, how do you know?"

"I've seen your file," Millie replied. "Before you have another melt-down, I'm the only one who has seen it other than Chris. He doesn't share files with the others. I saw it because I went through his things."

"You went through his things?"

Millie bobbed her head. "He keeps candy in his desk. I was looking for a Cadbury chocolate bar when I saw your file. I recognized the name because Chris said you were joining us. I took a peek."

"Oh, well, I guess you were curious." I forced out the words even as my stomach rolled. I knew people would find out about my past, about my parents, before too long. I didn't think it would be this soon, though. I hated answering questions about my parents.

"I'm nosy," Millie corrected. "I thought maybe there was something about you I might be able to exploit in case I ever wanted to blackmail you."

Now it was my turn to balk. "Excuse me?"

Millie's smile was impish. "How do you think I manage to handle

Laura so well? I've got a doozy on her. I thought I might need something on you, too. It turns out I don't, because I like you. But I didn't know that at the time."

"I suppose I should take that as a compliment, huh?"

"It's the closest you'll ever get from me," Millie confirmed.

"What did … um … what did the file say?" I kept my eyes focused on the ground, telling myself it was because I didn't want to trip, even though I knew in my heart that I was afraid to meet Millie's steady gaze lest she see into my soul and read the fear living there. The fear was always close. It wasn't the same sort of fear I felt the night before when I saw the figure near the tents. No, this fear was worse.

Much, much worse.

"It said that you were found abandoned when you were a child, put into the foster system and adopted by Kate and Caleb Rhodes." Millie recited the file with clinical detachment and exactitude. "The file said your adopted parents died when you were a teenager. You've been on your own since."

"That's all?"

Millie lifted an eyebrow. "Should there have been something more?"

I shrugged, noncommittal. "It's always humbling to see your entire life broken down into a few sentences. I had two sets of parents, and now I have none. That's all my life amounts to."

"I didn't mean that," Millie said hurriedly, and for the first time I saw something other than mischief on her face. I saw pity. I preferred the mischief. "You had a lot of academic accolades in there, too."

"Yes, well, I think I'll make that the title of my autobiography," I offered, going for levity. "Everyone loves academic accolades, right?"

"I think I'm doing this wrong," Millie muttered, scratching her cheek. "I can never tell because I'm so used to sticking my foot in my mouth. Most of the time I don't care. I care today, but I still managed to trip over it. I'm … sorry."

"Don't worry about it." I waved off the apology. "It's fine."

"I don't think it is, but I also don't know what I said to put you on edge. I truly am sorry."

"I said it was fine." I focused my attention on my shoes as I trudged forward. "The site is only a few minutes away."

"Uh-huh." Millie sounded thoughtful as she followed me. "You said that men are stupid," she prodded after a few moments of quiet. "Do you want to tell me what happened between you and Jack last night?"

"Not particularly."

Millie wasn't about to give up. "I know something happened. You guys went from constantly sitting next to one another to not even making eye contact."

"I think you're exaggerating," I said. "Jack and I are fine."

"Whatever." Millie rolled her eyes. "I'll bet you saw each other naked and have buyer's remorse. That's ridiculous. You're both under thirty, so what reason could you possibly have to be remorseful? Your thighs don't brush together when you walk and your boobs are still perky. Now is the time to get naked, honey."

It took me a moment to comprehend what she said. "We did not see each other naked!"

Millie's eyebrows flew up her forehead at my high-pitched tone. "Yeah, that convinces me."

I took all of my effort to lower my voice and remain calm. "We did not see each other naked. I swear it."

Millie searched my face, and apparently decided after a long time that I was telling the truth. "That's disappointing. I thought for sure you two rolled around on top of each other instead of looking for Bigfoot."

"Why would you think that?"

"Because you're suddenly uncomfortable with each other. You were fine yesterday," Millie replied, saddened now that I had kicked the legs out from under her assumption about Jack and me. "Actually, that's not entirely true. There's been a bit of tension here and there where you guys are concerned. I noticed it right away. I thought it was merely flirtatious energy, but now I think it's something more."

"Oh, yeah? What is that?"

Millie shrugged. "I think you guys are attracted to each other."

Well, that was just ridiculous. "Why do people keep saying that?" I asked, annoyed. "He's very bossy. It's not that he's not good looking, because he is – I mean he really is – but we have nothing in common."

"Relationships where you have everything in common are very boring," Millie supplied. "Why do you think Myron and I crashed and burned?"

That was an interesting question. "Because you're full of life and he's not."

Millie smiled. "Thank you for that, but on paper Myron and I had a lot in common. We were both academics who enjoy theater, reading and travel. We should've been a good match."

"What happened?"

"Life happened," Millie replied. "I didn't want to be a business-man's wife. All he wanted to be was a businessman. I saw us as equals. He didn't. There went the marriage."

"See, that's exactly why Jack and I would make a terrible couple," I said. "He's bossy and feels the need to tell me what to do. I can't put up with that."

Millie tapped her bottom lip as she stared at me. "He's not bossy. He's ... protective."

"That's not how I see it."

"Then you're looking at it wrong," Millie pressed. "Jack is a ... tortured ... boy. I say 'boy' but he's more of a man than anyone I've ever met. You guys seemed to have a nice talk last night before what-ever happened that you're pretending didn't happen, huh?" Amuse-ment flittered across Millie's face. "Do you know that you're the only one Jack has bothered to talk to since joining the group?"

"That's not true," I protested. "I see him talking to you all of the time."

"We talk, but not about anything heavy," Millie countered. "He's a good boy with a big heart. He's haunted, though. He talked to you, and I'm guessing it was more serious than any talk he's ever had with me. Why do you think that is?"

I shrugged, unsure. "We were bored and stuck out in the woods together. There was nothing to do besides watch the fire and chat."

"Yes, but why did he volunteer to go with you?" Millie prodded.

"He could've stayed behind and sent you by yourself. He volunteered to go with you despite the fact that he was agitated about you taking off for the resort with the blonde. Why do you think that is?"

"I … don't know." I wasn't being evasive. I honestly didn't have an answer. Millie's therapist shtick was getting old fast. "We didn't talk about anything all that deep. We talked briefly about my parents, then we went to sleep. Then I thought I saw something and climbed into his tent. That's it."

"Ha!" Millie barked out the exclamation, causing me to jolt, and pointed her finger in my direction. "There it is! I knew something happened between the two of you. You climbed in his tent. Were you naked?"

"No."

"Was he naked?"

"No."

"Did you kiss?"

"Absolutely not."

Millie's face fell. "It sounds like you did it wrong. Why didn't you make a move?"

"I barely know him and I'm not interested in a relationship," I replied, hiding my internal disgust when I realized I used the same words Jack had earlier. "Jack's not interested either. I came here for the job. Nothing more."

"You're an idiot," Millie muttered, shaking her head. "I think you'll figure that out on your own eventually."

"I think you're dreaming, but I don't feel like arguing," I shot back. "As for Jack … he didn't tell me much about himself. He did seem a bit … frustrated … this morning because we slept in the same tent and ended up a little closer than he felt was comfortable. He kept offering to resign if I felt that he crossed a line. It was very odd."

"He's had a traumatic past," Millie said, her voice low.

"What do you mean?"

"I mean that he's had a traumatic past," Millie replied. "Something happened when he was in the Marines … and, no, I don't know what it is. He was going to make the military his career, but then he cycled out at some point. I've heard Myron and Chris whisper about some incident, but I don't know what it entailed."

We moved toward the last hill before reaching the site. "You don't think he's dangerous, do you?"

"I think that depends on who he's up against," Millie replied. "I don't believe he's dangerous to you or me. He's dangerous to anyone who tries to hurt an individual under his protection. I've seen him in action a time or two, and he's good at his job. The thought of him being even better is terrifying."

I hadn't seen Jack in action, but I wouldn't challenge her assessment. "And you want me to hook up with ... that?"

Millie snorted, her dour expression melting. "I think you will hook up with that, but that's a discussion for another time. We're supposed to be looking for Bigfoot. Let's focus on that."

"I agree. I ... ." I didn't get a chance to finish my statement because when we reached the top of the hill we found Thistle, Clove and Bay searching the site. They didn't bother glancing in our direction, instead focusing on the ground for ... something. I had no idea why they were here, and I had trouble wrapping my head around the turn of events. Then Bay spoke, continuing what looked to be an easy conversation with her cousins as they traipsed around our hominid search site.

"Men are stupid," Bay announced. "I'm totally sick of them."

Thistle snorted. "Honey, you're preaching to the choir."

Millie met my gaze before focusing on the cousins. "Oh, this should be interesting."

I had no doubt she was right.

22
TWENTY-TWO

"*H*oney, you're preaching to the choir."

Millie, not one for awkward silences, filled the one in the clearing as soon as Thistle lifted her head and realized her group wasn't alone. Bay, who was mid-complaint, didn't bother to tamp down her surprise when she saw us standing on the other side of the tents.

"What are you doing here?" Bay blurted out, her cheeks flushed.

"What are you doing here?" I countered, suspicious.

Thistle mentioned twice over breakfast that she had something to do with Bay this afternoon. Were they always planning a visit out here? If so, why?

"What are you doing here?" Thistle asked, crossing her arms over her chest.

"I asked first."

"Uh-uh." Clove shook her head and pointed. "Bay asked first."

I stared down the trio, adopting the darkest expression in my arsenal. They didn't so much as shift from one foot to the other. "We're here to see if we can find more footprints," I replied after a few moments of silence. "We're here to do a job."

"I was simply asking what you were doing here," Bay replied. "I was under the impression that you were watching videos all afternoon."

"And not pornographic ones," Clove added. "I asked."

Thistle pressed her lips together. I could see her shoulders shaking from twenty-five feet away as she swallowed her silent laughter.

"We've seen the video. We came back to look for more prints," I said. "That's what we're doing here. What are you doing here?"

"Oh, well, we're looking for prints, too." Bay wasn't exactly what I would call a gifted liar. She kept exchanging unreadable looks with Thistle – looks that made me more suspicious than ever – while steadfastly avoiding eye contact with me.

"You're looking for prints?" I challenged. "May I ask why?"

"Because we're interested in Bigfoot," Thistle answered. She was calmer under pressure. I got the distinct impression that she would spout the same story until the end of time, never breaking until she ran out of oxygen. She was clearly a much better liar than Bay. I had a feeling that was the reason she took control of the conversation. "We wanted to see if we could find evidence of Bigfoot. I mean ... you don't own this land. We're allowed to come and go as we please."

"Yeah, it's a free country," Clove jeered.

I narrowed my eyes as I stared at the shorter girl. She seemed nervous, fluttery even. She kept glancing around the woods, as if she expected a creature to jump out at any time. Her reaction was almost comical. "I see." I tugged on my lower lip as I stared at them. "Well, if everyone is minding their own business, we can continue to do that separately. Sound good?"

"I was happier when it was just the three of us so we could speak freely, but I guess it will have to do," Thistle countered, grabbing Clove's shoulder and directing her toward the spot where Bay stood. "You guys can do your work and we'll do our work."

"Yes, that sounds lovely." I bobbed my head. "If you want to continue your discussion, feel free to do that, too. We won't get in the middle of it."

"That sounds great." Thistle offered me a wide smile that was much more "shark circling its prey" than "trustworthy woman" but I opted not to comment, instead leading Millie toward the spot where I saw the shadowy figure the night before while keeping my ears open.

"Go back to what you were saying, Bay," Thistle ordered. "Why are you mad at Landon?"

"I'm not technically angry," Bay replied, kneeling next to a spot on the side of the clearing and pulling out her phone. "He's just insensitive sometimes."

"That's a man thing," Clove pointed out. "He doesn't mean to be insensitive. What did he say?"

"He brought up the time he left as if it was funny and I was being stupid because it hurt my feelings."

"That's not what he said when he got trapped in Aunt Tillie's mind and had to relive it," Clove pointed out, making a sound like a wounded animal when Thistle kicked her knee. She recovered quickly. "I meant when Aunt Tillie brought it up in front of everyone that one time."

I rolled what Thistle said through my head. Landon got "trapped in Aunt Tillie's mind." There weren't a lot of ways to phrase that so it was believable. There also weren't a lot of ways to change it so that it made sense.

"I don't think he meant to hurt your feelings," Thistle said. "He loves you. Trust me. He's freaking whipped. He would never purposely hurt your feelings."

"In theory I believe that," Bay conceded. "In practice, well, it's hard to believe when he just brushes off my feelings. He doesn't understand why I'm agitated. He keeps telling me to calm down because I'm being a hysterical female."

Clove's eyebrows shot up her forehead. "Did he use those words?"

Bay shook her head. "That's what I heard, though. He thinks I'm overreacting. He told me to get over it because he has to spend the day with Chief Terry and didn't have time for a fight."

"A fight, huh?" Thistle was blasé. "You two don't really fight. You both pout until one of you apologizes. The problem you have is Landon's huge ego."

I didn't want to draw attention to myself, but couldn't stop from listening even more. I too was at my limit with the male ego today.

"Landon's ego is not that big," Bay argued, loyalty apparent despite her anger. "He's a good man."

"He's okay when he's not threatening to arrest us," Thistle corrected. "You need to crush his ego, though. It's out of control."

"I think that's a man thing," I interjected, realizing too late that I was letting them know I was eavesdropping.

"What's a man thing?" Bay asked blankly.

"The ego thing," I answered, opting to plow forward rather than retreat. "I had the same problem with Jack this morning. I'm pretty sure his ego is bigger than Landon's."

"No one's ego is bigger than Landon's ego," Thistle drawled.

Bay ignored the dig about her boyfriend and focused on me. "I saw you and Jack arguing. What did he do?"

"He decided to sit me down for a talk and explain why he wasn't interested in me … even though I'm not interested in him," I replied, the fury I thought forgotten rearing. "As if he's so good looking that people can't stop themselves from falling at his feet. It's just so … ridiculous!"

"I hear that," Clove said. "When we first started dating Sam actually told me not to cry if he didn't call me every single day, because he had a lot of work to do and he'd call as often as possible. Like I need someone to call me every day!"

Thistle shot Clove a dubious look. "You do need someone to call you every day."

"I do not."

"You do, too."

"I do not."

"You do, too."

"Knock it off," Millie ordered, shuffling closer. "Ladies, it's a good thing I'm here. I've discovered the key to dealing with men over the years – and it's nowhere near as difficult as you probably think. Do you want to hear it?"

Bay shrugged. "I don't see why not. It can't be worse than Aunt

Tillie's advice to tie a man to the bed once a month and leave him there for a full twenty-four hours so he's always thankful for his freedom and never gets clingy. What have you got?"

Millie beamed. "I'm so glad you asked. Sit down. This is going to be a long conversation. You'll thank me when I'm done."

Despite my misgivings, I was almost hopeful. "Lay it on us."

TWO HOURS LATER our original argument about who was allowed to go where and why was behind us. We headed into town for lunch. It didn't occur to me until we were in the rental vehicle following Thistle's car that the Winchesters had managed to completely avoid the question about what they were doing at the site.

"Do you think it's weird that they won't tell us what they were doing out there?" I asked Millie as she parked in front of the diner. "They completely evaded that question ... and they did it fairly easily."

Millie shrugged, seemingly unperturbed. "Does it really matter what they were doing out there? They didn't hurt anything or anyone."

It was a fair question, and yet ... . "It matters to me."

"Then I don't know what to tell you," Millie said. "We have no jurisdiction to close down that site and I have no idea who owns the property. Maybe we can track the owner and have him close it off to curiosity seekers. But that wouldn't stop law enforcement."

"Odds are that Sam Cornell owns that land," I added. "He'd be more willing to shut it down to us than them."

"And Sam is the short one's boyfriend, right?"

I nodded. "Clove."

"I can't keep them straight," Millie muttered, pocketing the keys and moving to the front of the vehicle. "They're named after herbs, for crying out loud."

Huh. I hadn't even put that together. "I wonder why."

"Why they're named after herbs?" Millie shrugged, making an exaggerated face as she stepped onto the curb. "You'll have to ask their mothers. There probably was some drinking involved. From what I understand, Tillie makes her own wine, and it's strong enough to knock you on your rear end."

I'd witnessed the power of the wine the night we caught them dancing under the full moon, but figured it was wise to keep that story to myself ... at least for now. "I'm still curious about what they were doing out there. It doesn't seem normal."

"What's normal?" Millie challenged, leaning her elbows on the hood of the sport-utility vehicle. "Are you normal? Am I normal?"

"You're definitely not normal."

Millie grinned. "Neither are you," she said. "The Winchesters definitely aren't normal either, and I doubt very much they'd declare themselves as such. The thing is, who decides what's normal? I was raised during a time when girls were expected to act a certain way. I refused to follow protocol. Look at me now!"

I couldn't help but smile at the wacky woman and her strong personality. "I think you turned out just fine."

"And I think you turned out just fine," Millie said. "I imagine that it's hard for you. You probably have a lot of questions regarding what happened to your birth parents. You probably want to know why they gave you up for adoption, right?"

"They didn't give me up for adoption," I corrected. "They abandoned me."

"Do you remember that?"

I shook my head. "I don't remember anything about that time. I don't remember being in the fire station either."

"Weren't you old enough to have a few memories?" Millie didn't sound accusatory, merely intrigued. I wasn't bothered by her questions. They'd plagued me for years and I'd asked them of myself many times.

"You would think so, but I don't."

"Which means you were probably traumatized by something," Millie mused, shaking her head. "Either way, it would be only natural for someone in your position to ask 'why me' and then dwell on it. You might think it's because you were abnormal in some way. Perhaps you even strived to be 'normal' as you were growing up. It's a mistake to focus on that now."

"I'm not interested in being normal." That was mostly true. I was fine being who I was born to be. That didn't stop me from keeping some very big secrets. I felt I had to, although I had no memories propelling me to that determination. "I just think there's something really off about the Winchesters. I can't help it."

"There is something off about them," Millie confirmed. "I still like them. Whatever they're keeping secret, I doubt very much it has to do with Penny Schilling. I also doubt very much that it's our business."

"I get what you're saying. You're not the first person to say it," I said. "Jack basically said the same thing. It's just ... they fascinate and frustrate me at the same time. I feel that they're keeping something from me. We're here investigating the death of a young woman, so it's hard for me to shove the feelings aside."

"Fair enough." Millie bobbed her head. "The odds of them having something to do with this woman's death are extremely slim, though. What's their motive?"

I shrugged. "They don't have one."

"So why are you so suspicious?"

"If I could answer that question I probably wouldn't be so fixated on them."

"I think your problem is that you want control," Millie supplied. "You didn't have control when your parents left you at the fire station. You didn't have control when your adopted parents died. You don't have control now because you're the newest employee and still learning the ropes. You want control of something ... and that something is apparently the Winchesters' secret."

"Aren't you curious?"

Millie shook her head. "None of my business," she replied. "If I thought they were a danger to others or even themselves I might worry. They're not. They're an extremely codependent and crazy family. They admit their faults and don't run from fights. I find that refreshing."

"I guess you're right." I heaved a sigh. "Why don't you go inside and find us a table. I want to take a minute to myself to get my head back in the game. All of that advice you gave us at the site made me loopy."

Millie's grin was impish, shaving a good twenty years from her face. "Use that advice, girl. It will get you far in life."

"I'll keep that in mind," I said dryly. Millie's advice was more prone to give me nightmares than inspiration, but I didn't tell her that for fear I would hurt her feelings.

I watched Millie walk inside, taking advantage of the quiet moment to suck in a few deep breaths and exhale slowly. Millie was right, yet I couldn't stop myself from wondering if the Winchesters' secret would lead me to answers regarding Penny Schilling's death. I had no idea why I believed that possible. I couldn't shake the feeling of unease that washed over me whenever I gave real thought to the Winchesters and their hijinks.

I was so lost in thought – disappointment with myself growing with each treacherous thought regarding the Winchesters – that I almost didn't notice the man standing at the other end of the sidewalk. I let my eyes drift in that direction and almost jolted when I locked gazes with a familiar face.

It took me a few moments to place the man, and when I did my stomach twisted. He made no effort to hide the fact that he was staring. We were the only two people on the street – everyone else already inside to enjoy lunch – so I couldn't help but feel exposed.

Shane Norman remained rooted to his spot. He practically dared me to say something in the way he glared. I took a step toward the diner instead, happy to increase the distance between us. I blindly reached for the door handle, not making contact. I felt a brief flare of power in my head and then the door handle hit my fingers. I made the door open with my powers. I couldn't manage the energy to care, though. Shane Norman's dark presence was enough to completely unnerve me.

And then things got worse.

"How did you do that?"

I jerked my head in the direction of the voice and found Bay staring at me. "Do what?" I asked, my mouth dry.

"Open the door like that."

"I … what?" I was legitimately confused, but I was also caught. I knew what Bay was asking, and found myself desperate to buy time to think of a convincing answer.

"The door," Bay prodded. "It kind of flew open. I thought it was the wind, but … there's no wind."

"I … um … have no idea what you're talking about." I'm not a very good liar, but I hoped Bay would drop it. She didn't.

"If I didn't know better I'd think you were a witch," Bay teased, smiling. "Is there something I should know? Maybe you want to move to Hemlock Cove and join the coven, huh?"

Uh-oh. Could this day get any worse?

TWENTY-THREE

"Witch?" The word felt alien on my tongue. I couldn't stop from laughing. "I guess everyone in Hemlock Cove has witches on the brain, huh?"

"Some more than others," Bay replied, furrowing her brow. "How did you open the door?"

"I grabbed the handle. That's how I normally open a door."

"But ... I would've seen your arm if that was the case," Bay argued. "I didn't see your arm."

"Maybe it was invisible." I offered a nervous chuckle and licked my lips. "Do you have any witches in town who can make themselves invisible?"

"Not that I know of." Bay was calm, but I could practically see her mind working. She was suspicious of my answers and dubious mannerisms, which was mildly hilarious given the fact that I'd spent the better part of two days grappling with wild thoughts about her family.

I decided to change the subject. "Do you know that man?" I inclined my head in the direction of Shane Norman.

Bay reluctantly dragged her gaze from my face and frowned when she saw him. "Yes. He works at the resort."

"I saw him there." I kept my voice low. "He works in the purchasing department. He was one of Penny Schilling's boyfriends."

"I know." Bay rubbed the back of her neck. "I wonder what he's doing in Hemlock Cove. I don't believe he lives here. I think he's from Bellaire, but I'm not a hundred percent sure. I know Landon talked to him the day we visited the resort."

"Did Landon happen to mention what he said?"

Bay shook her head. "I don't recall."

"And even if you did recall you wouldn't tell me, because I'm not a cop, right?"

Bay shrugged, refusing to bow down to the guilt trip I was trying to lay on her. "Probably not. Landon tells me a lot of things that aren't for public consumption. It hardly matters in this case. He didn't mention anything about his talk with Shane Norman."

"So why is he here?"

"That's a very good question." Bay moved closer to me, never removing her eyes from Shane. Finally, as if deciding after a lot of thought that he didn't want to deal with two of us, Shane turned and entered the shop closest to him.

"Should we follow him?" I asked, my heart rate increasing.

"Why?" Bay's expression was unreadable as she searched my face. "Do you think he's guilty?"

"I don't know," I answered, opting for honesty. "I'm leaning toward Bigfoot after what I saw in the woods last night. Still ... he was staring at me. It gave me the creeps."

Bay opened her mouth to say something, but I immediately started shaking my head to cut her off.

"No, I don't mean the witch creeps," I added. "I mean the general creeps. He was staring at me."

"Did he see you the day you were at the resort?"

"I think so," I said. "I made eye contact with him at one point when we were walking around the loading dock. It was brief. I don't see how he could know who I was or why I was there."

"Gossip travels fast," Bay replied.

"Do you know what store he went into?"

Bay nodded. "It's The Unicorn Emporium."

"He doesn't seem like the porcelain unicorn type to me."

"Me either." Bay chewed her lip, distracted. "That's Mrs. Little's store."

"The same Mrs. Little your great-aunt keeps stalking?"

"Yup."

"Can you think of any reason Shane Norman and Mrs. Little would spend time together?"

"Not off the top of my head," Bay answered, "but there's no harm in checking things out for ourselves. Let's see what they're doing."

I figured Bay would attempt to spy in stealth mode, maybe go around the back of the store and sneak in through another door so we could hide behind racks of goods and eavesdrop. What? I watch a lot of spy shows. Instead she shoved open the front door of The Unicorn Emporium and strolled inside as if she was part owner.

"Bay." Mrs. Little, her hair pulled back in a prim and proper bun, stiffly nodded her head when she caught sight of the blonde. She didn't so much as acknowledge me.

"Mrs. Little." Bay's greeting was equally cold as she scanned the store, her eyes falling on Shane Norman as he perused a display on the far side of the small boutique. Instead of approaching him, Bay shuffled toward the counter. "I thought I'd check in and see how things are going. How are they? I mean … how are things going?"

I hid a half-smile behind my hand. Even though she was outwardly cool on most occasions, Bay tended to fall into spaz mode now and then. This happened to be one of those times.

"Things will be fine, Bay." Mrs. Little's tone was clipped. "If that's all … ."

"That's not all." Bay's eyes moved back to Shane. "Have you heard about the body found behind the Dandridge?"

I jerked my head in her direction, surprised. I had no idea where she was going with this line of conversation, but I was fascinated. I risked a glance at Shane Norman and found his back to us. He continued to stare at the unicorns, but I was fairly certain his shoulders had stiffened in response to Bay's question.

"I did hear about that," Mrs. Little confirmed, squinting a bit as she watched Bay. "Why are you telling me? I didn't kill her."

"I didn't think you did," Bay supplied. "Chief Terry and Landon are investigating. We want to make sure that everyone is very careful right now given the new ... evidence ... that they discovered."

"What evidence?" Mrs. Little no longer looked annoyed. "Is the murderer a Hemlock Cove resident? I thought Bigfoot did it."

"I'm not at liberty to talk about the evidence," Bay cautioned. "Just make sure you're never alone, especially after dark, and that you have someone to walk you to your car."

"I ... um ... okay." Mrs. Little looked flustered. "Thank you for the warning."

"You're welcome." Bay kept her eyes on Shane Norman as she walked out of the store and stood on the sidewalk in front of the display window. I found her little act baffling more than enlightening.

"What was that?"

"I want to see what he'll do." Bay crossed her arms over her chest. "More importantly, I want to see if he talks to Mrs. Little."

"But ... why?"

"Because she's had her pudgy little fingers in some very unsavory pots over the years," Bay answered. "I doubt very much she has any ties to Shane Norman. I want to be sure, though."

"And if she is tied to him?"

"That explains why he's in town."

"And if she's not?"

"Then he's here for another reason," Bay replied, leaning against the nearest sidewalk bench and narrowing her eyes as Shane shuffled toward another display shelf. "Whatever reason he suddenly came to town can't be good. Something's going on here."

I couldn't agree more.

AFTER THIRTY MINUTES of looking at unicorn statues, Shane Norman made his escape from the store. He didn't glance in Mrs. Little's direction the entire time, and she seemed distracted by Bay's gossipy tidbit, so we headed back toward the diner relatively certain that they weren't in cahoots. I was less certain about Bay. She seemed to be playing a game that I didn't fully understand the rules of, so I was constantly behind.

By the time we hit the diner, Landon and Chief Davenport had joined our small group. Landon looked relieved when he caught sight of Bay and he stood to make sure he got her attention.

"I saved you a seat, sweetie."

Bay studied him a moment, her eyes flat. "I'm pretty sure I'm still angry with you."

"Bay," Landon cajoled, tilting his head to the side. "I said I was sorry. You know darned well I didn't mean that how it came out."

I risked a glance at her and didn't miss the way her lips curled at his reaction. "You already forgave him, didn't you?"

Bay shrugged. "It's hard to stay angry with him. He has a good heart."

"And he loves you."

Bay's smile was serene. "He does. I don't forgive him simply because I love him, though. I forgive him because intentions are as important as outcomes."

"Meaning?"

"Meaning that he wouldn't purposely hurt me for anything," Bay replied. "Sure, we tease each other, but he would take a bullet rather than hurt my feelings. Heck, he has taken a bullet for me. His intentions are always good."

I found the conversational shift curious. "Are your intentions always good?"

"For the most part. I won't deny I've had mayhem on the brain a few times over the years and acted out with bad intention. That was mostly during my teenage years. I hope I've grown out of that."

"What were your intentions today?"

Bay seemed surprised by the question. "They weren't bad, if that's what you're worried about. I was simply trying to get a read on Shane Norman."

"Because you think he's a killer?"

"We don't have nearly enough information to call him a killer." Bay took advantage of the lull in conversation sit between Landon and the chief. She greeted Chief Davenport with a hand on his shoulder and allowed Landon to lean close enough to whisper. Whatever he said amused her, because she laughed and kissed him on the cheek. He returned the show of affection by planting a loud kiss on her lips. It appeared that all was forgiven.

I sat between Millie and Thistle, grabbing a menu after getting comfortable, and letting the conversation wash over me as I rewound the day's events. Nothing in Hemlock Cove was at it seemed, and that included the Winchesters and my own team. I was in an awkward position. I was the only one who didn't have anyone to trust. I instinctively trusted Millie, of course, but I didn't know her well enough to share my biggest secrets. I was hopeful that one day I'd find loyalty in the group, but I was nowhere near that point yet.

"Where did you go?" Millie asked. "I thought you took off or something."

"I noticed a guy staring at me on the sidewalk, so Bay and I followed him into a store to see if he was up to something," I replied. "He was from the resort."

Landon stilled across the table, pursing his lips as he wrinkled his nose. "You followed a guy who was staring at you on the street?"

Bay's expression was murderous as she locked gazes with me. "Do you ever think before you speak?"

"I didn't realize it was a secret," I protested.

"It wasn't a secret, but you have to learn the right way to tell certain people particular bits of news," Bay snapped, pinching the bridge of her nose as Landon stared at her. "Just remember that I forgave you, so you shouldn't make a scene right now, Landon. We were never in any danger."

"Seems like a sound argument," Landon said. "Now tell me the story about who you saw on the street ... and then followed despite the fact that you might've been dealing with a murderer."

"It was Shane Norman," I supplied. "He was staring at me. When Bay found me on the sidewalk he hid in that unicorn store."

"Shane Norman." Landon cracked his neck as he searched his memory. "He's the head of purchasing, right?"

I nodded. "He's also one of Penny Schilling's many boyfriends."

"Did he say anything to you?" Chief Davenport asked, extending a finger in Landon's direction when it looked as if the FBI agent was going to push Bay on her actions. "You just got out of the doghouse. I had to listen to you whine about it all morning. How far are you willing to push things?"

"I haven't decided yet," Landon replied. "She shouldn't have followed a strange man into a store. It wasn't safe."

"It's broad daylight and it was The Unicorn Emporium," the chief pointed out. "How much danger do you really think she was in?"

"Fine." Landon blew out a frustrated sigh. "We're even, Bay. I'm not going to yell."

"I don't care if you do yell," Bay countered. "We didn't do anything. And I'm more than happy to resurrect my anger if you're going to be a butt itch."

I pressed my lips together to keep from laughing as Landon's cheeks flushed.

"A butt itch?" Landon looked caught between laughter and annoyance. "That's a new one."

"That's what you remind me of right now," Bay pressed.

"Well, I would hate to be a butt itch." Landon slid an arm around Bay's shoulders and rubbed his nose against her temple. "I'm not angry. I am, however, curious about what Shane Norman was doing in Hemlock Cove."

"I think he was interested in Charlie," Bay said, causing my heart to roll.

"Me? Why would he care about me?"

"He was staring at you when I came outside. I think he would've spoken to you if I hadn't interrupted," Bay explained. "You said he saw you the day you were at the resort. Maybe he discovered you were looking into Penny's death and wanted to pass on some information."

"Why not share that information with us?" Landon challenged. "When I talked to him he barely opened his mouth."

"Yes, but you're 'The Man,'" Bay answered. "People are nervous talking to law enforcement. Charlie is young and looks approachable."

"I think she's saying you look slutty," Thistle offered, slathering mustard on her chili dog. "You might want to lay off the hooker makeup."

I frowned. "I don't wear hooker makeup." Wait … do I? I craned my neck in an attempt to catch a glimpse of my reflection in the mirror behind the counter, letting my attention be drawn to Landon only when he tapped his fingers on the table.

"Your makeup is fine. Thistle is just being Thistle."

"She has teal hair," I muttered. "She doesn't have a lot of room to talk."

"Exactly," Landon said. "Get back to Shane Norman. Do you think he was trying to talk to you or did he have something else on his mind?"

"Like what?" I asked, confused. "I've never spoken to him. He stared a bit but couldn't run away fast enough when he saw Bay."

"That might be because the Winchester reputation is well known around these parts," the chief suggested. "In addition to being a Winchester, Bay has very clear ties to you and me, Landon. Maybe Shane Norman would be more willing to talk with Charlie."

"I guess there's only one way to find out," I suggested.

"We have to go back to the resort after lunch," Bay agreed, bobbing her head.

"You're not going alone," Landon interjected.

"He won't talk to us if you're there," Bay argued. "You have no choice but to step back."

"I have no problem taking a step back," Landon said. "As long as I can still see you it will be fine."

"You're being unreasonable."

"And I think I love you enough not to care." Landon reached for the ketchup. "Go ahead and pout, Bay. I'm still going with you to the resort."

"Maybe I should go alone," I suggested. "That might be the only way we can be reasonably sure that he'll talk to anyone."

"Absolutely not," Landon and Chief Davenport said in unison.

"We go as a group or not at all," Landon added.

"Just let them have their way," Bay muttered, her expression dour. "They won't ease up, so it's easier to compromise."

"Is that what you call it?" I questioned. "Compromise?"

Bay shrugged. "What do you call it?"

"Giving in."

Bay snorted, taking me by surprise. "Oh, Charlie, you'll find that a lot of the things you believe now aren't true. You're young and set in your ways. Things will appear different when you get older."

"I'm fairly certain that was an insult," I muttered.

"I'm fairly certain I don't care," Landon shot back. "We're going together. Get used to it."

He was still handsome. I would never say otherwise. But his tone was beyond grating Being low woman on the bossy totem pole well and truly sucked.

TWENTY-FOUR

O ur trip to the resort yielded nothing, not even a sighting of Shane Norman. His employees said he left early for the day, citing a headache, but it was clear something else was on his mind. Jim Green watched us from his perch above the lobby when we walked through the front doors, but other than that we garnered little attention.

Landon swung by Shane Norman's house on our way out of Bellaire. But the driveway was empty and the house dark, so we headed back to Hemlock Cove.

My mind was busy on the drive, and I could see Bay thinking just as hard in the passenger seat.

"I don't understand why he would come looking for me," I admitted, breaking the silence that had fallen over the Explorer. "Did he think I could help or something?"

Bay held up her hands. "I have no idea what to tell you," she said. "There are a hundred reasons he could be looking to talk to you."

I had trouble believing that. "Name one."

"Maybe he has information he's uncomfortable sharing with law enforcement," Bay suggested. "Police officers and FBI agents often make people uncomfortable. I've seen it numerous times since I started dating Landon. Even before then, when hanging around with Chief Terry, I saw it happen a lot, too."

"You mean the Dark Ages?" Landon teased, his eyes crinkling at the corners as he captured Bay's hand and squeezed it. "I often forget you had a working knowledge of law enforcement before I entered your life."

"That law enforcement didn't boss me around daily."

I pressed my lips together tightly, expecting Landon to blow. Instead he merely shook his head.

"If you think I'm going to apologize for wanting to keep you safe, you're wrong," he said. "It makes me nervous that this guy showed up in Hemlock Cove. Before this happened, he was furthest down my list of possible suspects."

Well, that was interesting. "Why is that?" I asked. "I thought there was something odd about him the day I saw him on the loading dock, so he was high on my list." In truth, I didn't have a list. I simply wanted Landon to justify his list so I could better understand.

"I usually don't base my opinion on feelings," Landon supplied.

"That's not true," Bay countered. "You had a feeling I was worth saving when you first met me. You even risked your status as an undercover agent to do it."

"No, I risked my status to save a bunch of civilians running around in a corn maze in the middle of the night," Landon clarified. "I would've done what I did no matter who was out there."

Bay looked almost disappointed. "Really?"

Landon sighed. "Probably not, no. I'm supposed to say that I would. You're the reason I was there that night. We both know it. You simply want to hear it because it makes you feel all girly and floaty."

Bay grinned. "You're kind of a sap."

"If the sap fits." Landon shrugged.

I watched the interaction with a pang of loneliness. I never realized I was missing someone until I saw how happy Bay and Landon were simply being together. I spent my college years studying and enjoying the occasional party, but I made sure not to let anyone – including roommates – get too close. My secret weighed heavily on me and I didn't want to risk letting anything slip at an inopportune time.

I cleared my throat to interrupt the moment and forced their attention back to me. "If he saw me and knew I was asking questions and that somehow triggered his attention, wouldn't it make more sense for him to be the guilty party? Maybe he wanted to silence me."

"That's a theory, but I'm not sure that feels right," Landon admitted.

"I thought you didn't base your opinion on feelings," I challenged.

Landon heaved a sigh, his annoyance evident. "This is why I need to hang around with more men. Women always throw things I say back in my face."

"She has a point." Bay adopted a pragmatic tone. "You said you don't base your investigative work on feelings. Why is this different?"

"Because I also applied logic when I thought about it," Landon answered. "Charlie wasn't at the resort alone. She was with Jack. What good would approaching Charlie do if she has an investigative partner? He can't possibly think he'll silence Jack, too. That guy is clearly trained."

"Trained as what?" Bay asked, confused. "Is he like a circus performer?"

Landon barked out a laugh, genuinely amused. "He's military, sweetie."

"He is?" Bay's eyebrows flew up her forehead. "How do you know? Did he tell you? He's not much of a talker."

"He's not much of a talker," I interjected. "Well, he's a talker when he wants to be bossy and tell everyone what to do. Other than that he's pretty quiet ... and judgmental ... and full of himself."

Bay shifted in her seat to look at me. "That's a man thing. You can't let him get away with it. You have to force him to talk to you."

"Well, I'm not in the mood to talk to him at all right now," I muttered, shifting my eyes to the window. "He's a butthead." I could see Bay's smile out of the corner of my eye and opted to ignore it. "Landon is right about him being ex-military, though. He was a Marine."

"So that means that he's probably intimidating to other men," Bay mused, tapping her chin and turning to Landon.

"He's not ex-military. Once a Marine, always a Marine," Landon nodded as though something had become clearer.

"You had Millie with you, right?" Bay asked.

I nodded. "I can't see people wanting to approach her either. I find her funny, but she has a cranky persona. From what I can tell, most people find her intimidating."

"She's like Aunt Tillie," Bay noted.

"No one is like Aunt Tillie," Landon countered. "Millie seems a bit eccentric but mostly stable. Perhaps Shane Norman didn't approach her simply because he didn't see her. Maybe he came to town to find anyone from your group and happened to stumble across you first."

"I don't understand why he would do that," I said. "How does he think we'll be able to help him?"

"Good question," Landon said. "Maybe he's the murderer and he's trying to push the animal angle. If he believes he can get you guys to look in the right direction he might've planted evidence somewhere in the woods. Maybe he's the person you saw out there last night."

I searched my memory, trying to overlap the dark figure from my memory with my picture of Shane's silhouette. "No way," I said after a beat. "Shane Norman isn't even six feet tall. What I saw in the woods was taller. Plus, well, I don't like casting aspersions on people's body types because I'm not about weight shaming, but Shane is kind of rotund."

"Yeah, I don't think Penny was interested in him because of his looks," Bay agreed.

"That's why you're interested in me, though, right?" Landon asked cheekily.

"Your looks are most of it, but I like the way you wash my car when it's dirty, too," Bay replied.

"Keep it up," Landon warned. "I'm going to sleep in the guest bedroom if you're not careful. We have that thing for a reason."

"We both know that's an empty threat," Bay shot back. "You'll cry if you're forced to sleep without me."

Landon didn't seem bothered by the assertion. "You'll cry, too."

"Yes, we'll be a couple of sad sacks."

Landon grinned as he leaned over to give her a quick kiss. Someone else – a lesser person, mind you – might find the display distasteful. It simply made me rueful.

"You can drop me in town," I offered as Hemlock Cove popped into view. "Millie is waiting for me. She was going to head back to the library for more research."

"Where will you go from here?" Landon asked.

I shrugged. "I have no idea."

"Do you still believe it was Bigfoot?" Bay asked, her sea-blue eyes somber as they locked with mine.

"I believe that something odd is going on," I clarified. "I know without a doubt that I can't leave this town until I find out what it is."

BAY AND LANDON dropped me in front of the diner. The rental vehicle remained in the same spot Millie had parked it in hours before, but she was nowhere in sight. I checked the diner to make sure she wasn't waiting for me, and then set out to walk to the library. Hemlock Cove was small, so it wouldn't take me long. It was a nice spring day, so I looked forward to the walk.

My joy lasted only a few minutes.

"I've been looking for you."

The woman detaching from the side of a Range Rover caught me by surprise. I took an involuntary step back when I recognized her. Phyllis Grimes looked different out of her resort uniform, and the dark glare she graced me with reminded me of a soap opera my mother used to watch. I braced myself for trouble ... and possibly the ire of an Erica Kane wannabe.

"Mrs. Grimes, I ... how are you?"

Phyllis arched a dubious eyebrow. "How am I? How do you think I am?"

"I honestly have no idea," I replied, looking around for the fastest escape route. "I'm not sure what you're doing here. In fact, I'm not sure how you found me."

"You were with Bay Winchester at the resort," Phyllis reminded me. "Everyone in the area knows the Winchesters on sight. They're ... famous."

"For what?"

"Being busybodies," Phyllis sneered. "That whole family is crazy. The great-aunt has a pot field behind the inn. She actually sells to high school students. Did you know that? The woman is out of control and no one does a thing to stop her."

I had no idea if that was true, but I wouldn't put it past Tillie Winchester. "Okay, well, I'm here. Are you looking for me for a reason?"

"I'm not sure you can help me, but I thought I would take a chance," Phyllis replied. "I know Bay won't listen to me. She works for the newspaper and she's looking for a story. She doesn't care how she gets it ... or how many lives she ruins in the process."

"I don't know her very well, but that doesn't seem likely," I argued. "She seems a genuinely nice woman."

"She was spawned by crazy people. That means she's crazy by extension," Phyllis shot back. "I'm not here to talk about Bay Winchester. I want nothing to do with any of the Winchesters. In fact, don't mention you saw me to them. If Tillie Winchester decides she's bored, she'll curse me and nobody wants that."

I stilled, surprised. "She'll ... curse you?" I had to bite the inside of my cheek to keep from laughing. "How will she curse you?"

"No one knows how she does it," Phyllis replied. "We simply know she does it ... and she takes joy in doing it. Why don't you ask Margaret Little about Tillie's curses and see what she says."

"Tillie has cursed Mrs. Little?"

"The woman runs a store that sells nothing but porcelain unicorns," Phyllis replied, rolling her eyes. "What do you think?"

I had no idea what to think, but I was fairly certain that fixating on Mrs. Little was a mistake. "So ... you wanted to talk to me?" I'm not good in social situations sometimes – especially if I'm uncomfortable.

I couldn't ever remember feeling more uncomfortable than I did right now.

"I do want to talk to you," Phyllis bobbed her head. "When Bay approached me yesterday I handled things badly. She caught me off guard because I knew why she was there. She wanted to embarrass my husband. He doesn't deserve it. I mean ... the man is a good provider."

Is that how a wife makes excuses for her husband's infidelity? If so, she should put a little more effort behind the lie. "I don't know your husband," I explained. "I mean ... I saw him, but I don't know him."

"I know you've heard the rumors," Phyllis countered. "You think he's a cheater. You think he slept with that Schilling slut. Well, he didn't. He wouldn't do that."

"Ma'am, I don't know what to tell you." I felt helpless and held up my hands in a placating manner. "I'm not a police investigator. I work for the Legacy Foundation. We're checking to see if an animal was involved in her death. If this is murder by human hands, well, we'll have nothing to do with the outcome."

"An animal?" Phyllis' expression was hard to read. "I heard that they thought it was an animal at first but ruled that out."

"And where did you hear that?" I was legitimately curious. I had a hard time believing Landon and Chief Davenport would share that sort of information with the media.

"It's just something I heard around the resort," Phyllis replied, averting her eyes. "Are you saying they don't know if a man or beast killed Penny?"

"I'm saying that if they do they haven't shared the information with me," I cautioned. "I can't say either way, because I'm not in the inner circle."

"But I saw you with Bay Winchester," Phyllis pressed. "She dates that FBI guy. It was the talk of the town for two straight months when it first happened."

"Yes, well, that's neither here nor there," I said. "I'm staying at The Overlook and I did ride to the resort with Bay, but our avenues of investigation aren't exactly overlapping."

"That's news to me." Phyllis swished her hips a bit, as if she was trying to let the new information wash over her. "It's important that you know that my husband was not having an affair with Penny. He's not the type of man who would do something like that. In fact, we're very much in love."

"I'm sure that you are."

Phyllis acted as if she didn't hear my comment. "My husband is faithful ... and loving ... and he's such a good provider."

She kept pulling out that "good provider" nonsense. I couldn't decide if she was really trying to convince me or herself of her husband's innocence and his beneficence. "I'm sure he is."

"He would never cheat on me." Phyllis was firm. "All of the women at the resort make up lies about him because they all want him to notice them. He's handsome and everyone has a crush on him. But I got him. They're jealous. I'm in a position of power at the resort, and the other women can't stand it. All of the whispers ... well ... they stem from jealousy. You must see that."

"I can see that when you work in that type of environment it's probably hard to stay clear of gossip," I offered. "As for your husband ... I don't know him, ma'am. I'm not part of the investigation. You'll have to take this up with Agent Michaels."

I'm not talking to that guy no matter what," Phyllis huffed. "Everyone knows he makes excuses to cover for the Winchesters. He's even willing to frame other people to do it."

"Why would he need to make excuses for the Winchesters?"

"Because they're crazy and evil," Phyllis replied. "Everyone knows it."

"I ... well ... okay." I wasn't sure what to say. The woman seemed manic, as if she was too scattered to focus on one part of the conversation. "I'll make sure that Bay and Landon are aware that your husband wasn't cheating on you."

"Yeah, you do that." Phyllis lowered her voice and I was almost certain she was going to shuffle away. Instead she lunged at me, taking me by surprise when she grabbed my shoulders and shoved her face in mine. Her ski-slope nose was only inches from me and I could feel her breath hot on my face. "My husband is a good man! You tell them!"

Even though I wasn't physically afraid of Phyllis I couldn't stop my heart rate from climbing. "I will."

"You tell them!"

"I … will."

"You tell them!" Phyllis gave me an exaggerated shake, snapping my head back and forth and making my mind go loopy. I lost my balance as I tried to remain upright. Thankfully someone moved in behind me before I could lose my footing and careen into the pavement.

It was Thistle, and she didn't look happy.

"What the heck is going on here?"

Phyllis managed to recover relatively quickly when she saw the teal-haired woman. "I … have to go."

"Why are you here in the first place?" Thistle challenged.

"That's none of your business."

And just like that, Phyllis scurried away from us and back to her car.

"What was that?" Thistle asked, turning to me.

"I have no idea, but it was really weird."

"Do you think? I always knew that woman was crazy."

"Funnily enough, that's exactly what she said about your family," I countered.

"Yes, but we're fun crazy, not 'I-need-a-straitjacket-and-electro-shock-therapy' crazy," Thistle replied dryly. "Come on. I'll get you some tea. Then you can tell me all about Phyllis Grimes and how freaking crazy she is. That's one story I can't wait to hear."

TWENTY-FIVE

"*A*re you okay?"

Thistle's gruff demeanor softened noticeably as she led me into her magic store, Hypnotic. I nodded as I glanced around, smiling at the homey interior. The store felt like the Winchesters. There was no other way to describe it. An aura of ease that was difficult to ignore washed over the store.

"She didn't attack me or anything, if that's what you're worried about," I said, forcing a smile. "She was just a little manic."

"Yeah? I know Phyllis Grimes a little bit, but only because she lived around here for years. She was about ten years older than us, but she had a certain ... um ... reputation."

Well, that was interesting. "What kind of reputation?"

Thistle's smile was enigmatic. "Do you want some tea?"

"Is it a long story?"

"It's certainly not a short one."

"Then I'd love some tea."

Thistle hurried around the counter and disappeared into the back room. Her absence gave me a chance to look at the bevy of items the store offered, all of which intrigued me. Thistle found me staring at a display shelf full of skull candles when she returned, wordlessly handing me a mug of tea before sipping her own.

"Do you make these?" I asked, rubbing my finger over the top of a purple calvera.

Thistle nodded. "I'm better with the crafty stuff. Clove is happier dealing with the customers. I don't think anyone would rate my customer service skills very highly, but Clove is amazing with the shoppers."

"So you're more behind the scenes and she's more in front of the crowd," I mused, tracing my fingers over the small table in the corner where a tarot deck sat. "Who does the readings?"

"Mostly Clove." Thistle's eyes were keen as she looked me over. "She has a certain … gift."

"Do you have a gift?" I asked.

Thistle shrugged. "Everyone has a gift, right? I'm good with crafts and artistic endeavors. Have you seen that metal witch down in the town square? I made that sculpture last year."

"I did see that." I nodded appreciatively. "You're gifted."

"I get that from my mother," Thistle clarified. "She's really good with craft projects, too."

"Is she the only one in your family good at crafts?"

Thistle tilted her head to the side, considering. "I guess it depends on what you define as 'crafts.' We all have our strengths. Aunt Tillie makes a mean bottle of wine. And she's a tremendous gardener."

"Pot?"

Thistle smirked. "Who told you?"

"Phyllis Grimes mentioned it," I answered without hesitation. "She said you were all crazy and that your great-aunt grows pot to sell to the local kids."

Thistle remained silent but didn't appear to be offended by the assertion.

"It's true?" I prodded.

Thistle shrugged and held her hands palms up. "It's true that Aunt Tillie has a horticultural streak that makes the two law enforcement officials in our lives unbearably agitated and uneasy."

I giggled at the way she phrased it. "I see."

"I'm not sure you do, but that's okay," Thistle said. "Aunt Tillie likes her pot. She claims she has glaucoma."

The idea of the feisty Winchester matriarch going blind made me inexorably sad. "Does she?"

"Not that any doctor has ever diagnosed," Thistle replied. "She simply likes her pot."

"I see." That lightened my worry. "Does the rest of the family mind?"

"The pot field keeps her busy, which keeps her out of everyone's business … at least to a limited degree. The only time people care is when she takes young Annie – she's the daughter of a close friend who used to work at the inn, and Aunt Tillie adores her – to the field. Then things get dicey."

"Even Landon doesn't mind?"

"Landon … um … Landon is all talk," Thistle replied after a beat. "He's an FBI agent and he believes in law and order, but he would never arrest Aunt Tillie."

"Because of Bay?"

"Because he loves Aunt Tillie as much as we do," Thistle answered. "Of course, she drives him just as nuts as she drives us, so it's a family thing. Landon is family. He loves Bay and would never purposely hurt her. Despite his threats to the contrary, he'd never arrest Aunt Tillie. He'd find a way around it."

"And Chief Davenport?"

"Terry has known about Aunt Tillie's field longer than Landon, but pretends he doesn't know about it," Thistle replied. "He's a good man with a wonderful heart. We've known him as long as I can remember. He wouldn't arrest Aunt Tillie either. He threatened her often when we were kids because she'd take us on adventures. He never once followed through … and yet he caught us numerous times when we were torturing Mrs. Little. Aunt Tillie claims he arrested her, but I don't believe it."

"So he keeps your secrets," I mused, carrying my tea to the couch that rested in the middle of the store and sitting. "What other kind of secrets does he keep for you?"

I had no idea why I asked the question. I didn't expect Thistle to own up to anything. The way she narrowed her eyes made me realize I caught her off guard, but she was on edge given the lackadaisical way I pressed her. As much as I wanted to know who or what killed Penny Schilling – and I desperately wanted to know – I was determined to uncover the Winchesters' secret, too.

"I guess you'll have to ask Bay about that," Thistle replied. "I believe he keeps a lot of dirty secrets for her."

It was a masterful deflection, I had to give her that. She wouldn't answer truthfully – that much was certain – so I let the topic drop. "I'm pretty sure all of his dirty secrets have to do with bacon, so they're not really secrets, are they?"

Thistle shrugged, her eyes weighted with worry as they locked with mine. "Everyone has secrets." She sipped her tea, never shifting her gaze, and then finally the atmosphere in the store relaxed as she crossed one leg over the other. "So, tell me what Phyllis Grimes wanted."

"She wanted to make sure that I realized her husband wasn't a sleaze who has affairs all over town ... especially with Penny Schilling."

"I don't know Bob Grimes all that well, but there've been rumors about him for as long as I can remember," Thistle mused, leaning back in the chair. "We're not exactly resort people. We don't golf or ski, so we don't have occasion to visit there very often."

"The dining room looks nice."

"It does, but my mother and aunts absolutely adore cooking. They'd pitch a fit if we ate a lot of meals there," Thistle explained. "Actually, I think Bay and Landon went up there for a romantic meal a couple of months ago. They wanted time to themselves. I think there was a fight about it."

"Isn't there always a fight in your family?"

"We simply call it communication," Thistle replied, unruffled. "As for Phyllis, there are some very unflattering stories about her. I guess it depends on who you talk to. There's a small group of women who think she's a victim, but the rest of the town believes she's earned what's happening to her."

Huh. I wasn't sure what to make of that. "I guess I'm missing part of the story."

"You are." Thistle smiled, clearly enjoying her role as narrator for what looked to be a torrid tale. "So, Bay ran down the list of Penny Schilling's boyfriends. It's like a blast from the past for Walkerville's Class of 1996."

I stared at her.

"Hemlock Cove used to be known as Walkerville," Thistle volunteered helpfully.

"Yeah, I know. I don't know what that has to do with the investigation."

"I'm getting to it," Thistle said grouchily. "Don't rush me."

"Sorry."

"Anyway, so Phyllis, Bob, Shane Norman and Jim Green all graduated together," Thistle said. "I don't know if they were friendly. When they were in high school I was still decorating tree houses with Clove and Bay."

"Got it."

"You have to understand that there aren't many job opportunities for people who choose to stay in Hemlock Cove," Thistle explained. "Back then there were even fewer good jobs. You either worked at the resort or you didn't get full-time wages and benefits. Walkerville's manufacturing base died with the tire factory that closed a long time ago. That's why the township council decided to rebrand the town as a tourist destination."

"Which seems to have worked out well for you," I pointed out.

"It has, but it was a big risk when the council members made the decision," Thistle said. "The resort was it for a lot of people. I remember listening to my mother and aunts talking when we were kids. They were worried we would have no choice but to move out of Walkerville after graduation if we wanted to get good jobs."

"You didn't want that?" It was hard for me to imagine purposely picking a town the size of Hemlock Cove to live in forever. I love travel and am fond of big cities. Hemlock Cove almost seemed stifling with everyone knowing everyone … and all the secrets they're desperate to keep.

"I always knew I would stay," Thistle replied. "I think Clove did, too. I had no idea what I would do, but the idea of leaving Walkerville freaked me out. Bay, on the other hand, couldn't wait to get out."

"But she's here."

"She's here now," Thistle clarified. "She moved to Detroit for several years after graduating from college. She wanted to work for a big newspaper – and she did – but I could tell she missed Walkerville at a certain point. She was excited to move back to Hemlock Cove in the end. Now I can't imagine her anywhere else. Neither can Landon, and that's why he moved here."

"Even though that has to be tough on his future prospects with the agency?"

"Landon has decided he wants Bay more than professional glory," Thistle answered, her lips curving. "I wasn't so sure at first. I was worried he would break her heart. Now the only thing I worry about is that they'll break each other because they're so freaking horny all of the time."

I pressed my lips together to keep from laughing. Unfortunately it didn't work and I choked out a hysterical giggle.

"Sorry." Thistle's smile was rueful. "Sometimes I simply say whatever comes to my mind."

"I have the same problem," I admitted. "Jack has been on me about it almost from the first moment we met."

"Jack seems like a good guy, so you might want to listen to him," Thistle argued. "I'm the last person who should be giving advice about being blunt, but sometimes it's a curse."

"I'm starting to see that." I rubbed the back of my neck and shifted on the chair. "You were telling me about the Class of 1996."

"Oh, right." Thistle seemed eager to return to her story. "So, all of those guys started at the resort right after graduation. They weren't in the jobs they're in now, of course. Bob and Phyllis started in the dining room. She was a waitress and he was a dishwasher. I believe Shane Norman and Jim Green started as members of the grounds crew. In the summer they worked on the golf greens to keep them lush and pretty. In the winter they made snow and groomed the ski runs."

"Okay, but I'm not sure what that has to do with Penny Schilling's death," I prompted.

"It doesn't necessarily have anything to do with her death," Thistle clarified. "I simply wanted you to have the background. The resort itself is like a small town. Everyone knows everyone and they're all up in each other's business."

"Like your family dinners?"

Thistle smirked. "Not quite as fun but you get the gist of it. That gossip doesn't stay at the resort. It spreads. There have been rumors about Bob Grimes for as long as I can remember. I have no idea if he's slept with hundreds of women – that's what the rumors indicate – but there are far too many whispers for some of it not to be true."

"So you think that Bob Grimes was screwing around on his wife, and that Phyllis might've killed Penny," I surmised. "She seems incredibly manic and determined to keep up appearances. She kept saying what a good provider her husband is, as if that somehow makes up for the fact that he betrayed her trust every chance he got."

"I think Phyllis is the type of person who can snap at the drop of a witch's hat," Thistle admitted. "I also think she's at a physical disadvantage if she wanted to kill Penny. Phyllis is small. She's, like, a few inches taller than five feet. Penny had to have at least five inches on Phyllis. She wasn't a big woman, but when you're dealing with dead weight that seems like an insurmountable difference in stature right there."

"Have you dealt with a lot of dead bodies?" I teased.

"You'd be surprised," Thistle replied, not missing a beat. "I've dealt with my fair share of a lot of things. Moving a body like that would be almost impossible for Phyllis to do alone."

"So you think she had help," I murmured, running the idea through my head. "Do you think her husband helped her?"

"I'm not saying it was her," Thistle cautioned. "She has her hands full with kids and a husband with a wandering eye. I think the odds of it being someone outside of that little group are slim, though."

"So you don't believe in Bigfoot, huh?"

Thistle shifted on her chair, the question clearly making her uncomfortable. "I'm not sure," she hedged. "I believe there are things in this world that we can't explain. I believe there are creatures we've never seen. I won't rule out Bigfoot being real."

"I can't say with any certainty what I saw last night, but it was big," I offered. "It felt … different … from a human being. I don't know how else to describe it."

"Just because there might be a creature out there doesn't mean the creature did the deed," Thistle reminded me. "If Bigfoot lived off human beings, I think we would've had more bodies drop over the years."

"Unless you never discovered the bodies," I pressed. "Maybe Bigfoot ate everything and there was nothing to discover. I'm sure you've had people go missing in this area."

"Fair point," Thistle conceded. "I still think we're dealing with a human who wanted the police to believe it was an animal attack."

"I don't know what to believe," I admitted. "On one hand, it would be great if we could track down a creature to blame. People aren't comfortable when human beings are revealed to be monsters. That's why they're happy to pin the crime on an animal.

"If it is an animal, it will most certainly be put to death for killing a human being," I continued. "I don't want some rare creature destroyed because it was merely following its instincts."

"Do you have anything concrete to go on?" Thistle asked. "Do you have anything other than those prints you found the first day?"

"Just the supposition from the medical examiner that the DNA found on the body didn't appear to be entirely human and could be a mishmash of other animal DNA."

"But didn't the medical examiner also say the sample was so small it could've been contaminated?" Thistle pressed. "That might've been on purpose."

"And it might be a creature," I argued. "We're still in the debate portion of the investigation. Until we can all agree on what killed Penny Schilling, we'll never be able to find the guilty party."

"I guess that's true." Thistle rubbed the back of her neck. "What will you do now?"

"I'll find Millie and head back to the inn so we can check in with Chris. I don't know what else to do until then."

"Well … good luck."

"Yes. I think I'm going to need it."

TWENTY-SIX

I spent another twenty minutes with Thistle before leaving her to work. She confirmed that she saw Millie walking toward the library a few hours earlier so I headed in that direction. I was lost in thought, trapped in my own head, so I didn't notice the figure pacing me on the opposite sidewalk until I walked a full block.

Slowly I let my attention drift in that direction, frowning when I realized that it was Jim Green. He wore worn jeans and a T-shirt instead of the suave suit he wore at the resort. His attention was in front of him and he didn't so much as look in my direction. I couldn't be sure he saw me ... yet it felt as if he did.

Green looped left at the intersection, heading toward the bakery. I made my decision quickly, scurrying across the street and following him rather than continuing to the library. My understanding was that none of the resort workers lived in Hemlock Cove. So why did they keep showing up here? I couldn't come up with a feasible answer.

Green ordered a coffee at the counter before sitting alone at a corner table. He didn't look at me, but I was certain he was aware of my presence. I could've pretended to accidentally bump into him, even order a fresh coffee, but I was already caffeinated from the tea and my patience couldn't hold out much longer.

I squared my shoulders as I headed straight for Green, grabbing the chair across from him and sitting without invitation. If Green was surprised he didn't show it. Instead he merely arched an eyebrow and locked gazes.

"Good morning."

"It's actually the afternoon," I corrected, drumming my fingers on the table as I looked him up and down. "I almost didn't recognize you without the suit and slicked-back hair. I saw you at the resort a few hours ago, so you must've gone home and changed, huh?"

Green pursed his lips. "I can run back home and take care of both issues if that makes you feel more comfortable."

"That's okay. I'm good." I hoped I came off as more of a badass than I felt. "Are you following me?"

Green's eyebrows hopped. "Excuse me?"

"Are you following me?" I repeated, refusing to back down. "I saw you on the street and you seemed to be matching my pace. That means you were following me."

"Why would I follow you?"

"That wasn't an answer," I pointed out. "A reporter I know says that answering a question with a question is a surefire way to prove guilt." Technically Bay didn't say that. Landon said something like it while talking about her, but I couldn't remember the exact nature of the conversation.

"Did Bay Winchester tell you that?" Green sneered. "I wouldn't put too much stock into her or that family. They're crazy."

"You're not the first person to tell me that," I supplied. "Phyllis Grimes was here about an hour ago and said the same thing."

Green's eyes flashed. "Phyllis was here? What did she want?"

"Why do you care?" I challenged, confused. "She's married to another man. Granted, that man was reportedly sleeping with the same woman you were involved with, but Phyllis should mean nothing to you."

"Phyllis and I graduated from high school together," Green noted, his tone even but icy. "We've known each other a long time. We're friends."

"That means you know Bob, too," I pointed out. "Are you friends with Bob?"

"Bob is … a diligent worker."

I didn't bother to hide my smirk. "And a good provider, according to his wife," I said. "Do you want to know what I find interesting about this little … ménage a whatever?"

Green remained silent, his hands wrapped around his mug.

"Phyllis waited for me on the street to make sure I knew her husband wasn't a philanderer," I started. "That only made me think he was even more of a turd. Shane Norman followed me around town yesterday. He acted as if he wanted to say something, but he practically ran into the unicorn store when he saw Bay. I have a hard time believing he had a burning need for a unicorn statue. How about you?"

Green's lips twitched. "I think Shane likes all sorts of fruity things."

"Are you saying that because you were sleeping with the same woman?"

"I'm saying that because he's an idiot," Green replied.

"You went to high school with him, right?"

Green shrugged. "It's a small area. If I remember correctly, he was there."

"Uh-huh." I looked around the bakery before leaning in closer. "Shane left before he said anything, but he acted as if he was afraid of Bay Winchester. Phyllis practically attacked me on the street and only backed off when Thistle Winchester showed up. You're here, but I didn't see you until I left the Winchester magic shop, which probably means you were watching me."

"I just came to town for coffee," Green countered. "I didn't see you in any magic shop. I try to avoid places like that. They're … unsavory."

"Yes, I'm often plagued by how unsavory candles and herbs are," I drawled, narrowing my eyes. "If you're not following me, why are you here?"

"This is a bakery. I'm here for the baked goods and coffee."

"Uh-huh. They don't have coffee in Bellaire?"

"I'm sure they do, but I grew up in Walkerville." Green maintained a calm demeanor, but I could tell he was fighting the urge to snap at me. Apparently he didn't think I'd call him on his actions. He wasn't good under pressure. "I like the coffee here."

"Yeah? I do, too. I just had tea with Thistle Winchester, so I'm going to take a break from caffeine." I pushed back my chair and got to my feet, never breaking eye contact with Green. "I'm going to pick up my co-worker at the library. Then we'll return to The Overlook. If you plan to follow me there, I'd be careful. Tillie Winchester is on a rampage, and she's looking for people to add to her list."

The threat had the desired effect as Green made a face and shifted in his chair.

"Enjoy your afternoon off," I added, moving toward the door. "Make sure to watch behind you. There's a rumor that Bigfoot is on the loose around these parts. Of course, you're more frightened of the Winchesters than Bigfoot, aren't you?"

"Anyone with a brain is frightened of the Winchesters," Green shot back. "They've earned their reputations. You have a nice day now."

"You, too."

I GLANCED over my shoulder multiple times upon leaving the bakery, but either Green was biding his time or wasn't interested in following me after all. I was determined to make it to the library without distraction this time, but that didn't happen. A blonde head in the cemetery caught my attention, and before I realized what I was doing I found myself watching Bay Winchester from several feet away as she did a bit of spring cleaning on a grave.

"That's better, huh?" Bay smiled at the headstone as she shoved a bit of garbage in a small plastic bag. She was talking to herself. Or, rather, she was talking to whoever rested beneath the stone. I recognized her efforts for what they were. I talked to my parents whenever I stopped by the cemetery, too.

"We'll plant flowers in a few weeks," Bay volunteered. "Aunt Tillie wants something bright this year. She said the flowers Marnie picked out last year were boring and that you don't like purple. She wants something blue."

Bay tilted her head to the side and laughed, almost as if she really was talking to someone. The way she focused on the headstone caused the hair on the back of my neck to rise. I couldn't stop myself from glancing around. Bay was clearly alone, yet I swear she was not only talking to someone but also hearing answers to her questions.

"She's feisty and good, as usual. I'm surprised she hasn't been out here yet. She's been busy torturing the guests and Thistle. You know how she is."

Bay paused and waited, her chin bobbing.

"Yes, well, her health is good," Bay offered. "I know you miss her, but we're not ready to let her go yet. No, I wasn't saying that you were trying to get her to go. I remember what you told me when … well … when we met in the fall."

I realized I was gaping – and out in the open – so I snapped my mouth shut and shuffled toward a tree to hide the fact that I was eavesdropping. The movement was enough to garner Bay's attention.

"There's no reason to hide," Bay said dryly, her eyes momentarily flicking to the stone before focusing on me. "I know you're there, Charlie."

I felt unbelievably embarrassed to be caught eavesdropping on a private moment. It was none of my business that Bay enjoyed conversations with dead relatives. I did the same with my parents. I didn't believe they talked back to me, but that hardly made Bay crazy. Although … everyone who worked at the resort said the whole Winchester clan was crazy. It was certainly possible that she was battier than a vampire stuck in a belfry, but she didn't appear that way to me.

"I'm sorry," I offered lamely, poking my head out from behind the tree. "I was walking by and saw you. I thought I'd see what you were doing. Then I realized you were talking to … someone you lost … and I thought I should give you some privacy."

"This is my Great-Uncle Calvin," Bay said, gesturing toward the stone. "That's my grandmother over there. Her name was Ginger."

"Oh, well, it's a beautiful cemetery."

"It is," Bay agreed, dusting off the knees of her jeans as she stood. "We generally do a spring cleanup as a family but I was passing by and thought I'd pick up the bigger pieces and get them out of the way. The wind blows through here in the winter and a lot of candy wrappers and empty bottles find their way through the fence."

"That's nice." I studied the headstones. "Did you know your grandmother?"

Bay shook her head. "She died before I was born. Aunt Tillie is our grandmother. Always has been."

"I guess that makes sense. Is Ginger her sister?"

"Yes. They were very close."

"Just the two of them?"

Bay chuckled, clearly amused by my discomfort. "They had a half-sister – Willa. They were raised to believe they were full sisters, but it turns out they weren't. They were never close with Willa. I guess it wasn't hard to sever the ties once the truth came out."

"It must've been hard on Willa."

"You would think so, but ... no." Bay tied the end of the bag so none of the garbage could escape. "What are you doing out here? I thought you were going to find Millie."

"I was looking for her when I ran into Phyllis Grimes."

Bay eyes widened. "Here? In town? What did she want?"

I related my conversation with the woman, including Thistle's appearance. There was no sense holding anything back because Thistle would tell Bay everything. Even though I remained suspicious of the Winchesters, I didn't believe they had anything to do with Penny's death.

"Thistle is right about the ties between that group," Bay noted. "I've been conducting a little research myself. I pulled an old high school yearbook and put it in my car. I plan to show the photos to Landon later."

"Where is Landon?"

"Investigating with Chief Terry. He really didn't say where they were going."

"I'm surprised he let you out of his sight," I admitted. "He seems keen on keeping you close. It's kind of … sweet."

"I thought you were going to say that it was kind of overbearing." Bay's grin was soft but earnest. "I told him I had work to do at the office. That wasn't a lie, but he does like to hover occasionally. He thinks I find trouble."

"Do you?"

Bay nodded. "I find it, it finds me. Sometimes I'm at fault. Sometimes I'm not. Sometimes Thistle is at fault. A good fifty percent of the time Aunt Tillie is at fault. Still, trouble seems to find us no matter who is at fault."

"It seems to be finding me, too, right now," I admitted, chewing my bottom lip. "Jim Green is in town, too. He followed me when I left the magic shop and then went into the bakery to cover his tracks."

"Did he say anything?"

"I followed him into the bakery and confronted him, so he didn't really have a choice," I replied. "He claims he only came to town for coffee, but I don't believe him."

"What do you believe?"

"I think there's something weird about that whole group," I confided. "They all went to high school together. Three men from that class were sleeping with the same woman. A fourth member from that class was married to one of the men, and she keeps insisting he is no cheater even though everyone knows he is. It's all too … weird."

"Weird is an apt word." Bay chuckled as she shook her head. "I thought you were leaning toward the probability of Bigfoot killing Penny."

"I know you guys think it's a joke, but I saw something the other night and I swear it was too tall to be a man," I said. "I don't know if it was Bigfoot, but it seemed too slim to be a bear. It reminded me of Chewbacca from *Star Wars*."

"I thought you couldn't see hair," Bay prodded.

"I couldn't, but … I saw something."

"I believe you." Bay's response was simple and succinct. "There are many things in this world that we can't explain. Whether Bigfoot is real or merely a figment of the public's imagination doesn't mean there's nothing out there."

"Do you believe in the paranormal?"

Bay nodded. "Don't you?"

"I wouldn't have joined the Legacy Foundation if I didn't." I rolled my neck, enjoying the way my joints popped. I had a chance to push Bay. Did I dare? Oh, what do I have to lose? "What are you?"

The question was barely a whisper. Bay raised her eyes to mine when she heard it. "What are you?"

"I'm just a person," I replied. "I graduated from college and joined the Legacy Foundation soon after. That's my complete and total life story."

"No, it's not." Bay crossed her arms over her chest as she stared at me. "I understand the urge to protect yourself. People attack what they don't understand. You don't have to be afraid to tell me what you are."

"I'm not afraid ... ."

Bay cut me off with a shake of her head. "I see it. You need something to bolster your courage."

"What are you afraid of?"

"Losing the people I love."

"I don't have anyone to love," I pointed out. "I'm alone."

"You're not, but you can't see the truth of that yet because you've been alone for a long time," Bay countered, heaving a sigh. "Do you really want to know what I am?"

I nodded, my heart rate increasing. "Yes." Was she really about to tell me?

"Okay then, I will confide in you even though it's a leap of faith," Bay offered, wetting her lips. "I'm not a normal human being. You're right about that."

"What are you?" My mouth was suddenly dry. I barely managed to croak out the words.

"I'm a witch."

And just like that my excitement faded. "Yeah. So is everyone in the town."

"Oh, you misunderstand," Bay cooed. "I'm a real witch. My entire family consists of real witches. We can perform magic, curse those we don't like or agree with, even control the weather on rare occasions."

"You're not serious?"

Bay nodded. "Your turn. What are you?"

"I have no idea," I admitted, staring at my hands. "Have you ever seen *Carrie?*"

Bay widened her eyes. "Yes."

"I think I might be Carrie."

Bay chuckled, the sound taking me by surprise. "Why don't you sit down and we'll go over this from the beginning. I doubt very much you're Carrie."

"I think you're wrong. The only difference is that no one has ever doused me in pig's blood."

"Why don't you tell me your story and we'll go from there? Let's not get dramatic until it's called for. Criminy, you remind me of Aunt Tillie. She would love to be Carrie, though you seemed terrified by the prospect."

I couldn't tell if the comparison was meant to be a compliment.

27

TWENTY-SEVEN

"So ... you're a witch?"

I followed Bay to a metal bench and sat, my mind working at a fantastic rate. I knew something was different about the Winchesters, yet ... this answer seemed somehow too simple.

"I am." Bay bobbed her head as she rested her hands on her knees. "All of the women in my family are witches."

"You have powers?"

"We have different gifts," Bay clarified. "As for powers ... well ... it's not like you see on television. Except for Aunt Tillie, of course. She lives her life by what she sees on television, so she often seems like a soap opera character."

I chuckled despite the surreal situation. "What can you do?"

"I can talk to ghosts and cast the occasional spell," Bay replied, choosing her words carefully. "We can do a little magic here or there, but we don't make it part of our normal lives. I'm nowhere near as strong as Aunt Tillie. Most of the spells I cast need power boosts from my cousins."

"Like ... what?"

"We call to the four corners," Bay explained. "That's how our line has always worked throughout the years. We're no different."

"Do you mean directions? You call to the corners of the north, south, east and west?"

Bay looked impressed. "How do you know that?"

"I conducted a lot of research on the supernatural in college. I remember reading something about it," I replied. "I tried to perform the spells in the book, but they didn't work."

"Did you try the spells because you suspected you were a witch?"

I shifted on the bench, finding it impossible to get comfortable. "I tried them because I didn't think I fit in and I was desperately looking for reasons for my odd detachment."

"You protect yourself, and that's probably wise," Bay noted. "We won't hurt you. We can generally tell when someone is evil, and you're not evil. I'm not sure if you've been worrying about that, but people aren't born evil. It's your heart that decides what you will or won't be, and your heart would never let you become evil."

"I ... um ... tell me about what you can do." I wasn't ready to admit my abilities until I saw proof of what Bay told me. I inherently trusted her – I probably always had because I sensed the goodness within – but I was understandably leery. "What kinds of things have you done?"

"Well, when we were little Aunt Tillie would take us on adventures. Those adventures almost always had something to do with her meting out vengeance on people." Bay smiled as her memories pushed to the forefront. "She enjoyed messing with Mrs. Little quite often. That often involved a spell or two. The Christmas after our fathers left I was in a bad mood because of ... well, a lot of things ... and she made it snow to save Christmas that year."

"She can control the weather?" That sounded unbelievably fantastical.

Bay nodded. "She's done it on more than one occasion. I've seen her bring lightning storms down on people threatening us on more than one occasion."

"Did she kill them?"

"A few. They were all bad people, so don't worry about that. We seem to attract a certain type of enemy. Aunt Tillie doesn't play favorites with her enemies. She enjoys smiting them no matter what they've done."

"What about your mother and aunts? What can they do?"

"They have their own blend of magic," Bay replied, her expression wistful. "They're all kitchen witches. Clove, Thistle and I tend to be elemental witches, drawing our magic from the earth and air. Mom, Marnie and Twila focus their energies in the kitchen. That doesn't mean they can't conjure a spell when necessary. I believe they did it more often when they were younger."

I bit my bottom lip as I ran the information through my head. "And you can talk to ghosts?"

"That's also a family gift." Bay's smile turned strained. "It's not exactly a comfortable gift, but I've learned to live with it."

"Is that what you were doing today? Talking to ghosts, I mean."

"I was here to clean graves because I do some of my best thinking when I have a secondary task to focus on," Bay explained. "I sometimes have a conversation with Uncle Calvin when I'm here. He only seems to talk to me when I'm alone."

"He was Tillie's husband?"

"Yes. I never met him in life. However, we've had some marvelous conversations. He was a good man. I often think he had to be a saint to marry Aunt Tillie. He really loved her."

"Was he talking to you today?"

"We had a brief conversation," Bay replied. "He doesn't talk to me often. I don't believe he's on this side. He manages to drift over occasionally, but he lives in a better place. Most ghosts who remain behind do so because they have unfinished business. They only stay until that business is settled."

"Do you help them move over?"

"When I can. It's not always possible."

"Have you seen Penny's ghost? I know you've been looking. I watched you at her apartment. You seemed to be searching for something, although at the time I couldn't figure out what. I saw you at the resort staring out into nothing, too. You were looking for her, weren't you?"

"I was," Bay confirmed. "Sometimes when people are killed they remember exactly what happened and point us in the right direction. Other times the truth of their death is so traumatizing that it takes time for answers to come. I was hopeful Penny was still around, but if she is, I haven't seen her."

"You don't believe Bigfoot killed her, do you?"

"No. I don't think you really do either."

"I saw something," I protested.

"You saw a shadow in the dark," Bay clarified. "I also saw your reaction when Jack mentioned the falling branch and how high up it was. I saw that branch. It wasn't ripped from the tree. Well, I mean it was, but a physical being didn't do it. Magic did."

I balked. "How can you possibly know that?"

"I've sensed something in you from the moment we met," Bay admitted, tilting her head to the side as she regarded me. "You're powerful in a different way from us. There's power inside of you. There's no sense denying it."

"I … does Landon know about all of this?" I had no idea why my mind immediately flew to him. He was such a straight arrow that I had trouble wrapping my head around the idea that he could deal with something this freaky.

"He knows," Bay confirmed. "I couldn't keep something like that from him. We were drawn together because we both chased the same case. When he initially found out about the Winchester witch gene he took a step back. I won't deny that it hurt."

"That's what you guys were talking about," I murmured. "That's why you were upset."

"I wasn't really upset," Bay clarified. "I was … all right, I was upset. Still, Landon came back. He needed time to think. There are people out there who will not only accept you for what you are but love you despite it.

"That's the key, of course," she continued. "You want to be wary of people who want to be close to you because of your abilities. They are not to be trusted. That's originally why we weren't fond of Sam. We thought he wanted to be close to Clove only because she's a witch."

"You obviously got over that," I pointed out.

"We have. Sam came to town because he researched the Winchester witches and wanted to get to know us. He fell in love with Clove because she's Clove."

"And what can she do?"

"Whine and complain." Bay smiled. "She has certain cognitive abilities. "If you want to talk to her she can share that information. It's not my place. I feel comfortable talking about my abilities, but I won't gossip about my cousins."

"And Landon really understands?"

"Landon is a unique individual who loves with his whole heart," Bay answered. "He understands and looks past the magic. He isn't always happy about the trouble it brings, but a good man will always follow his heart."

"Hmm." I tapped my lip as I considered the statement. "I always thought I would have no choice but to be alone. I didn't think people would understand. But there are times I can't hide the things I can do."

"And what can you do?"

"I ... um ... see things sometimes," I admitted. It was hard to grit out the words, but I immediately felt better after I did. "I can sometimes see the past or the near future when I touch things. I saw you when I touched Mrs. Gunderson the other day. That's why I tried to touch you later. I wanted to get another flash."

"That was odd, but I figured maybe you rolled that way." Bay's smile was impish. "What did you see when you touched Mrs. Gunderson?"

"I'm not sure. It's what made me suspicious of you guys. Well, to be fair, I was suspicious before I saw the flashes. The images sent my curiosity into overdrive. I saw you as a little girl. You were in this cemetery with Terry. He cried and hugged you."

"That was probably the day I talked to his mother after her death," Bay mused. "I told him what I saw. He believed me, although he never wants to talk about it. He likes to pretend he doesn't know about us. We let him because it's somehow easier."

"I also saw you and Landon," I offered. "He was upset, screaming your name. You were fighting some monster. I think it was made of mist."

Bay leaned forward, intrigued. "Really? I wonder if that was Floyd."

Something clicked in my head. "It had to be! I heard Tillie yelling, 'I'm coming for you, Floyd.' I wasn't sure they were part of the same memory."

"They were. Floyd was an angry poltergeist. We gave him what he deserved in the end."

"So ... he's gone?"

"More than a year now," Bay confirmed. "So you see flashes of the past and future. That's a cognitive gift. You can move things with your mind, too. I've seen you do it."

Admitting to the psychic flashes was one thing. Admitting to the other was quite another. "I ... ."

"It's okay." Bay rested her hand on mine to soothe me. "I won't tell. It's okay. I know about having a secret. I know how hard it is to deal with something you can't control."

"That's just it, I can't control the ... other," I admitted, tears swamping my eyes. "It started happening when I was ten. I saw flashes and it haunted me. My parents kept trying to get me to talk about it, but I couldn't.

"Then one night the neighbor's house went up in flames and I saw it before it happened," I continued. "I told my parents and they checked. It was too late to help the woman who lived there. It overwhelmed me and ... well ... I blew up a light bulb."

"That must've been difficult," Bay clucked, her expression sympathetic but free of judgment. "What did your parents say?"

"Oh, they were fine," I said hurriedly. "I mean, they were surprised, but they went out of their way to make sure I knew that it wasn't my fault. They were always good that way."

"That's good."

"They weren't my real parents, though." I felt guilty even uttering the words. "That came out wrong. They were my real parents. They weren't my birth parents. I have no idea who my birth parents were.

245

They dropped me off at a fire station in the middle of the night. I have no memory of them."

"How old were you?"

"Four."

Bay took me by surprise when she stroked the back of my head. It mirrored something my adoptive mother did to soothe me whenever I was upset. "You believe they abandoned you because of your abilities, don't you?"

"Why else?"

Bay shrugged, noncommittal. "It could've been a number of things," she replied. "Perhaps they were trying to protect you because they knew someone might come through them to try to use your powers. Perhaps they knew they weren't equipped to give you the life you deserved, so they opted to give you the best chance they could. You may never know why they did what they did.

"In truth, though, they might've done you a favor," she continued. "They might've put you in the system so you could get help. I'm a firm believer that things work out as they're supposed to. That's why I let Landon go without a fight when he opted to leave."

"Did you know he would come back?"

"No. I felt in my heart he would, but I didn't want to keep him if he didn't want to stay."

"That's how I want to feel about my parents," I said. "I can't help but wonder. Do you think they were like me?"

"In witch families, the power is handed down from the mother," Bay explained. "Boys sometimes get hints of magic, but they're never as powerful as the girls. Perhaps that's what happened to you."

"Do you know any telekinetic witches?"

"Yes."

"You do?" I couldn't stop the hope from expanding in my chest.

"Aunt Tillie can move things with her mind if she puts a lot of effort behind it," Bay offered. "I have on one or two occasions. It's draining for us. It doesn't sound as if it's draining for you."

"I try not to do it at all," I said. "I don't want people to notice. It pops up occasionally. That's what happened with the diner door when you noticed it flying out."

"I figured as much, but I didn't want to push you." Bay looked thoughtful. "It also happened at breakfast the first morning after you arrived … and the morning after you found us dancing in the field. You didn't realize it – and I don't think anyone else did, so don't panic – but your spoon stirred in your coffee mug without you touching it."

"Oh, my … ." I felt sick to my stomach. "I can't believe you noticed that."

"It's fine." Bay dismissed my potential freakout as if I were two years old and throwing a tantrum. "I understand why you're looking for answers. I understand why you don't volunteer information to anyone who asks for it. You should be careful. This is a dangerous world."

"But?"

"But you're not alone." Bay's smile was soothing. "You have help if you need it. You have us if you ever need to talk. You won't be here forever. Whether Bigfoot is to blame or one of Penny's suitors flipped his lid, you will eventually leave this place. But we'll always be here if you need answers. Don't forget that."

"Do you have the answers I need?"

"That's a good question. I'm not sure I can answer it."

"Can you help me find my parents?"

"I … ." Bay broke off and shook her head. "There are a few spells we might try, locator spells and the like, but I doubt very much they'd lead you to what you're really seeking."

"And what do you think I'm seeking?"

"A place where you belong," Bay answered without hesitation. "You need to give this job time, Charlie. You can't get every answer in the exact moment you ask the question. You need to reach out to others and let them help you."

"And how am I supposed to do that?" I challenged. "We're searching for paranormal beings and hoping magic is the answer to certain questions. All the while I'll be keeping a big secret from these people. How can I trust them if they can't trust me?"

Bay shrugged, her expression enigmatic. "I think that the easiest way to hide is to become the thing you believe is hunting you. Insulating yourself in this group was a smart move."

"But I'll never be able to trust them," I groused. "How am I supposed to build a life if I can't trust people? How am I supposed to get a Landon of my own if I'm always lying?"

"You don't always have to lie," Bay pointed out. "You merely have to protect yourself until you get a better feel for the people you've surrounded yourself with. When it comes down to it, I'll bet there are a few you can trust in that group."

"Laura?"

Bay immediately started shaking her head. "You'll never be able to trust Laura. She reminds me of a girl I went to high school with. She's a user and manipulator."

"Then who?"

"I think Millie is more than trustworthy," Bay offered. "Watch her a bit. I think she's keeping lots of secrets."

"She reminds me of Tillie."

"That's not necessarily a bad thing. I know you've only seen us complaining about Aunt Tillie, but we'd be lost without her."

"Who else?" I asked. "Do you think Chris will be okay with it?"

"Chris seems to be a man searching for something only he can explain," Bay replied. "I think Jack will be your greatest ally."

I balked, frustrated. "He's a jerk."

Bay smiled. "All men seem like jerks until you understand where they're coming from. I'm not telling you to confide in Jack right away. Simply … get to know him."

"So he can be more of a jerk?"

"So you and he can learn that trust is reciprocal," Bay corrected. "It'll be okay, Charlie Rhodes. I can't see the future like you, but I have faith. Now, come on. It's almost time for dinner, and I think we both could use the fuel. We need to decide where to look next in this investigation. I'm convinced Bigfoot isn't the culprit."

"I still believe in Bigfoot," I admitted as I trailed her toward the downtown hub. "I'll always believe."

"I believe in Bigfoot, too," Bay said. "I simply don't believe Bigfoot murdered Penny Schilling."

"Do you have any idea who did?"

"No, and she's not around to answer the question for us," Bay replied. "That's why we have to work together. Sometimes the dead rely on the living to provide answers. That's our job."

"Okay, but you still haven't told me what everyone was doing naked in the field the other night," I prodded. "Was that a spell?"

Bay shook her head. "Sometimes being naked is a form of magic all its own."

"I'll bet Landon told you that."

Bay chuckled. "He might've made the suggestion. Come on. We've got a long night ahead of us."

2 8

TWENTY-EIGHT

J texted Millie to tell her I'd ride back to The Overlook with Bay. The blonde witch drove around a bit so I could get myself together before facing her family and my team. I didn't mean to cry, but it was such a relief to share my story with someone I couldn't help myself.

Bay was a good listener. She went through everything with me from the beginning. Her more pragmatic approach when it came to my birth parents was much different from my scorched-earth policy, but I understood where she was coming from. I couldn't accept it … or forgive them … but I got it.

By the time we reached the inn I was breathing normally. Bay assured me that no one would notice I'd been crying. I was thankful for her presence. The Overlook was quiet when we entered. I was ready to make my escape – I figured a shower and change of clothes would allow me to shake off the remnants of an emotional afternoon – but the sound of voices in the library drew Bay's attention. I made the mistake of following.

"Hey, sweetie." Landon sat on the couch, a drink clutched in his hand. He looked happy to see his girlfriend. He lifted his chin to accept her kiss and made room for her on the couch. "Where have you been? I expected you an hour ago."

"I was hanging around with Charlie," Bay replied calmly, tipping Landon's glass so she could see inside of it. "Whiskey? Did you have a hard day?"

"It's always a hard day when I'm separated from you."

Bay made an exaggerated face. "Smooth talker."

"No, he's telling the truth. He's done nothing but worry about where you were for the past hour," Jack said, his presence taking me by surprise as I shifted my eyes to the other end of the room. He sat on one of the leather chairs in the corner, a drink in his hand. He looked happy and relaxed. I hadn't seen him since this morning ... and I wasn't keen to make up for lost time.

"Yes, well, he's a sap." Bay tapped her finger against Landon's cheek. "Strangely enough, even though I saw you just a few hours ago, I missed you."

"Yeah?" Landon's expression was hard to read. "I stopped by the newspaper office to surprise you with a doughnut from the bakery. You weren't there."

"I was there for a bit, and then I had something else to take care of." Bay remained strong in the face of Landon's accusatory tone. I felt my own annoyance bubbling up. It was almost as if he didn't trust her. Given how she'd taken care of me, I wasn't sure I could put up with that.

"What did you have to take care of?" Landon asked.

"Things." Bay flicked her eyes to me. "Do you want a drink, Charlie?"

"I can get it." I shuffled toward the cart, making sure to avoid eye contact with Jack. I could feel his gaze on me, but the last thing I wanted to do was deal with him. "Do you want something, Bay?"

"I'll take a Jack and Coke, Thank you, Charlie."

"You're welcome, Bay."

Landon pursed his lips as he glanced between us. "Why are you guys being so formal?"

"It's called being polite," Bay answered. "You should try it sometime. It does wonders for personal relationships."

"Uh-huh." Landon didn't look convinced. "Where were you, Bay?"

"I told you I was doing stuff," Bay replied icily. "I wasn't getting in trouble, so there's nothing to get worked up about."

"See, the fact that you're announcing that makes me nervous," Landon admitted. "Why won't you tell me where you were?"

"I was working. I didn't realize you were my keeper," Bay shot back, her blue eyes flashing. "Why are you being such a pain in the butt?"

"Because there's a murderer out there. You took off, and I couldn't find you," Landon gritted out, his cheeks flushing with color. "When you love someone – especially as much as I love you – it's natural to want to know that she's safe."

"You could've called or texted," Bay argued.

"I did. Eight times."

"Oh." Bay looked abashed as she dug in her pocket and retrieved her phone. Her expression was sheepish when she glanced up. "I didn't hear it because I turned it off."

Landon muttered, draining his drink. I wisely mixed two Jack and Cokes and carried them to the couple before taking mine to the empty chair and wishing it swallowed me whole.

"I'm sorry." Bay sounded earnest as she wrapped her hand around Landon's wrist. "I didn't mean to turn off the phone. I went to get coffee and got distracted by the cemetery."

"You were in the cemetery?" Landon's anger fled. I had to wonder if it was because he thought she was talking to ghosts rather than me. "Why were you there?"

"I like to think while I'm working, so I cleaned off Uncle Calvin's grave. Then I cleaned Grandma Ginger's before running into Charlie. After that we talked a bit and I lost track of time. I didn't do it to punish you."

"I know that, sweetie." Landon rested his hand on top of Bay's head. "I'm sorry. I don't like worrying about you. It makes me crazy. Your vehicle was in the parking lot at the newspaper office, so I thought you were in town with Thistle and Clove. They said they hadn't seen you, though, and by the time I got back to the newspaper office you were gone. I thought you were here, but … ."

"Charlie and I went for a drive," Bay volunteered. "We were just chatting. I didn't realize how long we'd be gone."

Landon arched a dubious eyebrow, but ceased all forms of argument. "Well, it's done. You're here and you're safe. They made pot roast for dinner. All is right with the world." He kissed the top of her head. I had a feeling Bay was looking at a serious conversation later, but Landon was smart enough to let it slide while he had an audience.

"All will be right with the world if you massage me later," Bay corrected, earning a smirk from Landon. "I want lotion and everything."

"Fine." Landon obviously didn't want to engage in an argument. "You're just lucky they made cake to bolster my energy."

"They always make cake."

"Not red velvet."

Bay brightened considerably. "Score!"

"You're easy to please, sweetie. That's one of my favorite things about you."

We lapsed into comfortable silence. All I could think about was taking a shower. Even though I knew it would mean drawing attention to myself, I drained my glass and got to my feet. "I'm going to get cleaned up."

"Are you okay?" Bay asked pointedly.

I nodded and averted my gaze. "I'm fine. Just tired. It's been a long day."

"You don't want to miss the pot roast and cake," Landon said. "Make sure you don't fall asleep."

"I have no intention of missing the pot roast and cake." I was thankful to make my escape. I made it back to my room door – and the emotional freedom so tantalizingly close on the other side – before being stopped by a hand on my arm. I wasn't surprised to find Jack behind me when I turned. "What?"

If he was bothered by my tone, Jack didn't show it. "Are you okay?"

"I'm fine. Why would you think otherwise?"

"Because your eyes are red and puffy, and all of your makeup has washed off."

Of course it had. I knew I shouldn't have believed Bay when she said I looked perfectly normal. Given the circumstances, that was impossible. "I'm fine, Jack." I forced myself to remain calm. "You don't have anything to worry about."

"Where have you been all day?"

"Why do you care?"

The question obviously caught him off guard, because he jerked his head back. "I ... you're my responsibility. I'm head of security."

"Oh, well, I didn't realize that being head of security also made you my babysitter," I groused. "For the record, I was working most of the afternoon. I ran into a few suspects and shared the information with Bay."

"You ran into a few suspects?" Jack was flabbergasted. "Are you okay? Why didn't you call me?"

"Because we're here looking for Bigfoot, not investigating the many corners of Penny Schilling's complicated love life," I answered. "I told Bay. I'm sure she'll share the information with Landon."

"Why didn't she already do it?"

I shrugged. "Perhaps she wanted privacy. You'll have to ask her. Now, if that's all, I need to take a shower. I wasn't lying about it being a long day."

Jack worked his jaw for a few seconds. Finally he snapped it shut and offered me a curt nod. "As long as you're okay."

"I'm fine, Jack." I forced a tight smile. "I made it through the day without a babysitter. I didn't put the moves on anyone, including you. That should make you happy."

The corners of Jack's mouth tipped down. "Listen, if you're still upset about what I said this morning ... ."

"I'm not upset." That wasn't a lie. I was far too drained to be upset. "I just want a bath."

"Knock yourself out." Jack looked furious as he swiveled, taking the steps with an attitude I couldn't put a name to. I was fairly certain I heard him muttering as he descended the stairs.

"I am so sick of people," I muttered, slipping my key in the door. "I can't wait for this case to be over."

"Something tells me you won't have to wait long," Tillie announced, appearing in the hallway, her combat helmet firmly in place and a whistle in her hand.

"What makes you say that?" I asked, eyeing the whistle.

"Intuition."

"Well ... okay." I pushed open the door. "I'm dying to ask ... what's the deal with the whistle?"

Tillie's smile was tinged with mayhem. "I like to put my lips together and blow."

Wait ... was that an answer?

BAY SHARED the gossip about my interaction with Jim Green and Phyllis Grimes while I was upstairs, so that by the time I joined everyone at the dining room table both groups were mired in heavy discussion. I preferred it that way.

The only open seat was between Jack and Landon. I took it without complaint, but focused on my plate rather than my dinner partners.

"Well, that can't be normal," Winnie noted, shaking her head. "I always knew Phyllis Grimes was wrapped a little tight, but I didn't think she'd go off the rails like this. I knew marrying Bob would backfire on her – the guy had a wandering eye in the womb, I swear – but she can't seriously believe that denying the fact that he can't keep it in his pants will make anyone believe her."

"I don't think that's what she's worried about," Bay countered, dipping a dinner roll into the pot roast gravy. "I think she's either covering for herself – which doesn't seem likely because I can't see her managing to drag a body into the woods without help – or she thinks there's a possibility her husband is a murderer and she's trying to cover for him."

"I'm not sure what this has to do with anything," Chris interjected. "We're clearly looking for a hominid. I saw the video footage from last night. There's a creature out there."

"There is?" That was news to me. I forced my questioning gaze to Jack. "Did you see it? I thought the footage was too blurry."

"It was too blurry," Jack confirmed. "Chris is convinced he saw something in the video. But no matter how we try to clean it up it still looks like a shadow in the woods at night."

"It's a sasquatch," Chris barked.

"It's a sasquatch-like shape," Jack said, his lips curving downward. "Either way, he wants all of us in the woods tomorrow."

"To do what?" I asked blankly.

"We're going to find Bigfoot," Laura replied. She looked irked more than anything else. "Chris is convinced having more of us out there tromping around will scare Bigfoot out of hiding so we can photograph him."

"Oh." That made absolutely no sense. I risked a glance at Bay. "I guess that sounds okay."

"I have a better idea," Bay offered, causing numerous heads to snap in her direction.

"No, you don't," Landon said automatically.

Bay refused to back down, her eyes flashing dark. "Yes, I do."

"No, sweetie, you don't." Landon almost sounded whiny. "Whenever you have an idea I end up in the lake or ducking so pottery doesn't hit my head."

"I don't understand the reference," Chris said.

"It's an inside joke," Bay said, grabbing Landon's knee under the table. "I think you're going to like this idea."

"Well, that means I definitely won't like it," Landon grumbled.

"Why don't you listen before shutting her down?" I snapped, causing Landon to glare in my direction. "You don't always have to talk over her, you know."

"I'm not talking over her." Landon kept his voice low. "Fine. Tell me your idea, sweetie. I'm sure I'll love it."

"The resort has a 5K run scheduled tomorrow," Bay said, ignoring

Landon's tone. "I have a copy of the list of participants because The Whistler needs it for coverage of the race. The money is for a local charity for abused children."

"Okay." Landon tilted his head to the side as he rubbed his index finger over the lip of his wine glass. "I've seen the signs for the race, but ... what does that mean for us?"

"All of our suspects are participating in the race, and the course happens to cross the Dandridge property," Bay explained.

"Oh?" Landon perked up. "You think whoever dumped Penny's body in the woods knew about the location because they'd already been there scouting it for the race."

"I do indeed," Bay agreed, bobbing her head. "I also told Penny Grimes and Shane Norman that you had more evidence than I was willing to share. I was thinking that if you put some police tape around an area and then left it alone ... maybe hid in the woods ... that you might be able to draw out a suspect."

"How would that work?" Chris asked, confused.

"The route doesn't pass by the area where the body was dumped," Bay explained. "I looked at the map this afternoon. All of our suspects are participating in the race, which means they'll be out there and have a reason to look around without drawing too much attention."

"It's still a hike off the main trail, but Bay thinks that the guilty party will check out the scene if he or she gets the chance," Landon supplied. "That means if we're hiding in the woods we'll be able to spot whoever it is."

"Exactly." Bay appeared to be overly pleased with herself. "It's not proof, but ... ."

"It gives us a solid direction," Landon said, his expression softening as he eyed his girlfriend. "You're kind of a genius sometimes. You know that, right?"

Bay smiled. "I know."

"Oh, barf," Tillie muttered as she mimed hanging herself with an invisible rope. "All of this planning only works if the killer is human. What if it really is Bigfoot?"

"A hominid," Chris corrected. "It's a hominid. I'm certain of it."

"Then things will work out well for you," Bay pointed out. "You want the area to be busy with people to scare your hominid out of the trees. If you guys are out there and look like you're working, that will unnerve runners and Bigfoot alike."

"Huh, that's not a bad idea," Jack admitted, rubbing his chin. "In fact, I think it's our best shot to draw out the guilty party."

"Which is a hominid," Chris pressed.

"Yes, it will draw out the hominid, too," Jack shot back, his temper bubbling. He was clearly at the end of his rope with Chris, working overtime not to run off at the mouth and endanger his job. "I'll need to see some maps so I can make sure my team is safe."

"Good," Landon enthused. "We'll discuss it after dinner."

"You're giving me a massage after dinner," Bay reminded him.

Landon opened his mouth to argue, but something in Bay's eyes clearly told him that was a bad idea. "We'll discuss it over breakfast tomorrow."

"That sounds fine," Jack said, smirking. "At least we're finally getting somewhere."

"Yes, we're getting close to immortality," Chris enthused, rubbing his hands together.

Jack rolled his eyes until they landed on me. "We're getting close to answers. That's the most important thing."

"I couldn't agree more," I said, reaching for my wine glass. "We all want answers."

Now we just needed to get them.

TWENTY-NINE

"*N*o way!"

Landon vehemently shook his head when Bay led us into Marcus' stable the next morning. He'd been arguing with Bay – and by extension Thistle and Marcus – for what seemed like forever. In real time it was probably two hours, but it felt a lot longer because he very rarely lost steam when arguing.

"I think it's a good idea," Bay pressed, running her hand over the nose of a black horse that poked his head out to see what all of the fuss was about. "We'll be able to cover more ground."

Landon was adamant. "No."

"Landon ... ."

"No, Bay." He gave his head a firm shake. "I don't want you on a horse."

"I've ridden horses since I was a kid." Bay adopted a pragmatic tone that she probably believed was reasonable and would somehow soothe Landon into agreeing with her. I had a feeling her tactics would push him in the opposite direction and she'd be better off screaming at him. She clearly knew him well, but it was obvious he had no intention of backing down. "I'll be perfectly safe."

"No." Landon crossed his arms over his chest. "I'm putting my foot down."

Bay pressed the heel of her hand to her forehead, her frustration evident. "Landon," she growled. "You're being unreasonable."

"I don't care. I'm putting my foot down. I mean it."

Thistle snorted, amused. "This should end well."

When Bay announced she had another brilliant idea over breakfast at The Overlook I was excited ... until I realized she wanted us to ride horses along the trails so we could cover more ground. I'd never been close to a horse – including the small ponies at festivals when I was a kid – and I wasn't keen on the idea of riding an animal that could kill me if it decided to throw me. Landon, it seemed, felt the same way.

"You can't tell me what to do," Bay argued. "I'm an adult."

"I don't care." The more Bay pushed, the more Landon dug in. "Do you remember what happened the last time you were on a horse?"

Bay and Thistle exchanged a weighted look.

"I do," Bay said, choosing her words carefully.

"Oh, I do, too." Thistle's smile was smug. "It was in the fall. We took horses out while you were on your undercover investigation – you know the one that almost ended with Bay being arrested for murder and you ruining your relationship – and we had a picnic by the Dandridge."

Landon stilled, a muscle straining in his jaw. "You went horse riding without telling me?"

"I couldn't get in touch with you, if you remember correctly," Bay reminded him.

It was clear the undercover assignment was still a sore subject between the two of them. My gossipy inner nature was dying to know what happened – I'm a busybody; I can't help it – but I figured inserting myself into this argument would be a terrible idea.

"Bay, I ... ." Landon worked his jaw. "I can't believe you went out on a horse without telling me. You could've been hurt."

"What happened last year was a fluke," Bay gritted out.

"You were thrown from a horse! I thought you were dead," Landon barked, taking me by surprise with his vehemence. "Hours, Bay! We spent hours looking for you. The horse came back without you. You didn't have your phone. I seriously thought you were dead."

Instead of reacting with anger, Bay brushed her hand over Landon's arm to soothe him. "I didn't die. I hit my head and was really sore for a few days, but I was fine. The horse just got spooked."

"Uh-huh. And do you think a bunch of people running in the woods while you're looking for a potential murderer might spook horses?" Landon challenged.

"I … um … hadn't considered that," Bay conceded, apologetic. "Maybe you're right."

"Oh, I'm right," Landon muttered.

"Not to mention the fact that we're really looking for a hominid," Chris added. He'd been against utilizing horses from the moment Bay mentioned it. He looked even less keen on the idea now that he'd seen the large beasts. "A hominid would be far more likely to upset a horse. I'm sure of it."

"Really?" Thistle asked dryly. "Have you conducted extensive research on that?"

Chris ignored her tone. "It's merely common sense."

"Well, I'm a Winchester," Thistle deadpanned. "We don't have common sense."

"None of you do," Landon complained, shaking his head. "No horses. Bay. You heard Chris. Bigfoot will eat you if you ride a horse. That's science."

I pursed my lips to keep from laughing at his reaction. He clearly didn't believe Bigfoot was to blame for Peggy's death, but he was determined to keep Bay off of a horse, and he was willing to use any means necessary.

"Fine," Bay said, resigned. "We won't use horses. I'm sorry I brought it up."

"Good." Landon pulled her to him, rubbing his hands up and down her arms as he rested his forehead against hers. "While you're in the mood to give me what I want, I don't suppose I could con you into staying close to the finish line so you'll be in town?"

Bay immediately started shaking her head. "Absolutely not! I won't ride a horse, but I'm doing what I want when it comes to searching the woods."

We spent a long time discussing strategy over breakfast. Everyone agreed to separate into pairs while searching the land surrounding the area where Penny Schilling's body was discovered. Landon didn't seem keen on Bay being part of the search team, but he hadn't outright forbid it. I wouldn't put it past him, of course, but Bay wouldn't stand for it. Then the fight would grow bigger and everyone would be caught in the middle of a huge dilemma that would tax our already frazzled nerves.

"Okay." Landon ran his tongue over his teeth as he regarded her. "Chief Terry and I will be close to the area that passes the Dandridge parking lot. We'll talk loudly when we can about evidence at the scene and mention we're waiting for a forensic team to arrive. That should propel the guilty party to move fast.

"Jack and Bernard will be close to the scene with two of Terry's officers," he continued. "Everyone else is allowed to wander through the woods in pairs, but don't get too close to the scene. We all agreed on that over breakfast and that rule stands. Understood?"

Chris bobbed his head. "The odds of the hominid returning to the exact same location are slim."

"I don't give a crap about your stupid hominid," Landon growled. "I'm worried about a murderer here."

"And won't you feel silly when we find evidence of the real culprit?" Chris pressed.

"I freaking hope so," Landon replied. "I'm a lot less worried about Bigfoot going after the woman I love than a maniacal human bent on covering up a crime." He shifted his eyes to Bay. "You don't go anywhere alone. Promise me."

"I promise, Landon." Bay sounded like a high school student talking to an overwrought parent. Everything probably went in one ear and out the other. "It'll be okay."

"Bay, you've almost died a good ten times since I met you," Landon said, lowering his voice. "I can't live with that. I need you alive … and safe … and with me tonight when I'll want a massage."

Bay's pretty face split with a wide grin. "I will be."

"You'd better." Landon pressed a kissed to her forehead and my heart hurt at the love shared between them. "No one goes anywhere alone," he stressed, his gaze bouncing from face to face before finally landing on me. "I don't know if Bigfoot or a human is guilty, but I have a feeling we're going to find out today."

"It's a sasquatch," Chris said happily. "I know it."

Landon didn't look convinced. I didn't miss the look he exchanged with Jack. They clearly worked on another wavelength, one the rest of us didn't fully grasp, and said much with a simple glance. "Good luck, everyone. I think we're going to need it."

"SO, WHAT HAPPENED WITH THE HORSE?"

Bay walked on one side of me, Jack on the other, and we made the trek to the spot where Penny Schilling's body was discovered largely in silence. I'm curious by nature, so I couldn't refrain from asking the question. Thankfully, Bay didn't seem bothered.

"It was last spring," Bay replied. "Landon's family came for a visit – it was the first time I met them – and we went for a ride on the trails behind the stable. My horse got spooked and bolted. I got knocked off and was unconscious for a long time.

"The horse made it back to the stable without me. My phone was in the saddlebag, so Landon panicked," she continued. "When I came to I was confused, but I kind of recognized the area. That's why I walked to the Dandridge. That's also how I found out that Clove and Sam were dating. She was keeping it a secret."

"I take it this was before they moved in together," Jack noted.

Bay nodded. "It seems like a lifetime ago. It's weird how things can change so fast. It's been a year, but it feels as if it happened just yesterday."

"What did Landon do when he found you?" I asked.

"He didn't find me," Bay answered. "I called Thistle from the Dandridge and she picked me up to take me back to the inn. She was more obsessed about Sam and Clove than about my health. As for Landon ... well ... he had a rough night."

"That's because he loves you," Jack argued. "You only remember it from your point of view. You were unconscious for most of it, so you couldn't be afraid. When you woke up, your first thought was to get home. Landon spent most of that time terrified that you wouldn't make it back to him."

"I understand that," Bay said. "I love riding horses. I always have. Landon wasn't keen on horses before this happened, which is a shame because I think he'd look good in a cowboy hat and chaps."

I smirked, amused. "Did he dote on you for days? I remember when I broke my arm when I was a kid and my mother tried to wrap me in pillows for weeks after."

"He was a little manic," Bay conceded. "He was more worked up the time I was almost shot."

"You were almost shot?" I couldn't help being impressed. "I guess he wasn't exaggerating when he said you're a trouble magnet, huh?"

Bay shook her head, rueful. "I do tend to find trouble, but I always manage to find a way out of it."

"Try not to find anything too dangerous today," Jack instructed. "I'll be close to the scene, so don't hesitate to sing out if you need anything. You should be safe, but ... if there's trouble I expect you to call for me rather than handle it yourself. Understood?"

Jack kept his eyes on Bay's face as he said the words, but I had a feeling he was talking directly to me.

"We understand," I said, rolling my eyes as I grabbed Bay's arm and dragged her away from the spot where Landon and Chief Terry had erected police tape after breakfast. "You won't have to worry about us."

Jack didn't look convinced. "Something tells me that I'll be worrying about you quite a bit ... and possibly for a long time. Stay frosty, and don't do anything stupid."

"Oh, you're so sweet," I deadpanned. "You worry about yourself and I'll worry about me. How's that sound?"

Jack shrugged. "It sounds as if I'll have an ulcer before this is over. I'm not joking. Be careful. While I agree with Landon that a human most likely killed Penny, I'd hate to rule out an animal and have it come back to bite me ... or one of you. Don't lower your guard. Be mindful of your surroundings and always look over your shoulder. Don't be heroes."

"Yes, Dad," I said dryly, rolling my eyes.

I could feel Jack's temper flare as he worked to remain professional. "Don't wander too far. Do you think you can handle that?"

"No promises."

BAY PURPOSELY PICKED an area for us to watch from that she was familiar with. It was close enough to the lake that we could sit and enjoy the wildlife while bored, but not so far from the scene that we'd be out of the loop should Jack and Bernard catch someone crossing the police tape.

That was the goal, anyway.

"What's the deal with the tanker," I asked, pointing at the large vessel anchored behind the lighthouse. I'd seen it on previous visits, but never bothered to ask about it. "Do you guys take that out on the lake or something?"

Bay chuckled and shook her head, grabbing a few flat stones so she could skip them across the water. "No. It floats but it you can't steer it. Sam had to hire someone to tow it in."

"But why?"

"This is a tourist area," Bay replied. "Sam opened the tanker around Halloween, but only allowed people to visit the top deck. This spring and summer we plan to turn it into the best haunted attraction in Hemlock Cove."

"It's pretty cool that you guys help each other out like that."

"Sam saved my life last year, so I figure I can help him with his tanker. Only seems fair."

I arched an eyebrow. "He saved your life?"

"He even got shot in the foot doing it."

I was a bit dumbfounded by the casual way she related it. "How many times have you almost died?"

Bay shrugged. "I forget."

"Landon hasn't forgotten."

"Landon will never forget," Bay said. "It haunts him. He almost died saving me the first time. I didn't even know him then. He was undercover. I didn't realize he was a good guy until he was almost a gone guy."

"That's kind of a romantic story." I grinned. "Just think; you'll be able to tell that story to your grandchildren one day."

"Yes, well, I'm sure it will have grown by that time," Bay said, dusting her hands on the back of her pants. "By the time Landon is done embellishing it he'll be superhuman and I'll be a crying mess."

"Does that bother you?"

Bay shook her head. "Not in the least. I already think he's superhuman. In fact … ." Bay broke off, tilting her head to the side as she glanced into the heavy foliage behind her.

I almost asked the obvious question, but the hair on my arms stood to attention as something dark and ominous washed over me. I lifted my eyes to the sky, half expecting a cloud to have passed over the sun or an eclipse to have taken place, but the darkness came from someplace else.

I opened my mouth to say something, but Bay pressed her finger to her lips as she crouched down, resting her palms on the ground as she peered into the foliage. I couldn't see what she stared at from my vantage point, but I knew we were in trouble by the way she widened her eyes and tumbled backward.

The explosion of movement from the bushes caught me by surprise as Phyllis Grimes, her eyes wide and manic, barreled through them. Her chest heaved, her race participation number hanging onto her tank top by a single safety pin at one corner. Her flushed face glanced between the two of us.

"What the … ?" She seemed as surprised to see Bay and me as we were to see her.

"It's you?" Bay looked a bit disappointed. "I didn't think it was going to be you."

"You didn't think what was going to be me?" Phyllis looked bewildered, sparing a worried glance over her shoulder. "Why are you hiding in the bushes?"

"We're not hiding in the bushes," Bay replied. "We're hanging out by the water in case Bigfoot comes calling."

"I … what?" Phyllis was flabbergasted as she rubbed her sweaty palms on her shorts. "You can't be here. You have to go right now!"

"What do you mean?" Bay asked, confused.

"It's not safe," Phyllis growled. "You have to go right now! He's almost here!"

Bay lifted her head and glanced in the direction Phyllis had approached from, her expression unreadable. "Who's almost here?"

I wanted to echo the question, but it was too late. I felt another presence before I could open my mouth to warn Bay, instinct taking over and causing me to take an unsteady step away from the trees.

"Run, you idiots," Phyllis shouted. "He'll kill you if he sees you!"

I watched as a set of legs moved through the bushes to my right, my stomach twisting as a tall figure stepped into the clearing.

"Oh, it's much too late for that," the new arrival pronounced, his eyes dark. "Well, well, well. I wasn't expecting such a big crowd. That's going to make what comes next difficult. I don't have a lot of choice in the matter, though, so I guess I'll start by asking for volunteers. Who wants to die first?"

30

THIRTY

*J*im Green didn't look happy as his gaze bounced between Bay, Phyllis and me. I could practically see his mind working as he surveyed the situation. When he shifted, I realized he had an ugly-looking knife clutched in his hand, one of those serrated blades hunters use to gut and skin a kill before carrying it to a waiting vehicle. He'd clearly been going after Phyllis when he came upon us, but that didn't mean he'd tuck tail and run now that he was outnumbered. The knife leveled the field ... and then some.

I hesitantly took another step back, increasing the distance between us. I was closest to him, but I had a bit of elbow room should I need to run. Every nerve ending in my body screamed to do just that, but the idea of turning my back on a deranged man with a knife didn't seem like a good idea.

"What's going on?" Bay asked, straightening and drawing Green's attention. "Are you hunting, Jim?"

"I think he's looking for Bigfoot," I offered, hoping I sounded calmer than I felt. Even though I knew we were trying to draw a killer to us I was flabbergasted it actually worked. It worked a bit too well. We drew a killer to us, yet our backup felt as if it was miles away.

"He's going to need that knife if he expects to fight the creature I saw out here the other night."

Green narrowed his eyes to dangerous brown slits. "What are you ladies doing out here? I was under the impression that volunteers were sticking close to the running trail. That was part of the arrangement we struck with the town council when we agreed to use Hemlock Cove's trails."

I had to hand it to him. He remained calm despite the untenable situation. His chest continued to rise and fall at a steady pace, but I knew the instant one of us tried to run he'd be on us. The only chance we had was keeping him distracted in the hope that Jack or Landon would come looking.

"Oh, we're here for you," Bay answered calmly. "The FBI and Chief Terry are running a joint operation to draw out a killer. Looks like it worked."

Green's shoulders stiffened. "What is that supposed to mean?"

"Yeah, what is that supposed to mean?" Phyllis asked, her eyes shifting to Bay.

"It means that you'll be okay, Phyllis." Bay offered the woman a half-smile. "Landon and Chief Terry will be here any minute. They only spread the word about new evidence at the scene to draw out the killer. It worked ... obviously. Apparently it worked too well, because it caused Jim here to chase you through the woods. Speaking of that, why was he chasing you?"

Phyllis' expression was hard to read, but when she locked gazes with Green a chill washed over me. A lot was said with the glance, none of it was good. I opened my mouth to warn Bay, but it was already too late.

"He's not chasing me," Phyllis replied, shuffling closer to Bay. "He was following behind me because we had something we needed to do together. There's a difference."

Bay realized her mistake. I could see the realization register on her features. She didn't back down, and I admired her courage. All I could think to do was run, but leaving Bay to fight the duo on her own simply wasn't an option.

"You're in this together," Bay mused, tilting her head to the side. "I guess it makes sense in a roundabout way, huh? You killed Penny and then panicked. You needed help getting rid of the body. You went to school with Jim and the two of you were tight. I saw photos of you together in the yearbook."

"We were in love," Green corrected, his voice dripping with disdain. "We were meant to be together until ... well ... until Bob ruined everything."

Bay arched a dubious eyebrow. "Bob ruined everything? How? No one forced Phyllis to marry him."

"He confused her," Green spat. "He made her believe things that weren't true. I tried telling her back then that it was a mistake, but she wouldn't listen. She wouldn't ... see him for what he was then. He only grew worse over the years."

I tugged on my ear – a nervous habit from when I was a kid that I thought I'd outgrown – and ran the series of events through my head. It made sense ... and yet it didn't. "You were in love with Phyllis when you were in high school, but she broke up with you because of Bob. You pined for her all of these years, didn't you?"

"I don't believe 'pined' is the word I'd use to describe it," Green replied stiffly.

"But it's clearly not the wrong word, is it?" Bay licked her lips and flicked her eyes to Phyllis. The woman didn't look to be armed, but that didn't mean she wasn't. I could practically see Bay's mind working. If it came down to it, fighting off Phyllis probably wouldn't be an issue. She was a bit chunky in the hips and thighs and had a few pounds on both of us, but we could outrun her. Green was the wildcard.

"I made a mistake," Phyllis offered, her demeanor suddenly grown eerily calm. "I should've followed my heart, but Bob twisted my head and I made a bad decision. I've regretted it ever since. Jim knows that. He accepts that. He ... forgives ... me."

The excuse sounded well-rehearsed but I didn't believe a word of it. "Let me hazard a guess as to how all of this played out," I interjected. "You fell for Bob because he was the hottest guy in your class.

Isn't that what you told us over dinner last night while we were looking at the yearbook, Bay?"

Bay nodded. "He even won that award in the mock election. It was in the yearbook."

"So he was considered the hottest guy in your class and everyone wanted him," I said. "Even though his prospects weren't great for making a living, once you were out of school you couldn't get him out of your head. So when he flirted with you one night you thought you had a chance to nab him.

"You were more than happy to dump Jim here, because you wanted Bob. You thought he'd go further," I continued. "You dated Bob, married him and even had a couple of kids. You thought you had everything you wanted ... but you couldn't keep him faithful."

"Bob is a good provider," Phyllis huffed. "He's a good ... man."

"No, he's not," Bay argued. "He has a certain reputation around this area. He'll nail anything with a pulse – including older women, young women, fat women, skinny women, ugly women and pretty women. He doesn't care as long as he gets off."

"You shut your mouth," Phyllis hissed, spittle forming at the corners of her mouth as she glared at Bay. "You have no idea what you're talking about!"

"But she does," I argued, drawing three sets of eyes to me. I figured the longer we could keep Phyllis and Green engaged in conversation the more time we bought for ourselves. Landon would come looking. He was too wired into Bay to abandon her. "Bob has quite the reputation. I'm new to this town, but at least five different people mentioned it to me." That was a bit of an exaggeration, but Phyllis didn't need to know. She looked easy enough to derange, which could only help us if it came down to a battle.

"You're a liar!" Phyllis' eyes flashed hot. "You have no idea what you're talking about. Just ... shut your mouth!"

"No, don't shut your mouth," Bay countered, shaking her head. "I think Phyllis needs to hear this. Of course, I think Phyllis hearing this over and over is what caused her to kill Penny. What happened? Did

Bob sleeping with someone who worked at the resort hit too close to home?"

"Oh, please," Green scoffed. "Everyone Bob slept with worked at the resort. He slept with guests and workers. He didn't care. The man was a walking billboard for Viagra, for crying out loud."

"Stop saying that," Phyllis hissed, glaring at Green. "That's not what happened."

I sensed an air of discomfort building between them. It was obvious they had different goals. I decided to play on that. "You killed Penny in an act of rage, didn't you, Phyllis?"

Phyllis jerked her eyes to me and swallowed hard. "It was an accident."

"Of course it was an accident," Green interjected. "You don't have a mean bone in your body. You could never purposely hurt someone. This is all on Bob. He's to blame for all of it."

Green was either deranged or blind to Phyllis' true nature. I couldn't decide which. "What happened? Did Penny confront you? Did she try to drive a wedge in your relationship with Bob?"

"That little tramp told me to let him go so she could have him," Phyllis replied icily. "She said that he loved her and wanted to be with her, and the only thing holding them back was the fact that he didn't want to create a hostile work environment by leaving me for someone else who worked at the resort. Can you believe that?"

Actually I could. Penny hadn't sounded like a very good person from everything I'd heard. To be fair, it wasn't that she was a bad person. It was more that she was a lost person. "What did you say to her?"

"I told her I'd weathered far worse than her," Phyllis replied. "Everyone at the resort knew about her. They knew she'd sleep with anyone to get ahead. Hell, do you think Bob was the only one she seduced?"

I shook my head. "No. She seduced Jim and Shane Norman, too. She also slept with a bunch of the grounds workers and bellboys. She wasn't discriminating."

Green grimaced at mention of his name. "She was a harlot! I had no idea she was sleeping with Bob and Shane. I didn't find that out until much later, until it was too late. I never would've touched her, but … she tricked me."

"Tricked you?" Bay's expression reflected doubt. "Did she trip you so you accidentally fell into her?"

"No one's talking to you, you foul-mouthed whore!" Green exploded, causing me to shrink back. Bay, however, remained standing steady. She didn't so much as let a muscle twitch.

"I bet I know how this all went down," Bay pressed. "She figured out you were still in love with Phyllis and used that to her advantage. That's what happened, right?"

"She wanted us to join forces," Green offered. "I thought she was crazy when she suggested it. She thought it would work out well for both of us if we broke up Phyllis and Bob. She brought it up after sex one night, as if it was nothing. Can you believe that?"

"What? You didn't tell me that?" Phyllis' surprise was palpable. "What did she want?"

"She said that if I helped her get Bob that you would come running to me," Green replied. "I considered it, but I wasn't sure it would really happen. We never really got past the planning stage."

"You were going to help her?" Phyllis' confusion turned to rage. "You were going to help her steal my husband?"

"You said you never should've married him," Green snapped, his attention focused on Phyllis. His distraction gave me a chance to meet Bay's gaze. I couldn't read her mind, but her intent was obvious when she gestured to the high branch over Green's head. I knew what she wanted me to do, but wasn't sure I could do it. My abilities hadn't always worked on demand.

"I never should've married him. But that doesn't mean you should've helped that terrible woman try to break up my family," Phyllis snapped. "What were you thinking? I can't believe you'd betray me like that."

"Betray you?" Green was beside himself as I narrowed my eyes and focused on the only target I had, willing myself to calm down and work the thick branch free from the stout trunk. "You broke up with me! You betrayed me!"

"I didn't betray you," Phyllis shot back, furious. "It was high school. No one marries their high school sweetheart."

"That's true," Bay said, trying to draw their attention back to her and free me to drop the branch. I could feel my power licking at the point of connection, yet nothing happened. My emotions were too wild for the magic to take hold. I needed to center myself. "You were holding onto the past, Jim, and Phyllis was looking forward to the future."

"What future?" Green sputtered. "She was never going to have a future with Bob. It was only a matter of time before he knocked up someone else and everyone in town found out about his extracurricular activities. We even had bets on when it would happen. All of the workers at the resort had a pool going. Bob was a disgusting piece of filth."

"Oh, trust me," Bay said, "that memo was sent out a long time ago. But get back to Penny. Phyllis killed her and then what? Did she come to you for help?"

"She killed her on the eighteenth green of the golf course," Green gritted out. "Everyone uses the ambulance codes to get back there. That's where Penny and Phyllis met to hash things out. Penny was already dead by the time I got there. I had a choice. I could either help Phyllis or leave her to do it herself and possibly go to jail. I refuse to let her go to jail, so ... I helped her."

"But how did you do it?" Bay asked. "The medical examiner said there was foreign DNA in the wounds. I'm guessing you used that knife there to open the wound a bit. Although ... did you stab her in the throat, Phyllis?"

"I didn't mean to." Phyllis managed to regroup a bit as she stared at her hands. "I told her I had no intention of divorcing Bob, but she wouldn't stop verbally attacking me. She kept saying that he loved her and not me, and that I was pathetic and clingy. I couldn't stand the sound of her voice."

"So you decided to shut her up," Bay deduced.

Phyllis nodded. "I didn't have a lot in my purse, but I did have a nail file. I stabbed her in the throat. I didn't even realize I was doing it until she was bleeding like a stuck pig. I stabbed her again ... and again ... and again. The wounds were small, but she went down quickly. But she wouldn't die!"

Bay pressed her lips together, horrified. "Oh, my ... why didn't you call for help when you came to your senses?"

"And go to prison? That's exactly what she wanted. She eventually died. It was almost four in the morning. I sat there and waited for her to quit breathing. I wanted it to go quicker, but I couldn't bring myself to hurry things along. I didn't know what to do when it was over, so I called Jim."

"And he came running," Bay muttered, shaking her head. "Then what happened?"

"We had to move her body," Jim answered, a form of grim detachment settling over him. "I carried the body to my truck, and then we did some brainstorming. I figured that someone would eventually notice Penny was gone and I would be a suspect because people knew we slept together. The fact that she slept with everyone gave the police plenty of other suspects to consider. We wanted to avoid becoming suspects altogether. That was our main goal. That meant we needed to make it look like an accident or ... ."

"The 'or' was easier," Bay surmised. "You took Peggy out behind the Dandridge and opened the wound in her throat with your knife. What about the DNA?"

"I hunt," Jim replied. "I had a few carcasses in my garage, so I rubbed the pelts into the wound. I thought if I could confuse the medical examiner enough he simply wouldn't be able to decide if it was an animal or human, and they'd have no choice but to let it go."

"And you almost got away with it," Bay muttered. "Then you heard a whisper on the trail, right? You heard the cops found some evidence, so you came out here to see if you could figure out what it was."

"Pretty much," Jim confirmed. "I planned to dump the knife in the lake. I bought a similar knife and planted it in Bob's truck so he'd become a suspect if the cops ever bothered to search. All I had left to do was dump my knife. That's when we found you."

"And now we have to kill you," Phyllis added. "We have no choice. I told you to run. I wanted you out of our hair. Now I'm kind of glad you didn't listen. You've made things easier. You stuck your noses where they didn't belong and ... it's time to die."

She was so matter-of-fact it caused me to jerk my head in her direction. She gripped something in her hand. It was small and silver, a pink handle poking out of her fist. It had to be the nail file she used to kill Penny. I opened my mouth to warn Bay, but that's when I realized Green was moving in my direction. Somehow they'd managed to communicate with each other without Bay and I noticing.

I was too surprised to make a sound. I tumbled backward, tripping over a fallen log in my haste to get away. I saw Bay grappling with Phyllis, but I couldn't risk focusing on her when I had my own problems crashing this way.

"I really am sorry about this," Green growled, grabbing the front of my shirt as he brandished the knife. "I have no choice. We need time to run."

My first instinct was to scream as the knife closed in on my throat. Instead, anger overtook me and I felt something powerful rip free from my chest and strike the branch over his head. I lifted my arms to protect my face. Green gave me an odd look before glancing over his shoulder.

When the branch hit him, he pitched forward. He was all dead weight when he hit me. Thankfully I managed to deflect the knife. I felt his breath on my face as I shifted. He was out, but not dead. His body was too heavy, though, pinning me to the ground.

"What was that?" Phyllis screeched, her hand tangled in Bay's hair. "I ... what was that?"

Bay didn't allow herself to become distracted, instead planting her foot in Phyllis' abdomen and launching the woman into the air as she kicked out. I couldn't see Phyllis' face, but I heard her hit the ground with a sickening thud.

"Is she alive?"

"Who cares?" Bay muttered, catching her breath. "I ... ."

The sound of pounding footsteps drew my attention. I saw two figures pushing through the foliage. "Is that more of Penny's harem coming to kill us?" I asked, shoving against Green's prone body with everything I had. "Good grief. I think I'm suffocating."

Instead of another potential killer, Jack's face swam into view. He was pale – almost completely white – but he looked relieved when we locked gazes.

"Are you okay?"

"Jack?" I couldn't keep the surprise from my voice. "What are you doing here?"

"Saving you," Jack muttered, wrapping his arms around Green's waist and tugging him off me. His hands were gentle as they roamed my shoulders and arms once I was free. "Is anything broken?"

"Just my pride," I admitted, ruefully rubbing my sore behind. "I smacked my butt when I fell."

"I saw." Jack's expression was hard to read, his dark eyes almost black as he stared. "You're lucky that branch fell when it did. I was trying to get to you, but you were too far away."

"You saw all of it?" Bay asked, her eyes accusatory as they fell on Landon. "Why didn't you come in sooner?"

"Because you were busy getting confessions out of them. I thought I had more time," Landon replied, stroking the back of her head. "We got here as fast as we could. It would've been helpful if you'd kept them talking a few minutes longer."

"Oh, whatever." Bay crossed her arms over her chest as she watched Chief Terry – I didn't even see him arrive – slap a pair of cuffs on a disoriented Phyllis. "You could've been quicker. I'm all dirty."

"Yes, well, that's the important thing," Landon teased, pressing a soft kiss to the corner of her mouth.

I risked a glance at Jack and found him staring in the same direction. "How did you know to come?"

"I didn't," Jack answered, turning back to me. "Landon somehow knew."

Landon nodded. "If there's trouble, it always finds Bay." He pulled his pouting blonde in for a hug, resting his cheek against her forehead. "She's a trouble magnet."

"I still can't figure out how that branch fell," Jack mused, shifting his attention to the broken limb on the ground. "I mean ... what are the odds?"

I exchanged a quick look with Bay and then mustered a watery smile. "I guess we were just lucky."

"Very lucky," Jack agreed, grabbing my hand and pulling me to a standing position. "Come on. Let's get you out of here. I'll bet you could use a soft place to sit."

"You don't know the half of it," I grumbled. "My butt will be black and blue for days."

"You should get someone to rub that for you," Bay said pointedly, inclining her chin in Jack's direction.

I pretended I didn't grasp the reference. "I'm fairly certain a bath will do."

"You don't know what you're missing," Landon offered, pulling Bay to her feet. "The post-takedown massage is the highlight of every dangerous situation Bay finds herself in."

"I'm not rubbing you," Bay growled.

Landon smiled as he slung an arm over her shoulders. "We'll see."

"Yeah, we will."

Despite my discomfort, I couldn't help but smile. "So ... it wasn't Bigfoot after all."

"No," Jack agreed. "But that doesn't mean he's not out there. It simply means he's not here right now."

"I guess not."

THIRTY-ONE

"How are you feeling?"

Chris' face was the first I saw the next morning when I trudged out of my room, suitcase in hand. He loitered in the hallway, a hangdog expression on his face. He'd been crushed upon hearing about the confessions, trying to muster an argument about them covering for a hominid-like creature, but no one would listen.

"I'm fine." Chris was listless as he stared at one of the family portraits, an oil painting featuring a formidable woman who shared Tillie's mischievous eyes. "I might be a little depressed."

I couldn't blame him. My adrenalin pumped for hours the previous day, but when it crashed, so did I. After ten hours of sleep I felt relaxed and refreshed. I figured the disappointment would set in eventually. I wasn't quite there yet.

"There will be other chances," I offered. "I'm sure of it."

Chris forced a tight smile. "Me too."

I watched him shuffle down the hallway, fighting the urge to chuckle at his depression. He had a dramatic streak that made me laugh, but even the determined scowl couldn't diminish his attractiveness.

The door next to the portrait opened, allowing Jack to exit. I shifted my eyes to him, pursing my lips as I debated how I wanted to deal with our relationship. Holding a grudge seemed petty. He did his best to save me, after all. Sure, he had a huge ego, but that didn't mean he was a bad guy.

"Are you depressed too?" I asked.

Jack shook his head, his eyes flashing. "No. It went largely how I thought it would. Er, well, I guess it went how I thought it would other than you almost getting stabbed."

"Yeah, I'm kind of upset," I admitted, shifting my suitcase from one hand to the other. "It is what it is, though."

"You're alive. That's the most important thing." Jack grabbed the suitcase from my hand, taking me by surprise. "I'll carry this."

"Why?"

"Because you fell and hurt yourself."

"I'm fine. Just a little sore."

"Because you almost got stabbed," Jack added.

"But I didn't get stabbed."

"Just let me carry the suitcase and pipe down," Jack grumbled, following me to the stairs. "Do you have to be so difficult?"

I shrugged as I descended the wide staircase. "You'll get used to me. Perhaps you'll even grow to like me. Of course, you won't like me in a romantic way – you've made your feelings on that perfectly clear, even though I don't like you that way either – but I'm sure we'll muddle through."

Jack made an exaggerated face as he shook his head. "You'll never let me live that down, will you?"

"Nope."

"Well, something to look forward to."

The Winchesters met us in the lobby so we could check out as a group. I caught a glimpse of Bay's hair through the window overlooking the front porch, so I said hasty goodbyes to Winnie, Twila and Marnie before stopping in front of Tillie. She looked me up and down a moment, her expression unreadable as she leaned against the panel next to the front door.

"I think I'm going to miss you," I admitted.

"I won't miss you," Tillie replied. "You guys have all been pains in the keister."

I leaned in and whispered. "I know you're all talk."

Tillie's lips curved a bit, but she didn't indulge in a full-on smile. "That's a possibility."

I moved to walk away, but she grabbed my wrist, lowering her voice so only I could hear as she leaned forward. "If you need help with something ... ."

"Bay told you." My stomach twisted. "I ... ."

"Don't worry about it," Tillie whispered. "I've kept more secrets than anyone knows. I'm good at it. Besides, Bay didn't tell me anything. I figured it out myself and grilled her. She rather reluctantly confirmed a few things, but she never betrayed you. I won't either."

"I ... well ... thank you."

Tillie nodded and released me, mustering a genuine smile as I stepped through the door. I felt Jack close the distance between us as he followed me outside.

"What was that?" he asked when we were clear of the Winchester matriarch.

"Just a little gossip between friends," I replied, turning to find Bay waiting for me at the bottom of the porch stairs. I hurried down, giving her a quick hug before she could wave off the gesture. "I'm glad you came. I wasn't sure you'd get here before we left."

"I wouldn't miss saying goodbye." Bay looked well rested. I didn't miss Landon dropping a conciliatory hand on Chris' shoulder behind her. He seemed amused by Chris' demeanor, but he didn't openly make fun of the man. For that I was thankful ... and also a little disappointed. "Did you and Landon make up last night?"

"We didn't fight."

"You kind of fought," I argued.

"That was nowhere near close to a fight," Bay countered. "Of course, that didn't stop us from making up just for the heck of it."

"I'm going to put your suitcase in the Tahoe and say goodbye to Landon," Jack interjected, his eyes bouncing between Bay and me. "We have to be at the airport in a few hours."

I nodded in gratitude. "Thank you."

"Don't mention it."

I waited until I was sure Jack was out of earshot, his head bent close to Landon's and his attention fully focused elsewhere. "Did Landon question you further about the branch?"

Bay shook her head. "You don't have to worry about that. Even if he suspected anything, he'd attribute it to me. You're fine on that front."

"I hope so."

"I know so." Bay pressed a card with her name and cell number into my hand. "If you need anything ... even just to talk ... don't hesitate to call."

"I will." I almost choked on the words and needed a moment to collect myself. "Thank you for everything you've done."

"I haven't done anything," Bay cautioned. "You did everything you needed to do on your own."

"I didn't find Bigfoot." It was meant to be a joke, but I sounded a bit bereft.

"Didn't you?" Bay arched an eyebrow. "You saw something in the woods that night. Landon questioned Phyllis and Jim extensively. They said they weren't out there that night. They've admitted to killing Penny and disposing of her body. They also admitted to breaking into Penny's apartment after the fact to make sure there was nothing to tie her to Bob or Jim. Why would they lie about that?"

"But ... ." I broke off, uncertain. "Do you think I really saw Bigfoot?"

Bay shrugged, holding her hands palms up. "I think there's more out there than meets the eye. I also think you'll find answers to all of your questions if you give it time."

"All of them?"

"All of them." Bay rested her hand on my wrist and leaned in closer. "I know you don't know the people in your group very well yet, but you have time. I think most of them are probably trustworthy."

I nodded in agreement. "Millie."

"And Jack."

I tried to hide my grimace ... and failed. "Jack won't understand. I don't know him well."

"I think you're wrong, but it will be up to him to decide," Bay argued. "Remember, Landon didn't stay the first go-around. He took a step back because he needed to think. That didn't mean he wasn't trustworthy."

"But he loved you."

"Not then he didn't. The love came later."

I shifted a glance to Landon and found him staring fondly at Bay's profile. "I'm not so sure about that. They say people don't fall in love at first sight – not really, I mean. I think Landon did. I think from the moment he saw you that you were it for him."

"That's a nice thought, but the reality was vastly different," Bay countered. "Still, you have plenty of time. You picked a career in which you're going to have plenty of adventures."

I brightened considerably at the notion. "I think you're probably right."

"And, even though I know you don't want to hear it because you're stubborn, I don't want you to rule out Jack," Bay pressed. "Landon said he was desperate to get to you when they realized we were unaccounted for. Men like Jack – men who are willing to risk their lives for the mere idea of someone else – are one in a million."

I flicked my eyes to Jack as he conversed with Landon, banter flying easily back and forth between them. "Maybe."

"If anyone should know that, it's me," Bay said, running her hands down my arms. "Don't shut him out before you know if you want to let him in. That's all I'm saying."

"I'll give it some thought."

"You do that." Bay gave me a hug and stepped back when Landon moved in to join us.

He extended his hand while slipping his free arm around Bay's shoulders. "Good luck, Charlie."

"You, too. Make sure you take care of Bay." I fought the urge to burst into tears. I barely knew these people, I reminded myself. I had no idea why it was so hard to leave them.

"You can count on it," Landon said. "You take care of yourself." He shifted his eyes to Jack. "Listen to your security chief, too. He knows what he's talking about."

"Did he pay you to say that?"

Landon grinned. "Call it … intuition."

"Yes, well, intuition tells me it's time to leave," Jack said, gesturing toward the Tahoe. "Saddle up, Charlie. It's time to say goodbye."

"Let's go." I nodded. "Adventure awaits, right?"

Jack's smile was small but heartfelt. "Adventure awaits. Now, let's roll. We can't start another one until we leave this one behind."

As much as I hated to admit it, he was right. So that's exactly what I did.

CPSIA information can be obtained
at www.ICGtesting.com
Printed in the USA
FFHW021247171219
57080830-62656FF